**Robert W. Walker takes you
to the EDGE of suspense with his thrilling series
starring Native American Police Detective
Lucas Stonecoat . . .**

CUTTING EDGE

*An on-line computer role-playing game leads Stonecoat and
psychiatrist Meredyth Sanger into a literal Web of intrigue,
murder and mutilation . . .*

**And don't miss
Walker's acclaimed INSTINCT series . . .**

KILLER INSTINCT

*The stunning debut of Dr. Jessica Coran, an FBI pathologist
tracking the blood-drinking "Vampire Killer" . . .*

FATAL INSTINCT

*Jessica Coran is summoned to New York City to find a
cunning, modern-day Jack the Ripper nicknamed "The
Claw" . . .*

continued . . .

PRIMAL INSTINCT

No killer in Jessica Coran's past can compare to Hawaii's relentless, psychotic "Trade Winds Killer" . . .

"A bone-chilling page-turner . . . Every bit as exciting as the chase is Coran's rigorous examination of the evidence."
—*Publishers Weekly*

"*Fatal Instinct* and *Killer Instinct* showed Walker at the top of his form. With *Primal Instinct,* he has arrived. [It is] a multilevel novel packed with detective work and an interesting look at the Hawaii that exists beyond beachfront hotels."

—*Daytona Beach News-Journal*

PURE INSTINCT

The "Queen of Hearts" killer is stalking New Orleans. And the police commissioner has requested—by name—Dr. Jessica Coran . . .

"Walker takes you into a world of suspense, thrills, and psychological gamesmanship."
—*Daytona Beach News-Journal*

DARKEST INSTINCT

In Florida, they call him the "Night Crawler." But when similar murders surface in London, Jessica Coran faces double jeopardy. One killer? Or two . . . ?

EXTREME INSTINCT

A murderer terrorizing the American West ties his victims down, drowns their sins in gasoline, and cleanses them with flame. Now Jessica must step into the fire.

DOUBLE EDGE

ROBERT W. WALKER

JOVE BOOKS, NEW YORK

DOUBLE EDGE

A Jove Book / published by arrangement with
the author

PRINTING HISTORY
Jove edition / November 1998

The Penguin Putnam Inc. World Wide Web site address is
http://www.penguinputnam.com

ISBN: 0-515-12384-6

A JOVE BOOK®
Jove Books are published by The Berkley Publishing Group,
a member of Penguin Putnam Inc.,
375 Hudson Street, New York, New York 10014.
JOVE and the "J" design are trademarks
belonging to Jove Publications, Inc.

PRINTED IN THE UNITED STATES OF AMERICA

10 9 8 7 6 5 4 3 2 1

Ironic how life has a way of kicking us in the teeth when we get the least bit complacent—from fire, flood, famine and other natural disasters, to disease, death, spiritual awakening, joy and love. This book is dedicated to another kind of "natural" disaster or "act of God." This is for Nicole Blankenship whose double-edged, dual spirit now and always touches me, teaches me and guides me to become a better spirit, a better man.

PROLOGUE

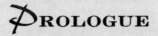

Lasso: captivity

The boy trailed behind the pack, a perfect selection. His basketball buddies had suddenly outdistanced him, having stepped quickly away after a brief shoving match, an exchange of accusations, counteraccusations, name-calling and gestures. The kid stood out as just right for the taking: a high-school-age boy, wrestling with his identity and the chaos of adolescence, skinny and bony as a starved jackal, that lean malnourished appearance. A hungry boy, hungry-eyed, the target a hunter always sought, for a hungry boy was easily led. And this boy looked the picture of a waif, his face grimy and dirty, as if he'd stepped from a page of a politically correct Dickens classic, a modern-day bug-eyed little Oliver Twist in blackface, looking for his next bowl of porridge.

The young boy's large black eyes, like grape plums, spoke of long years of neglect. The child's family took him for granted, those who by all rights should most prize him—brothers and sisters, mother and a likely absentee father—simply did not. Poor wretched thing stood in the shadows of the tenement house, a perfect choice—alone, abandoned by everyone . . . except by the devil, the shadow man now stalking the boy.

The young man had no idea that the battered old van, like an animal scouting its hunting grounds, had followed him from the school yard to here.

Absolute perfection . . . The perfect victim at dusk. A painting could easily have captured this moment, but a clicking camera inside the dark recesses of the van would have to do.

Obviously, the boy'd been wounded many times over, no doubt by those who were supposed to love him; instead, his small heart remained painfully unappeased. Needs, wishes, dreams and unfulfilled desires remained his constant companions. His so-called emotional quotient, his EQ, must fall extremely low on the scale, making the abduction that much easier. He'd be easily controlled, because of the very needs he wished to fulfill; in essence, the youthful animal's absolute needs equated out to his most basic weakness. *As is the case in all of nature,* thought the Snatcher, as the papers had dubbed him . . .

As is the case in all of nature, thought the FBI agent and psychic detective Dr. Kim Faith Desinor—identical thought patterns coming together in coincident harmony, a parallel unison, mysteriously measuring past, present and future on a timepiece belonging to the psychic detective, now telepathically tracking the Snatcher from a darkened hotel room . . .

The kid wanted that rarest of all human gifts: *attention,* real, unspoiled, unconditional, unequivocal and unadulterated attention. His needs were far more deeply rooted in the Jungian collective unconscious than such an untutored brain could possibly know or ever fully comprehend. Dr. Desinor knew this even though she had just arrived in Houston this day, even though she did not know the boy, even though she had never met the boy; she also knew that the stalking bastard who saw the boy as his prey also understood the boy's inherent weaknesses and counted on them. Deftly, devilishly, the Snatcher used the boy's own frailties, fears and emotions against him.

So, rightfully, the boy wanted and needed support to help carry a heavy heart, an adult heart, given to him by circumstances and a hard life no child should have to face. Then again, reality—which might well be a madman's delusion, Kim reasoned within—*sucked,* and so thought the man-shadow coming nearer the boy. The man-shadow meant to create his own reality, a reality built upon his fantasies, fantasies that involved lust-torture and lust-murder.

It was not material things the boy needed, although he certainly lacked material wealth as well, but it remained spiritual direction the boy most pined for. The boy had been born to be some angel's cause, right? Or had he been born to the opposite fate, to be yet another of the demon's unending victims? Which should he turn out to be?

At times the angels intervened to stop the demons, but at other times, they were far too late.

If not me, someone else'd come along, snatch the little bugger, the agent of lust and torture who meant to kill the child told himself as he clicked off a second and third photo of the boy. Kim heard the thought as if it had been spoken aloud, coming at her like a fist's blow.

Kim now watched from multiple directions and positions, ever changing: here above, here slightly to the side, outside looking on, but seeing only the dark shadow, and sometimes she *saw-felt* from within the shadowy figure—from inside his retinas.

She watched his seemingly massive hands as he opened the van door, tore out his cane and straightened up. *He walks with a cane. Remember this*, she ordered her second self, the one sitting precariously in a nearby tree with frail spectral branches and see-through leaves.

Meanwhile, the boy had turned his head, acutely aware of the railway-car-like noise of the van door as it rolled back on its rusted tracks. The boy watched the shadow man with only mild interest while the Snatcher, pretending nonchalance, now closed the van door on the driver's side with a weak push. The shadow man next turned and approached the boy, so light of foot he near flew, yet his cane beat a tap, tap, tapping along the wavy concrete as the floating human monster moved across the street like a Chagall creation, a harmless and lighter-than-air lover come to greet his prey.

The killer ignored and then walked through what bit of traffic he encountered here in the Raleigh Projects at Clayborne and Eustis streets—geography she knew from her reading of the abduction while in flight to Houston from Quantico, Virginia.

All the while, the boy's eyes remained on the Snatcher. Trained to be wary, the kid's animal instincts raised along with his hackles.

The young Turk should've stayed with the herd. . . .

The boy's eyes marked the slow gait taken by the dark man. The adolescent knew, if he had to, he could outrun any cripple with a cane. Still, he continued to eye the gimpy man with a malicious caution, his retinas itching with suspicion and a feral, savage look that served to sexually excite the man-shadow, inviting him to picture the boy trussed and helpless.

Click . . . a fourth shot. Picture of a kid just being wary for the moment, that moment of fear in which he might have easily bolted and run, but he didn't. Instead, he challenged the *old?* man approaching him with, "Whatchu takin' pictures of me fo? Huh?"

"I'm a pro, son. It's my job, takin' pictures."

Dr. Kim Desinor could not hear each word distinctly, but like a Geiger counter in a windstorm, she gathered in the general input and output of the two incorporeal conversationalists as they repeated a street performance some twenty-four hours ancient now.

"Pro? Pictures fo' what? *Entertainment Tonight* or something?" The boy laughed at his own joke. "You justa rag man."

The shadow man smiled wide and bellowed his laughter, too, but without overdoing it.

A certain arrogance and boyish curiosity about the shadow man and his camera sparked interest in the boy, kept his feet firmly planted. He stared at the strange pair of yellow eyes that looked back at him from the knobby head of the old man's cane, a bit mesmerized by it, saying under his young breath, "Cool . . . cool. . . ."

Kim desperately tried to will her astral eye and mind to see past the eerily stonelike, electric-yellow eyes of the strangely animated ornament atop the cane. It seemed to grimace back at her like some depiction of an Egyptian pharaoh on a pillar of stone, yet aside from the leering eyes and crooked smile, the exact features atop the ornamental cane remained static and unclear, like the man-shadow himself.

The spectral seesaw of their conversation continued, Kim promising herself to write down every word when she returned from her trance state to the four walls of her suite at the Houston Imperial Hotel. At the same time, she cursed herself for being able to see the color of the eyes on the cane but unable to decipher the color of the killer's eyes.

"Hey, son, what's your name, anyway?"

"Who's asking?"

This drew a laugh from the stranger, an old man's *hee, hee, hee* laugh. "Me, m'name's Cassell, Roosevelt B. Cassell."

"What's the B for?" asked the boy.

"Buck. Folks calls me Uncle Buck. Now, what be your name, boy?"

"Lamar."

"A fine name, Lamar. Lamar what?"

"Lamar Coleson."

"That's a fine name," he repeated for the boy, "and you looks like a fine, strong young man. If you can 'magine it, I oncet looked like you, m'self."

"What the fuck happen'?" the boy returned, laughing again, stepping along now, walking down the street, the shadow man keeping pace, his cane tapping the pavement. At times, his cane turned into a serpent, but this magician's stunt only intrigued the boy more.

"Time got caught up to me, you might say," continued Uncle Buck, "but it be true, son. I oncet was just like you. 'Magine dat?"

"No . . . can't 'magine dat you ever look good's me, mister. Hey, ain't I seen you 'round here befo'?" The boy stopped a moment in his walking to reconsider the raggedy man's clothing and appearance. The boy was sharp, and yes, he *had* seen the old man and his old van roaming about the neighborhood on more than one occasion, and the stranger knew this, and together—boy, monster man and psychic detective—contemplated its meaning.

"Sure . . . sure . . . ," he purred. "I been by your school yard some. Over by de park. Like to watch the chillen play, feed the birds some, takin' my pictures, stuff like 'at."

The boy stared hard at the *Nikon? 35mm?* camera dangling by a strap about Uncle Buck's neck, thinking that at some future time he might work the camera into his own possession, but Lamar said nothing, simply returning to his concerted walking, taking up a steady gait now, the shadow man beside him, the cane-beat asserting a steady threnody: *ta-thump, ta-thump, ta-thump* against the astral sidewalk where chocolate-layered brownstone buildings appeared and disappeared out of mist while the players moved along their *or Dr. Desinor's?* ethereal stage. . . .

The shadow man continued, "You prob'ly done saw me many times. I lives over a few blocks 'attaway." He eased into the easy rhythm of street slang to help allay any sense of discomfort the boy might have at talking with a strange old man. He next pointed with the cane north, in the direction of Parson Avenue, a street name that Kim had had no previous knowledge of, *a possible pure hit*, she told herself, urging her brain to store this fact in a special place, alongside the cane, the camera, the aged hands and ragged clothing.

Man-shadow continued, "But I jus' now moved into a new place—nice new place—but I needs some he'p, and I be willin' to pay good money, son."

Kind of long-winded for an old man, the boy thought, and Kim realized that much of the clarity of the psychic session was due to the boy, who now casually asked, "What kinda help? What kinda money?" The boy's eyes had widened just so, instantly curious at the mention of money. "And whatchu do with the pictures you take?" he finished.

Good, thought the killer, feeling a surge of excitement in his groin, a surge that disgusted Kim. "Well, I'm glad you're so curious, Lamar. I sell pictures to dem TV people and newspapers, big comp'nys like Mac—"

"TV, you gonna put my picture on TV?"

"Maybe . . . maybe, if dey buys it." Lamar's picture would be all over Houston by morning, if he'd just cooperate, thought the killer, furthering Kim's discomfort.

Lamar instantly asked, "Who? If *who* buys it?"

"Anybody in de news business all over dis country. My pictures been in de *New York Times*, *Look* magazine, de *Enquirer*, boy, but-but—"

"Really? The *Enquirer*?"

"—but I be gettin' old now. You see I'm an old man and can't do so much as—"

"Yeah, I see dat much be true. So how much money you got to spend?"

"Oh, I got plenty to get me by. Got dis cane to hold me up, but . . . well . . . truth of it is, can't always do for myself n'more, and I got no strong boys of my own like you to he'p me."

"He'p you how?"

"Got some furniture needs moving."

"That's a nice cane. How much you wan't fo' the cane?"

Lamar, focus on the cane, the cane, the cane, Kim chanted and willed him even as she willed herself to truly *see* the "candy" cane so attractive to Lamar. But the boy's netherworld eyes returned to the shadowed moon of the killer's face.

"I don't think I could sell it, son, Lamar."

The boy eyed him a moment longer. "You sure got a lotta wrinkles, mister."

The shadow man's laugh caused loose folds of skin about his neck to wriggle like Jell-O for the boy's amusement. The old stranger stood tall and heavyset, fat hands resting on the cane. He wasn't going hungry, the boy thought. Maybe he wasn't just blowing smoke about selling his pictures for big money. Maybe he'd spread some of it around if he liked the boy. He was well fed, heavy, this shadow man. *Or did he simply appear huge by the boy's standard of measure?* Kim wondered now, simultaneously upset with herself for interrupting her train of thought in this world of quickly fleeting moments.

"Call me Uncle Buck, son. Everybody always knows dey can make a buck from Uncle Buck." He laughed more, gaining a smile from the stone-faced boy. "Sho' beats pimpin' drugs."

But the boy only said, "I can't move no furniture. I ain't big 'nough, nor strong 'nough."

"Don't be talking lazy. Big boy like you? Betcha could move a hunerd-pound weight if I paid you well 'nough, but alls I got to move is just a few little things anyhow."

"Like what?" The boy came to an abrupt halt again, now standing before one of the project buildings, most likely home, but home faded in and out behind him.

"Tables, chairs."

The boy's hands opened wide in a defensive gesture, and he said, "I can't do no sofas or 'fridgrators or beds."

"Don't 'spect you to, Lamar. 'Sides, dem things got all took care of by the movers, son. But they put summa my things in the wrong rooms. I pay you ten dollars, how's zat?"

"Not 'nough."

"Twenty then."

The boy considered it, and pointing, said, "Twenty and the cane."

The old man grimaced sour, the wrinkles on his forehead and jowls turning his features into a Louis Armstrong mask. Lamar was right. The killer's face shimmied with loose folds of skin and mottled wrinkles, the road map of tendriled skin further masking the Snatcher's features.

"Can't give up my cane, boy," he finally said.

The shadow man is a black man, she told herself, *or a damned good imitation. . . .*

"Fifteen and the cane then."

The old man considered this, took a wheezing, deep breath and finally replied, "All right. I got 'nother cane in my closet, not so pretty as this'un, but I make it do. . . . I make it do."

Kim again tried to make out the ornamental cane head, but all she saw was a hazy, batlike globule of darkness out of which peered two painted yellow eyes.

Lamar wiped sweat from his forehead and said, "Gotta go tell my mama first."

"All right, you do just dat. Smart boy not to go off with no strangers 'fore you ask *your mommy*." It was said with just a trace of deprecation. "Where she at, just up this flight a stairs? Want me to go wid you, 'splain it all to her?" He smiled down at the boy, playing him like an instrument.

She wished with all her might that Lamar would walk him upstairs so that the mother would get a look at the abductor-killer, but she knew this hadn't happened in reality the day before, so it wasn't likely to happen now.

"No, I just gotta tell her where I be is all."

"Good, good boy. . . . Then you comes right back here, and we'll get dis business transaction out the way and done wid, and you'll get your money."

It must sound so logical to an early-teen brain, she thought.

"And the cane?" The boy was fascinated with the cane. *Why?* she wondered.

"And the cane, yes."

Lamar Coleson looked the shadow man over. A harmless, ambling old man, big in the shoulders, near as tall as the father on that silly Frankenstein spoof show, *The Munsters*. But again, she cautioned herself regarding the killer's physical size and age, seeing it through Lamar's from-the-pavement point of view.

Lamar now asked, "How long it goin' to take? How far is yow place, old man?"

"Few blocks over. We can take my van yonder, be there and back in, hmmmm . . ." He paused for effect. "Fifteen, maybe twenty minutes and you'll be back in your sweet mama's arms."

The trap was set.

The boy breathed deeply, looked around the isolated street, saw a solitary friend from the basketball court peeking from a doorway. Dr. Desinor desperately tried to focus on the witness, but Lamar, feeling a wave of pride swell with an image of himself, the cane and the money he'd be making, regained her attention. Another look in the direction of Lamar's friend and the comrade was gone—an eyewitness or merely another symbolic representation? Either way, she must recall the details intact later!

Now Lamar stared up at his bedroom window, the light casting a slice of warmth across a patch of the spongy, fog-strewn street into which his feet disappeared up to his ankles. A cold wind howled, screamed, went on past and was gone like a banshee, chased by another, sending a chill through Lamar and Kim. A sure iciness was in the air, yet the neighborhood boys had refused to give up the basketball court to winter just yet. And the street business of drug trafficking and prostitution, represented by zombies stalking about, continued at the fringe of the psychic scenario Kim had in some inexplicable way created with the help of either Lamar or the killer or both.

Since Lamar was presumed still alive and enduring the tortures of the mad abductor, Kim had faith in the boy, in the fact he might well be telegraphing a continual psychic plea from whatever hell he currently inhabited, that perhaps this version of events represented the boy's telepathic cry.

Frowning, Lamar studied first the old man and then his weathered dark *blue?* or *black?* van. His mind racing, he knew he should just go straight home. "All right," Lamar finally said defiantly, "but no more'n fifteen minutes."

The killer guessed Lamar's age at fifteen or sixteen, the age when a boy liked to assert his independence. Lamar going with him like this, without checking with his mother, was precisely what the Snatcher counted on. You didn't need a degree in psychiatry to understand the workings of an adolescent male mind. . . .

Besides, the boy was dealing with a harmless old man.

The boy went willingly now, forgetting about the beckoning light in the window above his head, about his mother's dinner on the stove, reaching out instead to caress the prize of his negotiations, the staff's head with its yellow-gold eyes. The boy's natural curiosity about the old man's battered black/blue van, his apartment, the money and opportunity for more odd jobs and goods in the future filled his thoughts now.

The old man took great care in placing his camera and cane in a protective box in the back of the van. The van itself reeked of spilt fluids, strange, medicinal and earthy odors. Pipe, conduit and assorted junk littered the van bed; the smells of construction dust and particleboard were heavy in the air, a fine white dust having thickly settled about the metal floor. Kim Desinor psychically gasped, acutely aware that the profiling team back at Quantico had strongly suggested the possibility that the Houston Snatcher drove a pickup truck or van that he used in his abductions, and that he likely worked in some capacity in the construction industry, given clues found on his previous victims, and that these quasi-facts might have influenced her psychic scenario.

As the boy climbed into the passenger seat in front, Lamar Coleson thankfully accepted two candy Life Savers from his smiling abductor. Dr. Kim Desinor's psychic vision came to a close, ending in a cloud-filled, peaceful white backdrop familiar to her. Slowly, carefully, all the fragmented pieces of her viewpoint selves gravitated into one whole. She no longer breathed the killer's breath or Lamar's breath, only her own. She breathed easier, longer breaths now, relaxing, consciously recovering.

Breathing easier allowed her eyes to slowly focus, to lose the gauzy, spiderweb haze, and to more clearly see the reality before her. Her eyes registered the great here and now of the darkened room she sat in. The return to this reality came as if entering from a dark tunnel. As planned, the first sight she saw, across from her, was the featureless outline of herself, reflected in the mirror where she sat upright on the bed in the lotus position. The shadowy reflection grinned evil back at her, an instant more of life for the shadow man, the Snatcher of her creation, moments before it suddenly tore its dark self from her mirrored form. It turned into a circling giant black bat wing as large as a blanket, filling the space overhead, hiding its gruesome features like some Phantom of the Opera, beating wings in a frantic attempt to disappear altogether, fearful of the light, fearful of her stare, and then it—or he—was gone.

Kim fearfully sought out the pencil and her professional notebook that she kept beside her bed at all times, hoping against hope to recall everything as it had happened, in its entirety, while counseling caution at interpretations even as she felt an overwhelming sense of accuracy in the cinematic insight that had played out in her mind's eye. It felt right; it felt solid, for the most part. It felt real, more so than any other single previous psychic experience she had ever encountered. It was far superior in clarity and detail to the impressions she'd gotten of the infamous Mad Matthew Matisak, or the now textbook case of the heart-eating killer she'd faced several years ago in New Orleans where she had worked hand in hand with FBI Medical Examiner Dr. Jessica Coran.

The local FBI here in Houston had called Quantico for profiling help, and they had requested any backup experts on serial killers available. She'd been assigned the case in typical thirteenth-hour fashion, now that it had gone beyond the control of local, state and federal authorities working through *normal* channels. Now FBI officials in D.C. turned to the paranormal, seeking answers to questions about the nature of this particular evil directed at young black boys in Houston, Texas, ghettos.

Kim's reputation in psychic detection for the bureau had grown impressively. This only increased proportionately when in 1997 the FBI had finally gone public with the information that tax dollars now supported psychic detection after a *Dateline* exclusive had raised speculation on the issue. Some supporters said that she was fast becoming the stuff of legend. But one misstep—should she make the wrong choices, should she trust too much her own literal interpretation of such nonexistent, ethereal conversations as that between Lamar Coleson and his abductor—and she knew that Kim Desinor could just as fast become the stuff of comedy. And if she wrongly interpreted the signs? And if Lamar lost his life as a result? And if the Snatcher were never caught as a result?

Doubt, as always, rose floodlike, seeped of its own nature through stone-edged conviction, even as she scripted the unfolding psychic impressions that had come to her in such sharp resolution.

Still, she felt good about this first psychic encounter between abductee and abductor, between innocent and violent, between torture victim and torturer, between soon-to-be murdered and established murderer.

The notebook on her knees moved, trembling with her anticipation, and the pencil in her hand soared as if possessed of a demon or an angel. She related the scene as closely as possible in her tight, yet conflicted, uncontrolled script. As she did so, she wondered anew who might believe it, who might scorn it, who might understand it, who might misunderstand. She cautioned, as she always must, against the source and clarity of the vision, and the symbolic nature of all things in the vision. Not one word of it could be taken at face value, not without verifiable substantiation, yet it felt so authentic, so real. . . .

ONE

Coyote track

Detective Lucas Stonecoat gave silent thanks to the computer
whiz kid who had accessed—lifted—the computer-generated
copy of the M.E.'s combined protocol on the Snatcher's
victims. The information included a report on the latest
murdered boy preceding Lamar Coleson's disappearance, a boy
named Theodore Melvin Ainsworth who might as well be
Lamar's brother, they were so alike in appearance. The
material—enclosed in an unmarked brown clasp envelope,
prepared by Dr. Leonard Chang and his civilian support
personnel, Randy Oglesby—burned in Lucas's hand.

He sought a private place to rip it open, to immediately and
carefully examine it.

The clock over Stonecoat's cluttered desk read 8:55 A.M., and
he'd long since become frustrated at having waited this
long—twenty-four hours—to get his hands on the M.E.'s
findings. Medical Examiner Chang, while eccentric, had earned a
reputation as the most thorough criminal forensics man in
Houston—in fact, in all of Texas. But finding a private place
in a police precinct, even here in the usually silent Cold Room,
this morning proved harder than locating an out-of-season
cactus blossom in the desert.

Several detectives involved in ongoing cases had come down

to Lucas's basement dungeon of unsolved murder, aptly named
the Cold Files Room, where every dead-letter murder case in the
city eventually resided. Each of this morning's visiting detectives from various precincts had come seeking enlightenment:
historical data on cases that'd gone unresolved that might be
relevant to the ongoing cases each worked. Since Lucas's
success a couple of summers ago in the reopening of cases that
he and Dr. Meredyth Sanger had successfully tied to the 1996
Mootry murder, netting an international ring of killers using
Internet cyberspace as their killing ground, every cop in the
city looked to be the next Lucas Stonecoat.

Lucas took it all in stride, but sometimes he became
disgusted by the lengths to which some of his white colleagues
were willing to go in an attempt to outperform the Native
American detective.

Adding to his annoyance, Lucas knew he'd be missed
upstairs in Dr. Meredyth Sanger's police group psychotherapy
session, which began at eight-thirty sharp. Meredyth ran
sessions for cops who'd discharged their weapons with result-
ant death or deaths of criminals, and sometimes citizens who
got in the way.

Lucas had come to work early, located Randy, Dr. Sanger's
male secretary, snatched the secreted report from him and
gotten clear of Dr. Sanger's arena. He had no intention of
swimming another lap in her pool of psychobabble. He'd
dodged last week's session, and he would dodge today's, but he
couldn't successfully dodge it and remain here beside his
phone where she could easily harangue him, so he desperately
sought an escape route, his eyes assessing the situation, his
mind calculating just how much he'd be missed if he stepped
out long enough to read over Chang's reports.

The roof, perhaps? he suggested to himself, going for the
seldom used service elevator.

On the roof, the U.S. flag snapped and fluttered in a bitter
October wind high overhead. Lucas watched the Stars and
Stripes, the Texas state flag and the city of Houston flag
alternating between full, flat-out and a limp, intertwining death

in the changing air currents. Metal pulleys clanged a dull rhythm against the three towering flagpoles, a perfect, hollow base; meanwhile, loose ropes danced as if some giant but invisible fingers played them. The ropes might've held invisible soldiers that rappelled down them. The wind also yanked and ripped at the soft blue shirt Lucas wore, first flattening it against him and then billowing it from his body, as if it were a sail on a boat at sea in a storm.

The several pages of the report were also being torn at, the wind threatening to steal them entirely. He located a walled alcove where some chilly pigeons reluctantly made room for him after a bit of squabbling and cooing.

He squatted and read the report as flecks of snow floated over him, so many fairy lights in the morning grayness. Overhead, white-bellied, roiling, somber clouds with bloated gray eyes watched over him. The same bloated gray eyes wept a silver-hued sleet that now pelted Lucas, dampening the pages of the report.

The report revealed some startling truths about the Snatcher, the killer of young black boys here in Houston. Still, many of what appeared to be revelations to Lucas seemed lost on Captain Gordon J. Lincoln. Lincoln had his hands full as the new replacement for Captain Phillip Lawrence, who, after judicial review by departmental brass, had found himself looking at early retirement, due in large part to his having misread all the salient clues in the case that had continued to make front page news all summer long, the Helsinger affair. It had been a case that had very nearly cost Meredyth Sanger, Randy Oglesby and Lucas Stonecoat their lives.

A particularly aggressive pigeon pecked at Lucas's foot, its persistence a clear enough sign for any Native American: The bird meant to urge the Cherokee detective along in his secret investigation.

"Yeah, I know," Lucas said, finally acknowledging the pigeon's help. "When I get back down to the Cold Room, I'll start a profile of the killer, and if you peck me one more fucking time, I'll test out my new microwave oven on you, bird."

He now closed the file Randy had created for him and stepped near the edge of the building, looking down at the sheer drop-off. The building sat squat and ugly amid the myriad of Texas-oil-rich skyscrapers all around the precinct house. Only four stories high, it had once been a city school named Wells High School. Randy Oglesby joked it must've been named after the weird science fiction writer and futurist, H. G. Wells. Maybe Randy had been right, but Lucas doubted it.

Randy *was* right about one thing, Lucas decided as he looked down at the dim recesses of a growing urban jungle. Houston, Texas, although a sprawling metropolis with an ever increasing population, remained a small town in many respects, living up to the state's single-word motto, "Friendship," and when a small town hurt, everyone hurt, or at least almost everyone.

For the past several months, Houston prayed for relief, but not all Houstonites prayed for the same relief. Some prayed for an end to the Houston Oilers' inglorious losing streak, while others prayed for an end to the bitter walkout at the Exxon refinery. Still others prayed for an end to the cold snap that had gripped the entire state with its biting winter wind that peeled paint from lampposts and skin from people unused to a thing called windchill factor. Agripeople prayed for an end to the months' long draught, while still others prayed for an end to the dull gray skies. But most Houstonites prayed to see an end to the horror of a string of disappearances that had yielded up a succession of small brutalized bodies from among the city's black population. Lamar Coleson appeared to be yet another victim—another spindly black youth lost to the ghetto stalker, a madman who roamed freely among Houston's seamier, darker streets, whom newshounds had dubbed the Snatcher.

The first six young teens to disappear had lived in the Bellaire District off Bypass Interstate 610, or had come from the Jacinto City area at the intersection of 610 and Interstate 90, areas where blacks and Latinos lived in a constant state of mild to seething unrest. Whoever the killer, he proved quite mobile, since these neighborhoods were parted by Houston's sprawling downtown business district. The geography of the crimes

supported the official belief that the killer used the highways as
a quick exit from locations where he abducted the children he
meant to torture to death.

Lucas, however, remained unconvinced of this official truth.
In fact, there proved a number of "detailed facts" regarding the
Snatcher case about which Lucas wasn't so sure.

But the Snatcher's satanic nature and the results the bastard
got proved true enough, and torture was the operative word.
The killer was what FBI insiders called a lust-murderer, as his
crimes were of an aberrant sexual nature. He got off on seeing,
hearing, tasting, feeling and smelling the suffering of these
young boys. His consolation, his gratification, his ease and
relief came by way of wounding, abusing and tormenting
children. He got off on the torture, on the beating, the cutting,
the crying and the bleeding. And so torture he did, for from
pain, anguish and agony, he achieved his only sexual release,
his only sexual satisfaction.

From the city medical examiner's reports that Lucas studied,
he learned the savage and ugly extent of the details. The youths
were ferociously trussed up, not dangled by their wrists or
ankles, which would cause bone fractures and separations at
the sockets and joints from the force of gravity. No, the victims
were tied in a "basket weave" fashion, the rope burns on rumps,
backs, shoulders telling the story of a netlike cradle in which
the boys had been trapped and made instantly helpless, unable
to defend against the brutality. The reports spoke of skin burns
of various kinds in hundreds of god-awful places on the body,
burns created by untold instruments, from cigar burns to
electrical and chemical burns, as if the bastard killer wished to
conduct experiments on his victims, to see what sort of burns
different household chemicals might raise.

Bruises and welts attested to repeated beatings and torture
until merciful death ensued. The report spoke of undisguised,
unremitting evil in its most pure form, that of the sociopath
who ironically, while unable to feel anything of the pain
inflicted on another living being, unable to experience normal

empathy, did feel a bizarre and twisted sexual high at the price of another's deepest agony and suffering.

Lucas imagined how the young victims agonized within the weblike trap, within a dangling net, unable to escape their captor, naked and bruised, burned and tortured, so that even sleep must hurt or frighten, given the rope burns and the sheer number of welts.

Downstairs, in the ready room for the precinct's task force on the Snatcher cases, the walls had been hung with the faces of the dead black children of Houston. Lucas's request to be a part of the task force had been denied by the new captain, Gordon Lincoln, who wanted Lucas's full attention on upcoming changes in Cold Room procedures. Despite this, Lucas had gotten the reports, which put the deaths at or about seven days after each disappearance. They showed that these young men, who might've survived their torture, would easily have starved to death nonetheless. Their stomachs were bloated and empty, lips parched, throats arid, bodies dehydrated.

Shaking his head over the mental images, Lucas made his way back inside, one of the pigeons attempting to follow. The wind rushing through the opened roof door clawed at Lucas and the pigeon, trying to snatch them both back, but succeeded only in gaining the pigeon. The knowledge Lucas had gleaned from Leonard Chang's coldly worded report also clawed at Lucas. He instinctively reached for some solid object to touch, a wall, a handrail, as he located the ancient stairs to the service elevator a half floor down. There he sleepwalked into the empty elevator car and pressed for the basement and the Cold Room.

The seventh in a string of child disappearances, Lamar Coleson's recent abduction infuriated, angered and frustrated everyone in the city, and the most frustrated guys in Houston at the moment were the local FBI's SAC and ASAC—special agent in charge and his assistant. Daily and nightly appeals on radio, TV and in print media, appeals by the city commissioner, the mayor, the FBI and the sad-faced single mother, including a spot on *America's Most Wanted*, had as much effect as cursing Satan, Lucas felt. The appeals pleaded for Lamar's safe return to his mother. The abductor, molester, brutalizer, killer's response: stone-cold heartless silence. A special airing of *Unsolved Mysteries* pleaded with the public to come forward with any shred of information that might lead authorities to Lamar. Everyone in officialdom knew that Lamar's time was running out with each passing hour, that from the moment of his disappearance, if he were indeed one of the Snatcher's victims, his remaining seven days of life began trickling through the killer's distorted hourglass. Everyone knew that if Lamar's abductor could not be found, the boy's life was forfeit. The facts stood stark and brutal; little hope survived among the police community.

Lucas hated to agree with the negative thinking, but young Lamar Coleson's disappearance almost assured tragedy for the boy and his mother, since Lamar so thoroughly fit the victim profile drawn up by authorities. Earlier victims of the crazed killer, all spindly youths, all black, all living at the poverty level, *all* had eventually been found mutilated.

Whoever the killer, he moved in and out of the Houston ghettos like a pale shadow—a ghost familiar with its haunts. All of the victims, like Lamar, had been young boys struggling with scarcity, street violence, gangs, delinquency, adolescence and their own identities, as anyone at this age and in this place must.

"Proving one thing," Lucas told himself in the empty elevator car. "The killer is one of us—all too human, and most likely a black man. . . ."

Many in Houston had armed themselves, and everyone with a child below the age of seventeen feared for his child's life. Fewer and fewer people walked the streets after dark, but this had not deterred the Snatcher, whose last three victims had been taken in broad daylight or at dusk.

Missing and presumed to be held against his will, callow Lamar Coleson would turn fifteen in two weeks. If he were a victim of the Snatcher, he'd not likely see that birthday.

Local FBI, the HPD Missing Persons personnel, augmented

by Violent Crimes and Homicide detectives, continued to scour the Texas tarmac for clues, seeking out anyone who might know Lamar or anyone who saw him in the hours before his disappearance. The headlines shouted in bold typeface the glaring and growing tragedy: news accounts bloated full with the Snatcher and his trail of death, a brief history of the young lives he'd snuffed out, a sidebar stating how helpless the Houston PD appeared in the face of such grotesque lust-torture murders and "experts" moaning how the FBI ought to have been called in weeks earlier.

The reality, known in police circles, played differently. In fact, the FBI had taken over orchestrating the case a month before, after the third disappearance. Truth be known, the venerable FBI had resorted to psychic detection, or so the word in police circles buzzed.

The intimation that the HPD hadn't cared about disappearing black boys in the ghettos angered everyone from the commissioner down to the beat cop, as did the intimation that the FBI had only recently been invited in, and that finally the HPD was abuzz with activity, every precinct set up as a command post, every precinct having a ready room as part of the citywide task force combining with FBI personnel to end the satanic career of the Snatcher. And all this activity, according to news reports, was thanks to FBI involvement. . . . So much bullshit, Lucas thought.

The elevator doors creaked open and deposited him in the dungeonlike, stone-walled hallway outside the Cold Room in the bowels of the ancient precinct building. He opened the door on a room filled with crates, boxes, files and murder books, all information relevant to what most any thinking person would call irrelevance—the stone-cold, dead files of cases gone unsolved over the years. He stepped through the creaky door, the squeal of the thing reminding him of the oil-needy Tin Man in *The Wizard of Oz*, and he found himself once again staring into the hole where the HPD kept its shame, its remorse, its guilt—all the room's graying manila folders so much fodder for mites and worms; still each murder book proved rich with story.

Once again the place prompted the question, "What good does it do to unearth ancient cases of incest, murder, suicide and death when today's headlines will do?" Lucas pondered the question even as his eye fell upon the headlines of the newspaper he'd left on his desk here. He now laid aside the M.E.'s protocol on Theodore Melvin Ainsworth for the *Houston Star-Dispatch*.

He looked over the front-page headlines for any glimpse of good or breaking news in the Snatcher story, but saw nothing new. He tossed aside the paper and glanced around the room at the hefty black, blue, red and manila binders—each a case book, a murder book, some requiring boxes—all the unsolved cases shivering on their shaky metal stacks, each calling out in a soft surreal whine, "*Taaake me up . . . tooouch me . . . reeead me. . . .*"

Each ancient case stood in disrepair, so to speak, like old houses in need of too much TLC, each just another moldy Cold File.

"Maybe you ought to stir the pot," his grandfather's advice came back to his ear like a resounding bell, "or steer clear of it altogether. . . ." In other words, Lucas knew he should simply stay out of the Coleson case and be content that Houston PD had given him a second chance, allowing him to start fresh. Still, the real action continued in the squad room upstairs, all this activity going on just overhead, and he held no part in it.

"Big favor they did for me," he'd complained to his grandfather when last he'd seen the old man at the Coushatta Indian Reservation in Huntsville. "Placing me, an Indian, in charge of their goddamned mistakes in that g'damn Cold Room. Bastards!"

Cranking up the heat in the Cold Room had little effect. The place was a dank cave, the walls wet with condensation. In this dragonless dungeon below Houston Police Precinct #31, Lucas had few visitors, but he daily heard many transcendent voices, saw many spectral faces, heard disturbing haunting interior noises, not the snake or mouse or spider or cockroach, not that distant trainlike rumble from somewhere beyond the basement window, not the sirens nor the semis of the nearby Interstate, not millions of volts of electrical current, not the pulse of the city, but the soft banshee cries of the long-ago dead who would not be denied.

Maybe the bastards who placed him here in this forced confinement with the dead, maybe . . . just maybe . . . on some subconscious, metaphysical level, maybe they knew that the ghosts of this place would speak only to a disgruntled, broken spirit like Stonecoat. Then again, maybe the bastards in brass simply knew enough to keep a Mad Hatter like Lucas Stonecoat off the street.

Dr. Meredyth Sanger stuck her head out from the conference room, looked angrily about and asked her secretary, Randy Oglesby, "Where the hell's Detective Stonecoat?"

Randy looked over his shoulder, showing annoyance from behind a ridiculously large pair of black, reflective dark glasses that Meredyth could have used as a mirror. Randy had taken to wearing the glasses after a spat between them in which Meredyth had insisted he keep the lights in the office turned on. He maintained that the hours he put in at the computer screen required a semidarkened environment, that the glare of fluorescent lights killed eyesight, but Meredyth had surmised that Randy's newly acquired interest in the dark side of the Internet had actually prompted his recent strange behavior.

Randy fit the profile of a computer nerd, but he'd been making real headway, coming out, as it were, up until the recent breakup with his Asian girlfriend, occuring as it had just after he'd proposed marriage to her.

"Stonecoat, Stonecoat . . ." Randy meanly teased. "You mean he's not inside with the others? You mean he's a no-show again? Maybe you ought to report him to his new boss." Randy returned to what stared back at him from his computer screen, clicking wildly for a screen saver to replace it.

Meredyth, seeing that he meant to hide what he had on the

screen, stepped out and stood beside him now. But all there was to see were the little fish being eaten by the big fish on the screen saver. A low rumble of talk from the assembled police personnel in the conference room behind her spilled out into the outer office until the door closed, dulling the talk to a soft oceanlike roar.

"You're certain you don't know where he is?" she asked.

"I called down to the Cold Room, like you asked. No answer."

"What're you hiding behind that screen saver?" she asked.

"Nothing."

Again Dr. Sanger thought how foolish Randy looked wearing the large, dark glasses—they made him look like a giant bug hunched over the computer screen. But Randy, acting like some teenager—although he was in his early twenties—claimed to enjoy his new look. She guessed that he rather appreciated the looks he received from others, and the overall effect he'd had on her, her reaction. To add to his new look, he'd gone out and purchased an entire line of Gant shirts and Guess jeans, which on him, she thought, looked not bad.

"Just what is it you're working on, Randy?" she asked, coming nearer.

Frowning, he brought back the Web site he'd been browsing, the fish disappearing in a nanosecond. Meredyth bit her lip, not knowing what to say to Randy, who had been using office time once again to cruise the strange site materializing before her eyes as he slowly scrolled down.

Meredyth could hardly believe just how dark cyberspace had become. She'd heard of child porn on the Net, of lewd and lascivious E-mail, but this—this was all new to her: electronic graveyards, casket shopping, headstone art, virtual scatological rites, burials, cremations, forays into virtual necrophilia—sex with the dead, even sex with one's favorite dead idol, say James Dean or Marilyn Monroe. Meredyth fleetingly thought she'd pick Jim Morrison to take to bed, then immediately scolded herself. But it came out as a scold for Randy. "Don't you have enough to do around here? You know they're cracking down on how our systems are being utilized, Randy. You want to get us both into trouble?"

"But I should think you, being a crime psychiatrist, that this stuff, you'd want to know about it, try to understand why it's so . . . so popular," he challenged. "I mean, it's . . . out there."

She saw now that a how-to on cannibalism was available to the casual browser, as was a how-to on dissecting a murder victim's body, to "virtually" do away with the evidence and all identifying marks, including teeth, and she began to see what Randy's last remark meant.

"Ouch," groaned Randy, reacting to the removing of the murder victim's teeth. "That's gotta mean applying some damned judicious force on the pliers."

Meredyth found herself mesmerized. "Plucking teeth from dead people . . ."

"*Virtually* dead people, Doctor."

"Your idea of fun?" Even as she said it, Meredyth realized that she, too, had been drawn into this morbidly fascinating world on Randy's screen. Still, she chastised Randy further, asking, "What does your ex-girlfriend think of your fascination with virtual corpses, Randy?"

"It's just a hobby."

"Rando—" She'd begun calling him Rando after Lucas Stonecoat had done so, since their encounter together with Lucas in which they'd faced down a band of computer Net killers a couple of summers ago. "Rando, it's hobbies and interests like . . . like pet iguanas and tarantulas that chase most girls out the door."

As if reading her thoughts, Randy replied, "I'm hardly alone in my interest, Doctor. Many cyberspace death-related destinations end in on-line obituaries, dead-pet memorials, tips on burials at sea, recycled rumors of reported deaths of famous people and a celebrity 'dead pool' for the genuinely gruesome gambler."

"You don't mean . . . You mean they take odds on—"

"The most overweight Hollywood stars, the most addicted

sports stars, the most feeble and ready-for-the-grave politicians, you name it."

"This gets stranger by the moment."

"Hey, I'm not actively participating in any of it. Just browsing, curious, you know, like—"

"Like me," she thought aloud.

On screen, Meredyth Sanger, police and forensic psychiatrist, saw the first full-service mortuary in cyberspace, the Carlos A. Howard Funeral Home, advertising the $1,192 Onyx Regal Velvet Coffin, equipped with adjustable bedsprings, mattress and a time capsule. Morose people from all over the nation wrote in to the billboard for the Virtual Memorial Gardens to immortalize a loved one by placing a eulogy on the Net. The Cemetery Gate placed obits on-line for a twenty-five-dollar fee, and with hundreds of takers a day, curator Bruce Armstrong offered a free list of resources on how to grieve, including E-mail support groups.

"All services available twenty-four/seven," Randy said to Meredyth's reflection on his screen.

A groan escaped Meredyth.

"A widow or widower waking up at three A.M. on a Sunday morning can't go to a bereavement group in any other fashion than by logging on," Randy defended.

As Randy scrolled the menu, Meredyth saw that the on-line death trend opened the user up to the world's most famous and inaccessible cemeteries, such as Paris's Cimetiere du Pere Lechaise—coincidentally the final whereabouts of Jim Morrison. She wondered if he'd found there in French soil a kind of peace alongside Oscar Wilde and Marcel Proust. Other such cyber sites opened up the Vietnam Memorial in Washington, D.C., various Boston, Chicago, New York and New Orleans graveyards, not to mention Egypt's tombs, and guides to worldwide disease and draught and famine and war cemeteries throughout history and the present.

"Cool," Randy muttered to his screen. "On some E-mail traffic, I've found messages to the deceased out there in cyberspace, while other messages go to survivors; some caring souls go to the trouble to forward electronic roses and other virtual flowers."

"Every girl's dream," Meredyth muttered.

"For E-mail enthusiasts with more macabre leanings, there's an even darker side of the Web."

"Such as?"

Randy stroked a key and highlighted a menu choice reading MORTUARY ON-LINE. "It's a Web site that offers gruesome autopsy photos, usually of the rich and famous or infamous from Judy Garland to Charlie Chaplin, Bonnie and Clyde, Mussolini and his mistress, the former Mrs. O. J. Simpson and Ronald Goldman, murdered children such as Susan Smith's kids, purported alien bodies, you name it."

"Ugh!" Meredyth replied, pointing at the screen with her pen and saying, "There's a cyber location depicting photos of a museum exhibit of exhumed corpses? Ugh," she repeated when Randy brought up the "holdings" of the Museo de las Momias. "God, next thing they'll have a Web site for that Summun Mummification Center I've read about."

"Yeah, in which ex-Mormon church elder Corky Ra describes his bizarre encounters with alien beings—"

"And promotes a service that mummifies dead pets—"

"And humans alike."

"In repose or in action," countered Meredyth.

Randy now brought up the Cannibalism Page—graphic and disturbing instructions for the preparation of humans for consumption. The Shroud of Turin Home Page offered one of the few religiously oriented entries in the computer death field. Another was the Jewish Burial Society's guide to Jewish funeral customs.

"What's that one?" she asked. "The Natural Death Centre."

"Provides a do-it-yourself funeral guide with primers on biodegradable body bags, burials at sea, backyard interments, that sort of thing."

"Backyard burials?"

"It's legal in some states, like Florida, with a permit."

"That'll bring the value of the old homestead down, won't it?"

"By twenty or thirty percent," mused Randy just before logging off the death field.

"I find it all quite . . . *interesting* from a purely professional stance, Randy, but I'm disturbed to find you surfing through this stuff on company time. You know about the department's crackdown on how we're spending our time and on what."

"But you need to know what the popular mind is up to every day, Doctor, in your line of work," he countered.

"Perhaps," she grudgingly half agreed. "But what about the transcription of yesterday's session with the ranking officers?"

"On your desk, Doctor." Randy knew Dr. Sanger would be far more upset about the time he'd put in on Detective Lucas Stonecoat's requests than about the cyber-death webs.

"What about the details of the Forester shooting? The Robinette case? You know I've got to be in court to testi—"

"On your desk."

"And the Snatcher stuff?"

"On your desk. I'd say, Doctor, that you're a lot further behind than I am at this point." He gave her a wide, devilish grin that reached the bottom of each lens of his dark glasses.

He could be so efficient as to be infuriating, she thought, and she realized that Randy's efficiency kept getting better, despite his sunglasses, his new hairstyle and his Net surfing. "All right. I've got to get back inside. Try to locate Lucas . . . Detective Stonecoat for me."

"Yes, ma'am, Doctor."

"I'll be in my session, then in my office by ten," she said. He took the cue to mean coffee, black, awaiting her at her desk at ten.

His morning duties for Dr. Sanger complete, Randy Oglesby returned to his computer, where he now entered data in his most businesslike manner, his bare feet hidden beneath the desk. His current search through all police inquiries related to the Snatcher case for Detective Lucas Stonecoat had not yet been exhausted, but he'd had to be careful so as not to arouse any suspicions from either Dr. Sanger or those in charge of the investigation. It could cost him dearly.

He'd already given Lucas a good deal of information, but there might yet be something mined from the Net on the detective's behalf. He liked and admired Stonecoat, although he wished that Lucas would lighten up. For a pencil-thin guy, Lucas was *heavy*.

While Randy's fingers worked over the keyboard and police files filled his screen, the depths of the dark side of the Net continued to wash over his mind. He was convinced that he could write a successful, perhaps bestselling book on the subject. He was well aware that for many people, this dark side represented a profound need, and that many hundreds of thousands of people were addicted to the bleak and macabre side of the Internet.

Either it was addiction or acceptance . . . acceptance of the dualism of human nature and reality, a reality of evil residing in all mankind. Part of the reality of evil must be the horrid, morbid fascination that evil evoked in the human heart. His book, Randy had concluded, would be a meaty study of the satanic in the computer and the physiology of evil, a phrase he had gleaned from Dr. Meredyth Sanger's press remarks on the serial killers of the Helsinger's Pit affair. However, his book would not condemn wholesale the Net's dark side. That would be a book written by a narrow-minded, fearful, idiotic, electronic prude bigot. Some computer users found a profound sense of release and relief in having the luxury of both an intimate and public forum for voicing their deepest emotions and/or darkest thoughts. Many a thank-you card to the curators and morticians who provided these death and dying services attested to this. Dr. Sanger, once she had time to review all the material on the subject, must agree. Perhaps she'd consent to doing an introduction to Randy's book—legitimize it, so to speak.

Randy Oglesby held ambitions and aspirations far greater

than most, and while a genius with computers, he believed life held more in store for him. His near death at the hands of E-mail assassins only two summers ago had spurred him on to meet the challenge of his deepest desires. But he was nobody's fool, not even his own. He'd keep his day job. He wished to skip over the starving artist/writer gig. Besides, he'd been highly instrumental in cracking the Helsinger's Pit murder-by-computer case, not that anyone had given him any citations or kudos for nearly getting himself killed. Still, he could confidently cite this fact, along with his having helped Detective Lucas Stonecoat and Dr. Meredyth Sanger in unmasking and zeroing in on the largest single evil ever to infiltrate cyberspace.

Now Lucas had again called on Randy and the computer to combat evil. It could be a whole chapter, no, an entire section, of his proposed book. The struggle to use machines for good or evil—the ancient, cosmic battle now being waged in cyberspace as well as inside the human cranium, all due to God's having given man free will, the will to do good and prosper or the will to do evil and wither the planet and the souls of humanity.

Randy knew that he had had as many daydreams and Walter Mitty schemes as most of the population of the precinct put together, but this idea, this one, felt doable. Randy had recently begun helping Lucas on the Snatcher affair out of a sense of duty, out of some warped notion that he and Stonecoat remained steadfast friends, blood brothers, in a manner of speaking, despite the Grand Canyon of differences lying between them. It had only been recently that he'd become convinced that *The Evil Computers Do—Satan in Cyberspace*— tentative title—written by Randall Oglesby, aka Mr. Squeegee, must be published so he could appear on Oprah Winfrey's show to discuss how the Antichrist got into the computer in the first place—who welcomed *it* in?

Forget it, Randy told himself. *Surely someone else already has such a book in the works. Surely it's beyond my abilities. Surely I'll never finish chapter one.*

Besides, Stonecoat probably never entertained the notion that he and Randy were figurative blood brothers, no way. Stonecoat courted no friends. He was as good as his name, that invisible armor all around him at all times. The goddamned Cold Room was the perfect place for the Indian bastard. Blood brothers . . . what a load of crap, no matter that the Indian himself had once jokingly said it.

Randy's anger rose incrementally with the minutes as they ticked away. Angry with himself as much as with Stonecoat, Randy felt used, abused, put-upon. He might as well be a computer, a piece of freaking furniture for all Stonecoat knew, yet Lucas continually came with his hand out for information on this and that, and this morning anything on the Snatcher case, "With particular emphasis on the Lamar Coleson disappearance." And what had Randy done but honored the great and powerful Stonecoat with insipid compliance—and now Lucas Stonecoat had Randy lying and covering for him!

Randy worried about how much Dr. Sanger knew, and if her trust in him might be irreparably eroded. Talk about nobody's fool! She had an uncanny ability to read a lie. And while Randy felt awful about lying to her, he'd had to—for the sake of a pseudo-brotherhood and a chance for a new chapter in his projected bestseller.

To further complicate matters, a recent HPD gestapo rule about evidence-gathering on-line meant that big brother watched every byte, and while Randy had no problem accessing information, he'd done so on Lucas's behalf by logging on as Dr. Meredyth Sanger, using the password that Randy had created for her.

Oddly, or perhaps not so oddly, given the high visibility of the Snatcher case, Dr. Sanger had now requested all information on the case herself, and making a duplicate copy for her from Detective Stonecoat's material had been only a minor inconvenience. More worrisome: the fact that both Dr. Sanger and Stonecoat had each expressly told him not to tell the other of their interest in the Snatcher case.

Amazingly enough, like a tightrope walker, Randy had been

able to do both: provide each with what he or she needed without violating either trust—so far. But this was no small feat, the juggling act becoming more complicated hour by hour, an undeniable web of deceit.

Why couldn't the two of them, shrink and cop, play together in the same sandbox? Why all the freaking cloak-and-dagger?

Randy had noticed that the lady shrink and the Texas Cherokee cop had distanced themselves from one another since their work on Helsinger's Pit. Perhaps it had something to do with Lucas's having been decorated for bravery in the affair, and for having brought down the Helsinger's Pit computer conspiracy "single-handedly," as the papers and the toastmasters had put it. Certainly Meredyth, like Randy himself, deserved more credit for the downfall of the villains than either of them had received, and perhaps this fact bothered her, as it did Randy. More likely, Randy thought, the flickering and flaring emotions Stonecoat and Sanger displayed toward each other simply frightened the other one off.

Just beyond the conference room door, the sound of men and women who'd fired their weapons in the line of duty rumbled and ebbed and flowed.

To Randy the muffled sounds coming from the session had a soothing effect, despite the fact he knew the level of energy and emotion in the room next door must be intensely high. Once he'd heard Lucas Stonecoat shouting at Dr. Sanger, and he'd clearly made out the words, "Bullshit! It was kill or be killed!" In another instance, he had heard Stonecoat shout, "I'd do the same with a rabid animal!"

Sanger, speaking on the subject of Timothy McVeigh and whether or not he deserved the electric chair, had yelled back, "Evil is more to be pitied than hated, Lucas!"

From there, the two of them had gotten nowhere, Randy had surmised when Lucas stormed out over Meredyth's protest. His parting shot: "I'm cured!"

"You're afraid of looking too deeply at yourself, Lucas. It's fear that drives you!" she'd countered, but he was gone, with no plans for returning.

The conference room door opened now, Dr. Sanger breaking up the session early, saying a good-bye to each of the six officers and two detectives who'd recently been ordered into psychiatric counseling. When they had all filed out, Dr. Sanger asked Randy, "No news from Lucas?"

"Sorry, none."

"I'll be in my office, catching up on this Snatcher business— and thanks, Randy, for getting all the data on the case for me."

"No problem. Coffee's coming up."

"Yeah, that'd be nice, and again, thanks."

"Don't mention it."

Randy, once more alone with his thoughts and his computer screen, pushed the print button, the printer blipping into action. *I'll run Dr. Sanger a copy of what new stuff I've pulled up on the screen for Lucas Stonecoat. I'll give it to her first. Maybe that'll count for something, if I can later say that I merely made copies for Lucas, but that she got first dibs. . . .* But he doubted it would help when she learned the truth, and learning was what a psychotherapist did.

$\mathcal{T}wo$

Fence: guarding good luck

LATER THE SAME DAY . . .

The Cold Room, with its stacks of unsolved, dust-laden murder files, felt even colder than usual today. Lucas found a handful of files and murder books dropped on his desk alongside the sign-in/sign-out clipboard. One stack, clean and neat, heralded the arrival of new, incoming unsolved murder cases, an always steady flow since they came in from all over the city. Not every precinct housed a cold room. The smaller, dingier stack of files and books represented cases recently cracked open and looked into, cases from the past, dusted off and examined. There had been more activity in the basement file room lately than at any other time in Lucas's short reign here as the Keeper of the Dying Embers, his pet name for the necro-file duties foisted upon him by the department

Still, for the moment, the place was empty and quiet, stultifyingly so, save for the dead voices reaching out from each file.

Lucas swiveled back and forth in his recently oiled chair, working in the WD-40 as he visually scanned the ledger to see if any files had been removed in his absence, and if so by whom. He saw that Detective Mich Harrelson had taken a file labeled 1967 THERESA PASSERO, someone somehow linked to an ongoing case, perhaps? Detective Dave Casey had taken away a case labeled 1959 EMIL NUENBERGER, no doubt of interest to Casey alone. Still, Lucas silently wished Detectives Harrelson and Casey luck. Both men had been tapped as possible assistants to Lucas Stonecoat on special assignment in attacking the enormous backlog of unsolved murders warehoused here.

Captain Lincoln, short of ordering Harrelson and Casey to join COMIT, the name of the new program that Lucas would spearhead, had given the men a grace period in which to "volunteer." Lucas knew that no detective working active cases wanted the duty. He himself didn't want the duty.

At least with the promised funds for Lincoln's "bullish" plan for COMIT, he'd be getting a secretary to file away all this stuff, someone with computer smarts to scan every file in the place from hard copy print and photos to three-and-a-half-inch diskettes for easy access and use on the computer, which would eliminate a great deal of dust, dust mites and the growing problem of space; but first they'd have to get some decent lighting down here. These thoughts played through his mind as he continued to poke through the clutter lying about his desktop.

He next lifted a rather thin and worm-eaten murder file left amid the others. A quick check and double-check of the ledger revealed nothing about who had left the ancient file on his desk. He snatched down a second clipboard and scanned back through the months preceding. Nothing. The book, dated 1948, could not be accounted for, as it had not been logged out or in.

Had someone merely come in, cased the book here at his desk and dropped it, not bothering to sign the ledger, out of carelessness? Or had the reader intentionally wished to leave no tracks? Careless casualness about the handling of evidence and materials relevant to criminal acts had in the past cost the HPD and every major police department in the country dearly, as witnessed by the O. J. Simpson trial. Still, some people played fast and loose with evidence, particularly "ancient" evidence. And this murder book, labeled 1948 MINERVA ROUND-POINT, AKA CLARICE DANE, apparently was no exception.

Roundpoint . . . the name rolled easily off his mind. Round-point was an American Indian name, one Lucas recognized and knew to be of Fox or Sauk origin, but some said Mohawk. With so much intertribal marriage since the end of the Indian Wars, there was little telling. In any case, like Lucas's ancestors who'd migrated first from Georgia to Oklahoma in the 1820s and '30s, and then from Oklahoma to Texas, Minerva Round-point, when she died in 1948, was a long way from her homeland, whether she considered it Canada, northern New York, Illinois or Kansas.

Uprooted and rootless when she died, she'd almost been buried in a potter's field in Houston, Texas, before her body was finally claimed by a minister named Father Michael Avi from a Kansas Indian reservation.

Lucas stared now at a photograph depicting Minerva in life, likely taken from her personal effects for the file so long ago; the photo revealed a beautiful young Indian face with large, luminous eyes. Lucas's fingers now worked independently of his mind to ferret through the file while questions pursued him: How had she come to be here in Houston at the age of twenty? How had she come to die so young and so ignobly? How had she become the victim of a mutilation murder? Had she been raped or merely sliced to ribbons? The number of cuts and slashes to her face mocked the number of questions Lucas instantly felt flooding in.

The photographs of the body spoke a complicated story to Lucas. No one who destroys a body so completely, and with such violence, does so on a stranger, unless he does so on a battlefield, to mark his kill.

Still, he cautioned himself, knowing that then as now there lived madmen capable of turning strangers into *replicas* of the object of their maniacal hatred. The file said Minerva was the victim of an unknown assailant, probably some lunatic who had left town immediately after killing her and disposing of the body—the bogeyman did it, was always the hope. People slept better at night believing the monster had returned to its faraway lair, like the creature Grendel in *Beowulf*, shunning the company of "normal" men and society. As if the killer couldn't possibly be human, or of the white man's race. Yet time and again serial killers and mutilation murderers and lust-murderers turned out to be middle-aged white men.

Certainly, it had been a human monster that had dumped Minerva's body in a drainpipe near a railroad yard. Detectives surmised the killer might have hopped a train, but which car and going in which direction? In any case, detectives working the case, most likely overloaded then as now, watched it go unsolved.

A quick check told him that there had been no sexual attack, although semen had been found. Lucas checked the detectives' notes and a crude sketch of the crime scene, but these items told him very little. A city map pinned on the corkboard over his desk helped to pinpoint the location of the railroad yard in question. The sketch remained incomplete all these years, leaving Lucas to wonder exactly how far the drainage pipe lay from the train yard.

The cursory remarks and sketch also made Lucas wonder if the train yard and hobo-killer theory hadn't simply been, as he'd earlier wondered, an easy way out for those 1948 dicks, both of whom might be hell to locate today. Even if they were alive, having given Minerva such short shrift in 1948, it wasn't likely they'd have any vivid memories.

Something disturbed Lucas about the photos and the murder book, but he could not quite lock down on what it was. Like a roadrunner, the mental angst kept two steps ahead of him. Maybe it was simply his anger at the brevity of Minerva's reports, as if the detectives in charge hadn't felt it worth their time to fill out the paperwork, despite the rank horror inherent in the crime, or perhaps due to the level of absolute evil displayed by Minerva's killer. *Husband* instantly came to mind. *Boyfriend*, a close second. *Father* ran third. *Other*, such as a mad rail-rider, came in a distant fourth, Lucas felt, speaking from a purely rational 1998 stance, at a time when a great deal more was known about human weaknesses, murder and the psychology of evil.

Lucas faintly wondered who Minerva's closest friends and relatives were, and why her slender murder book had been disturbed now, in this time and place, and by whom? He half suspected Dr. Meredyth Sanger of dropping it before his eyes in this fashion, but what interest might she have in this particular dust-laden case from among the thousands stacked to the ceiling? If it were Sanger, why had she chosen so slight a murder book from so many other larger, three- and four-inch-thick murder books on other, more "important" murders? The sheer size of many murder books bespoke the death of a politically powerful individual. Minerva was hardly that.

The incongruity of the death books also showed the inequality of death investigation, but it also pointed to the times — 1948, post–World War II America, just before the true boom times of the Texas oil industry. Murder books that dated back to the thirties, forties, fifties, even the more enlightened sixties were, as a rule, far less thick than today's counterparts. With less emphasis on pathology reports, fewer scientific methods of detection, detectives of the day having no help from such advances as the electron microscope and gas chromatography, infrared photography and DNA, so much of modern scientific police work was denied detectives of an earlier era. For example, he noted the poor quality of the photographs of the body, which had a dull veneer and halo effect that looked like a light surrounding the deceased. In '48, there existed no fiber evidence, no secretor evidence, and blood told only a partial tale since no one knew how to read blood trailings and spatters. Even ballistics had a long way to go at the time, as did the science of gunpowder residue. As for lust-murders, no one aside from the fictional Sherlock Holmes understood the psychology of evil behind a Jack the Ripper responsible for such heinous acts; few men in 1948 knew that loved ones, in the name of love, in the name of Christ, in the name of decency, often murdered with "moral" impunity. Certainly, no one knew of criminal profiling then. There hadn't been reams upon reams of interviews with the likes of Jeffrey Dahmer, Ted Bundy, John Wayne Gacy, Richard Speck and a host of other such evil spirits who, out of sick obsession, slew the object of twisted affection.

So Lucas realized that the further one traveled back in time, the thinner the death files were. Indeed, the science of detection and humanity had advanced a long way since Minerva Round-point's murder-mutilation case—thus, her lean murder book. Perhaps by applying today's methods against the slender information known about Minerva's death, the unsolved mystery of her last moments on earth might come clear. But again he sternly wondered *why*. Why focus on her amid the thousands waiting here? Had Captain Lincoln some secret interest in the case? Or had Meredyth stumbled onto the case, seeing a Native American connection and thinking Lucas might automatically respond, salivating like Pavlov's dog?

He stared again at the awful and overwhelming photos that had lain silent in the slender case file for so long, the photos of a mutilated corpse, the eyes wide and staring into vacant space, staring out over time until they found Lucas's eyes staring back. Long gashes across the upper torso, down the arms, along the thighs—deep, dark wells of blood arising from more cuts than anyone could endure. He'd seen literally hundreds of crime scene photos of dead men, women and children staring blankly back at him. In most cases, it appeared the deceased held a photographic image of either God or his killer in the retinas, somehow just behind the iris. How simple murder detection might be in a future where the mind's film could be processed as easily as that of a camera, he thought.

In Minerva's blank film, this gentle, accepting look of awe in her eyes seemed somehow intensified. Had she known her killer?

In any event, her search for whatever brought her to Houston so long ago had ended with her life. Meanwhile, her killer continued to live a life, the bastard never apprehended except for that one moment when he'd been captured in her eye, perhaps so that her Maker might have a record of the offender.

Still, he wondered why . . . Why did her strange black eyes, staring from the black-and-white photo fifty years old, disturb him to the core? He wanted to know why. . . . Why did he feel a sudden attachment to the deceased? Was it due to her Indian blood? Was it due to her long, black hair or soulful eyes? Was it due to her having had no one hear her at the time of her death, what she so wanted to tell them concerning her killer?

No one in 1948 to read the signs? Her soul hovered about the crime scene photo now, still crying out to deaf ears. Why did he, now, so clearly hear her cry?

Had the HPD merely chalked it up to the victim having asked for it? Such attitudes still prevailed today. Had Minerva been given short shrift as both a no-account Indian and a street slut, Lucas wondered, and if so, why expect anything resembling a complete investigation?

Still, something in the photos . . . something in the dead woman's eyes . . . something reaching out across time and space . . . as if her spirit had secretly entered Lucas's Cold Room, had lifted her murder book from among thousands to place it before Stonecoat's eyes. He felt an overwhelming sense of playful, elflike fate pervade his being, ordering him to make time and room for serendipity.

Had he come to be here in this place so that this dead Indian woman might speak to him?

But he didn't have time or room for it—not fate and not Minerva Roundpoint's aged case. He slammed it down with a decisive thud, gathered up all the file material and tossed it back into the official oblivion from which it came—the to-be-filed in-box. He heroically attempted to put the case and Minerva's haunting eyes out of his mind.

Still Lucas felt a sense of frustration when he tossed Minerva Roundpoint's file aside, relegating it back to its decades-long slumber slot. He knew he could not devote attention to it at present. To deal with a case of such vintage, or to play games with Meredyth Sanger or anyone else who may've dropped the file in his lap, could cost a young boy's life, a life that hung in the balance *today*.

His full attention must be on the Snatcher monster and each

detail of the previous victims, particularly the last two, The-odore Melvin Ainsworth and Raule deJesus Milton.

After again reviewing all the information he'd squeezed from Mr. Squeegee concerning the Snatcher case, Lucas had a revelation. He immediately dialed Randy Oglesby again. Randy pleaded for Lucas to leave him alone before finally asking, "What more can you possibly need?"

"The man—the killer—must have a history of assaultive behavior."

Randy's pause at the other end told Lucas that he had the young man's attention, perhaps curiosity. Finally, Randy said, "With you . . . so far."

"Go to battery files."

"Assault and battery files. You have any idea how many A and B files there are in the system?"

"Check those recently searched. See what's already been pulled by the task force."

"Now that really brings it down." Randy's sarcasm spit like static.

"Check and double-check and do that cross-reference thing you do between child molestation and abduction charges, as well as battery cases and child abuse cases, known child molesters in the area, wife beaters."

"Why stop at that?" Randy continued in a facetious tone. "Why not target those who've injured themselves?"

"The man's going to be a police buff, a fanatic of crime detection and police procedure," Lucas replied, thinking aloud. "He will likely be reading the works of Stephen Robertson, Glen Hale and other writers such as William Bayer and Ed McBain, or following cop shows on TV from *Homicide* to *NYPD Blue* for how the cops work a case. He might even hang out at known cop bars."

"You mean like Max's and the Guardrail?"

"Precisely, and if he's not caught, he'll go on killing. And if he's not caught within the next week, the Coleson boy's death is a sure bet."

"You think the oddsmakers are putting down on it?"

"I'm sure they are, both here and in Vegas, sure." The idea that people placed bets on the outcome of a child abduction turned Lucas's stomach, but human nature knew no bounds when it came to tasteless entertainment—witness the novels of Geoffrey Caine.

Randy's silence at the other end spoke volumes.

"The creep's going to be in his late twenties, early thirties, I'd guess. Put that in as a cross-ref, too."

"How can you know his age?" Randy wondered aloud.

Lucas cleared his throat and replied, "I draw my conclusions from previous experience with offenders of his type."

"I see," Randy lied.

"Think it through, Rando. . . . Each abduction's been well planned and expertly executed, which points to a killer with some poise, some prior experience that translates into ease of effort, you might say."

"Sure, I get it. We're *not* dealing with some punk kid on an acid trip, then."

"Precisely. And this . . . well, this almost guarantees that the killer has had practice in abduction and possibly a street sense of child psychology, if not a textbook knowledge; perhaps he's even done time on abduction charges in the past. So this area means yet another cross-check must be—"

"I get it. I get it."

"We've got to act now. We can't put this off," he told Randy. "Every minute counts for Lamar Coleson. We can't help the others who've gone before, but . . ."

Randy heard the abiding concern in Lucas's voice. "Cross-check for abduction cases, got it. For that, I'd best go back ten, maybe fifteen years on any charges brought. If the guy did time . . ."

Lucas added, "The level of organized behavior put into the planning of these crimes is textbook, Randy. It means this mother's adept and casual about his crime, and such casualness seldom belongs to the uninitiated."

"Gotcha, but aren't you assuming too much to assume he's a he?"

"There're extremely few female serial killers who act alone, and fewer still who kill outside their sex. I'd say, given the victims are all boys, this creep's a male who is angry at males, maleness, his own masculinity or lack of masculinity. Answer your question?"

"Yeah, thanks. I'm maybe going to write a book someday."

Lucas, taking it as a joke, laughed before saying, "And thanks, Randy."

"Yeah . . . sure . . ." Lucas detected a note of concern in the younger man's voice, but he couldn't quite tap into the problem. He imagined Randy was having difficulties serving two masters at the moment. He hoped that Meredyth Sanger hadn't been grilling the kid on why Randy's time seemed taken up with matters other than her office. But somehow, he rather knew that Meredyth—true to her nature—must be curious to bursting.

"Any problem in my being a no-show this morning?" he asked, fishing.

"No," lied Randy. "But I sure hope all this sees a payout, Lucas."

"You and me and most of Houston hopes so, kid. And Rando . . ."

"Yeah?"

"I do appreciate the position I've put you in; I know it can't be easy for you. Is Mere . . . Dr. Sanger in your face on this?"

"No . . . nothing I can't handle," Randy replied, again coloring the truth. "I'll see what Vanessa has to say about your suggestions, Lucas."

"Vanessa?"

"My computer."

"Randy, my friend . . ."

Randy smiled at Stonecoat's use of the term *friend*. "Yes, my friend?"

"You may want to one day get a life. . . ." Lucas hung up, leaned back in his desk chair and groaned with the fixed and constant back pain that was his reminder of his near-death accident and the subsequent multiple operations and a yearlong rehabilitation program. His in-the-line-of-duty injuries had left him with a limp and in chronic agony. He looked forward to reducing and masking the pain tonight through his ritual of meditation and his stash of drugs.

In the van . . . dark interior . . . story of my life, thinks Lamar Coleson. Dr. Kim Desinor sits alongside him, her spectral, astral form actually converging with Lamar's there on the seat. They sit high up, able to see a long distance ahead in the coming darkness of night.

I like the van, like riding in it, until I look back over my shoulder, Lamar and Kim think in tandem. In the rear of the dark van, she sees a rat's nest of materials—*building materials, grain sacks? pipes, tools and some containers, like cement containers before the cement is mixed with water.* It's a strange and vast array of supplies. Kim wonders about the little grain sacks and several small round canisters with lots of writing on them, large labels with directions for use. *Chemicals?*

Something about the smell in the cab slowly infiltrating Lamar's and Kim's nostrils fills each with a revulsion, a nameless fear. The doors locked automatically. They'd been locked by Uncle Buck, Roosevelt B. Cassell, and he'd strapped Lamar into his seat belt, telling him how important it was to be safe, to follow the rules, that there was a reason for the rules.

Cars pass by. Lamar/Kim sees people along the route. It is farther than the old man promised. He drives in zombie fashion to the interstate, now swearing to Lamar that their journey is not a far one.

Lamar grows increasingly jittery, frightened. He's heard about the Snatcher, and as if reading his mind, the old man begins to talk about the terrible business in the news lately about all those boys disappearing and being found tortured to death.

Lamar/Kim sees the cane lying in the back of the van, just out of reach, the cane the old man had earlier promised him. The boy and Kim feel and simultaneously smell something suddenly bite into their shared/combined ethereal forearm. The old man, his eyes displaying a naked pleasure now, has plunged a needle into Lamar and has sent some strange, dark fluid into his veins, causing Lamar to scream and pull away, tearing at the seat belt and the door lock while the old man laughs at the useless resistance.

Kim now stares into the eyes of the cane, the snout and countenance of an angry animal staring back, and then blackness. . . .

She started, coming back to consciousness, her lips cracked, his throat—Lamar's throat—like her own now, parched and sandpapery, filled with a nasty taste she could not place. It was her last sense of Lamar's being with her.

Harrison Vorel, SAC—Special Agent in Charge—and Loren Wells, his ASAC—Assistant Special Agent in Charge— watched Kim in the semidarkened room, Vorel's office, a place filled with negative energy fueled by both men, but Vorel in particular. Dr. Kim Desinor had detected the negative "vibes" on entering this morning.

They had a copy of her previous night's vision made, and she watched as Wells took it from Vorel and officiously dropped it into a manila file folder he'd carried in with him. *Formally handled*, she thought. *As prescribed, according to form, in an established manner.* She knew where she stood with these good ol' Texas boys.

"So, anything new to add, Dr. Desinor?" asked Vorel, in a thick Texas drawl.

But she could not talk. Her throat was filled with desert sand. The bastard made Lamar swallow some of the grain from those sacks he'd seen in the van. Was it desert sand? "Wa . . . wa-ter?" she managed, pointing to the pitcher and glasses on Vorel's credenza.

Vorel indicated it was Wells's job to fetch water, that, like an assistant coach, it was what assistant special agents did. Wells having performed well, Vorel now watched her repeatedly swallow, trying to clear her throat of the spectral grain there. She noticed the globular sand had a smell, a mineral-rich smell, and a gagging taste. Something about it made her think of dead fish and decay, but she dismissed this thought, grabbing for a second glass of water offered her by Wells, who sympathetically nodded as she thirstily drank.

Finally recovering her voice, Kim said, "Yes, I have a great deal to add, sir."

"Why don't you write it all down, Doctor, like you did the earlier stuff," suggested the paunchy Vorel, "and we'll get it all transcribed and copies in the hands of all my agents, I assure you."

Kim distrusted people who used phrases like *I assure you.* "If that's how you wish to work it," she replied, "all right."

"Take your time. Meanwhile, we've got a debriefing on the Snatcher case within the hour that Wells and I have to prepare for. You're welcome, of course, to present your . . . findings at the meeting, if you care to this early in the game, but time's limited, as you know, for the latest abductee-victim, so you'll have to keep your remarks to what's pertinent, you understand."

I understand more than you know, she thought, but realized she could only say, "Thank you, sir. I will do that, yes."

"Later in the day, I've scheduled my key task force people to spend a little time with you, you understand. At that time, if you care to go into more depth, perhaps then you can share precisely . . . ahh, how you glean your information for my boys."

My boys? she mentally questioned. Just how far behind the times was the Houston field office? Tucking her thoughts away, she said, "That would be—" but Vorel was already out the door.

Wells, following his boss like a puppy dog, turned at the door, and giving her a little nod and a thumbs-up, said, "Check with the secretary about times. See you later, Doctor."

"Yes, well, thank you, too, Agent Wells."

Welcome to the Wild West, welcome to Houston, she thought, shaking her head.

THREE

Cactus flower: courtship

It was past one in the afternoon, and Lucas still could not pull himself from the stack of M.E.'s reports on all the previous Snatcher victims. He leaned in over them in the silence of the Cold Room, his lamp seeming to burn a hole through each page and photo.

He'd driven by to see the last victim at the crime scene, or rather, the dump site. No true crime scene had actually been unearthed to date. Every beat cop and detective in the city wanted a look at what this monster of monsters had done. Every cop wanted to locate the bastard animal and his lair. Lucas was no exception.

At both the Milton and the Ainsworth boys' dump sites, Lucas had merely flashed his newly minted Houston detective's badge, and he was allowed close enough access to see the results of the torture that the last two boys, a fourteen-year-old named Raule deJesus Milton and a seventeen-year-old named Theodore Melvin Ainsworth, had endured. As with all previous victims, there were ligature marks on the throats, wrists and ankles. The M.E.'s guesswork—Chang liked to hold court—held that each victim had been trussed up turkey fashion from ankle to neck to wrist, "Quite like the Asian method of torture"—a remark that found its way into the press only to cause more trouble than usual between the black and Asian communities in Houston. "All one connective cord, the sort of tying off one sees in such child porno books as *Bizarro Internationale.*"

Medical Examiner Leonard "No Waste" Chang believed it a one-piece fishnet apparatus in which the boys had been suspended, saying he'd never encountered the like of it before, and that the truss or net most likely had been purchased at a hunting store or an Army-Navy outlet, if not homemade, customized to the task, because while it cut wrists and ankles, it also burned generalized areas of the backside, shoulders and legs. It appeared to be a coarse rope.

Other marks, marks of brutality and torture, were everywhere on the bodies. These included burns determined to be electrical burns and electrical shocks. The killer seemed to have an affinity for electrical apparatus, such as automobile jumper cables, that would send painful jolts of juice through the victim's body. The killer used a variety of additional instruments from an electrician's toolbox, such as needle-nosed and blunt-nosed pliers. Medical Examiner Chang had surmised that the killer's repertoire of horror included coat hangers, belt buckles, ice picks, corkscrews, and other snatchers, scratchers, rippers and twisters. But one pattern mark found on all previous victims could not be identified beyond Chang's lame remark calling it, "A blunt trauma instrument capable of shattering the skull, causing shock, subcutaneous edema and ultimately death." This final trauma the killer delivered to the head, leaving a strangely symmetrical shape—roughly speaking, a three-pronged, star-shaped indelible mark.

Lucas recalled how oddly shaped the final death injury looked. It lay alongside the left ear, and a second similar bruise discolored the forehead, above the left eye, as if the killer had struck out blindly in this general area twice, finally ending the young man's pain and suffering. Each of the two blows had punctured the skull inward. *Like the heel of a woman's shoe*, Chang's report concluded. But it wasn't a clean puncture with ice pick precision. Rather it was flared outward, leaving a wide, slightly larger than a half-dollar blaze.

Lucas had closely studied the welts believed to have finally put Theodore, Raule and the preceding four boys out of a weeklong misery. He had to agree with Chang. A strange, irregular-shaped star pattern emerged, but it fit no known, specific murder weapon. Ever the hedger, Leonard Chang reported that between two and three blows to the cranium had killed each victim, only after each boy endured unimaginable torture.

The very minutia of clues left upon the bodies mocked everyone: remnants of gauze and duct tape in each victim's hair and eyebrows, fiber evidence, hairs not matching the victim's, oil adhering to the body. Any of it might have been picked up at the scenes of discovery, construction site Dumpsters, all of which were now being watched since Chang's advice to, "Watch the Dumpsters. Every construction site Dumpster. Keep a surveillance on them."

There remained one clue, however, discovered during autopsy in each and every victim. Every boy had been force-fed a bizarre dry mixture of chemicals. Chang listed the strange combination of chemicals he found, citing that particles clung to the mouth and throat and were harmless in and of themselves, mere fish food.

The bastard force-fed his victims fish food.

The M.E. suspected, too, that the victims were all kept blindfolded during the entire ordeal. The tape residue adhering to the eyelids and eyebrows attested to this. But there had been no such evidence the boys' mouths had been taped shut.

"The bastard kept their air passages free, so that they could breathe easy?" asked one detective of Chang.

"Not so, not at all," countered Chang. "Only so he could hear the cries, their screams, and so he could torture them by way of this orifice as well. Stuff fish meal and whatever else he wants into their mouths."

Lucas imagined the fear, pain and utter darkness these children had suffered at the hands of this miscreant. A wave of revulsion washed over him. Lucas recalled a Jungian battlefield where, in a repeating, unconscious ancestral memory, his soul wanted to escape this world. He was no stranger to tormenting pain. On the battlefield of his forefathers, he'd fallen, wounded and left for dead, the weight of other men, struck down by a rain of bullets, pinning him to the arid earth. His seemingly frozen, lifeless body then was thrown over a cliff into a pile of rotting flesh alongside others of his kind. It amounted to *dream time* pain, and Lucas generally shook it off with sleep, but Lucas also knew and lived with real time pain, due to having taken a real bullet and due to the fiery police-chase accident that'd claimed the life of his partner, Wallace L. Jackson, and had left Lucas permanently scarred.

Lucas unconsciously reached up now and traced the fire scar that began as a thin line at his left cheek and flared the length of his neck and shoulder, most of it covered by his collar. He concentrated instead on the M.E.'s reports. Discovery of each defiled and emaciated body came at various construction sites all around the city, inside a Dumpster where waste from the used building materials was thrown. Quite a number of jokes about "No Waste" Chang and the Dumpster deaths now circulated around headquarters, and Lucas smiled, recalling how Chang, a big proponent of recycling paper cups and human organs to begin with, got the nickname when a detective, overseeing an autopsy Chang was conducting, had brought a lunch and was about to toss it out when Chang stopped him, saying, "No waste food in here."

"It's makin' me sick," replied the detective.

Chang countered, "There are many people in my country and all over the world starving, and you going to throw away good sandwiches? I take them." He then reportedly placed them into the nearest lab freezer.

Lucas read again that the left breast of each victim, about the nipple, in the area of the heart, had been sliced off with what Chang believed to be a tile knife, mutilated along with the genitals. Each teen's buttocks also had chunks of flesh cut away, and each child's buttocks had been beaten severely with a paddle as well as other instruments. What significance the left nipple—or the right nipple being left intact—had to the killer remained unknown, but speculation said that the killer was *souveniring* them up, saving them for times when he could not catch another victim, using the old remnants of earlier victims to rekindle the moment in his mind, to relive the fantasy and get off sexually all over again.

The genitals and breast must then be kept in some state of preservation by the killer, which meant embalming fluids, a refrigerator or possibly a deep freezer.

The Snatcher had to do his work in remote locations in a van or truck, Lucas guessed. If not, he had to have a soundproof room somewhere, unless he lived in so remote an area that no one could hear the screams he created in his macabre and twisted artistry. If the killer was in construction, he might easily have constructed his own soundproof torture chamber complete with ropes, pulleys and joists for dangling his victims.

DNA tests on blood and hair evidence, tests on fiber evidence, this all took time; Chang's way slowly yielded information that might prove useless. DNA experts with the FBI had been called in and were working day and night to discover what they might from the minutia left in the killer's wake, but such tests took weeks. Lamar Coleson didn't have that kind of time before he would be recycled.

Seven-day cycles. The killer worked within a seven-day cycle of abduction, torture, murder, disposal.

The monster's chosen cycle must somehow be interrupted, but Lucas feared since he knew so little of the killer and his habits, with no witnesses, no clue as to the bastard's identity. Besides, Lucas had received no invitation in on the case from his new captain, Gordon J. Lincoln; in fact, Lincoln remained cold to the idea when Lucas had let it be known he wanted in. Perhaps if his old captain, Phil Lawrence—who knew what Lucas was capable of—had remained . . .

But now, with the case in the hands of Harrison Vorel, the FBI's SAC officer, Houston, Texas, branch FBI, Lincoln'd figuratively washed his hands in his best Pontius Pilate imitation, while putting up a front operation he called a "precinct-specific task force to combine with leads generated by ongoing circumstances and to *assist* Vorel's people." It was a combined stroke of PR genius and political savvy or gobbledygook, however one looked at it, from whatever viewpoint. At least the official HPD stance had the advantage of sending the press scurrying to FBI headquarters and away from police precincts.

Still, a chill of concern spread through Lucas Stonecoat's bone marrow here where he sat in the glare of his desk lamp, a cold whisper that could neither be denied nor stopped any more than time itself. From a young age, Lucas had always hated injustice, especially as it fell on children. And he hated this feeling of helplessness welling up in him now, a feeling created in him by a child killer.

But it was not his case, and in fact, he faced walls of casebooks and files he remained ultimately accountable for. According to Captain Lincoln, in regard to the Cold Room with its cold cases dating back to the turn of the century, "The heat's on!"

With Lucas's success in uncovering the murderers of former appellate judge Charles Mootry and a string of related deaths, the new police commissioner wanted more unsolved cases put to true rest rather than in acceptable limbo. Laziness, a smug self-satisfaction of narcissistic proportion in the matter of unsolved cases, would no longer be tolerated, or so the press and public had been told first by Phil Lawrence, and now Gordon Lincoln, who had inherited the torch along with all the other headaches of leadership in a precinct. To this end, the FBI and the HPD would be teaming up to crack unsolved cases, working in cooperation. Despite the fact the state prosecutor's office had figuratively stamped CLOSED on all these unsolved cases, while in the real world, they'd never been closed, now a new FBI/HPD collaboration, code-named COMIT for Cooperative Murder Investigative Team, meant to commit to cases dating back sometimes more than thirty and forty years!

Lucas again looked at the list of objectives for COMIT. The effort, modeled after a successful program in Los Angeles, meant a promotion for Lucas from Officer Stonecoat to Detective Stonecoat, and it granted his status as curator of the Cold Room file collection some dignity—dignity that it'd failed to possess only days before.

Still, the Cold Room itself hadn't changed. It remained the dumping ground where unsolved murder rested in what were to most useless, mute files. What had changed—if it had changed—was the official attitude toward unsolveds. Some skepticism remained firmly entrenched in Lucas, however, and not simply because of what Meredyth Sanger might say, but due to the fact change always came on a reluctant horse.

In a city that averaged a murder every two or three days, no one but immediate family remembered yesterday's victim. The new commissioner believed a high percentage of cases given up as stone-cold, dead in the water must be revived and revisited, rethought, actually, in light of today's technology, investigative technique and know-how. The theory proved sound. The operation might not be.

Profiling techniques, for instance, were a relatively new device in crime detection, not available to criminalists of the '20s, '30s, '40s and even up through the early '70s. So why not apply victim and criminal profiling to the dead files?

Still, these dead files circling him, left to themselves, remained voiceless to everyone, it seemed, but Lucas, so he naturally wondered how precise his newly acquired FBI partner or partners' hearing might be.

How quietly this cement-encased dead file place breathed. Nowadays referred to as Lucas's necro-file, the Cold Room put people off. It remained a place men felt obliged to step around, not unlike a cemetery, this necropolis of paper, and not wholly unlike the lonely labyrinth of stacks he'd explored as a young man at Boone Township College in Boone, Texas, where he'd gone on from his reservation high school, the first in his family to enter college, the first male from his reservation to go to college.

He didn't finish college, but he managed to get through two grueling years there, and he'd come away with two tools useful to a police detective, the only two items, in effect, college could help him with: knowing how to research a subject, and controlling and valuing time to the point of making it work for him instead of against him. He recalled Professor Abel Kessler's words exactly: "You control your time, then you control your life."

He'd dropped out of college not because it was too difficult or because his grades were mediocre, but because the money had run out. Some years later, little by little, in Dallas, he'd finally compiled enough credits to graduate from Dallas City College while working as a police officer and later as a detective, the first full-blooded Native American Indian to reach such a rank in Dallas history.

Lucas had finished at the police academy in Dallas before he'd finished college, but determination had kept him at City College, going nights, weekends, whatever it took. Determination and persistence he had no shortage of, but such stuff came of a stubbornness borne of some jerk's telling him he shouldn't bother, or that maybe college ought best be left to people of a different turn or skin color. Lucas's Texas Cherokee Indian blood boiled whenever someone suggested that he ought to be happy with the level of education he had attained, as if to say, "Any more, boy, and you're pushing the limits of what's expected or natural. . . ."

The city of Dallas had also been the scene of his near death, where his partner, Wallace Layfette Jackson, had in fact died during the high-speed chase of a gunman. The gunman had died during the chase, as well, when Lucas, bloodied, burned and dizzy from his own wounds, still had somehow managed to put a bullet into the cretin's brain. The street punk had earlier wounded both him and Jackson in return fire.

The unmarked police car had careened out of control into a truck, bursting into flames from which Lucas dragged Jackson's lifeless body. The gunshot wounds, the second- and third-degree burns and his broken insides left Lucas with pain that dissolved only when he drank enough or smoked enough to curb the jagged, cutting edge of distress into a smoother, more rounded blade.

In Houston, he'd had to go through additional police academy training after his long rehabilitation, training that he had successfully completed. He now worked as a detective with the Houston PD, assigned to the Cold Room by small-minded bureaucrats who thought it safest to keep a lid on the "wild Indian with a reputation" whom they'd inherited from Dallas.

Lucas at first hated the Cold Room, and he still held reservations about the duty he'd pulled. However, with the success of the Mootry case, he saw the need for COMIT and a thorough review of every case in HPD's long history. This meant manpower, and Gordon Lincoln, at the urging of the commissioner, found funds for a renovation of the storage room itself, plus the extra personnel in the form of more HPD cops and the invitation extended to the FBI. . . . It all appeared a giant step forward.

These thoughts ran freely through Lucas's mind when Dr. Meredyth Sanger noisily entered through the ancient door, which made Lucas cringe each time it squealed, reminding him of the WD-40 oiling he'd promised it. Lucas quickly snatched up the M.E.'s report and slid it under his desk blotter and newspaper. He feared if she saw the report in his possession, she'd get ideas, and she would also know of his great interest in the Snatcher case. It was more than he wanted her to know.

No greetings, no hellos, Meredyth simply jumped in with, "I can't believe they've not placed you on the Snatcher case, Lucas."

Lucas leaned back in his chair, almost turning it over with his weight, studying her, wondering if her words should be interpreted as taunt or challenge. How much did she already know? How much had Randy blabbed to her? he wondered. "Doesn't surprise me," he replied noncommittally.

While pacing the small area before his desk here in the dungeon, Meredyth continued to sputter, her reading glasses clutched between white knuckles. "Damn fool Phil Lawrence was . . . well, unable to learn from his own mistakes, and so he buried you—and your talents—down here, and then the bastard gets himself booted."

"Phil wasn't so bad."

"Do you really think Lincoln's going to be any better?" Venom seeped from her every word, making Lucas smile. She could be a smoking pistol, Lucas thought as he studied this light-skinned, silver-blond professional woman, this beautiful off-limits woman pacing before him like a sleek, sexy mountain cat.

"What're you laughing at?" She prodded him with a pointed finger.

"I know your anger actually stems from the fact that you have to break in a new captain, but so do the rest of us! It's probably got to do with your having been raised a spoiled brat with a silver spoon in your mouth."

"Bullshit, my parents were teachers! We lived quite middle-class lives!"

"My heart bleeds," he replied. "As for Lincoln, he's really not so bad. . . . You know he's following through on Phil Lawrence's COMIT program idea."

"That was my idea," she countered.

"All I'm saying is that it would have been simple and easy for Gordon Lincoln to toss your idea out, since it wasn't his baby to begin with."

Dr. Meredyth Sanger's forehead pinched in consternation, but rather than admit to defeat—not a word in her vocabulary— she sarcastically sped on, saying, "Inspires confidence, does he? So far as I can tell, Lincoln's a classic example of a power-addicted male, with male-on-male . . . penis envy. And it's your penis he most envies, so watch yourself."

Lucas's red face reddened more, but he tried to cover his embarrassment with a smile. "You're off and running again," he said, still smiling at his friend, recalling how she'd saved his life during the Helsinger/Mootry investigation. "Look, Lincoln simply decided that I'm not needed on the Snatcher case. End of story."

"But why?"

"Because, he's got an army crawling all over that one, and—"

"What do you think about the speculation going round that the killer's maybe a cop gone bad? Or that he's possibly of Asian descent?"

"I don't think so, no."

"No to which one?"

"No to both theories."

She breathed deeply and asked, "How can you be so flaming sure?"

"No cop's ever gone *that* bad," protested Lucas. "I mean, sure . . . rape, murder to cover a crime, blackmail, excessive use of force, prejudicial attitudes, preferential treatment, fixing tickets, but murdering kids . . . torturing them to death, starving them? No, my instincts tell me no to the cop theory. And as for it being an Asian killer, no way."

"Might make sense, cop theory, I mean. Killer comes and goes unnoticed, snatches these kids within sight of their homes in broad daylight. . . . I mean, what kid wouldn't go off with a cop in uniform who promises him a ride in a patrol car where he can play with the siren, maybe get an ice cream cone?"

Lucas openly and heartily laughed at the image. "Sooner be a Ninja killer as a cop."

"Stop that," she demanded, stamping her expensive Gucci pumps against the cement floor. She wore a beautiful matching powder blue dress suit that highlighted her fiery blue eyes.

Lucas explained, "No way are these kids that stupid. These street-smart kids're not going to fall for a friendly cop routine. They hate and suspect the cops. Remember Rodney King?"

"How much do you know about child psychology? If they feel safe, they'll walk off the face of the earth with this guy. Whoever he is, he's got some smooth, friendly routine. Damn, but it's awful, what's happening out there."

"It's not my case."

"Simple as that, huh?"

God, how her eyes blistered him, he thought. "It's not my g'damn case, Mere."

"The latest abductee, that Coleson kid, they figure he's only got five or six days to live, Lucas. Days! And they've been screwing around since the kid's disappearance."

"It's not my . . . freaking case, Meredyth."

"I see," she said, nodding as if it had all come clear now. "Playing it safe these days, huh?"

He didn't answer. The implication lay in the space between them, clear and stark.

"Damn it, Lucas, I know you're interested in the case."

He merely stared at her.

This only infuriated her. "You were at the last kid's autopsy."

"Rumor. No basis in fact."

"You got the M.E.'s report."

Damn that Randy Oglesby, he must have told her, despite his promise not to. Lucas only stared back at her, stubbornly matching her glare.

"Damn it," she again swore, shook her head and leaned against his desk, close enough that he could smell her Venice perfume. But her eyes wandered now over the stacked-to-the-ceiling dead files in the room. "I just can't believe that they're wasting your talents here, that they didn't immediately place you on the Snatcher case and move you the hell out of here, Lucas." She grasped him firmly by the arm, and he sighed heavily, in vaudevillian fashion. But she ignored his theatrics, ranting on. "We've got to fight this . . . this injustice, Lucas. All we did for these moronic, imbecilic, lamebrained nitwits, and this is how they repay us?"

"Mere . . . Mere. . . ."

"They can't treat us this way, and they don't need a detective of your caliber working these files. Any number of other—"

"What *us*? I'm okay with things as they are, Doctor. Don't go stirring up the pot again. Besides, I don't get you. You believe the Cold Room files are worth our effort, and yet you come on with this attitude?" Lucas knew to keep his plea mild, that Meredyth didn't respond well to angry retort.

"Stirring up the pot?" She pulled back, looking as if he'd struck her. *Talk about theatrics*, he thought. She continued, saying, "And what do you mean, 'What us'? It was the two of us who cracked Helsinger's Pit and explained to the world why Judge Charles Mootry, along with a string of other prominent folk, had been murdered by crossbow-wielding assassins, remember? You, me . . . us! And as for these blasted blame g'damn files, they've been here for fifty, sixty years, so they can just wait. That boy has only a matter of days left."

Lucas stood and paced, a head taller than her. He looked down into her deep blue eyes. "I'm not officially on the case, Mere."

"Granted, but you . . . damn it, you deserve a crack at the Snatcher. You know, as recognition for your work on the Helsinger thing."

Was she stringing him along, trying to get him to open up about just how involved he'd already become in the Snatcher affair, or was she being sincere? "I got a citation and a promotion to detective rank, Mere."

"Then why not a proper caseload, *current* cases?"

"I'm getting . . . plenty. . . ."

"Plenty of what?"

"Recognition."

"I'm not talking about your picture in the paper or groupies on your arm, Lucas."

"Neither am I."

"What, then? What're you getting from Lincoln? A dog-catcher's license?"

He frowned at this, raised his right hand but only joked, "Dream-catcher's license, maybe."

"Meaning?"

"Look, the captain's promised me a . . . a squad. I'll be in charge. . . ." He handed her the memo detailing plans for COMIT. "If I keep my eyes pinned on the prize, I can't lose."

"Do you know how long I pushed Lawrence on this COMIT program?"

"No, but I'm sure you'll tell me."

"COMIT's in memos dating back to before you came on here, Lucas."

"I see."

"And I reasserted the need again after the Helsinger's Pit fiasco, a perfect example of what can be unearthed in all this dust-gathering paper down here, if we just commit to it." Meredyth's crime psychiatrist's eyes read Lucas's little half shrug as well as his memo; she next read his smug grin as supplemental fact to her own conclusion that his words and stance meant a wall-building defense against pain.

Lucas in turn read her reading of him and didn't like what he saw in her eyes. "Don't start, Mere. I'll have two teams of two working under me, day and night, double-teaming the files, scanning them to disk, analyzing, rethinking, reading, actual investigation, you know?"

"You've been talking to Randy O. about this, haven't you?" She knew Lucas was, while not computer illiterate, not altogether comfortable with the language he'd begun to employ.

"Matter of fact, Rando's explained to me how all these murder books can be scanned onto diskettes, yes. Anyway, with more manpower poring over these dust-laden tombstones in here, who knows? You yourself have officially championed the idea, like you said."

She nodded, saying, "And I stand by what I said, but you're an excellent investigator, Lucas, and you're needed on this boy's case *now*. Why the brass isn't seeing clearly, I don't under—"

"Well, why not expand our understanding of this . . . this . . ."

"Database?" she furnished the word for him.

". . . treasure buried down here?" He waved a hand in a flourish about the dark room. "Think of it. We go over everything in the place, and we'll have FBI backup and access to FBI files, computers and maybe lab assistance. And all this"—he raised his hands and opened his arms to the roomful of dead files—"all of it, will be scanned into the computers.

Captain's excited about COMIT. Committed to it," he lied. "Says it'll be *my* squad."

"Which captain said that? Lincoln or Lawrence? And either way, Lucas, is that what you want? Or is it something you've convinced yourself you want?"

"Where's the difference?"

"Is this why you're too busy to make yourself available for therapy? Is this why you've been buddying up to Randy? Next thing you'll want is to steal him away from me, too."

"Hold up there! I didn't steal COMIT."

Their voices had risen, spilling out into the corridor.

"You don't really give a damn about COMIT," she challenged. "It's just a safe plan, a kind of paid retirement for—"

"Does it matter . . . to you . . . what I want?"

Now she slowed, understanding all too well his innuendo. She knew exactly how Lucas felt about her, that he cared more about her than he did anyone in his small circle of friends. A moment's truth caught and held between them, snared in their mutual gaze.

Lucas had tried to interest her in a relationship, but she had managed to hold him at arm's distance, perhaps because of the canyon of difference between them and their worlds—he a Texas Cherokee raised on U.S. government rations on a reservation, she a well-to-do upper-crust white girl who'd graduated from Duke University with a degree in shrinkology.

She had money, too; lots of it, thanks in large part to her private practice, which she'd somehow managed to make a thriving business while also working for the HPD. It was rumored that her private clients, while hardly the healthiest people in Houston, *were* the wealthiest. While the list remained a carefully guarded secret, Randy had let slip a few names to impress Lucas, among them a senator and a certain actress whose star had risen meteorlike due to a hit television show filming in Houston. Because Meredyth's time had become so preciously limited, her rates for private consultation matched those of the shrinks at Betty Ford.

He got to his feet, stopped her in her pacing, stared deeply into her eyes and challenged, "I'll be in charge of *something*. Something good could come of it. And hell, at least I won't be *alone* down here anymore. That's got to count for something," he joked to lighten the mood.

Meredyth wasn't happy with the department or the city's handling of the aftermath of the Helsinger/Mootry case. Spokespeople, publicity department guys and Captain Lawrence had all taken the credit for Lucas's daring and bold work, as far as she was concerned. It was just so typical, she wanted to spit every time she saw a news report on the affair.

"Despite the tremendous success you and I had in collaring a national ring of cyberspace murderers whose berserko religion became so twisted and tangled that brutal murder was rationalized away—*despite all that*—the department deems it necessary for you—for some unaccountable reason no one can fathom—to continue as a baby-sitter for a room full of vexing, unsolvable murder investigations? And you let Phil Asshole Lawrence and now Lincoln get away with it, and then you *thank him for the privilege*? Sorry, but I don't see where—"

"The hell I did. I didn't thank anyone," countered Lucas.

"But you are thankful, appreciative?"

"Somewhat, yes."

"All right, so we proved two things: Old cases can be solved, hence they're going to supply the manpower, and two—"

When she hesitated, he urged her on with, "And two, what?"

"And two, Lucas Stonecoat *can* actually be *thankful*!"

"Hey, this means I regain my old Dallas status of detective, Meredyth, and for that, I guess I did willingly—"

"Cave?"

"Call it what you will. . . . I now carry a bona fide Houston Police Detective's gold shield. It's what I've fought for; it's what I returned to the force for."

"God, I go on vacation and everybody's back to machismo Joe. You men . . ."

"God, I hate when you revert to such useless, syllogistic reasoning, Meredyth. Why don't you just write bumper stickers?"

Fuck you, she wanted to reply, looking coolly into his mesmerizing whiskey-brown stare. "Okay, then, you cops and your shields, that's what I'm talking about. What's that make it now? You've got three shields? Does that make you the most well-endowed cop on the force?"

"Two detective's shields." Lucas had, in all the confusion of leaving Dallas, somehow held on to his Dallas gold shield. "And one officer's badge." Having been sworn in as a detective third grade with the Houston Police Department, Lucas need never flash his beat cop's badge again, and perhaps he'd never have need of his Dallas shield, which he'd used on occasion even here in Houston to get past yellow and sometimes red tape.

She apologized, her eyes downcast, saying, "I'm sorry I was unable to make the ceremony, Lucas. I know it meant a lot to you."

"No big deal," he replied, covering his emotions with a grin.

"So," she fumbled, "number three badge is . . . in your collection."

"Lincoln conferred it on me . . . same day he walked in with this." He pointed to the COMIT program papers. "I've earned all of it, Mere."

"I *know* you have, Lucas, and you've earned more than that. You've earned every cop's respect along with . . . along with mine. But are you sure you're making the right career move, Lucas, staying in the Cold Room on a program ironically called COMIT put together by people who can't commit?"

"Lincoln is committed to it."

She shook her head. "I hope you're right, but I'm afraid they're just stringing you along, Lucas."

Lucas clambered to his feet again and paced to the frosted glass windowpane where he stared up to the street. "I'm in no position to argue with the brass, Doctor. Look, the lighting in here will be improved, the new addition'll add more windows, and—"

"Big woooo!"

"And maybe they'll replace that damned door, my chair and

desk. It won't be so bad, and for once in my miserable excuse for a career . . . I'll be in charge of . . . of something."

Outside, the hum of the city was held in check by the thick, durable glass. A light dusting of snow had crept catlike into the city from the surrounding prairie land, and a bitter wind clutched at and wrapped about the tall skyscrapers of Houston, pelting the stone and leaving invisible scars in its wake. It had proven an unusually cold and wintry November in Houston, and the radio stations filled the airwaves with the white man's idea of music for the season of Christ's birth. Lucas wondered if the Christ child had ever heard "Rudolph the Red-Nosed Reindeer." He also wondered how the white Christian majority would welcome Christ on His return—eggnog, mistletoe and a hearty rendition of "Santa Claus is Coming to Town"?

The station house was decorated in Christmas doodads and ornaments and lights. As for Lucas's little corner, there remained only bare bulbs suspended from worn fixtures. "What is it with you white people and Christmas, Mere?" He wanted to change the subject, and he felt hateful, felt like striking out at her, and this seemed a fine way to do it, by attacking her beliefs. "I mean, first you make your God a Santa Claus–like figure on a chariotlike throne somewhere in the sky, and next you make the birth of God's child on earth into a toyland merchandiser's dream of paradise. Want to explain that to me?"

"Don't change the subject on me."

"Christmas ever depress you, Meredyth?"

"Oh, is that it? Does this time of the year get you down? No surprise. It brings on the blues for many Americans, regardless of color or nationality. I've got some self-help tips for you, if you care to listen."

Neither of them spoke for a long moment. He kept his back to her. Finally, Meredyth sighed and said, "Look, Lucas, it's just a suggestion, but if you want, I could talk to a few people about your . . . situation."

He turned back to face her, asking, "Oh, really?"

"I still have some friends left here and there who—"

Lucas bristled. "No, no! I don't want or need any bleeping help in that department, *Doctor . . .*"

"Hold on! I'm not talking about the Christmas blues, now. I'm talking about getting you out on the street, working a desk upstairs on current cases. Like you wanted all along before this COMIT smoke screen blurred your vision."

"Where do you get off calling it a smoke screen? And my vision is perfectly clear. And why do you persist in condemning your own program?"

"Was my program. No longer. Lifted out of my hands, Lucas, and it hurts like hell, like having an adopted child taken away."

"I'm sorry."

"And they'll do the same to you, if you let them. You know they're not going to deliver on this, Lucas. That it's all a bunch of crap for the press and public relations. You're smart enough to know they'll never commit to it, not fully, not in the way needed, not in the way either one of us could be satisfied with, no!"

He glowered at her, his chest heaving, looking as if he either wanted to strike her for being so damned right, or to take her in his arms. She didn't know which prospect frightened her more. Steeling herself, she returned his stare, looking long and hard at him. "Have I thanked you today for saving my life?" she suddenly asked.

"You've thanked me for three months now. *Enough.*"

"Has it been that long?"

"Besides, in the end, you saved my life as well, and in any Indian's book, that makes us even, Meredyth. Now, get out of here and let me get some work done."

"Now I know you don't mean that."

"You are an evil . . . distraction." He laced his fingers behind her neck now, looking even more intently into her eyes as his powerful fingers massaged her shoulders, his every thought, his complete attention on her. Time faded for this moment, this now. . . . Her powder blue suit and white blouse and a necklace with a multifaceted crystal shining at her breast created an enticing package. Her radiant, vibrant eyes touched something in Lucas, and the crystal beckoned his fingers to wrap about it, feel its warmth. She allowed him the moment, seeing that his eyes reflected the light coming through the nearby window and bouncing off her crystal amulet.

It felt like a mystical moment.

His dark hair, long and raven-black, whispered across her face as he leaned to kiss her. She started when the phone rang, and he cursed aloud and said in singsong rhythm, "Damn, whoever the hell it is. *Let 'em ring, let 'em ring, let 'em ring*."

"And if it's your boss man, Lincoln, or some other brass to kiss?" she intentionally derided, thinking it the easy way out—out of his embrace.

Her words, spoken in cold clarity, angered him, but he kept hold of her and lifted the receiver at the same time. "Captain Lincoln," he said, his eyes still pinned on her.

She took this moment and his half-smile and deepening gaze as her cue to pull free of him and leave. She still felt like a weak child around Lucas, uneasy about the fact he could so easily disarm her, so quickly turn her backbone to jelly, and she hated this power he held over her, this feeling of helplessness. She was caught off guard when a memory flashed into her mind of the night that Lucas and she were nearly silenced forever when they stumbled upon the final solution to the Helsinger's Pit affair. She thought of the moment when she saw Lucas lying near death in that cleft of rock in the canyon where she'd climbed down to him to take his head in her lap, how she'd remained there with him all that night, until dawn and help had finally arrived. She remembered how much he'd meant to her at that moment, how deeply she'd felt, how terrifying it had been, and how much she'd wanted him at the same time.

Around Lucas, alone like this, she feared how easy it would be to fall into a deep chasm of love from which she might never climb.

Meredyth Sanger now hardly heard Lucas's conversation with his captain. She moved off and away from Lucas, as if her feet—like a pair of mischievous gnomes—operated independently of her heart and brain. Her feet were smarter, yes. At least they knew she must remove herself from his touch, so they inched closer to the door and further from him and that energy he threw off.

"I'll do that, Captain." He dropped the phone back onto its cradle and looked up, searching for her now, seeing her halfway out the door, staring back at him.

Out of some sense of politeness, likely drummed into her pretty white brain, she allowed the door to close. Or was there hope she wanted him to take her in his arms again? he wondered.

He knew he'd lost the moment when she started talking again. "It should prove interesting, Lucas, your being in charge of a squad working out of here, throwing in with the FBI and all that, but where're you going to put two more men in rotating teams down here?" She feigned nonchalance. But she was swallowing hard and feeling warm, a bit dizzy, sweaty. How had it become so hot in here, she wondered.

"They're knocking out a wall, building on. Construction begins next week."

"If the city's on time," she countered.

He nodded, smiled. "If they're on time." Lucas took a step toward her.

She liked his smile. He didn't smile often, but when he did, it brightened his entire being. "Which wall?" she asked, looking around, again stepping further from him as she did so.

"Don't worry, the architects have it all worked out, all without your help, Mere." He brought forth a healthy laugh.

"What's that supposed to mean?"

"That you are *all* woman."

"*Oooooowww*, now that hurt, but hardly necessary, stooping to such flagrant sexist reason—"

"You always have to know everything before everyone, Mere, and—"

"Bull!"

"—and you have to get in the first and last word before anyone, even if it's about nothing. If that's sexist, then so be it."

"Shut up, damn you!" She didn't join in his fun but took this opportunity to stomp noisily toward the door in a show of anger. It made perfect sense to exit now, but holding the door open once again, she glared back at him, and just before disappearing, she coolly muttered in her best Lauren Bacall voice, "One of these days, Lucas Stonecoat, you're going to make me angry, but for now, if you need me, just give a whistle. You do know how to whistle, don'tcha?"

Then she was gone. And Lucas wondered what she'd come for. Why she felt compelled to push him around, acting as if she might truly be concerned about his future, his career at the 31st. Her job as police shrink, he guessed. Keep the troops happy in their work, or at least find out if they *can be* and report back to Lincoln. Or had she some more sinister, compulsive or manipulative reason for visiting him down here in his dungeon, to see if the monster needed a crumb thrown his way? God, but she sometimes played the white rich bitch too well; it could not all be an act. She made it clear with her every word and move that he wasn't and could never be "right" for her. That he could never possess her, so why bother?

Still she came to see him, to test him—possibly to confirm whether or not he had seen and read Minerva Roundpoint's file? Or was it more personal than that? To see if he remained interested in her? If she could still get a rise out of him?

Sure, that had to be it.

And she'd done exactly that.

And now he wanted in the worst way to pound a fist into the stone wall in front of him.

A siren wail overhead signaled the changing of the guard, one set of street cops coming home to the station house, another set exiting. It was common practice for the men to blip-siren one another as they passed. Duty aboveground, out in the open where a man could flex his muscles, operate his body to full max . . . this is what Lucas had wanted from day one; it was what his body and Indian soul and spirit required, demanded. Meredyth instinctually knew this, knew of his need for open spaces. But now, for the first time in his miserable excuse of a career in law enforcement, Lucas had been offered a position of authority, a shot at running his own show, a shot at being in charge, and he wanted to rise to the challenge.

He had a four-thirty meeting with members of the FBI to go over initial plans for COMIT. The sirens reminded him of the hour and that he had to run if he wished to make the meeting at FBI headquarters on time. But at the door to the Cold Room files, as if the file screamed at him, Lucas stopped, stared back at the 1948 case file in his return bin, walked over to it, lifted it and carried it out with him to go over in more detail at home. He quickly locked up the Cold Room and left by way of a basement back door, which he had jimmied open and placed a padlock on so as to have quick and easy exit and entry to the Cold Room. The door opened on a half flight of stone steps that took him to street level in the back alley.

He decided to walk the short distance to the FBI building, feeling a need for the exercise. Maybe tonight he'd find some sleep, if he could escape the constant pain he lived with. Not to mention the worry over Meredyth Sanger keeping him restless. Meredyth knew about him; knew he was a fraud, a liar, a cheat. She knew that he'd bluffed his way through the police academy training here in Houston after Dallas refused his return to active duty there. This in itself hardly presented a secret she might hurt him with, but his medical problems, his self-administered painkillers in the form of booze and drugs, and his infrequent blackouts *were*. And Meredyth had discovered these problems the hard way, when they'd cooperated together on the Helsinger's Pit conspiracy, when they'd come so terribly close to being killed by the men behind that ugly connivance.

Lucas now wondered how long and how strong their friendship might endure; how long could the rule-conscious police psychiatrist go without reporting him? *Too dangerous to work cases*, official brass might be easily persuaded. Yet she had just been here in an effort to get him working on current cases, the Coleson boy's case in particular. Perhaps his fear of her all this time had been unwarranted.

Despite the fact she'd said nothing to him beyond suggesting he continue to seek medical help, he worried. Despite the fact he'd saved her life along with Randy's only a few months before, he worried. Despite the fact that she'd also saved his life by calling in the cavalry that day, it remained Meredyth's job as the resident precinct shrink, as well as crime psychiatrist, to report on the weaknesses and chinks in the army of men and women who made up the Houston Police Department. Shielding Stonecoat could cost her a career and a reputation in a field where reputation meant all.

Still, after all was thought and done, she had remained silent for this long. Perhaps Meredyth was as gutsy as she let on. Perhaps she *would* keep his secret, even take it to her grave. Perhaps she'd never threaten him with it or use it against him, no matter what the future might bring. Perhaps she cunningly wished to hold on to this knowledge of him, keeping this power over him, in a feminine attempt to remain alluring. Women liked to be quixotic, he knew. And perhaps he wanted it this way, too; perhaps he *needed* someone—her in particular—to fully know and completely understand his darkest side, and accept it . . . accept it as natural. Perhaps he'd misjudged her, and maybe he'd also misjudged his own motives where Meredyth Sanger was concerned.

Lucas waved at officers in slow-rolling patrol cars as they came into the shadow of the precinct building, and he was soon out of that shadow, setting a strong pace despite his limp. It felt good to breathe in the cold, bracing air. He let his overcoat flap in the breeze.

Straddling a desk five days a week meant his back muscles and leg muscles would atrophy. He needed to push himself physically, to challenge his body, not because his doctors had said so, but because his spirit instinct had said so.

To this end, he'd joined Adair's Gym near where he lived, and for a three-hundred-dollar annual fee, he had full run of the equipment and the lap pool, which he loved. Adair, the owner, was Texas Cherokee, at least three-quarters of him, and a good and valued friend. Lucas's major problem was fitting the gym time into his already hectic schedule, but Jim Adair wouldn't listen to such nonsense, so Lucas worked out whenever he could. And whether at the gym or on his hardwood floor doing sit-ups and push-ups, he worked out all the aches and pains, believing in feeding the pain, playing to it, keeping it always at bay by biting the dog that continually nipped and tore at him.

"The more painful the workout to the body, the less internalized in the mind becomes the pain," Adair said in a prescriptive, philosophical tone, the same one he used for the New Age crowd of yuppies lately filling his gym. "You can send the pain out into the world through sweat glands and pores."

Lucas took the advice with a smile, knowing that an element of primary, deep-rooted pain always remained to torture him from within, and it could only be helped by the ancient Indian herbal weed that he sometimes chewed, sometimes smoked before bed. Meditation helped, but not so well as it did in combination with drugs.

As for the white man's painkillers, he'd become so enamored of them that he popped them like Excedrin all day long, but like the giant Texas roach or gila monster, nothing in the white man's scientific arsenal of answers to nature any longer touched Stonecoat's eternal internal pain.

So Stonecoat lived with the pain most every hour; the only relief came when a case completely captivated his mind, as had the recent rash of disappearances here in Houston. They reminded him of the Atlanta child murder cases of 1979, which Lucas had studied with extreme care, making himself intimately familiar with the details. And this case of the so-called Indian prostitute of 1948 also fascinated him, to the point where his mind played over the minute particulars.

A driver blared his horn at Stonecoat as he walked across the street, absorbed in thought, thinking once more how little time the Coleson boy had left on this earth and how much time had passed before Minerva Roundpoint was heard. The two cases seemed in extreme juxtaposition to one another, far more than mere miles apart, and yet both tugged at Stonecoat equally.

Four

Deer track: ample game

LATER THE SAME DAY

"Talk about pressure on a case."

Kim Desinor heard Chief Harrison Vorel's lament the moment she'd stepped down from the small jet that had brought her to Houston from Quantico. They had been standing on the tarmac, her bag in hand, while Vorel continued like a man incapable of remaining silent on the point, a man obviously uncomfortable with a psychic hotline partner being shipped out to fix his problem in Houston.

"As you know," he'd said at their first meeting, standing like a big Texas wall between Kim and the car brought for her, "we've got full press interest, the mayor and the governor are at our throats, and D.C.'s unhappy as well. It's damned relentless. No lead too small to cover. Got four agents working full-time, every lead. We're going to get this mother."

He took her bag, escorted her to the car and continued his officious, nervous prattle. "It's just a matter of time before we get this guy."

Time . . . a commodity that Lamar Coleson didn't have, she had thought then as now, but she'd remained calm, polite even in her thoughts, simply nodding in response, going for the car.

"So, they sent you as our profiler," he remarked, a hint of

acid in his tone. "Hear tell you're . . . that you've been effective in eighty percent of the cases you've . . . worked. Impressive! Don't deny we need all the help we can get, even if it's of the sort . . . the variety . . . you know, un—"

"Unorthodox?" She read Houston's number-one, overweight, chief of agents' remarks as riddled with lies. The man's unstated remarks screamed as clearly as his spoken words; he was an easy read. At the car door, she'd turned and replied, "Yes, Quantico believes I can help you profile and identify both the victim and the assailant in the case, Chief Vorel, and yes, I've had some successes in the past."

"Pressure, like I said, Doctor."

"Funny, I've never thought of myself as pressure, Chief."

He laughed like a politician, she thought. "I didn't mean you personally. Just that there's a push on, big pressure, knowing I can ask for *anything* from D.C. and I won't be turned down. That puts pressure on my department, pressure for results, you see."

Was this a veiled threat? she wondered. Did he mean to ask D.C. to remove her before she'd even gotten started on the case? "Sorry, you're stuck with me, Chief Vorel."

"Hey, don't get me wrong. But I did ask for a profiler, not a psychic. I was pleased—surprised, actually—with the turn-around time. Like I said, on this case there's nothing I can ask for that I *won't* get."

"Yes, scary, isn't it? When they give you everything you need to do the task? No one else responsible for screwing it up but you. I know; I've been there, Chief."

He'd attempted a smile. "So you understand my position."

"Precisely. This is a case you can't screw up."

"Precisely."

"So, you've rounded up the usual suspects, I imagine."

"And more."

She had then climbed into the backseat of the car where Chief Vorel joined her, telling the driver to take them to the Houston Imperial Hotel. Then he turned to her, his eyes agitated, his brain filled with questions, his curiosity itching to be scratched, to know something. "Tell me one thing," he began. "Will you be reporting to me, or directly to the man?"

His dramatic choice of words made her smile inwardly. "The director of the FBI is watching, of course, but he hasn't asked me to report to him, nor has Chief Santiva. I'm to do nothing to supersede or undermine your authority, sir."

He had visibly relaxed, let out a long, sigh-filled, "Good!" But some part of his brain did not believe her, and she knew this.

The scene at the airport had kept replaying in Kim Desinor's mind since the first night she'd spent in Houston, Texas. She wondered if all Texas FBI men were like Vorel, or if the man was a throwback to an earlier time when Texas Ranger machismo ruled. She wondered if he carried a bottle of Brute aftershave in his glove compartment, if he drove a Ford pickup sporting a gun rack across the rear window. The man hadn't even introduced himself, hadn't even asked her name when she alighted the plane, and to date, he'd been nothing but rude. The little mannerisms, the way Vorel and his men behaved toward her told the story. They believed now that the FBI had sent her as a one-time-only "psychic experiment" in the pursuit of the elusive Snatcher.

Up till now, she'd been treated with grudging courtesy, only because Vorel and company had suspected her of being some low-level informant, a spy sending back messages to D.C. about these fuckups in Houston. The attitude and their feigned courtesy only pissed her off. Meanwhile, young adult males—boys, really—were being victimized in twisted, brutal fashion on the average of one a week here in Houston, and instead of welcoming her help, the FBI field operatives saw her as some sort of ghoul escaped from an episode of TV's *X-Files*. "Grasping at straws," the Texas brains thought.

Oddly, the public displayed only a positive reaction to the FBI's footing the bill for a psychic manhunt for the killer, and the press liked the idea of a psychic solution as well, assenting to the notion of "try anything at this point," and perhaps as a

result, the attitude at the Houston field office had only grown
more sour.

All these distracting thoughts now impinged on Kim's ability
to find a state of unconscious grace in which to tap into Lamar
Coleson's signals again. She desperately attempted to regain
her foothold in the psychic realm, but her every fiber was here
where she sat upright in a chair in the middle of Field Chief
Harrison Vorel's office at 4:10 P.M.

Around her sat a small group of Houston FBI agents, ill at
ease in the semidarkened business office. The blinds were
drawn, lights off, the darkness heightened by Vorel's dark-
wood bookcases lined with criminal psychology and law
books. . . . Everyone's attention focused for a brief moment
on the strange FBI agent and psychic from Quantico.

The psychic's trance state had just come over her like a veil
of ethereal webbing. The light and shadow danced elflike on
her pretty face, illuminating the fragile web as a cracked mirror
of many refracted colors. From somewhere deep inside, she felt
a calm wash over her. At the same time, she could feel the
distrust and discomfort of the others, though her eyes were
closed.

Light and shadow danced away from her now. Reflections of
light and dark alternated to pace the room like so many
disembodied tiger stripes. The men became increasingly jittery,
more uncomfortable. Each man silently worked up a small joke
to share with the others later, some snappy line to cover any
possibility that they might be taken in by this *witch*. Their
minds were consumed with the need to laugh. Anything to ease
the discomfort, she thought.

Dr. Desinor sat stiffly upright in the center of the room, yet
she stood psychically on the threshold of a discovery. That
discovery flitted about butterfly fashion just ahead of her,
making her feel like a floating hang glider, able to reach out
and *nearly* touch the butterfly, but not quite. Each time she
reached out, the image fled just ahead of her grasp.

"Damn, damn, damn," she cursed, feeling herself lifting out
of the trance and back to the now. The damned stuffy,

overcrowded room didn't help matters any, nor did the glare of FBI men before her, their eyes and mouths clearly showing their skepticism. She didn't give a damn if they believed in psychic or paranormal powers, but she did give a damn that they were, as a group, blocking her efforts.

None of the FBI men in the Houston field office believed her to be like them, an FBI agent. And she had to admit, she wasn't like them. She had been different all her life. Still, she resented their hypocrisy: While accepting the fact that she worked for the FBI, they still considered her a hired gun. As far as Harrison Vorel and his Houston guys felt, she'd been brought in to second-guess their work. To them, it was just short of installing an inspector, an agent given the status of deputy assistant director, reporting only to the director of the FBI. This did often occur in high-profile cases. Perhaps they saw her as a vanguard, a precursor to installing a special agent who would ostensibly come in and take over the case on temporary assignment, remaining until the case came to a resolution. And perhaps their insecurities were warranted, but damned if she could work with such animosity, given the need for peace of mind in psychic detection.

Houston was one of the fifteen largest field offices, known as major offices. Because of its importance, only an agent who had previously managed other offices was named to it. Houston, with 201 agents, barely made it into the league, and now it was saddled with a case that interested not only headquarters but the director of the FBI himself. The *number one* FBI agent in the country had begun to call daily to ask about progress toward a resolution to the case.

Damn these bozos, Kim thought now. *Surrounding me . . . one or more of them blocking my receptors without even knowing why . . . without even knowing they can do so. . . .*

She opened her eyes, refocusing on a faded, water-stained photo laid out before her, a photo that had been blown up for their use, a photo of a young black boy with wide, inquiring eyes. She'd been told that the outdated picture was of Lamar, that they couldn't get anything more recent from the family.

Beside the photo, a small and pitiful pile of his things—things belonging to Lamar—lay in a heap.

She looked from the photo to Vorel's blank expression, and she said, "I need time alone with the kid's image and his things."

"I'm sorry it took so long to get these items to you, Doctor," he replied.

She waved this off. "Alone, please?"

Vorel glanced past her and tightened his lips before nodding his okay.

"These items do belong to Lamar Coleson, right?"

"You tell me. You're the psychic, remember?"

Vorel's agents all wore a contented look, feeling that their boss had scored one for the skeptics. They had, until now, argued only in their collective subconscious, a collective her single unconscious strength could not fight against and win. "Clear the room, please, all of you."

"Are you sure, Dr. Desinor, you wouldn't rather have a witness or two present?"

"I'll record my session. You'll have it on tape."

She saw in his eyes the unspoken reply: *Your hand is faster than my eye*. As if she would slip a prerecorded tape into the machine during their absence.

She knew that Vorel had accessed her file, that he had inspected her credentials and her history, that he knew she'd once worked as a Miami police officer, and when circumstances changed, she had worked for a time out of a storefront in Key Biscayne, Florida, as—and he'd put it so delicately— "some sort of private eye with psychic detective abilities."

Kim had noticed how the words *psychic* and *detective* caught in his craw.

Vorel had also read of and dismissed her successes in previous FBI manhunts. His only response came out as a snide remark, for the benefit of his men, about the going rate for psychics in police detection these days, and how the retirement villas in Florida seemed filled with psychics of every stripe.

Kim's thoughts raced back to New Orleans, to how distrust-

ful the NOPD's detectives had been, especially Alex Sincebaugh, who'd become a believer when her psychic powers had
helped to corner a murderer there. Sincebaugh had in fact
become a convert both to her psychic ability and her personal
charms. He'd followed her back to Quantico, Virginia, located
police detective work in nearby Baltimore and carried on a
romantic relationship with her ever since.

She'd even helped Alex on several of his cases in Baltimore,
with varying degrees of success, and they had become the best
of lovers and friends. They'd talked about marriage, but both
were willing to give it time. Still, when Alex had first met Kim,
he had treated her like a piranha, believing that she wanted only
to dupe the city of New Orleans out of as much money as
possible by milking a series of tragic, horrid deaths there for all
she could take away.

So, why did today's efforts here at FBI headquarters in
Houston feel like reinventing the wheel? Sad enough to cry
over, she thought.

"Ahh, yeah, well, we've all got plenty on our plates to keep
us busy, guys," Vorel now told his men. As SAC, Special Agent
in Charge, with such a red ball case on his hands, Kim well
understood the perspiration beads on his forehead. He was both
an ass and a heavy secretor who found himself, late in life and
career, in charge of a most sensitive operation, one that could
destroy a lifetime's work.

Vorel constantly dabbed at his forehead with an already
sopping handkerchief; he might be a poster boy for heart and
lung disease—certainly the man's blood pressure had risen like
mercury in a thermometer between the time of Lamar Coleson's disappearance and Kim's arrival in the city. A chain-
smoker, Vorel's lungs worked for every breath as he spoke, in
desperate need of every oxygen cell available. Kim imagined
his normal routine involved any number of fund-raisers, parties
and political gatherings. But someone had recently gotten on
his ass and ridden him hard, she told herself; someone had
ordered him to "get results" in the Snatcher case *now*. For all
these reasons, she knew instinctively that Vorel felt threatened

by her, that he believed her capable of fortune-telling, and that she might easily foretell his imminent death—death of a career, death of a man, death of a personality . . . whatever form it came in, for Vorel, it meant one and the same. Little wonder her being near him unsettled the man.

Eriq Santiva, Headquarters Chief over the BSU, the Behavioral Science Unit at Quantico, where profiles of killers and victims were drawn up, had called Kim into his office only the day before, detailing what they had in Houston. He first asked and then ordered her to Houston. She'd wanted to stay put in D.C., to continue work on important research projects— several of which she had gained funds for and now directed. Too many projects back at the lab, all awaiting her attention, she'd argued, but Santiva didn't want to hear it.

If she'd been honest with Santiva, perhaps he would have laid off her and found another avenue. If only she'd been strong enough to tell him the truth: that her stint in New Orleans had frightened all hell out of her, and worse fears had arisen with her last case, that of the Washington, D.C., serial killer known as the Capital Punisher. The bastard had nearly destroyed her emotionally.

She dreaded going after another serial killer in the field again, out from behind the safe confines of the lab and Quantico's walls, but she also feared telling Eriq, or anyone in authority over her, this truth. All she knew for certain was that the more she had her nose psychically rubbed into evil, and the more evil she saw, the more danger of becoming the very evil she chased. It was not an unfounded fear. It was widely rumored that the FBI Medical Examiner, Dr. Jessica Coran, a friend and associate of Kim's, had for a time turned to alcohol in response to the evil she chased, and it was no secret that Jessica had been in therapy for years for the same reason. Until now, Kim had been able to hide her disturbing fears, and to successfully avoid any real confrontation of the issue, even with herself. She'd thought to turn to Coran and other agents who had dealt with the same issues for support, but she feared showing any more weakness than she had already shown during the dark days of the Capital Punisher case.

She hadn't had a field assignment since that case, which had ended successfully only after the deaths of a number of children. Still, she knew that she was here in Houston due to her success in D.C., hard-won both physically and spiritually. And while the case had taken a grave psychic toll on her, Santiva and others pointed to it as a test case, along with New Orleans, for the use of psychic detection as a *regular* part of the FBI arsenal in profiling.

She'd just gotten comfortable in her lab again when Santiva threw the Houston case at her. She'd wanted to work the case from a physically safe distance within a controlled environment. Coming to Houston to literally "look into" the Snatcher case placed an enormous burden on one person's shoulders. Being psychic didn't in the least lighten the emotional burden, but rather heightened it.

To become the killer, to crawl into his skin, to see from within his contorted features as he meted out his torture, to think from within his cranium, and to taste the blood of children . . . perhaps this explained why she'd crawled so quickly and easily into the boy's head instead, seeing everything from the victim's point of view. But rather than lighten the burden, it had had the opposite effect. She remained unconvinced that she was the right person for—or ready for—this formidable task.

And while Eriq Santiva had felt differently, Chief Vorel and his men obviously agreed with her own assessment and not Santiva's. They willingly left her alone, as per her request, filing out noisily, like an unruly class, talking just loud enough about her failed attempt that she might feel the sting of their skepticism, not realizing that no sting was felt. Rather, she felt a great sense of relief waft over her on seeing them close the door on her.

"To hell with them," she said in a low growl.

They were all Vorel's good sheep. She'd earlier given Vorel a photocopy of the notes she'd taken after her first dream/vision the night before when both killer and victim had visited with her in her hotel room. She also had her second visit from Lamar in the killer's van transcribed from tape by one of Vorel's support staff, and she'd given this to Vorel, who shared it with his team. They were following up leads on anyone in the city named Roosevelt Cassell and Uncle Buck, and they promised to question Lamar's associates and friends again in search of an eyewitness, but Vorel's body language sent the clear message that no one believed any of her visions had the slightest thing to do with reality.

The team had read the reports with an official circumspection that said, "Thanks for the fiction."

Alone now, she thought, alone with Lamar's most prized, personal possessions . . . items from his bedroom, from his bureau drawers. . . . *Good, perhaps now I can relocate Lamar or that astral part of Lamar who reached out to me.*

"Alone now." She said it aloud, like a mantra, repeating the two words, and although it felt good, a curl of anxiety slowly crept in as well, for she also knew that she was alone with the devil who called himself Uncle Buck.

Now that everyone had left her in peace, Kim Desinor found her focus. Earlier, with others present, she had turned down the lights and set a tape recorder in motion. She now rewound the tape, starting over. She also went about the room, closing more blinds, darkening the room further before kicking off her shoes and climbing onto the center of the conference table, locating the geographic center of the room, where she assumed the lotus position, surrounded by Lamar Coleson's most prized possessions.

Alone with the remnants of what Lamar Coleson's mother had left of her son: a faded photo a few years old, a handful of items of clothing. A belt with a cowboy buckle, a pair of bleached and shopworn denims, a backpack, a pair of wrinkly, curled sneakers, a comb, a set of keys, a small wallet, a superheroes comic book, a favored, well-worn T-shirt screaming: Jefferson Elementary Hornets.

Kim set aside all items not Lamar's, stating aloud, "I am putting aside the wallet, the comic book, the comb, the keys and backpack. And I'd like to state for the record," she continued for the recorder, "that none of these 'control' items belonged to Lamar Coleson. Some of them, however, once belonged to previous victims—the comb and comic book to Ainsworth and the wallet and keys to young Milton. The other items are from the police property room."

After pushing all items removed from consideration off the table, Kim pulled the remaining items even closer. She thanked Vorel on the record, saying, "Hopefully, I've passed the obligatory test."

She next pulled two articles of clothing to her breast. She held tight to the sad gray T-shirt, its basketball team logo near worn off, along with the pair of boy's faded jeans, realizing that the T-shirt had once belonged to Lamar's big brother, someone deceased now, a casualty of the streets. She held the other item of clothing close now: denims with belt and cowboy buckle intact. She draped herself in the missing boy's clothing, pulling it about her shoulders, laying it across her lap, clutching the cloth tightly in her grasp, her nails biting into each garment. At the same time, she willed herself calm, a necessary state, by working in several deep, abiding breaths.

Touching Lamar's apparel gave her a sense of him. She cleared her conscious mind to get in touch with the god of unconscious awareness. She knew that conscious and unconscious must be in tune with one another to be successful, to touch the god place in herself, to work a miracle.

Her eyelids closed, fluttered, closed, fluttered. . . .

"Darkness, utter, whole, solid, biting darkness," she muttered in response more to a feeling than a sight, the tape recorder picking up her deep, guttural tones. "Cold is absolute . . . as is the darkness. Unable to breathe, can't breathe; can't move hands, limbs, body." She tried to move her arms and hands, but the arms were jammed to the sides of her body, the hands tied ferociously behind her. "Like being in a coffin . . . Smell of wood . . . Pinewood smell . . . Like being in a box . . . Smell of animals and rope and blood; odor of burnt flesh. My flesh? Burning . . . painfully burning, yet not my flesh, for Lamar's flesh is aflame . . . fiery suffering. . . ."

She next whimpered like a child, like an animal in the throes of agony. She smelled animal odors all about her, musk, animal fur, wet fur, earth, feces and urine.

She didn't sense or hear anyone enter the office, where she remained in the lotus position.

Can't move. Boxed in, but pain . . . insufferable . . . horrible. Want the pain to end. She shouted aloud, "Want to die. Let me diiiiiiieeeee. . . ." The plea tore at her own heart as it coiled about in her mind, and she realized that she'd tapped into Lamar Coleson's mind, wherever he presently resided. "Kill me, damn you! End it! End it. . . ." A terrifying series of screams erupted from Kim, but these abruptly stopped.

She desperately tried to get a fix on Lamar's surroundings. But she was blindfolded both physically and mentally—while in Lamar's state, his head, his eyes behind a black wall, a blindfold?

She now fought for sounds—to *hear* her way—but all noise here filtered through a muffler—some rumbling, continual noise, like the sound of a fan or other machine nearby, and beyond this came a strange collection of crying beasts, whimpering puppies, a cacophony of jungle sounds all confused and pleading for attention at once. Symbolic sounds, real sounds, she could not say. Then she realized the tomblike effect came of being wrapped about the head like a mummy, layer on layer of bandages, tape blocking out the noises and sounds all around.

Lamar lived, for the moment, in a tomb, but he could flex his mouth, and he could scream freely, scream as freely and as openly as he liked through an aperture in the tape tomb.

A flash of white darkness—a lightning bolt straight to the brain like a screaming siren. Blotting out all sight, a kind of mental whiteout swooped down over Kim's—no, Lamar's— ethereal self. It blanketed her and Lamar like a single moving wing—a spectral white stealth bomber—engulfing her mind. Something huge, lumbering just out of sight, but she could feel it, an approaching monster, as if on second or third attack, an evil all-white monster.

This charge came on hoofed feet, thundering, bellowing, cackling all at once as the beast came out of the whiteness and rammed its thick, ugly rhinoceros horn into her, drawing gory blood to the surface, sprinkling the horn and the head of the monster, which showed now a pointed beak and extravagant plumage, looking for all the world like a cross between an ostrich and a rhinoceros.

Having forgotten the tape recorder on the desk beside her, having forgotten that she sat now in Harrison Vorel's office, Kim tried desperately to see the salient features, the true features of the symbolic beast, but the features eluded her, congealing into a wall of solid white construction—like drywall, an empty slate, with feathers drifting around and through it now. The smell of the beast, pungent and stale and sickening, filled her and Lamar's nostrils: urine, feces, animal odors, all perhaps products of Lamar's own animal fear, the smell of his own fear and perspiration, as each new attack came wavelike, unstoppable, pendulumlike, unceasing, the pain increasing with each pulse beat.

The whiteness became white ink, spreading over him/her. Kim remembered now who she was, where she was in real time and place—past four in the afternoon in Vorel's office—and she attempted her best description of what she saw, felt, smelled, heard, tasted. The recorder and the focusing of her attention on the device suddenly detached her from him, the boy, and it effectively detached her from the vision.

Kim still pushed on, concentrating on Lamar's location in the astral stratosphere, putting the *now* out of her psyche. It took great effort and courage to return to that dirty, secret place where Lamar languished. But the boy, too, was reaching out, reaching toward her. He had felt her touch him. She knew she must return.

The excruciating pain, cuts, slashes, burns flare up like

biting insects all over his/her body now, and Kim's reactions violently reflect her vision as blow after blow is rained down on her/him from some invisible phantom, the dark wall standing over her—his—helpless form. She feels the burns turn into real welts as each appears on her arms, back, shoulders, buttocks, breasts, hands, feet, some below her clothing, others clearly visible to anyone who might be in the room to see, but the FBI men had abandoned her, hadn't they?

She feels the blood now trickling from slash wounds caused by the killer. She feels her breath coming shorter and shorter, knowing she is going to pass out if she does not claw and climb from the white suffering well of the vision, when a pair of strange porcelain monkey paws with upturned thumbs reach out from the white behemoth before her. Then a metamorphosis occurs, the smooth, polished, alabaster hands turn rough, dusky, and they grasp not Lamar but her in the center of the room in Vorel's office where she sits in the now time. . . .

His touch is surprisingly warm and healing, immediately taking all the pain away. She is stunned, having expected the scaly, even scaldingly cold white hands of a frigid creature of the grave or the branding burn of Hades itself. Instead, she receives the sensation of caring, a searing yet warmly inviting touch from dark hands and warm fingers that now have hold of her.

Her eyes explode open to meet those of the man whose hands have warmed her and saved her from another moment's anguish in the presence of the white demon.

"Are you all right?" asked the tall, angular, copper-skinned man whose clothes, a gray suit and London Fog overcoat—now bloodstained—and surroundings marked him as FBI. He'd tied a handkerchief around her bare left arm, high up, to end the flow of blood at the bicep, and his eyes remained concerned. He called over his shoulder for emergency help, for 911 assistance, through the door left ajar, but the only response either of them heard was laughter from outside.

Secretly pleased to have been delivered from her pain, Kim found herself being helped down from the table where she'd

been sitting in a trance. But she was also angered at having
been disturbed and immediately sought to reassert her professional demeanor, pushing the stranger away even as she
found her footing beside the table. But the dizziness and nausea
told her to sit back down, and she obeyed, gasping for air and
blinking at the red welts and blood spots that had mysteriously
appeared on her body, discoloring her clothing and dripping
onto Lamar's clothing, still clutched tightly against her. The
ethereal blood had dripped onto the table and onto crime scene
photos and continued creeping toward the table's edge.

Seated, again with the help of strong, insistent hands, she
cursed. "Damn, damn it, you've interrupted my trance." Her
complaint rolled from her tongue in a sad calm, her face contorted in pain. Her eyes flared fire toward his. "Who the hell let
you in here?"

"I must've picked the wrong door," the handsome, dark-
featured agent—his face slashed in half by the semidarkened
state of the room and a healed-over burn scar—replied
casually, while his eyes spoke of deep concern. She noticed that
the slender, long burn scar flared out along his throat.

She studied him a moment. The stranger's staring eyes
registered in earth-brown hues, a burnt umber intensity, telegraphing the amazement he felt over the results of her
psychometric exorcism of Lamar's things. Astonished, a bit
frightened even, the big agent must have felt as if he'd walked
in on an eighteenth-century witch at work. "Maybe I should put
a sign around my neck? Maybe a scarlet letter for sorceress at
work?"

Finally, he spoke, saying, "My God, but you are some
psychic manipulator, or else you're the best damned magician
I've ever seen aside from David Copperfield." He indicated the
welts and blood.

She saw that the cuts and welts were already fading. Soon
the stigmata disappeared, going back into the spectral world
from which it'd been forged. Each ghostly wound disappeared
like a lost negative.

"You're the psychic the FBI's called in on the Coleson case, aren't you? I read something about it in the papers."

Breathing in deeply now, Kim Desinor gathered her scattered energies enough to yell at him. "I thought I . . . I told your boss that everyone was to leave me in peace? That it's the only way! I can't work with distractions at every turn, agent ahhh . . ."

"My boss is across town."

She stared again at his long, black hair and his Native American features as he in turn studied her dark features. "Aren't you one of Vorel's agents?" she asked.

"No, no . . . I'm HPD." He flashed his badge. "My name's Stonecoat, Lucas Stonecoat."

"Stonecoat? I know that name. You're the guy who broke that international ring of killers, that Helsinger's Pit thing on the Internet."

"Couldn't've done it without computer-aided assistance."

"Just the same, I was impressed. Hell, everybody in Quantico was impressed."

Lucas laughed nervously, not knowing what to say. Changing the direction of the conversation, he replied, "It was quite a big step on the part of the FBI to go public with the fact that you, that they . . ."

"For my bosses to confess my existence? Yes, it's been rough on the FBI engine, indeed. Major step for them to send me here without any pretenses, nonsense or excuses; to send me out as an actual FBI agent, badge in hand."

"I heard about your work on the D.C. and New Orleans serial killer cases, but I thought you were a private psychic detective."

"Before now, I maintained an office and lab, my psychic detection unit within the FBI's Behavioral Science Unit, all rather quiet and hush-hush. In two years' time, it's been quite a step up: FBI HEADQUARTERS UNVEILS SECRET WEAPON AGAINST SNATCHER: FBI PSYCHIC DETECTIVE IN SEARCH OF ELUSIVE SNATCHER. Yesterday's rumor confirmed by today's headlines."

He smiled at her rueful tone. "I hope I didn't say anything to offend you, Doctor."

"Look, how did you get in here in the first place to disturb me?" She believed she knew the answer to this question, but she wanted to hear it from this hapless Houston cop.

"I'm here to meet with a couple of agents who're going to be assigned to COMIT, and I was *told* to step inside here and wait."

Her nose and forehead wrinkled. "Commit, huh?" She closed her eyes to battle the anger growing within. "Look, do you always do as you're told, Detective Stonecoat?"

"Not hardly. People who know me don't think so, especially my captain, but I had no reason to believe I, you . . . that is, *we* were being set up."

"What *did* you think?"

His shrug and expression were both pained. "I thought you were one of my new partners for COMIT."

"Commit? Commit who? What're you talking about?"

"Well, ma'am, it's C-O-M-I-T," he spelled it out. "A new partnership we're to build between the local FBI field office and the HPD to look into dead files, ahhh, unsolved cases, that is."

"I see." She knew full well what had happened. "So, the yo-yos outside sent you in here to wait for further instruction?"

"That's about it; yes, ma'am."

He's a caveman, a throwback, and he's so damned polite, she thought as she frowned and shook her head.

"Played me like a fiddle, huh, ma'am."

"Yes, Stonecoat, I'm afraid they did it to both of us."

"So, you . . . you are the . . . the psychic we've heard so much about?"

He seemed nervous, sparks flying like quicksilver around his brilliant blue-green aura as she stared up at him. Was there something about psychics and mystics that frightened him? Secrets, she guessed. He was full of secrets, and she threatened the sanctity of his petty secrets.

"That'd be me," she finally said. She started to stand, but she found herself still a bit woozy, so she plopped back down. "Poor Lamar," she muttered, feeling again his pain and suffering.

He stepped closer and asked if he could get her anything. "Anything at all," he repeated.

"No, no. . . . Unless you can find a frightened, lost teenager for me. You think you could do that, Lucas Stonecoat?" She realized the moment she said it that her sarcasm was lost on the Indian, who took her literally.

He leaned in to her and whispered conspiratorially, in his most deadly serious tone, "Funny you should ask."

"Meaning?"

"Well, I'm not officially or otherwise on the case, but I drew up a profile. I'd be happy to share it with you. You know, send it over, and you . . . well, you could take it from there."

Clear me of any further responsibility for Lamar Coleson, she thought she heard him think. "A victim profile? We have—"

"A profile of the killer."

She regarded him anew. "I see. But so has the FBI."

"I haven't seen the FBI profile. Have you?" he asked.

She nodded. "It's seared into my brain, you might say."

He nodded. "Interesting." He could hardly keep from staring at her. She was a beautiful woman, tall with striking features. "About as interesting as those welts and cuts I saw on your arms and neck which've all gone away now." He continued to stare hard into her hypnotic dark eyes, the element of risk and fear still present in him; but he seemed to be flirting now with the danger she represented.

She looked down at the wounds that had dematerialized like so many spectral markings, ectoplasmic ghost globules, stigmata; but the blood on Vorel's chair and carpet, on her own blouse and skirt, on Lamar's clothing, and on Lucas's trench coat were real in the sense they remained behind in this world. "Don't be alarmed. It's part of my ESP. I somehow became Lamar for a brief time, literally speaking."

"Literally bleeding, you mean to say?" he added. "So the wounds . . . they were real. They hurt?"

"Like all hell, and the blood is mine."

"You . . . you are a brave woman." He thought she might easily find a seat in the council house of the Wolf Clan.

"Not so brave. I was easily led away, part of me springing back, so please don't place any laurels at my feet, Detective. Look, I would like to see your profile, compare it, you know, to what we—*they* came up with at Quantico."

"And vice versa."

"A team of experienced professionals formulated the FBI profile, but they were some distance removed, using statistical averages. Who knows, maybe there're some significant differences in the two profiles, and you guys in the HPD may be closer."

"I don't think I made myself clear," he countered. "I'm not officially on the case. And I did the profile on yellow-lined paper at my desk and in bed at night, just thinking."

She laughed lightly at this. "Officially, neither am I on the case. That is, no one believes so, not really. Everyone—or almost everyone—will discount my involvement; occupational hazard. You see it's already begun with Vorel and the men here."

He bit his lip and nodded, understanding. "It certainly appears that Vorel and his boys feel that way."

"Look, I'll just return Lamar's belongings to them, give them my tape, and I'll meet you later somewhere where we can talk about your profile, the case."

Lucas wondered if he ought to become involved to the degree she wanted. "It isn't my case. Fact is, I've got a roomful of cases needing my attention," he told her, shuffling his feet. It might easily jeopardize what little he had finally gotten from Captain Lincoln, he thought. Still, a part of him wanted to help this passionate, psychic woman and, by extension, Lamar Coleson.

"Why so hesitant, Detective? Too risky?" she challenged as

if she knew precisely the button to push. He wasn't sure he liked this any better than her more demure plea for help.

Unsure what to say, he blurted out, "There's a bar and grill not far from here, two blocks north, called the Guardrail. I can meet you there when I'm done here, say in an hour?"

"Will you bring the profile you worked up?"

"I'll have to fetch it."

"Will you bring it?"

"If I can do so without upsetting any apple carts, sure I will."

"Don't bother typing it up or putting it on WordPerfect or anything. Just bring it as it is." She smiled radiantly, making him respond with his own smile.

"I'm sorry to've barged in on your . . . séance."

She laughed at the use of the term. "Psychometric vision, not séance. I reserve séances for the raising of the dead." Again she got no laugh from the stone-faced man whose angular features gave a sculptured, hard edge to him. He seemed spiked with edges both physical and mental, living on the brink of some cataclysmic psychic and spiritual edge . . . like a man balanced on a stone ledge.

"Oh, yeah, raising the dead, guess that's more in keeping with what *I* do."

She looked up at him quizzically, determined now to stand and look him in the eye. Lucas held out a hand to her, helping her from her chair and back onto her feet. "What exactly do you mean, more in keeping with what you do?"

He told her about the Cold Room's dungeon of dead files, and how files from the Cold Room had led to a break in the Mootry case, which led to uncovering the Internet murder game–religion called Helsinger's Pit.

"It must be interesting work," she suggested, "and apparently you were 'chosen'."

"Chosen?"

"Something about you tells me that you are comfortable with the dead, that you have been there, perhaps, taken the journey? Perhaps in a war zone, say Vietnam? No, you're too young to've been in Vietnam. Desert Storm, perhaps?"

He self-consciously touched the scar tissue on his neck. How did she know about his dream-time war? His father had fought in World War II, his father before him in World War I. Other ancestors had fought in the American Civil War on one side or the other when the Cherokees, along with the other so-called Five Civilized Tribes, had gotten suckered in over the white man's issues because for a generation they'd been living out the white man's dream, following the "white" path of peace, rather than the "red" path of war. But Lucas had managed, so far, to avoid going into the white man's wars. Yet he warred often in a dreamscape. How had she guessed this truth? Was her accuracy due to the obvious wound—his scar? "Yeah, you might say I've been through a war, but it wasn't 'Nam or Desert Storm," he assured her.

"Korea?"

"No, never been to war, aside from the street war out there." He indicated the window. "I'd have a hell of a time fighting in a war created by politicians for oil consumption on the side armed with space-age technology against a primitive people in a remote jungle or desert. Sort of makes us look like the Empire burning up the Ewoks."

"I think I believe you would have trouble in that role, yes."

Emboldened by her reply, he added, "Desert Storm was a hollow victory much needed after the debacle of Vietnam. Both wars were wars fought to defend lies we tell ourselves and want to believe. The kind of lies Lyndon Johnson and Richard Nixon based their presidencies on."

"Whoa, I'm not up for a foreign policy argument right now. Suffice it to say, I agree in principle."

"Sorry." He realized that she was right, that he'd gotten carried away. Yet it had been her question about war that had triggered his strong reaction. It brought back a memory of lying in a field of dead men, hiding beneath another man's body, injured and expecting to die, pretending death in order to survive. It remained an ancestral memory, one lodged in his unconscious, born of a century of genocide carried out against his people—tribal memory.

"So, I'll be waiting at the Guardrail for you, Detective Stonecoat."

"I . . . I read about you . . . you know . . . what you did in D.C., stopping the madness there, and Dr. Desinor——"

"Please," she corrected. "Call me Kim."

"I'm Lucas. I just wanted to say, what you did in D.C. and in New Orleans before that, I thought . . . well, remarkable and wonderful."

"Thank you, Lucas."

"How you read the minds of those killers . . ."

"Well, I'm a criminal psychologist as well as a paranormal investigator."

Damn, he muttered deep within, *another shrink. They're falling out of the trees these days. Why am I surrounded by beautiful headshrinkers?* "Oh, then your doctorate is in psychiatry? Psychology?" he managed to get out.

"Both," she replied with a resplendent smile.

"Great," he replied flatly, his mind reeling. *Playboy ought to do a spread.* "Perhaps you know Dr. Meredyth Sanger, then? Our resident crime psychiatrist at the 31st Precinct?"

"Name sounds a little familiar, but no . . . I don't believe I know her."

He nodded. "Probably read about her. She was instrumental in helping me solve the Helsinger's Pit case."

"Ahh, yes, of course. Look, I need to get out of here and——"

"Oh, yeah, of course."

"——freshen up. Maybe touch base with the hotel . . . before I see you later?" she questioned with her eyes as well as her words.

He stood there nodding but saying nothing.

"At the Guardrail? In about an hour?"

"Oh, yeah, see you then at the Guardrail. Better make it an hour and a half," he hedged.

Guardrail, a fitting name for the place where they'd secretly meet, her thoughts raced. "Yes, I look forward to it, Detective Stonecoat."

"Lucas," he corrected.

"You're sure it's not too public?"

"It's kind of public. It's a cop bar."

"We could meet at my hotel room, if that suits you better."

Was she making a pass or simply being pleasant, trying to reassure him? he wondered. "No, the Guardrail . . . at six, six-thirty?" He backed from the darkened room to get on with COMIT.

FIVE

Crossing Paths

Kim Desinor turned on the light and cursed, realizing only now that their entire conversation had been captured on the tape that'd been running the whole time behind her on Vorel's desk. She'd have to go back, erase the section she—and no doubt Stonecoat—wished to keep private. Only after seeing to this did she feel ready to face Harrison Vorel and his agents, hoping to get by them all with her dignity intact—if she could manage. She hoped to remain above their level.

She had been patient. She'd given Vorel the benefit of the doubt. Now she knew him for the closed-minded bastard he was; he and his men *planned* to be as cooperative as a pack of rutting hyenas. But this man Lucas Stonecoat was a natural mystic—something about him felt spiritually connected, cabalistic, and yet earthy and natural all at once. She knew Lamar Coleson needed an angel, perhaps a pair of angels to save him; she knew that time now flowed riverlike *away* from Lamar, and had been from the moment the boy disappeared, and no one knew—aside from Lamar and the killer and herself—just how trapped Lamar had become in a web of continually spinning, spiraling pain. The more he struggled, the more he fed the monster that fed on his suffering; the more tangled and pained Lamar became, the more sated the brutal torturer became.

The pain would only end with Lamar's death or discovery, whichever came first, and right now the sand in the hourglass ran down and down, and the river of time flowing against Lamar washed like a flash flood over the boy. And her major obstacle to locating Lamar was not Harrison Vorel, nor his men, nor even Lucas Stonecoat's interruption, but the boy's own intense pain, which she so sharply felt and shared. She hardly wished to return *there*, yet she must.

She had no time for Vorel's fun and games; she had no time to waste on the small-minded men in the department of skepticism. Obviously, Eriq Santiva hadn't paved her way in Houston any better than her former boss at the FBI had paved her way into officialdom in New Orleans.

Getting Santiva to contact Vorel and make him see the error of his officious ways meant only more friction and more wasted effort, time that none of them had to play about with. Certainly Lamar didn't.

In that moment when Lucas Stonecoat had entered the room, she had displayed to Stonecoat her stigmatalike injuries. She *became* Lamar in that instant, and this had impressed the Native American. Obviously, he understood something about the metaphysical nature of all things, the invisible skein sustaining and connecting all the tissue called life. She had felt no negative emotions or mind trips with this man Stonecoat, beyond his desire to remain a private person. Rather, he had put her at ease.

She could work with Stonecoat. She knew it. And despite his situation, his precinct captain, the fact he was not on the case, she knew that Eriq Santiva could arrange the impossible.

After erasing the section of tape she didn't care to share with anyone else, Kim used Vorel's desk phone to contact Santiva. She must make Eriq believe her best chance at ending Houston's nightmare came in the form of a man named Stonecoat who worked out of the 31st Precinct.

It'd been a long day, and after a workout at Adair's Gym, Lucas stopped off for coffee and dinner at a favorite restaurant, avoiding the Guardrail and standing up Dr. Kim Desinor, deciding against getting involved in the FBI psychic's plans. After dinner, he headed back to his desk in the Cold Room, intending to spend a bit more time studying the 1948 murder file on Minerva Roundpoint.

Still, there was something in the Roundpoint file that drew him like a teenager to trouble. Helplessly, he again began browsing the dusty casebook.

Thumbing through the stone-cold, brittle-with-age file, the murder of a streetwalker known to the police as Clarice Dane, Lucas learned that the woman had had her body completely hacked up by some maniac no one ever saw or heard from again. It was as if the madman had simply come out of the dark after Clarice, taking pleasure in wielding hatchet, meat cleaver or bowie knife like the one Lucas carried at all times. The perverted exercise ended in the killer's having butchered her in the fashion of a swine, her stomach slit, long gashes on arms and legs. Bastard might've been a butcher or a slaughterhouse man carving a roasting chicken, but all the parts were left intact. Whoever the sicko was, he didn't walk off with any of Minerva's body parts.

Small comfort . . . Rather, he cut her hair, leaving a long lock of it in the ditch outside the drainage pipe where her body had been discovered.

Footprint casts were taken from the muddy embankment of the drainage ditch, and they matched a man of average height and build, weighing some 160 to 170 pounds, but this evidence pointed as much to the man who had discovered the body as the assailant, except that the shoes were determined by their sole impression to be boots made of fine leather, brand name Lariat, long since extinct now. Lariats left a distinctive heel mark.

They weren't cheap boots. If the suspect was a hobo, surely the boots must have been stolen. Photos showed deep knife wounds in the body, cuts reminiscent of the long slashes left by American Indians on the plains after battle with an enemy. The taking of the woman's hair, too, while not exactly a scalping, had given Lucas reason to think it might be the act of a Native

American. Statistically speaking, people killed within their own race.

Back in 1948, when the murder occurred, Houston, still a cow town crowded with cattle and stockyards where major butchering of livestock went on, surely meant home to many hundreds of butchers of every size, stripe, nationality and ability. And a good butcher could afford Lariat boots, even if he were Native American. And stockyards abounded near train yards.

He wondered how much was known of Minerva Round-point. In the photo, taken with an ancient camera, a strange glow, like a radiant halo, encircled the corpse where it lay in a waste-filled drainpipe behind a tenement. A separate "before" photo displayed a lively, smiling young woman, hardly out of her teens, with distinctively dark features. Was she a half-breed or full-blood? She certainly looked Indian, but the alias she'd chosen was distinctly not Native American. Who was Clarice Dane? Who was she trying to be? Why had she used an alias? Was she recently escaped from a bad marriage? Did she want to hide from reservation relatives? Who was the minister who came to Houston to claim her body?

Still, her change of name meant little, as Indians all over the nation had by then adopted white names to satisfy census takers, while retaining their Indian names for friends, family and reservation life alone. Maybe she thought life as a Dane would be easier than life as a Roundpoint. Obviously, it didn't work.

Lucas thumbed ahead, searching for any background on Minerva/Clarice. There were two sets of photos of Minerva/Clarice, one outdoors after her remains were pulled from the drainage pipe where, due to drought that summer, her wounds hadn't been washed clean. Rats had fed on her bleeding corpse until she was discovered by a homeless man who found his way into a nearby tavern some twenty-four hours after the murder—or so the 1948 coroner had estimated.

Night photos were taken of Minerva in repose inside the large pipe to record exact location of the body in accordance with a triangulated sketch of the crime scene; but for overhead frontal shots, the cameraman had had to wait until the body had been hauled out and repositioned just outside the drainage pipe, and by then daylight had come to reveal the gruesome extent of her fatal wounds.

The photos were cruel: grisly, grim, ghastly items in their every aspect. Still, something in the shots forced Lucas to study them more closely and at length, despite their power to induce agitation and nausea. He kept coming back to the questioning, open eyes, the eyes that called out to him across time.

The second set of photos were taken in a fairly well lit morgue, and while the wounds were clean now, they proved even more disturbing in the harsh light of the old-time morgue. Her eyes remained open, fixed in death. Had no one the mercy to close them? Her eyes telegraphed a message through the camera lens to Lucas here and now.

Yes, that was it. There remained something about Minerva's large black eyes staring out from her "slab" photo—the one taken in the morgue—like two black plums, each with a shining seed of hope deep within, and each holding a plea in them, reminding him of the eyes he'd seen when looking at a photo of the recently abducted Lamar Coleson. Little wonder the doelike appeal of those eyes had such significant impact on Lucas. He didn't really want to know any more about Minerva; he didn't want to know who she had been, what her dream-time stories told her, what disappointments she'd faced or run from. He did not wonder to whom she'd belonged. His powerful reaction to her had simply mirrored his earlier reaction to having seen the photo of young Lamar Coleson, whose eyes looked the same—though the boy in the photo wasn't dead, not yet, but alive and presently being tortured to death. Yet in Lamar's living eyes, from his photo, and in Minerva's dead eyes, from her death photo, there existed a connection, cosmic and powerful.

Maybe, he chastised himself, he'd managed to get his emotions in a jumbled, tangled web, so much so that every victim looked and felt like Lamar Coleson, maybe . . .

A few lines scribbled here and there had pointed to Minerva's having been labeled a vagrant, which meant she was both homeless and destitute at the time of her death. Some detective named Cormack had quoted a building super, a single jotted line, like an excuse, saying, "She'd just been evicted from her apartment for nonpayment of rent." She had been going by the name of Clarice Dane, dodging debt, according to Cormack. She had most likely entered into prostitution simply to make her rent in the big city. Had some pimp tossed her out? Had some pimp killed her as a show for his other girls, to keep them all in line? Or had some psycho-john gotten off on butchering her thin body?

Officially, the police had not been too kind to Minerva/ Clarice as a victim, soiling her memory in the bargain. In fact, she'd been treated as the nobody that she was—a vagrant Indian squaw turning tricks in the burgeoning city in 1948.

Lucas bit his lower lip, contemplating the ingrained callousness of the times and the men who wore badges. Then he saw something that caught his eye, a single phrase: *victim of Native Indian and Negro descent.* The phrase was stitched in alongside the other words used for nonessential human beings, words like streetwalker, vagrant, vagabond.

"The bastards weren't even aware of their own blind prejudices," he muttered to the silent room. "Why did you come to Houston?" he asked the dead woman.

"Why do the young leave any reservation?" He heard the answer as if she whispered in his ear now, and he cursed his ability to hear her reply.

"Restlessness, passions uncontrollable, to seek a better life, to follow a man?"

He read on to learn that Minerva's maiden name had been Chechepinquay, an Indian name with roots to the Fox, originally of Illinois and Iowa origin, now holding tribal lands in Kansas. Then Roundpoint was in fact her married name. Roundpoint, a familiar name among the Cherokee and other Indian families. It was a name Lucas had some familiarity with; in fact, some of his relatives were Roundpoints. There was a family of Roundpoints—Texas Cherokees—at the nearby

Coushatta and Alabama Indian Reservation where they and other Texas Cherokees had intermarried, some with black slaves who'd run from captivity and found refuge among the Indians; but Roundpoint had its origins in the Mohawk, whose tribal land remained the borderlands between upper New York State and Canada, along the St. Lawrence Seaway.

He wondered if anyone at the nearby Coushatta Reserve might have any knowledge of a young woman named Minerva Roundpoint, aka Clarice Dane, a 1948 murder victim in Houston, Texas. He wondered who might care enough to know about this long-ago death. He wondered if his grandfather might have any knowledge of the woman's death. He wondered if she'd spent time at the Coushatta Reserve before coming to Houston. It was not unusual for Native Americans to travel from reservation to reservation, seeking shelter and hospitality along their way, and no Native American was ever turned away from a council house on an Indian reservation.

Lucas really wanted to let it go. Yet he again wondered what manner of man could be so malevolent in 1948 to so desecrate the woman's body. Was it simply the work of an itinerant madman who had left the area by boxcar as police of the day suspected, or wanted to suspect? They had canvassed the mental institutions for anyone considered criminally psychotic who could not account for his or her whereabouts. Some city-supported transient mental case was almost put away for Minerva's murder, but there hadn't been quite enough evidence to do the job, and since the mental patient was a white man . . .

So, had the brutal murder of this young woman been a stranger killing, as those '48 cops assumed when coming across the horrid remains in their city's gutter? With what Lucas and all of law enforcement knew today, wouldn't it make more sense to believe that Minerva's killer may well have known her intimately? That the ferocity of the murder might well be in direct proportion to exactly how closely and dearly the woman held her killer, or how closely and dearly the killer held her? That some sort of a perverted reciprocation had gone on between killer and victim?

When her identity was learned, it came as a result of a search instituted by a priest from her home reservation in Kansas. There had been no word from her in weeks. Her son was an infant at the time, and according to the kindly priest, the child desperately needed her. She'd left him in the care of his reluctant father, an alcoholic. The priest, a Father Michael Avi, had been receiving money from Minerva for the boy's upbringing. Father Avi had begun to worry when the money stopped coming in. Minerva was about to be buried in a potter's field when lucky coincidence—which always made Lucas suspicious—supposedly alerted the priest to her whereabouts and the grim circumstances of her death. The priest told police that Minerva had at one time been forwarding large banknotes, beyond her means, and he prayed for her soul.

Minerva's remains traveled back to the reservation in Kansas where she'd grown up, and she was interred there. Her family had consisted of a husband and a son, an aged mother and father.

Perhaps Dr. Sanger would agree with Lucas's assessment that Minerva's killer quite possibly knew her, that he was not an absolute stranger to her. Perhaps he should run the facts by Meredyth. Get her reaction. See what she might say. Perhaps it was exactly what Meredyth wanted, if she had planted the file before him. Perhaps her earlier visit had all to do with finding out if he'd read Minerva's file yet. She dearly loved yanking people's chains, he thought.

But doubt filtered into his string of pure speculation. Some fifty years had gone by, and this file had sat in the quiet gloom of this place, buried below HPD headquarters in a city office building older than Minerva Roundpoint's case file. He pushed the file from the glow of the tensor lamp, but one photo of the dead woman refused to leave the circle of light, as if stuck to the desk. He ignored it for the moment and leaned back into the chair, his back aching, a painful reminder to take his painkillers. He downed two pills with a stash of whiskey he kept in his London Fog overcoat, which hung on a rack beside the door.

Returning to his desk, he saw the death photo staring with

fresh intensity back at him. She'd been so beautiful, this Minerva Roundpoint, a young Indian girl of mixed Fox, Sauk, Black and possibly Mohawk blood.

Still, with a case as old as Minerva's, going so long unsolved, there'd be little or no hope of finding any new answers now, Lucas cautioned himself. But damned if he liked taking no for an answer; damned if he liked *no answers* any better. Such things drove him mad, and here he sat, slowly becoming the Mad Hatter in this teacup room of unsolved mayhem, when in fact he preferred the character of Alice who, at every topsy-turvy turn, proved the methodical, logical investigator in every sense, while all the people and the world itself around her remained chaotic and absurd. The Cold Room seemed little different than Alice's Wonderland, here where every box and file taunted Lucas, gloating its success over him and the entire collective army of police detectives that'd come before him, each file holding *secrets*—the creatures he most despised—clawing at his basic nature, the bedrock that was Lucas Stonecoat.

"Screw it," he mumbled to himself, closing Minerva Roundpoint's file with a heavy, definitive hand, still unsure how it had gotten on his desk. The mystery of it made him wonder if he hadn't picked up the file himself, acting in a fog. Or perhaps a drug-induced stupor or hangover? He'd smoked some marijuana the night before, followed up by Indian locoweed, peyote. Prior to that, he'd been drinking Black Label.

It irked, irritated and troubled Lucas that he could not recall the exact moment he'd reached out and taken down Minerva's file off the shelf before him—if, in fact, he had. And if he had, what had prompted his action? Nothing came . . . and it was getting late, so he said again, "Screw it."

Minerva suddenly gave him a final shove—a ghost clutching at his mind. The effort on Minerva's part violently pushed all petty considerations from his cluttered brain, demanding that all else besides *her* register as unimportant, including Lamar Coleson and his abductor-soon-to-be-executioner. In fact, Minerva might well be his way out—a rationale that he could live with when he stopped thinking about little Lamar's impending execution. She had now gained his full attention as Lamar's big, oval, pleading eyes nestled far back into the recesses of his mind, replaced by a focus on Minerva's plight some fifty years ago.

She now taunted him, saying, "Screw you back, *Detective* Stonecoat. If you're such a hot detective, detect me."

He could almost make out her dialect. She was, like him, an angry American Indian, but now his head and the Cold Room had gone stonily, eerily silent again. He tossed the file down a final time, and one of the photos, the one taken of Minerva when her body was pulled from the pipe, fell out, and he saw what he had seen before, but he also spied what had been hidden from him before his eyes: *her hands!*

He dared not think it possible, that Minerva had left them all a sign all these years but no one could read her sign language, no one but another Indian.

She had died with her right hand clasped tightly about her left wrist, and left hand. It was an Indian hand signal understood by every plains and prairie Indian in America, meaning *capture* and/or *imprison.* Had someone followed Minerva to Houston, angry with her for having forsaken the old ways, for daring to escape reservation life, married life, life as a mother in a hovel with no future? Lucas wondered. Her killer had "captured" her in some way, but how and in what sense? Her killer was not only the enemy, but a known enemy, and most likely another Indian.

What was it the FBI claimed as the most probable statistic in murder investigation in America? Same-race murder . . .

Lucas finally reached his apartment, pulling up in his new car, a striking cherry-red Dodge Intrepid that had put the joy of driving back into his life. It was the one extravagance he'd allowed himself since being promoted to detective status with the Houston Police Department.

He felt a little guilty about having dodged Dr. Kim Desinor at the Guardrail. If she still wanted his profile input, he'd fax it to her at FBI headquarters tomorrow morning, *during working hours*. He just wanted to protect the fences he had built at this point, to not rock the proverbial white man's boat. Women of all races knew it to be a man's world, and he knew it to be a white man's world. Piss Lincoln off as he had Lawrence before him, and Lucas might never see COMIT get off the ground.

Lucas lived in a flat over a bar named Bovey's, and Bovey owned both the bar and the building. Lucas had never seen or met his absentee landlord, only the bartender/manager of Bovey's, a spindly old saw named Jake, and the second "front man" for Bovey, the building superintendent, a grimy little man named Frank Finley.

Lucas watched a crowd spilling from the bar, revelers having fun with one another; most had had a bit too much to drink. The noise level brought the super to the window, and he shouted down at the three men who'd opted to use the curb as their social club and urinal. All three men simultaneously gave the superintendent the finger. One of the drunks sent a beer bottle hurtling up at the man.

"That guy comin' there's a cop!" shouted the super from the safety of the overhead window. "Stonecoat, arrest these bums for disturbing my peace!'

Damn, but Lucas hated it when someone like Frank Finley wanted to use his position as a cop whenever it was expedient. Every citizen wanted the law enforced, so long as the rules weren't too stiffly applied to one's own self.

Off duty, Lucas liked to remain that way. He knew about expediencies. And if he was off duty, it was expedient to remain off duty. Besides, it really pissed him off that Finley was telling the whole damned neighborhood that he was a cop. Just who had given Finley license to blab that all over the building and the neighborhood?

"Do somethin', will you, Lucas?"

"Let 'em be, and let it go, Finley," Lucas, fighting with an armload of groceries, yelled up to Finley, who now hung dangerously far out of the window.

"So, you're a cop," one of the drunks said, pushing into Lucas's face the moment Lucas spoke up, his message to Finley still reverberating down the street.

"Don't look like a cop," complained another, staring at Lucas's plainclothes outfit, his long black hair, tortoiseshell necklace and stud earring, which he'd recently taken to wearing.

"Looks like a fugitive from *Dances With Bears*," joked the third man.

"Wolves," corrected his friend.

"Bears, wolves, Indians do it with anything on four feet."

This brought a hail of laughter from the threesome.

"You better watch that damned lip of yours, Swenson!" shouted Finley from above. "Casting racial epithets and asper . . . aspersions on Lucas's heritage."

Lucas realized only now that Finley, too, had had too much to drink. He imagined how little work law enforcement would have if an alien mother ship landed tomorrow and made all alcoholic beverages disappear for everyone but Lucas himself.

"This guy's no cop. Tall enough, big enough, but *waaaaay tooooo* faggy to be a cop. Check out the earring and necklace."

"Out of my way, fellas," Lucas said, gritting his teeth to keep calm.

"Whattaya, undercover operations?"

"Fag patrol or what?" came the taunting remarks, while the third man moved to block Lucas.

"Break up the party, Lucas!" shouted Finley from overhead.

"I'm a detective with the HPD," he finally said. "And it's been a long day, so if you'll let me by."

"Creep Finley says you're going to bust up our party," replied the biggest of the three menacing men now surrounding Lucas.

"You do look like a goddamned Indian or half-breed to me," said the one on Lucas's right. "You take scalps for the Houston Police Department?"

"Sure, I've been known to, yeah." Lucas tried a smile. "Now, you fellas go on about your business, and I'll mind mine, and Finley can go to hell."

This caused the one on Lucas's immediate right to laugh, but the other two remained stone-faced.

"What kinda Indian are you?" asked the man at Lucas's left.

Lucas's eyes trained on the man directly in front of him, the one who insisted on blocking his path, the largest of the threesome. Lucas's features turned to granite in the blink of an eye. "I'm going through those gates behind you, going to my place, so let's just say I'm a *good* Indian."

"Going beddie-bye?" mocked the one on his left.

"Only good Indian's a dead Indian," retorted the big fellow who persisted in standing in Lucas's way. Lucas saw in the man's eyes there could be no peaceful resolution here, no matter that they had no reason for disagreement whatsoever.

"Ever see an Indian sweat, Tom?" asked the big one now.

Tom, on Lucas's right, grinned and replied, "Not till now."

"What kinda red man is yellow?" asked the one on Lucas's left.

"Enough with the fun, gentlemen," Lucas said, dropping to one knee to set down the bag in his hands. A metal-toed boot came up to meet his jaw, but Lucas yanked back at the precise moment that Big's reinforced foot whisked beneath his chin, missing by a hair. Lucas's instantaneous reaction brought his 9mm. Glock directly in line with Big's crotch.

"Summabitch's got a gun!"

"He really *is* a cop!" came the chorus while Big trembled like a vibrating signpost in a hurricane.

Lucas put up the index finger of his free left hand, indicating the fight to be over. He backed off. The men watched, wide-eyed, as Lucas popped the clip of his sleek, black 9mm., and in an exaggerated show of peace, held up the clip with its live rounds for the three drunks' inspection. He then dropped the clip into his coat pocket and returned the gun to its holster below his coat. None of them had seen him draw.

"Want to make this as fair a fight as possible, gentlemen," he told them in his most appropriate public relations tone.

"Wouldn't be fair of me to come at you all with my cannon, so now . . . where were we?"

The two smaller men had backed off while their big friend still stood frozen in his tracks. "Are we done here?" Lucas impatiently asked Big.

The man swallowed, his pale skin visibly running with perspiration. "Good," Lucas said, stooping once more for his bag, lifting and stepping around the man Finley had called Swenson. Overhead, Lucas heard snickering laughter escaping Finley.

Lucas also heard Swenson's movement the way a basketball player hears someone coming up from behind, and he dropped the bag, its contents littering the sidewalk as he tried to dodge the blow that came down full force on his shoulder, causing a shooting pain to burst starlike through his mind. But he refused to concentrate on the pain Big Swenson had caused him, instead rolling to the pavement and coming up on his feet to face the charging bear who growled an unintelligible epithet.

Lucas easily sidestepped the blind charge, sending the angry bully into the concrete wall that was Bovey's Bar and Grill. The other two, emboldened by their leader, now rushed Lucas, one sporting a pipe he'd lifted from the gutter.

Lucas's foot went into the shorter man's stomach, doubling him over, and at the same time, Lucas caught and held firm the pipe leveled at his skull. The pipe wielder held firmly to his weapon as well, and together they struggled, each fighting to pry loose the other's grip.

Overhead, Lucas heard Finley whistling and clapping and shouting for Lucas to kick butt. Finley had the best seat in the house.

Lucas yanked viciously at the pipe, sending the pipe wielder, who stupidly held on, through the neon sign and blinking lights of Bovey's window. He then straightened up the doubled-over smaller man, only to find him vomiting. He pushed the little one into the gutter, and then hurled the pipe halfway down the alley.

By now the big man had stumbled to his feet, his forehead

gashed and bleeding where the red brick wall had so brutally bitten into him. Crumbling bits of brick mixed with blood trickled down the man's forehead and nose. He'd taken a hell of a blow and was dazed.

"You've had enough," Lucas warned as the man tried desperately to focus on where to direct the blows he meant to hurl.

Lucas continued to try to reason with Swenson as the man's blinking, glazed eyes fought for focus. Obviously the man already needed emergency treatment. Lucas held his hands up, saying, "That's enough, Swenson. . . . Enough . . ."

But Swenson continued to circle, continued to search for his target, his huge, skillet-sized hands now two fists, gavels prepared to pummel Lucas if only he could get his eyes in working order.

Now, as the one who'd gone through the window climbed back through the broken glass, bleeding from multiple cuts, a stranger stepped up and one-twoed the drunk into unconsciousness on the pavement below the window. The tall shadow figure had streaks of gray in a long, dark mane of hair, and he gave out an unmistakable Indian war whoop as he chased the third drunk down the block.

Meanwhile, Swenson expended more breath and energy on his bleary target, Lucas. One great swing came at Lucas, like an aged and sad baseball player wielding his last effort at the plate. Lucas sidestepped the powerful blow, which threw Swenson off balance, causing the fool to fall through Bovey's already broken window, where Lucas saw the stunned faces of the bartender and patrons.

Swenson lay half in, half out of the window, a huge clod, still and clownish. Patrons inside were doing little boxing dances in an effort to keep up with the action that had so suddenly spilled from the street and into their lives. The pack loved it.

Overhead, Finley hoisted a Killian's Red, cheered and laughed in one fluid motion.

Lucas found his groceries, reclaimed errant cans and finally got past his gate as sirens sounded in the distance. He'd turned to close the gate when the stranger who'd helped him out stepped up and asked, "Mr. Stonecoat, can I have a moment of your time? It's important . . . about a case you're working on."

Lucas stared through the bars into the face of a man who resembled him in stature and general appearance—dark-skinned, long-haired, face cut into hard edges. Hardly a young man, the stranger appeared older than Lucas. In the poor light here, Lucas guessed him to be in his late forties, possibly early fifties. Rivers and tributaries of worry lines creased the man's face, giving something of his nature away. On closer inspection, Lucas found him to be a Lance Henriksen look-alike in need of a face-lift.

Again, the approaching sirens alerted Lucas, who thanked the man for his help and added, "Damn sure wouldn't look good for one of HPD's finest to be arrested for street brawling. Come on up."

Lucas unlocked and pushed open the gate, the stranger following him through the building's door and to the waiting elevator, a calm and patient man, Lucas observed, as, with grocery bag in hand, he rifled through a series of keys.

They took the elevator, Lucas seeing that his new acquaintance obviously abhorred the tight, closed-in space as much as Lucas detested the coffinlike box of the elevator. Always a bit of a claustrophobic, Lucas usually opted for the stairs, but he had to hurry to keep Finley from blabbing to the uniform patrol about how Stonecoat had single-handedly avenged the Chero-kee Nation when three drunken fools had insulted his heritage.

"I've got to detour to the super's place," he told the stranger when they reached his floor. "I'll be right with you, if you don't mind."

"Not at all. I'll wait here for you."

The stranger spoke English well, Lucas thought as he went for Frank Finley's place; he knew he had to shut Finley up, and keep him out of that damned window until the mess below was cleaned up.

SIX

Teepee: home, temporary

Lucas found Finley's door ajar, and Finley, half expecting him, smiled wide and raised his bottle of Irish red beer to Lucas in respectful, solemn salute to the conquering hero. After a sip, he said, "I want to shake your hand. Let me get you a drink, Lucas. Hoist one with old Frank Fin—"

"Close that damned window and get the hell away from it!" Lucas ordered him, cutting him off and causing a look of mild shock and disdain in the drunken features. But Lucas's command sent the slight man scurrying. Finley rushed as if something urgent was about to be imparted, closing the windows and blinds, obeying and returning to Lucas like a retriever. Then Finley, sounding like Humphrey Bogart, conspiratorially asked, "What's going on?"

"I don't want to answer any stupid questions. The cops'll take care of those clowns downstairs, run 'em to the closest hospital or drunk tank just fine without me."

"Rough day, huh?"

Lucas frowned and shook his head at the man. "Thanks to you. *You* got me into that fight."

Finley's hands flew up, causing his beer to slop over. "What're you talking about?"

"I'm saying this, Frank! I'm not living in this building to

fight your fights for you or to fix your tickets, or to do any
police chores, you got that? I live here because it's close to the
precinct, and it suits my budget. I pay rent here, and I want you
to stop telling everybody you see on the street that your best
tenant and your best friend is a cop, because we both know
that's more lie than truth, now, don't we, Frank? Frank?"

Finley was asleep on the couch.

"Bastard . . ."

Lucas snatched the beer Finley had offered earlier off the
table beside the window. The beer, still unopened, was frosty
cold, so Lucas held tight to it, lifted his grocery bag once again
and pulled the apartment door closed behind him. Finley owed
him a great deal more than a bottle of beer. "Dumb shit," he
cursed the spindle-legged, pot-bellied man.

Lucas continued cursing Finley under his breath while going
down the hall to his place, where his mysterious visitor now
joined him. Lucas, his hands full, fumbled again with his keys.
The stranger offered to take the grocery bag, but Lucas
stubbornly refused help, balancing beer and bag while working
the key in the lock. "What the hell is it? A full moon out there
tonight?" he asked the stranger, neither expecting nor wanting
an answer.

The stranger stood lean and tall in the narrow hallway, his
head threatening to hit the light fixtures, and Lucas found him
as angular and resolute and persuasive as the uprights of a
wrought iron fence. Damned if he could take a hint, though;
damned if he would leave Lucas in peace anytime soon.
Damned if the older, sophisticated-looking man with the gray-
streaked hair and expensive shoes and suit didn't cut quite a
figure. He looked on the one hand like a Kevin Costner Indian,
straight out of *Dances With Wolves*, and on the other an
executive with Neiman-Marcus. His clothes marked him as
a successful businessman of some sort, and Lucas respected
any Native American successful in white-dominated Anglo-
America.

"Last quarter moon, actually," the stranger now said.

"What?"

"The moon . . . it's in its waning last quarter," he corrected Lucas.

"Oh . . . oh, yeah," replied Lucas, finally getting both the point and the door unlocked. He kicked it open, sending a resounding thud through the darkness within. "I didn't thank you for your help downstairs, but you know, I didn't ask for it, sir, and it's very late, so . . ."

"I know you didn't need my help, but I wanted to gain favor with you, Mr. Stonecoat."

It was the second time he had used Stonecoat's name. Lucas held him at bay at the threshold, now staring hard at the man. "You know my name, but I don't know you. . . ."

"Every Indian in the country knows of the great Detective Lucas Stonecoat by now. I heard stories in Kansas about you. I've come a long way to find you. May I come in?"

The mention of Kansas instantly alerted Lucas. The last person he'd met from Kansas was a dead woman whose file someone had placed before him, Minerva Roundpoint. Lucas's features softened, knowing he must invite the stranger in and talk to him. An unwritten Native American law stated that, as an Indian—one of the First People—Lucas must oblige the journeying stranger, must welcome him into his home, shelter him, feed him, give him a place to sleep if he requested it. "You've just come from Kansas?" It was rude to push for such details. But the man's clothes didn't fit the picture of a reservation Indian. "Whereabouts in Kansas?"

"You know very well whereabouts."

"The Fox and Sauk reservation?" Lucas studied the classic Fox Indian features.

"I've just come from the deathbed of my priest," replied the man solemnly.

"The reservation priest," commented Lucas. "A Catholic priest." The Catholic Church had spent a fortune and several hundred years trying to convert the heathens, Lucas thought.

"A man who was like a father to me. His name was Avi."

Lucas recognized the name from the 1948 file. He realized that the man before him could well have culled all this information from the tattered file. "And your name would be?"

"Roundpoint."

"Roundpoint, of course." Lucas swallowed hard. Should he give in to an eerie feeling of mystical proportion and cosmic coincidence? Not so long as charging doubt blunted his thoughts. What kind of coincidence brought someone named Roundpoint looking for him on the very day he began reading Minerva Roundpoint's long-dead murder book? The answer appeared too clear. He recalled how equally mysteriously Minerva's too weak and thin case file had come into his hands earlier that day. How the file had just appeared on his desk out of thin air, no routing sheet, nothing to tell him where it had been, or who had previously handled the documents or why—of all the thousands in the cold pit—Minerva's case had come to be under his tensor lamp. And now comes another Roundpoint knocking at his door.

It had to be Meredyth, he surmised. She must have some tie to this man Roundpoint.

"Roundpoint," Lucas repeated. "How did you find me?"

"I am Minerva's son. And in my business, finding people . . . well, that's what I do."

"Minerva's son . . ." Lucas's surprised expression was half real, half show. "You found me through your line of work? Are you some sort of detective?"

"In a manner of speaking, yes."

If Meredyth Sanger had anything to do with giving this man any false hopes—and giving this man Lucas's home address—he'd chew her up and spit her out. But if so, just what was her interest? Then it dawned on Lucas.

"Are you a patient—ahhh, client—of Dr. Sanger's?" Lucas asked point-blank, watching for his reaction.

Stone-faced, Roundpoint immediately shook his head, saying, "I know no one by that name. I've not spoken to any of your doctors, no."

If he lied, Lucas couldn't tell. "How did you know I'd shown an interest in Minerva's . . . in your mother's case?"

"I arranged for it to come into your hands. I want the case to gain your full attention."

"You arranged it?"

"I am, Detective, resourceful, like you. . . . May I sit?"

Lucas nodded. "Yes, yes, of course, come on in. Let's talk further."

Lucas sensed a certain danger and coldness in the other man, a resolute determination, admirable in and of itself, yet something of the carnivore aura surrounded this man as well.

Turning his back on Roundpoint, stepping into the darkened apartment, Lucas felt a flutter of fear, like a flickering candle, burn just below his heart. Lucas's grandfather had taught him to never ignore his instincts, or his body when it spoke to his mind. And knowing his instincts to be good, Lucas realized exactly how helpless, at the moment, he appeared: grocery bag in one hand, Finley's beer in the other, his empty gun in his holster, the clip still in his coat pocket. There remained the bowie knife tucked into its sheath in the small of his back, but for now, Lucas tried to remain calm in the face of the strange turn of events. While something told him that Roundpoint could be a dangerous man, he knew at the moment Roundpoint needed him alive.

Lucas quickly snapped on a light and placed his groceries and keys on the kitchenette counter, holding firm to the beer bottle as his only weapon, feeling foolish even as his knuckles turned white around the bottle. Roundpoint casually closed the door on them. Sensing Lucas's nervousness, the older man now stared at the unopened beer that Lucas held like a weapon.

Roundpoint began speaking to calm him, saying, "I am Indian, like you, not so young as you. I come with my hand out." He extended his hand for Lucas to take.

They shook, Lucas feeling the strength and power residing in Roundpoint, who now said, "I need your help, your professional help, and I can pay you well, far better than the city of Houston."

"Really?" Lucas replied, and began putting his groceries away.

Roundpoint now strolled in a small circle about the flat, taking it in the way an animal explores another's territory. "You have learned to live well with the Anglo world around you," he said to Lucas, "but still you are one of us."

Lucas opened his refrigerator, snatched out a beer for his guest, opened both beers and offered one to the stranger, who accepted it and found a chair to sit in. "Seems you know all about me, but I don't know a thing about you, Mr. Roundpoint. I knew some Roundpoints when I was a kid on the reservation, but you . . . no, I never forget a face. We've never met."

"If we have ever met before, we both would have been children. My family travels, like most Indian families, between the reservations, and most in my family have barely eked out a living through the selling of Native American crafts and what the U.S. government gives us, not much."

"But not you?" Lucas combined putting away his groceries with reclipping his gun. "You're different. I can sense that."

Roundpoint watched Lucas work with his 9mm., curiously interested, but he simply said, "I am different, yes."

"So I can see," replied Lucas. "You didn't purchase those clothes in any reservation store."

Roundpoint, crossing his legs, fingering his expensive boots, tried compliments. "You're as observant as I've been told. You have the instincts of a hunter, as I've been told."

"So, what do you do for a living? No amount of Indian handicraft's buying the kind of clothes and boots you're obviously accustomed to."

Roundpoint laughed lightly. "They're not rentals. You got that right." Then he turned in an instant to a cold stone speaking. "I am like you . . . a tracker."

"What kind of tracker?" Wall Street tracker? Lucas wondered.

"A hunter-tracker, for hire."

"Where precisely do you hire out from?"

"Anywhere the work takes me. You see, Detective, I am an assassin. Does that clear it up?"

Lucas laughed, disbelieving his ears.

"Like you, Mr. Stonecoat, I am very good at what I do. At the top of my game, as the white man says, and I'm something of a perfectionist, type-A personality."

"An anal-retentive assassin for hire?" Lucas remained incredulous that the man so arrogantly admitted to him his ugly profession.

"Being neat and tidy has kept me alive and in business, Detective."

"You kill for money? You work for anyone who meets your price? You walk into my home, a cop's home, and you tell me that you kill people for money? What kind of balls is that?"

"I am at a point in my . . . business dealings . . . in which I have the luxury to pick and choose as I see fit, although it wasn't always so."

Stonecoat felt good about having replaced his clip in his gun. "And you've chosen to do me," Lucas said matter-of-factly. "And the whole scam with Minerva's file and your claiming to be her son, all a ruse to set me up? Get close enough to see me sweat before you did me? Very clever, like a fox."

Now Roundpoint laughed, shaking his head. "Men like you and me, we are what is left of our warrior kind, Stonecoat."

Lucas stared across at Roundpoint, sizing him up anew. He had heard of a handful of Native Americans or partial breeds who'd bought into the Mafia. Rumor had it that some were so good at what they did that they left no tracks whatsoever. And this made them invaluable to men who routinely needed someone somewhere snuffed out.

"I tried locating you about two weeks ago," the man calling himself Roundpoint now said, "but you'd left the city on some business, I was told."

Lucas mentally calculated the time frame. With Roundpoint conducting business in Houston two weeks prior, had anyone died? There had been something in the news, a still clueless, unsolved hit man–styled murder of three. The victims, all male, suffered single shots to the back of the head from a .44-caliber weapon. One had been a labor leader named Kiley, long suspected of running in rough circles.

"What sort of weapon do you use?"

"That is none of your concern, Detective."

"A .44, maybe?"

"It's not your concern how I work, Detective. This is your concern." He reached into his coat pocket.

Lucas instantly brought his weapon up, prepared to put a bullet through Roundpoint's brain when he realized the man held out a thick white envelope. Lucas stepped closer, his gun now leveled between Roundpoint's eyes. He ordered the other man to his feet and shouted, "Open the envelope. Empty it on the countertop, now!"

Lucas saw the hundred-dollar bills, amounting to thousands, skid across his countertop. "It's all yours, Detective. A down payment for services."

Lucas frisked the other man but found nothing else on him. He lowered his gun and ordered Roundpoint to pick up the money, place it in the envelope and return the envelope to his pocket, all over Roundpoint's quarrelsome objections.

"Take the money! It's more than you'll see in years working for Houston. You'll earn every cent."

"Shut up and get back to that chair," Lucas countered, pushing the other man toward the chair he'd come out of.

"So, where were you last week? Visiting a sick relative, I understand," Roundpoint said, unruffled, calmly icy.

It irked Lucas to know that this complete and total stranger knew his comings and goings. Lucas had taken time off to visit his ailing uncle on the reservation. It had been a difficult time. His uncle was in spirit ready to pass over, but his body would not make the journey, or so Lucas was led to believe when the old man had relatives telephone him. Lucas had remained on the res for ten days, and still his uncle had not died, and it appeared on the last day that he was not going to die. Instead, Uncle Ray sat up and asked for Lucas's help in winning over a woman who lived several doors down. They laughed over the request, but the old man'd been deadly serious.

His uncle Ray was the brother of Lucas's paternal grandfather, who'd passed away only the year before. Lucas, wishing to help his aged uncle, acted as messenger and go-between in the budding romance, doing what he could, and somehow he managed to get the two would-be lovers together. When he left, his uncle was well again.

Reservation living was difficult now for Lucas. He hated looking into the ugly face of poverty, sickness and depression, seeing the old ones interested only in drink, and the young ones without spirit or power. It only brought back old depressions he'd spent a lifetime avoiding. So once Ray was up and about, Lucas knew that he had slept long enough in a straw-tick bed, and so Lucas had raced back to Houston and his more civilized new self—where great comfort came in being anonymous.

Now here sat a self-proclaimed killer in his living room, sharing a beer with his anonymous self. Something in the whole scenario felt threatening on more levels than he cared to count.

It occurred to Lucas that Roundpoint could be telling the truth about being an assassin and about being Minerva Roundpoint's son. Still, he might simply be on the trail as a hired killer for someone else, parties unknown. Lucas held judgment.

"I am sworn to uphold the law, Mr. Roundpoint. One phone call and you're put away for life, if you are who you say you are."

"We are not enemies, Lucas Stonecoat."

"What's your first name?"

"I have none."

"Just Roundpoint?"

"Just Roundpoint."

The gray-streaked hair shone like slate in Lucas's apartment. Roundpoint stood up, paced the room, looked out at the police mop-up activity below. Roundpoint had sat here, with Lucas's gun in his face, with threat of arrest hanging over him, calm, collected, strong, virile, proud and menacing. He was an Indian's Indian, his sun-bronzed manly features covering any possible sign of weakness. He appeared in excellent health, his body responsive, on autopilot, so to speak, a body that Lucas helplessly envied, his own body having turned against him since the accident. Lucas hoped that at fifty-plus, that he himself might have such straight height and tight girth.

Roundpoint's ruddy complexion was dappled like a rain-drenched pond by pockmarks about the chin, cheeks, eyes. With his flowing black hair, he appeared a man out of time.

Lucas decided that the other man assuredly had an alias he went by, that he had long before dropped the name of Roundpoint for the sake of his professional facade and would not tell Lucas any more about the web of pretense he daily lived. "So, Minerva Roundpoint was your mother?" Lucas finally asked, standing opposite the man, drawing on all his own reserves to remain calm, relaxing his hold on his weapon.

"I learned this from my priest on his deathbed."

"This Avi guy?"

"Yes."

Lucas thought it odd how often killers confessed to priests. "What precisely did you learn from Father Avi? That Minerva was your mother, or that she was murdered here in Houston in 1948?"

"The murder part. I learned how she died."

"And you just happened to hear about me, and you managed to get hold of the case file and dangle it in front of me, all without the courtesy of simply coming to me and asking in straightforward fashion if I'd look into it for you?"

"Did it not work my way? Aren't you interested, curious?"

Lucas felt a surge of anger. The man read him too well. "You must have known your mother was murdered before now, before this priest told you on his dying bed. You're too smart not to know that what is whispered on a reservation is at least partially true."

"I always knew that she died badly somewhere far away, even as a child. I didn't always know where it happened, and I still don't know how. . . ." He sat back down, and Lucas sat opposite him, the gun relaxed.

"Why—you mean why. . . ."

"What?"

"You damn well know *how* it happened. You saw the autopsy report, the photos."

"I did."

"Then you know the how of it, and what you want me to find out is the why of it. Why was your mother murdered, right? Who had reason to kill her, isn't that it? So you can go gunning for them or him or her?"

"I want to see her avenged, justice done. Is there anything wrong in that?"

Down deep, in his heart, Lucas could not find any wrong in the ancient tribal law that called for blood vengeance. It was as old and true a tradition in Native American culture as the first mantras chanted by the first Cherokee to take breath.

Lucas made a show of putting his weapon back into his shoulder holster, and then he nudged the conversation in another direction. "So, you never knew your mother?"

"I have scraps, bits of memory . . . a certain odor, a certain touch, but no . . . other than vague dream visions, no . . . very little survives. Seeing her picture in the case file . . ." He stopped to collect himself, the first display of any chink in his armor. "Seeing the pictures helped to bring her face into focus."

And a lot more, Lucas imagined. What had the crime scene photos done for Roundpoint's dreams? Lucas wondered. "And exactly *how* did you get hold of the case file?"

"At this time, that is unimportant, don't you think?"

Lucas wanted an answer, but he chose not to press the issue any further for now. "And now, after all this time has elapsed, you want her killer brought to justice?" Lucas asked, draining his beer and setting the bottle on the end table beside him.

"Yes."

"And you want *me* to be the instrument of that justice?"

"You are a man interested in justice, yes?"

Lucas stood up, paced to the other side of the room, turned and stared across at the man. He wondered how much was lie, how much half-truth and how much fabrication born of an obsession. He wondered how many years Roundpoint had searched for some clue as to the truth about what'd happened to his mother. He also wondered if the man before him mightn't've been hired by someone else to locate Minerva Roundpoint's killer. How many people were involved in this thing? Finally, Lucas asked, "How many people have you murdered?"

"I don't murder people."

"Funny, what *do* you assassinate, then? Pets? Are you a pet assassinator? Or do you do Cabbage Patch dolls, what?"

"*Animals,* yes—people who *deserve* what they get."

"And who decides who deserves what? Are you judge, jury and executioner?"

"I only take on cases that . . . that interest me."

Lucas laughed lightly. "A kind of Robin Hood of hit men, you mean. Rob, cheat people of their lives, but only those who don't deserve life; I see."

"Not unlike yourself, except that you carry a badge . . ."

"And here I thought assassins for hire weren't choosy."

"This one is. In any case, I don't *murder* people; that is, I don't do murders, not in the sense that policemen think of murder."

"What exactly is the term you use for what you do, then?" Stonecoat sat across from him now, leaning in, wanting his reaction, absolutely curious now.

Roundpoint didn't flinch or hedge. "I carry out a plan."

"As opposed to murder. Nice spin."

"So long as I can live with it, it's not your bother. All you have to do is find the worthless bastard fuck who butchered my mother in 1948."

"You were there in the Cold Room sometime *today,* weren't you? Or you had someone intervene on your behalf to place the file under my nose."

"You are quite good, Detective."

Lucas offered the other man a second beer, and when Roundpoint accepted, Lucas stepped to the refrigerator and produced a bottled Blue Moon. The professed assassin took the offering. "I can blend in when I want," stated the Fox Indian.

"Is that what makes you so good as a killer for hire?"

"In the white man's world, Stonecoat, a man like me, a man like you, we are the same. We must do what we must do."

"What makes you think I'll look into your mother's death?"

"You are curious, aren't you?"

Lucas sat down again, putting the other man at ease. Roundpoint looked like Minerva, especially around the eyes and mouth, Lucas thought. Some might take him for an Apache or Arapaho but never a Texas Cherokee or a part Mexican Indian.

"You know I could lose my job, my career, just talking here with you? How do I know you haven't been put up to this by, say, Internal Affairs?"

He nodded. "I know you've had your troubles with them. You've already frisked me. You know I'm not wearing a wire."

"Taking money from you to work a case, even if you were the Pope, could get me canned."

He nodded. "You saw the money. I can pay you enough that it won't matter."

Lucas sat shaking his head, saying, "No, you can't."

"Try me."

"No amount of money thrown at me will convince me to jeopardize what I've got going with the HPD. I've worked too damned hard to get where I am."

"Yeah, I know about your accident in Dallas, and your miraculous return from death there."

"You know a lot about me."

"Part of my technique."

Lucas eyed him again. "You might've made a good cop."

"I was a cop, once, on the reservation. A man could starve. It's not glamorous, not like in a Tony Hillerman novel."

"Well, if you know so much about me, then you know I've just been returned to duty as a detective. I enjoy working as a detective. Do you understand that?"

"I believe I do, but hell, man, you could set up your own detective agency with the bread and clientele I can send your way, if you cooperate with me."

Looking at Roundpoint was like looking into a mirror that

reflected an image ten or fifteen years older than Lucas; but while the mirror reflected a physical truth, it distorted the psychological truth. Lucas, no longer the angst-filled youth who blamed all his problems on others, particularly the white-controlled world, saw that Roundpoint did exactly that. Still, maybe Roundpoint was right; maybe the two of them were alike, the similarities outweighing the differences . . . maybe.

"Look, Roundpoint," he began, "you're born Fox, full-blood of the Fox tribe, right?"

"Close enough to full-blood that it doesn't matter, yes. So, you know more about me than you let on. Perhaps you are as good as I've heard."

Lucas surmised as much from what he knew of the Round-point name and the amulet the man wore around his neck. He modestly said, "The folks we knew on the res with the same name, they were part Fox, part Mohawk."

Roundpoint smiled, nodding his approval, fingering the amulet.

"In any case, if I pursue your mother's murder, it will become a matter of public record as a test case for a new program we're implementing at headquarters, so if I pursue it, I do so for my own reasons, not for financial gain, understood?"

Roundpoint's eyes widened in amazement. "You want nothing in return?"

"That's not entirely true."

"What, then?"

Lucas studied him closely. "We follow my rules, not those of assassins or tribal traditions, you hear what I'm saying? I want none of that blood vengeance crap, got it?"

He nodded, muttered an okay.

"And I call you, not the other way around, when I want or need something."

"But I must be kept informed."

"I don't want anyone seeing you coming and going here."

"All right, but you must keep me apprised every step of the way," he argued.

"Finally, once I begin, there's no backing out, no matter where it leads or to whom."

"I just want the man who killed my mother brought to justice."

"Whose justice?"

"Yours, of course." It smelled of a lie, and Lucas knew he'd be doing a tightrope walk with this Fox from beginning to end.

"We're both assuming a great deal," began Lucas, repositioning himself in the chair where he sat. "We're assuming the killer's alive, for instance. There's been a lot of time flowing downriver since your mother's death." Lucas thought of the priest, Father Avi, who had, upon his deathbed, become the catalyst for Roundpoint's sudden insight into what had really happened to his mother after all these years of wondering. For Roundpoint, the revelations of the priest combined with the crime scene copy and photos must have come as a shock, a powerful crisis of identity, confusing the man, sending him on a quest for his past and his previously forgotten mother. Whether he'd heard rumors and rumors of rumors all his life, the priest's dying words must have sealed it firmly for him, sending him down this avenue.

Lucas suddenly asked, "What were you called as a child?"

He shook his head. "That does not matter."

"I have to have a place to begin."

"How do I know you won't simply turn me over to the FBI?"

Lucas glared at him. "You don't. Now, what was your name among the People?"

"I am called Three-Hands by my council brothers; Zachary was the name the priests at the school gave me. I am known as Roundpoint by those who pay me."

"And you were once a reservation cop, on the Fox and Sauk res?"

"That information stays with me."

"Fox reservation, then."

"As you say . . ."

"Kansas."

"Right again. They told me you were good." A mirthful half-smile escaped Roundpoint, but the curling lip menaced like a disturbed snake.

"Who are *they*?"

"Oh, everyone. Word gets around the moccasin grapevine better than the Internet. How you cracked that computer murder ring . . . I first heard of it in the stories of the old men before I read about it in newspapers. Now those guys you stopped back then, those people were some sicko white men, huh? White men, always got something nasty going, you know? Anyway, heard about the good work you did in Dallas, too."

Lucas cynically wondered how much of the flattery Roundpoint had practiced. "Yeah, we've established that you've done your homework."

"You've gained a reputation among the People."

"Not everyone would agree. You did talk to Dr. Sanger about me, didn't you?"

His confused look didn't keep him from answering instantly. "No, I told you, I thought I'd do the direct-route thing; get in touch with you directly, and no, I haven't spoken to any of your doctors."

"You call your approach direct?"

"For me, the way I usually work, yes. It has been direct."

Lucas broke off eye contact, stood and paced before the man alleging to be Roundpoint. Lucas finally said, "What do you suggest I do with this case?"

Roundpoint's shoulders lifted. "Do with it?"

"It's from 1948. That's fifty years ago, Three-Hands, and why did they name you Three-Hands? Because you were a thief?"

"No, no . . . Because my hands moved so fast around the girls."

Lucas, amused, found himself laughing with the assassin.

Roundpoint then said, "Fifty years . . . That's older than

you, almost as old as me. It is a long time for a death to go un . . . unsolved."

"You mean unavenged, don't you?" The old ways demanded vengeance for such a loss, and Roundpoint appeared a man who clung to the old ways. "I mean it. If I take on this case, we go by my rules, and my rules say, we bring the killer to justice, American justice, not the blood justice of our ancestors. Can you agree to that? Can you abide by that?"

"I can live with that. I just want the truth, and the guilty punished. And since you obviously are refusing payment, then I come to you with my hand out. I can give you nothing but this." Roundpoint fished from a beautifully crafted medicine bag a necklace with a Fox amulet like the one dangling from his neck.

Lucas took the amulet extended to him by the other man. It was a beautiful gold-and-turquoise ancient Indian cross, much like the swastika in shape and appearance.

"I can't take payment for working a case, Mr. Roundpoint," he repeated. "It's against section four of—"

"No, not as payment . . . It was hers, my mother's. Supposedly something she treasured and kept with her at all times."

"I see, and exactly how did you come by it?"

"Father Avi received it when he claimed the body, along with her other personal effects."

Lucas dropped his gaze now, studying the extraordinary amulet. It represented the old, exquisite Indian craftsmanship of a kind near impossible to find anymore.

"This is going to take some time to check out, Roundpoint." Lucas offered the other man a third beer, which he gladly accepted. They got comfortable and Roundpoint looked about the room, obviously interested in the wall hangings, the rugs and Lucas's mounted gun collection.

"Nice things you've surrounded yourself with, Stonecoat," said Roundpoint, now staring at a collection of mounted Indian arrowheads. "You've not forgotten who you are, where you've come from. I like that in a man."

"Yeah, I like the old ways if I can *control* them."

"I know what you mean."

"Now, about this priest?"

"Yes, Catholic, Jesuit . . . Frenchman, actually, but part Blackfoot. He was a good man."

Lucas smiled at this. "I can tell you learned a lot about Christian forgiveness from him."

Roundpoint's head bowed, and he shook it from side to side. "Life often tells us what we must do, what we must be. Is this not true?"

"Did this Avi . . . did he tell the authorities anything about the amulet? How she came by it? It was either purchased at great expense or someone gifted it to her, I would imagine. Did he know anything of its history?"

"Only that she never let it out of her sight. She slept with it around her neck."

"Perhaps if we knew how she got it, it might tell us something."

"Father Avi told me that they—the white authorities conducting the investigation—didn't pay him much attention; they believed my mother sold or traded her body for money and such expensive jewelry as they found in her possession."

"Like the amulet, you mean? Was there much jewelry?"

"Father Avi sold it all to give me what I needed at the time. All except this piece, which he refused to part with until he gave it to me."

"On his deathbed, I see."

"She had the amulet from when she was very young, before she married my father, I was told."

Lucas wondered how important the amulet was in relation to the woman's death, if at all.

Roundpoint continued, his voice a calm treble. "It may have been handed down from her mother. I'm not certain. I am certain of only one thing—as Father Avi said, she would never have parted with it."

"Was this Father Avi, was he like a father to you? Where was your father during all this time?"

"My father died a drunken Indian in a dirty little mud puddle on the reservation a few days after my mother's death. He took her death very badly."

"Are you sure he didn't give the amulet to your mother?"

"He gave her nothing but bruises. No, she owned the amulet before she married. Father Avi was clear on that."

Lucas looked into Roundpoint's eyes. "Are you sure you want to pursue this, because—"

"It's haunted me my entire life. Yes, of course, I'm sure."

"No matter where it leads?"

"My father did not kill my mother."

"And should evidence prove otherwise?"

"He . . . he stopped caring about her; he stopped living with her long before. He had no reason to murder her."

"Despite his abuse of her?"

"He didn't care enough about her to kill her."

"Interesting take," Lucas replied, realizing that Roundpoint had astutely arrived at the same belief that Lucas himself held about Minerva's killer. "Still, you've got to be absolutely, one hundred percent sure. . . . Despite where the evidence leads, do you want this matter pursued?"

"My father died within a week of my mother's death, with much regret in his heart, or so Father Avi told me. The priest likely lied about that, to spare me, give me some cause to find some measure of respect for my father, I don't know. Some said that my father died of a broken heart, but more cynical folk tell a tale of alcoholism. He drowned in a lousy ditch filled with rainwater on a drunk. Sound familiar?"

It did indeed, as Lucas's own father had died by drowning in a lake on the reservation, stumbling out into the water in a drunken stupor. He'd been a decorated soldier, returned from the War for the Pacific, returned to the reservation where he sank back into oblivion, poverty and alcoholism. Obviously, Roundpoint had done his homework on Lucas's personal life as well.

Roundpoint interrupted Lucas's thoughts, consumed by his own obsession. "Anyway, the damned cops on the case gave

Avi the amulet in an envelope with all her other belongings when he picked up the body."

"Then the amulet was found on or near the body. . . ." Lucas mused, holding it up to the light where its turquoise blue recalled the desert sky. "Why are you handing it over to me?"

"I want you to feel something for her; I thought if you had something that belonged to her, then perhaps . . ."

"Do you find it odd that your father should die so close in time after your mother was murdered?"

"Yes, I've had my thoughts along those lines, but I do not believe my mother's killer will be found on a reservation in Kansas."

"Where do you think he will be found?"

"I can't say. That's why I am here, pleading for your help, tracker."

Lucas leaned back in his chair and sighed deeply. "So, your mother left the reservation when you were . . ."

"Hardly more than an infant."

"And she left you in the care of the community?" Common enough practice on a reservation, Lucas knew.

"She had no choice."

How much had Roundpoint romanticized Minerva and her decision to leave his alcoholic father? Lucas wondered. The woman had abandoned her infant son, and for what? Promise of a better life in Houston, Texas? Whispers from a lover there, one who promptly abandoned her? Did she leave her son due to a hopeless love affair? "There's always choice," muttered Lucas.

"She left to find a new life." Roundpoint's voice rose incrementally now. "She intended to send for me. Father Avi told me so."

In search of a new life, but all she found was death, thought Lucas, who now asked, "And you believed and still believe everything Father Avi had to say?"

"He treated me like his own son. He had no cause to lie to me."

"But he withheld the story of her murder until his own death. Why?"

"To spare a boy, her boy, any further pain." Then he erupted, shouting, "Look, damn it! I want to know what kind of man butchers a woman like that!" Roundpoint's fist came down on the table beside him, knocking over his empty beer bottle. He apologized, straightening up the mess he'd made, and then added, "Look, I eliminate people for a living, Stonecoat, but nobody suffers. Nobody's disfigured. I don't butcher women."

"Do you have any relatives from that time who are still alive? Anyone who might offer me a lead? Anyone who knew your mother personally? Anyone who might explain why she had chosen to go by the name of Dane? Does that name, Dane, have any significance to you?"

"No . . . none."

Lucas saw a flicker in his eye, a movement in his body.There was something he wasn't saying, and Lucas's brain sent a warning, an ancient police truism: Everybody lies. "Spit it out," he ordered.

"There've always been stories, but no proof . . ."

"Proof of what?"

"She took up with a lover, ran off with a lover."

"Whose name may've been Dane?"

"I have never heard the name, not before I saw the police report."

"And just how did you manage that? Getting a look at the murder book on the case?"

"I bribed someone. It was easy enough."

"Then it was you who placed it on my desk for me to see."

"I saw to it, yes."

"Who'd you bribe to get at it?" Lucas thought it unlikely that Dr. Meredyth Sanger would be led into bribery over police documents unless something was terribly awry here. Did the assassin threaten her or a loved one in some fashion? Or had Roundpoint worked his lethal Fox charm in some other form. He guessed the assassin to be a man of many faces, capable of charm, enchantment, spinning an intricate web, possibly drawing on maudlin sentiment. Lucas quickly asked, "Did you come to any conclusions about the case?" He again wondered if the assassin might not be seeing Dr. Sanger in the guise of gaining professional help from the shrink. Meredyth, true to her workaholic nature, saw a number of wealthy clients on an individual basis at her high-priced uptown office.

Roundpoint nodded, biting his lower lip. "Yes, I know her body was badly used, that she'd had sex previous to the attack, that the cops treated her remains like those of a dog."

"Anything else besides the obvious?" Lucas wondered if Roundpoint had been composed enough to have taken notice of the hand signal left behind . . . *for her son? Or for Lucas Stonecoat?*

"I saw enough to turn my stomach." Roundpoint stood, now pacing restlessly about the room. Outside, the noise and lights of the street disturbance neither Indian wanted any part of no longer existed, so Roundpoint saw only a silent city street and a rising veil of night fog.

Lucas decided that Roundpoint, too emotionally involved in the gruesome police photos, likely had not noticed the sign language. It wouldn't be hard for the man to overlook, not in his emotionally charged state. It'd only been in one of the crime scene shots. Lucas himself had only stumbled on it. He thought of it again: the shot of Minerva's hands clearly seen in that frozen state of rigor, the clasped hand over wrist indicating imprisonment, capture by an enemy . . . Lucas momentarily flashed on a scene in a 1948 morgue—*an ancient M.E. prying the Indian's hands apart, thinking their position perhaps peculiar, an anomaly but nothing of grave import.* Only the photo remained, allowing Minerva's signal to pass down through the years.

Leaning in toward Roundpoint and changing his tact, Lucas asked, "Again, is there anyone living now on the res in Kansas, or here in Texas, who might provide me with a lead, or some insight into Minerva's personal history, her character? What her interests were? Her weaknesses, frailties, faults?"

Again the assassin bit down hard on his quivering lower lip and thought. "No one but Great-grandfather Osheeniwah."

"O-shee-nee-wa?" Lucas lifted a pencil and pad and asked him to spell the Indian name. "Where might I find him?"

"He is nearly a hundred years old. He is on the res in Kansas, dying."

"Do you think he will . . . can speak to me?"

"If he is able, yes. But I don't believe the killer will be found by going back to Kansas."

"I'll do what I can to find your mother's killer, but it may take some time, and I do have other, more pressing cases."

"Like the disappearing black boys?"

"Yeah, that too. . . . ," Lucas hedged.

"If you wish to speak to the old man, don't wait too long."

Lucas nodded, understanding. "I'll go to him as soon as I can."

Roundpoint stood, placed his empty beer bottle aside and raised both his hands, saying, "That's all I ask. Thank you for looking into this for me."

Lucas thought for a moment that Roundpoint might say something about professional courtesy as one Indian hunter-tracker to another, but he didn't. Roundpoint simply found the door and stepped through it as quietly as a deer in the forest and was gone, leaving Lucas to clutch the ancient and beautiful amulet in his hands. It was an old Indian shape, the ancient sign for all the elements in harmony: earth, wind, fire, water. It also represented the cycle of life-death-life and the seasons in all of nature. Obviously, the amulet hadn't been lucky in Minerva's case.

Lucas went to the window in an effort to see Roundpoint's shape disappear into the night gloom, but he had already done exactly that, like the Fox he was, leaving no trace of himself.

SEVEN

Morning stars: to direct, guide

DAY THREE, 12:24 A.M.

Alone now, Lucas wondered anew if the man calling himself Roundpoint spoke the truth, if he were in fact who he claimed to be, or if he had been sent to do a job, and playing Minerva's long-lost son was a simple enough disguise. Lucas further wondered about the ghost of Minerva Roundpoint, aka Clarice Dane. But for the moment, he felt overwhelmed, and to control the sensory overload, he sat square on the carpet in the lotus position, meditating on just being, on the easy rhythms of his extremities, tracing each pulse beat from heart to toe, concentrating on the electrochemical activity of his brain as the beautiful fireworks display that it was.

He sensed his mind's most primal essence, feeling both the biological organism and metaphysical soul, the *I AM*ness of self, trying to touch that universal part of himself that became one with God and his cosmic power, a power capable of taking all the day's pain away, so that he might defend against tomorrow's.

Lucas thought he might finally find some peace this evening when his bell rang, disturbing his trancelike state. He swore, realizing it was the doorbell and not the phone that beckoned him, the sound of it coming as if from a long way off. Whoever the disturber, he might well have seen Roundpoint leaving

Lucas's place. Lucas cursed the timing and went to the intercom and barked into it, "Who is it?"

"It's me, Lucas, Meredyth, and I have to see you. I need to be with . . . to talk to you, now. . . . It's urgent."

"Mere?"

"Let me come up to your room, Lucas, now!" she admonished, and laughed a laugh that came out sultry and full. "Are you going to keep me down here, or are you going to buzz me up so I can rub your back for you? I know you're in pain. Let me help, sweetie, huh?"

"Mere?" He wondered what she really wanted.

Some part of Lucas's mind told him to beware, that she had to have something on her mind other than massaging his back. He joked into the intercom, saying, "Why Meredyth, I didn't know you *delivered* to the doorstep."

"Damn it, let me up!"

Perhaps she *could* help him forget his problems for a while, soothe and smooth out the stress and reduce his pain, if only he could get her hands moving and her mouth to stop moving. He could always go back to the meditation and the medications after, he reasoned, giving in to Meredyth's tempting offer. "Sure, darlin'," he replied, "why not?" He buzzed her through, again noting how damned far away the buzzer sounded, and how soft the door felt, and how spongy the walls and floor felt. His head, when he reached up to touch it, also felt soft and large.

He realized only now that he was tightly clutching the necklace and amulet that had been Minerva Roundpoint's. He didn't want Meredyth to see the jewelry. She'd want it. He didn't know why he believed so, but she would defintely want the amulet; she'd fall madly in love with it, in fact. He didn't know how he knew but he just knew that she'd act the rabid animal about anything Native American, in the categories of both jewelry and men.

Lucas stumbled about, feeling the effects of the Native American drugs he'd been smoking, managing to find a drawer to stash the amulet in, and as he closed the drawer on the swastika-shaped amulet, he realized that something to do with the thing nagged at him, tugging at his attention, but he couldn't quite grasp what it might be. Meredyth knocked at his outer door. . . .

The sound of the knocking was soft, like knocking one's knuckles against a pillow.

Time lost.

Inside his night-streaked apartment, Lucas lay now on his back amid the tousled sheets, meditating to the rhythm of the overhead ceiling fan, meditating away the constant pain that—like a second shadow—remained with him daily, nightly. The pain he felt for the Coleson boy surely had its roots in the physical suffering he himself felt at all times.

Lucas watched the ceiling fan rotate at the velocity of an idling propeller. The drugs he'd shared with Meredyth helped relax his mind, got the clutter of this day off his eyelids, lulled him into reflection. He stared hard at the fan now, realizing it was slowing, so much so that he could see the individual blades. Dully, his mind asked his body how he'd gotten himself into bed with Meredyth; his body replied that he hadn't, asking his mind to quit playing games. But someone else must be in the room with him to've turned the fan down, so it must be Meredyth. He'd spoken to her, buzzed her up, hadn't he?

She must be here with him, and she must be the one who'd turned the fan to slow.

Or had someone else turned the fan down? No way . . . No one else occupied the room, only Lucas and Meredyth—*maybe*—and his ghosts. He reached out and found that if Meredyth had been here with him in his bedroom, she was now long gone, the mattress beside him cool to the touch.

Now he remembered. The sex had been lukewarm at best, because Meredyth had talked the entire time! Meredyth hadn't come for sex, but she tolerated it because she wanted to talk about problems she'd been having with just about everybody in her sphere of existence—landlady, sister, mother, uncle, aunt, friend, mother-in-law-to-be, psychic adviser. Still, she'd provided a fast and easy answer to his pain and loneliness; but the answer left him with even more questions about her, because again they wound up fighting, disturbing the place where he sought peace. Thinking the drugs would quiet her need for talk, if only he could wait her out, Lucas finally blew up at Meredyth—whose hair for some reason tonight had been dyed a flaming red hue to go with her flaming green eyes. He recalled simply begging her to shut up while she spewed forth on the subject of her fiancé's mother, her soon-to-be mother-in-law. And that's when it hit him. She'd come only to use him, to test her sincerity in marrying that twerp she'd been seeing for a number of years now.

Angry at what she perceived to be *his* insensitivity, she staggered out, shoes in hand, taking what she called her pride with her, promising he'd never be bothered by her in his life again, ever!

Peace replaced her, peace and silence, and for this Lucas had been grateful. Still, he knew that Meredyth had never really in actuality been past his threshold, that she never actually rang his bell, that it'd only been a drug-induced visitation.

Now he thought about another woman, a woman whom he had disappointed earlier today.

He wasn't sure why he'd stood Desinor up. He'd simply opted out. He'd gone to the gym instead, and from there to eat, and from there to do his shopping, and then he'd come home to a street brawl, followed by his meeting an Indian assassin in his home. He topped off the night with sweet Meredyth's astral form in his bed. And now he lay awake, numb to all the pain, the drugs taking hold.

He'd done the sensible thing, taken the intelligent route, he told himself now. Still, a nagging sense of guilt clawed at Lucas, even in his drugged state. Perhaps more due to his drugged state, he sullenly told himself. The drugs might ward off and deaden some of the demons, the pain and anguish he suffered, but the same drugs seemed to induce a sentimental, even sophomoric belief that maybe, just maybe he ought to jump with both feet into the cesspool created by Lamar

Coleson's abductor, the Snatcher, since maybe, just maybe he could make a difference, and that maybe, just maybe fate said so—fate whispering windlike in his ear again, reminding him who he was, who his ancestors were, that he was a hunter-tracker. . . .

He had let Kim Desinor down, but he'd also let himself down, let Lamar Coleson down, opting instead for a drug-induced stupor, one from which not even the long legs and red hair of Irish Meredyth Sanger could excite him.

Sometimes Lucas hated what he'd become. . . .

He flinched and squinted at what he saw in the whirring, slowed fan blades, and when did it catch fire? Smoke accumulated around the damned thing; perhaps the motor had blown, but it showed no sign of slowing. Simultaneously, Wallace Jackson's face congealed from the smoke amid the whirring overhead—smiling, laughing as he might normally appear. Wallace's great, grinning eyes came clearer and clearer, staring out of an amorphous black face, like some sort of Jacob Marley come to haunt Scrooge. Behind Jackson, or in front of him, or all around him, other more faceless images floated, smaller images, going-away images, descending in size, downscaled, down, down and away, as if two mirrors were held up on either side of Wallace's eyes, and mirror and eyes—*all one now*—shone off into an ethereal eternity: *infinite regress,* the effect created when two mirrors faced one another.

In the mirrored eyes of the ghost, Lucas saw the Coleson boy struggling against his bonds, trussed turkey fashion and dangling over a spit.

"And here you are, doped up, on your ass, you junkie bastard," Wallace mercilessly indicted him in a banshee voice.

Jackson's image represented the second specter today, along with Minerva, to call Lucas up short. *Surely, the spirit world is angry with me*, he believed. *Either that or the drugs're taking effect* . . . the slow-motion fan blades, the smoke-fog, Wallace's image, but now Jackson's black face metamorphosed into that of a young boy. He looked for all the world to *be*

Lamar Coleson, but his features were distorted . . . contorted in pain.

The boy's silent screams now became audible, coming forth from a spiraling, wobbling mouth made of Jell-O. The ugly music of pain wafted over Lucas. He'd traded in his pain for the boy's, it appeared. And the boy's pain outdistanced his own, for it was a pain of infinite humiliation and torture.

He turned his eyes from the fan. He tried to shut out Lamar Coleson's image and Wallace Jackson's derision.

Despite his protestations to Meredyth Sanger, his hands-off attitude now clearly displayed toward Dr. Desinor, and despite what he'd told himself, Lucas had given a great deal of thought to the Snatcher case. The plight of these poor boys, children of the street, being made sacrificial lambs to some sicko's penile lust, tore at him, reached into some subterranean part of him and tugged without relief.

Lucas recalled again the Atlanta child murders of 1979 that he had followed with such obsession. Just turning eighteen that fall, Lucas's fascination with the investigative technique of those involved in locating Wayne Williams, the imagination and science that went into the chase, convinced him that he, too, wanted to go into criminal investigation as a career. In fact, today's Houston child murders looked in so many ways like the Atlanta cases that some experts and retired FBI agents were mouthing off in public that maybe they had the wrong guy behind bars, that maybe the Atlanta child killer had reemerged as the Houston child killer. Lucas didn't believe this for a moment.

At the time of the Atlanta slayings, Lucas was just enrolling in college, but even then the fate of the children of Atlanta, all black children, just as in today's kill spree, became something of a passionate preoccupation. Without fully understanding why, he wanted to know the secret reasoning of a child butcher. He now recalled discussing it with his grandfather, the man who had raised him. His maternal grandfather, whose tribal name Keeowskowee meant Spiritual Leader, told him, "Follow your heart, but first know what is in your heart, what it speaks."

The old man had then taken Lucas far out into the desert and canyon valleys of a wild region of uninhabited Texas country-side known to the Spanish as Diablo Spinata, the Devil's Backbone, where only the gila monsters and a host of reported phantoms converged: the spirits of wandering Indians on ponies and afoot, and entire ghostly regiments of Civil War vintage thundering through the landscape. Other sightings spoke of marching conquistadors, Spanish monks in full regalia, starving Apache Indians. Whatever the garb, ghosts were the order of the night at Diablo Spinata.

Along the rough terrain of the Devil's Backbone—a dragon-backed promontory of ridges and valleys—the spirits of the dead of all races made an ethereal home, roaming in lost circles, caught up in some sort of magnetic vortex that kept their images alive here. There appeared no accountable reason as to why this phenomenon existed at the Devil's Backbone, but it had been known and passed down for generations among Texas Indian tribes and Mexicans.

It had been along the Devil's gnarled backbone, amid the canyon walls and cliffs, that Lucas, as a young man, had gone out alone to search for manhood, and his spirit guide, his manitou. In isolation, left to his own devices for seven days and seven nights of ritual fasting, which no one but his grandfather believed in any longer, Lucas nearly starved to death before seeing visions that grew from his heart—or his mind—visions of wild beasts that flew and ran over the earth with horns and wings, unrecognizable monsters that came to devour him. The visions did almost devour him, but one vision—the yellow-eyed wolf with bared teeth—guided him, showing him where to find fresh water and how to locate food to sustain his body. Later, his grandfather reminded him that through his ancestors he was a member of the Wolf Clan, and that the wolf had selected him specifically to guide him, that his god, his manitou, was the wolf.

After a week's time in the wilderness of Diablo Spinata, his grandfather returned for Lucas in their old Chevy pickup, and by then, Lucas—even starving—knew what he wanted to do with his life. He wanted to chase monsters—the human, demented kind, the sort that did the work of a Wayne Williams, a John Wayne Gacy, Charles Manson or a Juan Corona.

As a boy, he'd learned the ways of the tracker. His grandfather made a hunter of him. His grandfather made a survivor of him, but there was scarce enough game to hunt on their reservation lands. In the white man's world, he could survive as a man who upheld the laws by which all men might live together. It was an idealistic, young man's dream at the time, perhaps foolish, but nonetheless, Lucas's heart had spoken, telling him to get an education and to become a detective. His hunter's heart could not survive on a reservation where—despite the fact there was no game to hunt—there were more laws restricting hunting than anyone could memorize. His hunter's heart needed broader horizons. He had the heart of a detective, so he must become a policeman and build a career as a detective in the white man's world. Policing the reservation, he knew from early on, was too small an assignment for him.

He told this to his grandfather all along their route back to the reservation. His grandfather merely grunted and nodded and said, "You see your way clearly now. This is good. To leave us, this is bad."

There came many arguments after this, but in the end, Lucas found his way from the res to the streets of Dallas, Texas, where he became a beat cop for three years while attending college. He soon passed the detective's exam and was partnered with Wallace Layfette Jackson. Ironically, he found there were more rules to hunting human prey than animal, that the Texas State Legislature and the Officer's Rules of Conduct—a telephone-book-sized manual kept in the trunk of every police vehicle—tied a cop's hands behind his back even while asking him to risk his life in the performance of his duty. It meant one hell of a job.

In Atlanta in 1979, police had been slow to see a pattern in the disappearances and deaths of young black boys, but today, with better computer networking and cooperation between precincts and local, state and federal law enforcement agencies, the patterns had crystallized and emerged far more quickly here in Houston for any thinking cop.

The Atlanta culprit had been captured when a single FBI field operative suggested that law enforcement throughout the city "watch the bridges," since the killer's chosen method of disposal of the bodies was via water—rivers, lakes, ponds. As coincidence would have it, psychics brought in on the Atlanta case had also thrown up the cry to watch the bridges.

After well over a month of watching the bridges, the notion was about to be abandoned when on the last night before an official pullout, the very agent who'd suggested they watch Atlanta's bridges heard the sound of something hitting the water and watched a car slowly move off a bridge.

It led to the arrest of the killer, Wayne Williams, now serving consecutive life sentences. In that case, all the victims had been black male children, and just as in today's case in Houston, nearly a continent away, the popular thinking had it that some crazed white man or KKK member was killing the city's black male children in a one-man effort at racial genocide, or that some survivalist nut was attempting to start the so-called doomsday, end-of-the-world race war. And this notion fired a cauldron of racial bitterness growing rapidly toward a boil in Atlanta then, and in Houston now.

But Lucas knew better. He knew that if law enforcement, like all else, did not learn from mistakes—from history—they were all bound to repeat those same mistakes. Despite the acceptance that history repeats itself, and so does war, and so does murder, and so does fear and panic, despite this knowledge, men failed to learn from previous history, war, murder, fear and panic. In Atlanta, as it turned out, the killer shared the same race as the children, and statistically speaking, one fact emerged about serial killers: *They ate their own.* The Houston child killer had to be a black man.

Knowing this, Lucas had developed his own theories and a working profile of the Snatcher. He had done so early on, not because he expected anyone to ask his opinion, but simply for his own peace of mind and edification. He had passed along his thoughts to the principal detectives working the case at the 31st Precinct, but had taken them no further.

And now, like the Cherokee snake lightning of old, sluicing pendulum fashion into his consciousness, he knew one immutable fact: The Coleson boy took precedence over the Cold Room files, the COMIT program, Minerva/Clarice Roundpoint/Dane and everything else.

He again opened his eyes on the dizzying fan, knowing the image of the Coleson boy stared down on him, and knowing it was as much the drugs as any preternatural abilities on his part to grasp straws from the supernatural. But now, suddenly, the boy's image smoked away, and a nagging, insistent ringing filled Lucas's ears. He realized after a moment the ringing phone beside him had turned his vision into floating away pieces. This ringing bell had a solidity to it. He reached out from his trancelike state and clutched the rooted reality of the phone and placed the receiver to his ear.

"Detective Stonecoat?" asked a soft, fluttering female voice on the other end. Not Meredyth . . .

Through a haze, Lucas muttered, "Yeah, that's right. Who's this?"

"We met today at FBI headquarters. It's Dr. Desinor."

He tried to focus on the clock. Thought her resourceful for getting his unlisted number. Felt a pang of irritation that she'd disturbed him in his place of privacy. "What time is it?"

"You stood me up. For all you know, I'm still sitting at that cop bar you sent me to. Look, I'm sorry to disturb you at such a late hour, but—"

"No, no . . . That's quite all right." He read the red numbers on his clock as 1:19. "Sorry about earlier. Something . . . well, came up. You're not still at the Guardrail, are you?"

"No, I'm not that . . ." She let her words trail off. "Never mind that now."

"How can I help you?" he asked.

"I am most anxious to see that profile you mentioned, see where we agree and disagree."

"I can get it to you tomorrow."

"Tomorrow's a long way away for Lamar Coleson." A note of controlled annoyance filtered through to Lucas. "Look, whatever your reasons for failing to show up at the Guardrail this evening, I—"

"Things got real . . . *involved* when I met with the two FBI detectives who're going to be cooperating on COMIT." *She's a goddamned psychic,* he told himself. *You're lying to a psychic, hesitantly, badly. She's got to know it.*

"How about we all commit to Lamar Coleson? I need your input."

Do you really now? he wondered silently, picturing her waiting until closing time at the Guardrail for him. "Where are you now?" he asked aloud.

"My hotel room."

"I'll shower and come over. You got any booze?"

"We can raid the dry bar, if you think it'll help, and if you're paying."

"Where are you?" he fuzzily repeated.

"Imperial, downtown Houston, room 1348."

"Gotcha. Be there ASAP."

He hung up and stood too suddenly, his brain dizzy, his bad hip clutching him in a spasm of pain, his back stabbing him. The drugs had at first lulled him into a feeling of numbness, and they might've induced a sexual romp with Meredyth and a vision of Wallace Jackson and the Coleson boy, but getting to his feet cleared up one thing: The drugs had not as yet completely induced any respite from his physical pains.

He clenched his teeth, gnashing hard, swallowing the pain while making for the shower. When he flicked on the light in the bathroom, it burned his eyes, so he instantly cut it off. Showering in the dark, he soaked in the hottest water he could stand, turning it up increment by increment until the scalding took the place of the pain.

He tried to forget the images of Jackson and Coleson that

had appeared in his dark room, and to condemn any feelings of remorse and guilt—all the work of the drugs. The drugs hadn't completely killed the pain, but they had brought on a flood of sentimental nonsense about how he must, beyond all reason and protocol, go after the Snatcher to save the boy and all future victims of this bastard, as if he could single-handedly do so—the way the press painted him after the Helsinger's Pit affair. He reminded himself now that it was when a man began to believe his own press that he was doomed to failure.

Still, he mentally ran through the Snatcher profile he'd put together on a yellow-lined legal pad; at the same time, he tried to remember where he'd left it in the apartment. His plan included physically taking the profile to Dr. Desinor, leaving it with her and at once distancing himself from her. He'd soon be cooperating with some of the men under Harrison Vorel, and both Vorel and Lincoln might have something to say about Lucas's becoming entangled in the psychic's investigation. And while he didn't completely understand why, this Desinor woman made him nervous. Perhaps he simply feared the demands she intended placing on him. Perhaps it had been seeing the evidence of her power, the stigmata displayed in Vorel's office that had so unnerved him. Another Meredyth— this one psychic to boot—he didn't need, he assured himself.

Rinsing and toweling off now, he realized that Dr. Desinor's stubbornness and resourcefulness impressed him. She had somehow managed to learn his unlisted phone number. And why did she continue to pursue him when he'd decided to stand her up at the Guardrail? How much did she already know about him and his reason for standing her up: *fear*. Fear that his involvement in her psychic investigation of the Coleson case jeopardized too much what he currently had going for him— the COMIT program, Gordon Lincoln's backing and support, the possibility of renovation, additional manpower in the Cold Room, placing all the cold cases on computer—all admirable goals. He might easily be tossing all that out the window if he started stepping on FBI toes now. And how would it look?

Lucas Stonecoat teaming up with this so-called psychic detective whom he hardly knew.

But Wallace Jackson's insistent plea played continuously in his ear. Only it wasn't Wallace's voice, but that of a child.

Perhaps somehow the psychic had conjured Wallace and the Coleson boy up for Lucas. Too far-fetched? An impossibility? He'd known one other psychic personally, his mother's father, his grandfather who had insisted he fast in Diablo Spinata. So Lucas knew how devious psychic folk could be. Cunning folk, is what the Cherokee called them. Besides, he'd seen with his own eyes the blood, the cuts, the welts rise on her skin in Vorel's office, hadn't he? Perhaps Desinor was capable of long-distance manipulations and machinations of a metaphysical nature . . . perhaps.

Lucas had experienced stranger things while under the influence . . . yet he'd also seen what his grandfather was capable of, the reprobate old shaman who worked magic with everyday household items from Borax to hand-twisted tobacco.

He dressed quickly, pulling on a pair of loose-fitting jeans, his worn sneakers and a pullover sweater and jacket. He grabbed his keys and caught sight of himself—or rather his black shape—in the dark room's mirror, seeing the eagerness with which he ran from his nightly demons and the boredom here; the sight made him feel a bit foolish, like a little man, rushing out to meet with Dr. Kim Faith Desinor in the middle of the night, wondering if she were interested in him personally, wondering if he shouldn't change into something a bit more elegant for the Imperial—and for her—wondering if their combining on the Coleson case made any sense whatsoever.

He stepped out into the hallway, about to lock the door to his place when he again thought of the amulet that'd been Minerva Roundpoint's, the necklace the priest had kept all those years until the boy who was now a man was made privy to the fact. He rushed back inside, grabbed up the amulet, thinking that perhaps he might prevail upon Kim Desinor to run her incredible hands over it, to read it and unlock its secrets. Also, as an afterthought, he grabbed up the manila folder with the ancient crime scene photos, just on the off chance Dr. Desinor might become interested in the 1948 case. Perhaps with her help, he would have something for Roundpoint sooner rather than later.

Lucas now left his place in a swirl of emotions and a cloud of confusion, much of which had been brought on by his own personal seven percent solution: his medications and painkillers as he called his drugs, booze and the Native remedies given him by Grandfather Keeowskowee.

ᎬIGHT

Headdress: ceremonial dance

At the Imperial in downtown Houston, Lucas found some clear vision when Kim Desinor opened her door. The psychic detective, dressed in a pair of jeans and tailored lime-green shirt, her rich, black hair pulled back in a ponytail, looked both natural and radiant, he thought. She obviously hadn't had any sleep this night, and Lucas felt a pang of remorse at not having met with her earlier. He was amazed when she smiled at him, agreeably invited him in and asked what he'd like to drink.

"I'd best have whiskey. Lots of ice," he replied, stepping through the doorway, instantly filling the room.

She was drinking coffee, a swirling plume of steam rising from her cup.

Lucas found a comfortable position in one of two chairs near a window that overlooked Houston's fantastic evening light display, several downtown buildings decorated year-round in brilliant lights. The incredible lit sphere over the Standard Oil building gave off an otherworldly, alien glow. Christmas lights added to the effect. A dusting of snow—less snow than sand—tornadoed about, lapping at the chilled windowpane. But it was warm here in the room.

Kim joined him at the table, placing his drink before him. Raising her coffee to her full lips, she sat and looked down at the yellow legal-sized pad he'd brought with him. "The profile?" she asked.

"Sketchy, at best," he replied. "Again, I'm sorry I stood you up earlier."

"Understood, I think."

"Meaning?"

"Few men of your profession trust psychics or what we claim to do, Detective, although I'd gotten a different feeling about you."

Lucas, staring while taking a sip of his whiskey, squinted, his eyes narrowing down to slits. "What do you mean? What kind of . . . feeling?"

"I can see you're of Native American descent, but tell me, are you of the Christian belief?"

"What's it matter?"

"Important what a man believes. It defines who he is."

He took a deep breath. "The Christian belief, as it is taught in the church, is a bastardization of Christ's teachings. I admire Christ and his teachings, and I live by his word as much as it is within my power to do so, but I don't exclude Hindus, Buddhists, Jews, Muslims, Cherokees or other races and religions from the opportunity of attaining a higher plane and peace any more or less than—"

"A higher peace?" she interrupted. "Higher than what?"

He stopped to consider this, finally saying, "Higher than we can find by ourselves, higher than we might find in this world alone. Does that answer your question?"

"Yes, to some degree, and thank you for your frankness."

"What about you? What're your religious . . . leanings?"

"I've gone through a series of metamorphoses with regard to my religion, as I suspect you have."

Is she hedging? he wondered.

She seemed able to read his thoughts. "The very word: religion . . . Ask yourself why it's so closely aligned with legion. Allegiance to God and country, all that."

"Doesn't exactly answer my question," he pressed, taking a sip of his whiskey as if it were a rare wine. "There's something different about you, Dr. Desinor. I see it in the pigmentation of your skin, and I saw it in your blood earlier today."

"All right, you've found me out. I was born in New Orleans, a Creole."

"And you pass for white."

"No, I never deny my heritage, although sometimes I'm appalled by it." She laughed after this. It was the sort of laugh that invited others in. He liked it. She continued more seriously. "I was born Creole, into Catholicism, but you might say it wore off—particularly the Catholicism, thanks in large measure to those who profess its doctrines while harming others in the bargain."

"Poor role models in robes?"

"Try ugly and destructive role models in robes. Read a short story called 'The Butterfly' by James Hanley, and you'll get some sense of what I endured back in New Orleans as a child in a convent orphanage."

"Tell me more about this Hanley story you mention."

"Suffice it to say that the so-called religious Brother Timothy in the story crushes the butterfly."

"Did your religion let you down, or the people running the institution?"

"One and the same, according to their own doctrines; besides, I'm not an idol-worshipping person. A statue of the Virgin Mary leaves me . . . cold."

"But your main argument with the Church involves its inability to meet your spiritual needs, which are many, right? Sometime while you're here in Texas, I'd like to show you the desert, Diablo Spinata, perhaps."

"Diablo Spinata?"

"My church. A place of ancestral spirits."

"I'd like that. Is that where your spiritual needs are met, the desert?"

"Some, yes. It is a place of beauty."

"Then your needs are also many?"

"Absolutely."

"I should think the desert a place of death, ugliness. . . ."

"No more so than the ocean, the Grand Canyon, Yellowstone or any wilderness or mountain range. As in all natural places, the living must be respectful and watchful, and if not they join the spirits who peacefully dwell there."

"Diablo Spinata? The Devil's Backbone—no, Spine, right?" she mentally translated as she spoke. Very quick and intelligent, he thought. "This is a desert place, right?"

"Yes, some distance from here, but well worth the trip."

"I'd like to see this place," she repeated. "Perhaps someday you can show it to me."

"You know some Spanish. Good."

"My Creole upbringing? I'd better know some Spanish."

"Yes, well, I'd like you to see Diablo sometime. With your psychic energy . . . well, it would be quite an experience for you."

"The place might just recharge my psychic energies. Certain places can do that, you know. Perhaps I can find myself there in the desert. Tell me more about this place, and how you became so familiar with it. . . ."

Lucas described the ghost-ridden land in some detail, explaining how he first came to explore it. At one point, Lucas saw himself as a third party, as if standing in a corner, looking on, and he wondered why he was talking so freely with this stranger about his most intimate beliefs; yet he kept talking.

When Lucas finished, Kim said, "I will only see this place if you take me, you know."

"Then we'll have to find the time."

She smiled at his invitation before abruptly returning to the topic of religion, saying, "The limitations of organized religion, any organized religion, confine me, and the nuns tried to confine and limit and define me, and they tried to shame me for being both Creole and worse—clairvoyant. Strange thing about a lot of so-called Christians . . ."

"What's that?" he asked, again sipping at his whiskey, eyeing her.

"Most are very close to metaphysical thinking, though the

thought surely would send them into paroxysms of denial if it were suggested."

He nodded, understanding. "My own Indian metaphysical beliefs work in tandem with Christian teachings, those actual teachings of Christ, that is, minus the array of rituals, props and dubious 'word of God' reruns, such as Revelations, for instance."

"Oh, please! Spare me. Don't get me started. You know how many people assume the identity of the John who wrote Revelation to be that of John the Baptist, when in fact it was written by the apostle John? By the way, it's Revelation, not Revelations."

"It was written during the time of the Roman persecution of Christians."

"Exactly," she agreed.

"At a time when the Roman Empire became a near religion in and of itself."

"Yeah, when the Christians refused to bow and burn incense before a statue of Caesar," she enthusiastically agreed, "because to do so meant a denial of worship of God. Nowadays Caesar's statue has been replaced with statues of the saints, the Virgin Mary and Christ himself. What's that?"

Lucas added, "Revelation was written some eighty or ninety years *after* the death of Christ."

"John was exiled to some remote island, and he wrote the Book of Revelation for churches being persecuted in Asia Minor. The great message he passed on to Christians was that the Lord Jesus, risen from death, stood stronger than Rome."

Lucas added, "Yeah, that Christ was stronger than all the power of evil unleashed by Roman tyranny."

"John couldn't use the name Rome for fear of persecution and death, so he called it Babylon."

"Exactly," agreed Lucas. "It was too dangerous to use factual names. He could be beheaded or thrown to the lions."

"And even if the Romans failed to see his meaning, Christians everywhere would, and so, in a terrible account of the fall of Babylon, he actually prophesied the fall of Rome as the pouring out of God's judgment on earth, hence Revelation."

"The great dragon beast, Satan, along with his evil Babylon, would also be destroyed, the saints of God rescued to stand about God's throne, alongside Christ, the Lamb, all to live for ever and ever." Lucas leaned back in the chair where he sat, contemplating it all.

With a grunt and a shake of her head, Kim said in a sad voice, "So now Revelation has since been used to bear witness against every corruption and corrupt government——"

"Since Rome!" he interjected.

"Including the good old U.S. of A.," she added.

Lucas laughed and said, "Some people think the Romans have been replaced by the U.S. military, like there's some plot to revive Caesar and bring down the moral majority, all that shit, and why? Because Revelation tells them so. Because God's word is clear on this. Because John, author of Revelation, foresees it."

"And some, mostly survivalist-minded folk, think the FBI's part of the new unholy Roman Empire called the Industrial Military Complex."

Both sat in silence for a moment, contemplating the absurdities of the day.

Lucas, raising his near-empty glass as if toasting, finally broke the silence, saying, "In their day, the Christians facing Roman persecution understood John's writings and Revelation brought comfort and courage to them."

She nodded, adding, "And at the end of John's words, there's that wonderful promise of a new Jerusalem out of the heavens, and an end to all mourning and crying and pain, and 'men shall need no light of lamp nor sun, for the Lord God will be their light.'"

"Revelation, twenty-two?"

"Twenty-two five."

They smiled across at one another, bridging a gulf between them. She laughed lightly and said, "There's a TV evangelist in Ft. Lauderdale, Florida, who says that bad things happen to good people because that's God's pink ticket, God's way of getting their attention or getting even."

"Pink ticket? God's giving out pink tickets? This guy actually used this term?"

"I kid you not."

"Yeah, I've run into that logic, or lack of logic, sure," replied Lucas after taking another sip of whiskey.

"I shudder to think what such a person might say of Lamar Coleson's 'getting his comeuppance.' He'd say Lamar Coleson was getting a sign about now from God."

The mention of the Coleson boy's guilt in his own abduction brought Lucas up short, and he feared she read his mental flinching as a weakness, so he casually toasted and spewed forth a mock indictment of the abducted child, saying, "That rotten little kid's getting exactly what's coming to him for breaking the commandments."

She joined in the mockery, asking, "You think?"

"Ain't it obvious? God is good, God is great, so long's you ain't outta yow bed too damn late."

This made Kim laugh again, more heartily this time. Her laugh, he thought, sounded melodic and pure. But in an instant, the pure melody disappeared, replaced by angry words.

"Hell, when you look at life with such blinders on, that God and not man is responsible for the evil men do to men, women and children in this life, God then becomes the most notorious and cunning serial killer of all time . . . if you believe He's holding the puppet strings, if you don't believe in free will."

Lucas quickly added, "But the white man likes his reality bundled up in neat little moral syllogisms to fit on bumper stickers."

This made her laugh again.

Lucas continued sipping whiskey, and after looking into her eyes, studying the soft contours of her mouth, nose, brow, he said, "It occurs to me that because we give our gods the attributes we want them to have, firmness, fairness, judiciousness, gentleness or anger, large genitalia—"

"And all races and nationalities do this," she judiciously added.

"Yes, agreed, this may be one more way of *blaming the victim.*"

"Interesting conclusion indeed, Holmes . . . But how so, ol' boy?" she teased.

"Elementary, Watson. Lamar brought it on himself. His getting tortured to death by some crazed psycho is atonement for sins the boy was born with, for Original Sin. God and the Bible have said so."

She nodded, and raising her coffee cup to his toast, she now sipped the lukewarm liquid. "Exactly my point. If not Original Sin, then some sin the boy committed, or will commit, in a future he'll never see."

"So it all evens out, or so a lot of people believe."

"It's certainly the simplest explanation for the unexplainable, and with the turn of the century coming—"

"The technological race on for the unknown ahead of us," he added.

"—and the human race afraid of the unknown, we're only going to see more and more of such irrational crime, random violence and a senseless knee-jerk religious reaction to such crimes."

Lucas warmed inwardly with the whiskey and outwardly to the topic. He found himself enjoying Kim Desinor's wit. "God is again the great, cosmic scapegoat."

"Yes, exactly, the greatest escape from mortal responsibility ever concocted. Even more sublime than Satan himself, wouldn't you say?"

"Lamar did something bad, maybe did a lot of things bad. Therefore, he deserves whatever the Snatcher does to him, might even save the boy's soul, if he sees the light amid the horror." He grimaced as he finished.

"Easy to confuse God and the devil, isn't it?"

"Where's the distinction?" He noticed the blurred reflection of himself in the mirrored surface of the darkened window-pane. He chose to study her reflection instead, finding it sharper, more in focus, and a great deal more pleasant. He never lingered before a mirror, never searched his own eyes or the crevices of his brow or the rugged lines about his eyes. Never dwell on the scars, the burned tissue down his neck, he always told himself. It was only self-indulgent and weak to do so, he believed. He caught her studying his reflection, however, and she lingered on the scar tissue. She did so without flinching.

"Things like what the Snatcher does to Lamar and other people like Lamar, that will never happen to *me* because I'm a good person," she facetiously continued with the train of thought launched earlier.

"And *I* don't have to do a damn thing about any of it. It's in God's hands," Lucas added. "Nothing *I* can do about it."

"That's the Church I don't ascribe to."

He looked admiringly across at her. "Me neither . . ."

"So, let me have a look at these pages you've worked up, my metaphysical friend."

Lucas handed her the legal pad, stood and helped himself to another glass of whiskey while she glanced over the clear, sharp lettering. His script held a hard, biting edge to it, she thought. Kim knew something of handwriting analysis, just enough to diagnose him as an energetic and enigmatic man, given to a cryptic nature that perhaps she'd chinked away at, to some degree, in the short time they'd known one another. His ink markings appeared tight, like Indian pictographs, revealing some sort of phobia or phobias, a bit of pulling back, a secretiveness; not forthcoming in all his dealings, she thought. Yet his hand showed great imagination and daring and a love of raw, unfettered sex, which she would be wary of, as she'd gained a whole new hidden meaning behind his desire to show her the devil's spine out in the desert.

She pushed these thoughts aside, trying to concentrate on the profile itself, but first she dug into a briefcase left on her bed, found some papers and placed them before him when he returned to the table. "Look over these two transcribed . . . visits with Lamar."

"Visits?"

"Just read."

After some concentration, both reading in silence, Lucas mumbled, "This vision of yours, it's . . . it's remarkable." Lucas felt a sense of awe, his former fear of the "witch" beside him creeping back. What he read added up to an amazing insight.

Once each had finished reading the other's reports, they looked again into one another's eyes. She finally broke the silence, saying, "You appear to be quite accurate in predicting much about the killer in your profile, Lucas. That he's an organized offender. Thinks through his every move. Plots every step. That he's between the ages of twenty-eight and forty. That he uses a van or pickup. That he talks his victims into his snare. That he's above average in intelligence. That he does the torturing at some remote location or in some soundproof place where he feels at great comfort. That he's killed in the past, that he doesn't come to Houston with clean hands, that he's a black man—all most likely true, statistically speaking."

"I've put a lot of thought into it, and I think the bastard likes to hear them scream, that he gets off on it. He wraps them in tape, shutting off the eyes and ears, but leaves the nose and mouth free. He force-feeds them some vile concoction that only chokes them, according to Chang—the M.E."

"I didn't see that in the M.E.'s report."

"I spoke to him, off the record. It's something he found in the last victim, and he's checking to see if it might not also be found in the previous victim's mouth. Wheat germ meal, corn gluten, something called torula dried yeast, algae meal, sorbitol and a preservative called ethoxyquin or something. Chang thinks it's fish meal. It's in his last protocol."

"What?"

"You know, fish food."

She recalled how choked and dry she had become the second time she had visited Lamar. "The bastard's doing the same with Lamar. Makes him vomit. Stench of the fish food is disgusting.

It was overwhelming for me, and I was safely in an office, presumably miles away."

"Damn," muttered Lucas, wondering if he hadn't simply been supplying the psychic with more information that she then turned to her advantage; but Dr. Desinor didn't seem to be a liar, he told himself. Still, cunning is as cunning does, he reminded himself, thinking of his own grandfather.

"All part of the SOB's turn-on," she was saying now. "The killer has to mask the noise, though, control it. When I was in a trance, inside Lamar at times, I heard a clattering of noises, all muffled."

"What sort of noises?"

"The ones I could make out, I think, seemed barnlike, animal noises, but I can't be sure. It was as if I were locked away in a soundproof box. It all felt coffinlike, and I was wrapped like a mummy, and every sound around me was muffled except for my own screams."

Lucas felt the depth of her pain as she rejoined the moment she and Lamar had shared. However, Lucas went on matter-of-factly when he saw her look away. "The moment the kid entered his van or truck, the killer 'owned' the victim. Lamar became an object of torture, no longer a stranger or a human being."

"Yes, yes. . . . The kid was prey until that moment, an object—a possession—after that moment."

Lucas finished his drink and said, "The killer lives or works in the area in which he kills, or so it appears, and since there were two areas from which these boys have disappeared, the animal might well live in one area and work in the other. Two lairs, possibly three if you count a van."

She read aloud the rest of Lucas's words. " 'Or he lives somewhere between the two areas where he hunts. He knows the terrain over which he hunts. He is in the construction trade or some related field, hence the tile knife, the dump sites. He knows every construction site in his killing territory. The van or pickup truck he uses will be somewhat old with high mileage since he cruises for hours just looking for the perfect victim.' "

She again looked up at Lucas, who was nodding affirmatively, remembering when he had written down and dated the same or similar conclusions Kim had come to independent of him. The most significant difference was that Lucas had been working with the previous victims, she only with Lamar.

Kim ended with, "You have a damn sight more here than the remote FBI profile worked up in D.C."

"Thank you."

"FBI has him living alone with his mother, just an educated guess," she added, "but you think the guy has an ongoing regular, straight sex relationship with a woman, either a girlfriend or a wife who knows nothing of his perverted side."

"That'd be my guess, yeah."

She nodded her understanding, and continued, "The wife or girlfriend, if our killer has a significant other, might suspect him of an interest in child pornography or other lewd behavior, but she likely hasn't a clue he's butchering children."

Lucas stood to stretch, his lower back and hip throbbing, the familiar pain spreading through him, troubling him. She sensed his discomfort and asked if he were okay. He made an offhand remark, dismissing the pain, returning to his seat and what he knew—or thought he knew—of the killer, saying, "During the abduction, he's emotionally flat, although he might be playing a part that calls for emotional responses in enticing his victim."

"Playing a part, yes . . . agreed." She thought of the sweet temptations she'd seen exhibited in her vision of the killer. "But during the torturing of the victim, he's far from emotionally flat. In fact, he's on an emotional high, a roller-coaster ride ending in a climactic moment," she quickly added.

Nodding in agreement, Lucas said, "Up, up, up, down! Up, up, up, down! And on one of those downturns, he finally kills the kid, quite possibly in an uncontrollable, blinding rage that comes simultaneously with his sexual climax, at which time he strikes the victim with that unidentified blunt instrument, which not even the coroner's been able to identify." Lucas placed his empty glass on the table between them, the gunshot sound of it punctuating his frustration.

Her brain blipped and she saw the yellow-eyed cane staring back at her, but she didn't have time for the image just now. "Don't apologize for this bastard child molester murderer."

"Who's apologizing for him?"

"If the killing urge is so *uncontrollable*, done in a rage, then why is it so damnably predictable? Coming in seven-day cycles?"

"The ritual is ingrained? Becomes a part of the fantasy? I don't know."

"The cause of death is some mysterious blunt instrument trauma to the head," she said matter-of-factly, suddenly standing and staring out at the cold city below. What was it that Lamar wanted to gain from the relationship with the old man more than anything else in that ethereal street scene that kept playing in her head? *The cane* . . . Was he ironically to be killed with the cane, the yellow-eyed bird or beast atop the cane?

She suggested the possibility to Lucas.

"The M.E.'s people are taking bets on what the murder weapon'll turn out to be. Anything from a woman's heeled slipper to a baseball bat has been suggested. But your theory, an ornamental cane, is as good as any, yes, maybe more so."

She returned to the table, sat and slapped the legal pad down between them, sighing as she did so. "So, that's the ugly truth of it all. But there is one area where we sharply disagree," she summarized.

He had seen nothing in her written words to indicate any such thing. "Whataya mean?"

"You're convinced the Snatcher is a black male between the ages of twenty-eight and forty."

"So, you've got him older. Not a big problem."

"It's more than that, Lucas. In my third vision, I saw him as a white man, not a black man, and that skews things."

"That's crazy. He's clearly black in your vision. Chalk it up to one of those symbols of yours. Maybe he's one of those Uncle Toms instead of an Uncle Buck. Maybe he's a black man who outwardly does everything to appear white, and you picked up on that element of his personality."

"Perhaps, but the image was powerful, and as such it can't be ignored or treated lightly. In any case, I think we should put the press to work for us on this case."

"How so?"

"Put it out there in the *Morning Star News* and the *Constitution* that we know more about Uncle Buck than this creep thinks. Work up a combined profile from your work, the FBI profile and my notes to throw a little scare into the bastard, and at the same time alert the public to two things: who the Snatcher in fact is; and that authorities are not sitting on their thumbs. What do you say?"

"If we indict him as a black man in the press, it could have repercussions all the way back to Vorel and Lincoln, my boss, not to mention the NAACP and whatever and whoever. Besides, I'm not officially on the case."

"So we stop short of giving him a racial makeup, and as for your not being on the case, we don't have to say it came from you, if you want your name kept out of it."

Lucas knew that his profile ended with the fact the killer likely followed the news about his crimes, voraciously feeding on police reports and the like. He might even have been at some of the crime scenes to watch as police cleaned up his leavings. "Whatever you think's best, but yeah, I'd like my name kept out. Like I said, it's not *my* investigation."

"Do you want it to be?"

"Pardon?"

"The case . . . do you want in?"

"There's no freakin' way."

"If there were a way, would you want in on the case?" she pressed.

Lucas gave it a moment's hesitation. "Maybe . . . yeah, perhaps, but—"

"Good, then you're in."

"Per your say-so?"

"I've got some influence with Quantico leadership."

He raised an eyebrow. "Really now? I'm impressed."

"Consider yourself in on the Coleson boy's disappearance, Lucas."

"Just like that?"

"Just like that . . ."

He stared at her, disbelieving.

Kim ignored his stare and simply muttered, almost under her breath, "I really hate this bastard, don't you?"

"Yeah, makes two of us . . ."

"Torturing young boys is all that this freak lives for. All else in his life is a deception, a front, an edifice. Everything he does, including his charade and sham of a 'normal' life, all cover-up for a twisted sexual perversion in him. No one, not his neighbors, his coworkers, his boss, nor family . . . none of them know his secret self, that he lives on the sacrificial lambs he slaughters."

Lucas, feeling the depth of her empathy with the victims, wanted to take her hands in his to reassure her. Instead, he firmly said, "You understand the monster as well as his prey."

"No, not entirely, nor may anyone ever. You don't, do you?"

"I know that this is likely his only sexual outlet, the only way he can, pardon the expression, get off. Only through the cries of tortured children can he feel sexually sated. Where a man gets that need from, I'll never understand, but there it is."

"Through the smell of their burnt flesh, the sight and odor of their blood, he gains ecstasy, exaltation. It's the ultimate narcissistic evil, pure and heartless. . . ."

Lucas agreed, saying, "The notion of their being sacrificial lambs, the torture and peeling of skin and rending of parts and pieces—it's what the bastard dreams of, fantasizes about."

"No longer just fantasy," she countered, her hands now playing with her empty coffee cup.

"Reading tea leaves?" he asked with a straight face, leaving her to wonder if he were serious or joking. She had no doubt that he'd had too damned much to drink before his arrival.

Unsure what to say, she continued with her earlier train of thought, adding, "No, it's no longer just a fantasy he's content to play out in his head. Now he has finally found the aberrant and distorted courage to *make it so*, to bring into reality his vile and demonic visions, thereby altering and controlling his and his victims' reality."

"So it's about power. . . . It's a power trip for this guy."

"I think so, yes."

They stared across at one another, both understanding. It was the ultimate power trip, what the FBI termed a lust-kill fantasy, and it was about subordination and domination, subjugation and regulation, a monopoly held on a life.

"Can I use your phone to wake up someone?" he suddenly asked.

In your condition? she wondered, but kept silent, simply pointing to the phone, somewhat disappointed in Stonecoat now for the second time today, still stinging from his having not shown up at the Guardrail.

He explained in a guttural voice as he dialed, saying, "I got a contact in the police Internet who's been some help. He's searched out new information for me. Hold on . . . he's picking up. . . ."

NINE

Crossed arrows: friendship

Lucas heard Randy Oglesby's sleepy voice asking, "Who the hell is this?"

"Anything pop out?" Lucas asked.

"Pop out? What the—Lucas? That you?"

"Any of your cross-checks pan out on the Snatcher case we're runnin', Randy? Par'ner?"

Partner? Randy thought, noticing the detective's slurred words, realizing that Lucas had been drinking, possibly doing more than drinking. Since when did he call Randy partner? Randy almost hung up, but decided he'd best give Stonecoat what he had. "Between the task force and the FBI, there've been several hundred perverts arrested and released in connection with the abductions and murders of these boys, Lucas, any one of which could be our—*your* man. I'm running a cross on all the items you requested as we speak. It's on autopilot. It'll be in tomorrow's mail to you."

"Thanks, buddy, Randy . . . Rando. . . ."

"You okay, Lucas?"

"Go back to bed."

"Wait, something I ought to tell you, Lucas."

"What's that?"

"It's Dr. Sanger."

"What about her?"

"She knows."

"She knows? She knows what?"

"*She knows,*" Randy angrily repeated.

"Knows I've got my nose in the Snatcher case?"

"'Fraid so. Sorry, but it became impossible to keep it from her any longer."

"When?"

"When?"

"When did she know?"

"Found out today."

"What time today?"

"First thing, after you missed your session . . . today."

Lucas groaned and said, "Oh, shit . . ."

"She figured it out, all on her own. You know, Lucas, she *is* an intelligent woman."

"I hadn't noticed," he replied facetiously.

"Was bound to happen, Lucas," Randy finished with a note of apology.

So, Meredyth knew all along, even as she pretended not to today in his office. "Thanks for the warning, Randy."

Young Oglesby added with a heavy sigh, "You can't keep a strong-willed female shrink down. Believe me," Randy joked, recalling how once, in a moment of extreme anxiety, fearing he and Meredyth were facing the last moments of life, he had made sexual advances, only to be soundly rebuffed when Meredyth Sanger had bodily pushed him aside. "She's stronger than she looks."

"No . . . no you can't ever count Meredyth out," Lucas muttered to the dial tone. Randy had gotten off the line.

Lucas now saw that Kim Desinor stared across at him, wondering about the strange one-sided conversation she'd overheard, and wondering what his final comment about Meredyth meant.

"Anything wrong?" she asked. She'd gotten up, poured another cup of coffee for herself, pretending not to listen in, keeping a polite distance, but Lucas knew that she'd heard every word and could surmise Randy's responses.

"No," he lied, "nothing important. How 'bout another drink?"

She shook her head firmly, one hand on her hip, the other extending the newly poured cup of steaming coffee. "No more booze for you, Lucas," she said, pushing the coffee on him instead. "You need to be clearheaded."

Lucas, taking the coffee, returned to his ruminations about Randy's revelation regarding Meredyth, that she knew Lucas had been pursuing information relative to the Snatcher case. Even as he wondered what kind of game Meredyth was playing, he politely explained the phone call to Kim, clarifying what it meant, minus the disconcerting news about what Meredyth Sanger knew.

Lucas had a good mind to wring Meredyth's pretty neck, or better yet ring her apartment and wake her up. She ought to be losing sleep, too. He wondered how much he could trust Randy Oglesby; he was, after all, *her* computer whiz, not his, and Randy did, by rights, owe his allegiance to the good doctor. Perhaps her little discovery of his interest in the Snatcher case had been helped along?

Lucas looked at his watch. It was nearing three A.M. He hesitated a moment before dialing Meredyth's number, his hand perched over the phone like an egret preparing to strike and spear a fish. "What the hell," he mumbled, lifted the receiver and dialed. He almost dropped the phone back on its cradle when suddenly the ringing at the other end stopped and a man answered.

The male voice on the other end of the line was smooth, silky, melodic and refined, a kind of Brooks Brothers style. It was Meredyth's intended, Conrad McThuen, big shot in public relations. "This is Detective Lucas Stonecoat, calling for Dr. Meredyth Sanger. Got a situation here for the doctor." He used his most officious voice, not wanting to talk to the boyfriend.

"Oh, yes, Detective Stonecoat, Lucas rather. I'll roust her. Just a minute."

"Yeah, thanks . . ." Lucas pictured Meredyth lying beside McThuen, whom he'd met only twice.

Meredyth's slurred voice coalesced into questions at the other end. "Stonecoat? What's this about?"

"The Snatcher."

"Not another one?"

"No, nothing new's developed, and that's the problem. Fact is, the damned case is at a standstill. Listen . . ."

"Where are you, Lucas?"

"Listen, Dr. Kim Desinor and I are working over a profile of the killer, combining the FBI sketch, you know, with my own homemade model."

"Dr. Desinor? Kim Desinor?"

"Yeah, you know her?"

"I know of her . . . of her work, that is. Read she was in town. She's made some remarkable . . . showings in psychic detection. I've read some of her papers on the subject."

"We've concluded the killer's a person of color, black that is, in his late twenties, early thirties, most likely, and . . . and he possesses a high IQ and a high level of comfort in these parts as . . . as a hunter-gatherer chicken hawk. Likely has a history as a pedophile, and his pedophilia has taken on a nastier and uglier edge as he's scored successfully. Getting away with it makes you bolder and bolder. He's also a black man. Did I say that?"

"Are you on something, Lucas?"

"Never mind."

"How can you be sure of his age and race?"

"Both profiles say so."

"Profiles can be wrong, and they can lead you astray. Be cautious. Use your gut instinct. Instinct's better than statistics, be—"

"Okay, all right, shut up!" he ordered, silencing her. Without being direct, Meredyth had declared her knowledge about him, that he used drugs to dull his chronic pain, that she knew long ago that, in his own resolute style, he'd begun investigating the Snatcher deaths. Damn her . . . He continued on about the case, adding, "The restraints and other methods of control used by the killer also indicate his level of organization, thus age, if stats can be counted on."

"Like I said, beware of statistics," she again warned.

"You know me. I take everything with salt."

"So, why're you calling here in the middle of the night? What can I do to help?"

"We're going to knock on some doors tonight, including the newspapers and wire services. Are you up for it?"

"You're asking me if I'm up for it?" He heard her stifle a laugh.

"You've been in from the beginning, according to Randy."

"What has that silicon-chip junkie been telling you?"

"'Nuff for me to deduce . . . you follow my comings and goings a bit too closely, Doctor. In the future, I may have to get a restraining order."

"Very funny. Where do you want me and when?"

He chuckled, causing Kim Desinor to regard him with a smile. "That sounds like one hell of a Freudian wide-open you've left us with, dear Doctor: *Where do you want me and when.*"

"Lucas, damn you. Shut up and give me an answer."

"Imperial downtown. Meet us in the lobby in fifteen?"

"Imperial. Got it," Meredyth repeated.

Kim came on the line, asking, "Is this Dr. Sanger?"

"Why, yes, it is. Dr. Desinor?"

"Lucas has praised you highly," Kim automatically replied.

"I'm sure."

"Do you know the Imperial?"

"Yes."

"I'm in the tower, room 1348."

"Give me twenty, no thirty minutes," Meredyth replied.

"Looking forward to it."

"How did you get Lucas to commit?" Meredyth couldn't hold back the question.

Kim snickered and replied, "He did that all by himself."

"I'll see you shortly."

Kim hung up and looked over at Lucas, who was lying flat on his back on her couch, a snore escaping him.

Kim took a few minutes to touch up her makeup and to make more coffee for Lucas as well as herself. Seeing no need for changing her clothes, she somehow managed now to get Lucas into an upright position and to convince him that he must drink the black coffee. She was amazed when he finally found his feet, went to the washroom and threw cold water on his face, shuddered and bellowed out a wild war whoop. She was even more amazed when he escorted her down to the lobby in his zombielike condition, saying, "Enough time's been wasted already. We've only got five, no, four lousy days left before . . . before it's lights out for Lamar Coleson."

Introductions in the lobby ricocheted between awkward and curious, as Meredyth Sanger and Kim Desinor sized one another up, while Lucas continued to sober up. Somehow, being between the two women had a more sobering effect on him than all the coffee in the hotel could have. . . .

Meredyth gained the upper hand with a series of questions about Kim's recent D.C. case, and her case in New Orleans, where she'd been instrumental in nabbing the Queen of Hearts killer, with the help of FBI specialist and medical examiner Dr. Jessica Coran and the New Orleans Police Department.

Lucas ushered them from the hotel lobby to his car in the parking garage. The entire trip, from Kim's room to the lobby, waiting for Meredyth, and then down the elevator to subbasement level, they'd argued about who would drive, Lucas shouting the ladies down, "I am driving! I'm fine to drive."

Silenced for a moment, Kim and Meredyth turned to talking about the Washington, D.C., case, dubbed in the press as the Capital Punisher case. Kim filled them in on little-known facts about the sequence of events leading up to the case's resolution. When they located Lucas's car, the two women opted for the rear of the vehicle, where they might more readily talk. Meredyth, now asking for more details on the New Orleans case, was fascinated with the criminal psychology aspects of both cases.

As Lucas pulled the car from the parking garage, he heard Dr. Desinor saying from behind him, "It took more than detective work in New Orleans. . . . It took *pure instinct*."

"The NOPD caught a lot of flak about utilizing your services there, but you proved everyone wrong in the end," Meredyth complimented Dr. Desinor as Lucas pulled out into traffic.

"Trust me," Kim replied. "Success in New Orleans and D.C. was the result of teamwork."

Lucas attempted to force in a word or a question here and there, but Meredyth monopolized Dr. Desinor's attention, now asking, "What initial impressions, Dr. Desinor, have you had of the situation here in Houston?"

"Yeah," piped up Lucas, "tell Dr. Sanger what your instincts tell you about our killer."

"Frankly, Lucas," the psychic detective replied, "I believe you have as good a fix on this guy as anyone, and except for one reservation, I'm inclined to agree with your workup of the killer's profile."

Lucas's attention was riveted on the rearview mirror, his eyes focused on Dr. Desinor. She sat stone-faced while Meredyth asked, "You're in what, eighty, eighty-five percent agreement with Lucas's profile, then?"

"More like ninety percent."

"Where do you differ?"

"On the racial makeup of the perpetrator."

Meredyth gasped and said, "That's a significant difference, Doctor."

"Really? You think?" Lucas asked facetiously, finishing with a snort. "You have to agree, Dr. Desinor, that statistically speaking, the Snatcher's most likely a black male."

"Agreed. My own profile team—the best the FBI has to offer—says as much. And analytically speaking, yes. Intuitively speaking, no."

"How can you make that distinction?" Lucas asked.

"I wouldn't make that assertion too near any newsman," added Meredyth.

"We've already got every corner tavern in Houston breaking out with fights over the issue of the killer's racial identity, Dr. Desinor," explained Lucas from the front seat.

Meredyth asked point-blank, "What have you seen to make you think the killer is a white man, Doctor?"

"Nothing specific, just a feeling."

"A feeling isn't enough," Lucas muttered.

"It's not a vague, amorphous feeling, Lucas. It's a crystallized feeling, one I can't ignore."

"And if it's wrong? It leads us astray, taking time away from Lamar, and Lamar hasn't got a lot of time," countered Lucas.

"And if you're wrong, about its being a black man, ditto."

Lucas's reflected eyes in the rearview mirror met her determined, grim, set stare. He finally said, "You'd better be certain, then."

"When I was in the boy's head the first and second time, I saw the killer as an elderly, even kindly looking, black gentleman with a walking cane. But the third time . . ."

"Go on," encouraged Meredyth.

"The third time, I saw him as a huge animal standing granitelike . . . like a wall in my way." The lights of the city played across Kim's features. Lucas watched her closely in the rectangle of the rearview, sober enough now to wonder if she wasn't playing some elaborate fortune-telling, tarot-reading game with authorities; but if so, how had she created the spontaneous stigmata in Vorel's office?

Meredyth urged Kim on. "Tell us more about this wall."

"Not a wall. Large and in the way like a wall, but an animal, a fire-breathing animal, like a mythical dragon or beast. It was not an animal I recognized, not a rhinoceros, although it had a rhino's horn, but it also had wings, big, feathered wings like an ostrich or huge stork, stark white with blood dripping from its feathers, and its rhino horn was in *addition* to its beak, and it gored me with the horn which became bloody, bloody with my—Lamar's—blood dripping from it. This enormous white bird—the wall it became—blocked every escape and exit. That wall was not a wall of blackness but a wall of whiteness."

"And so you surmise," Meredyth began, nodding repeatedly, trying to follow, "that this wall in your vision, symbolically speaking, the wall equates to the killer, you mean?"

"His hands turned to white, feathered, birdlike claws."

"Was this in the vision I interrupted?" asked Lucas, thinking again of the blood, the stigmata.

"It hadn't fully gelled then, but earlier tonight I entered Lamar again, and I picked up these images, the vile odors, the bad taste in my mouth, the stifling air, the feeling of being bound and trapped and unable to move, and a variety of strange sounds all vying for attention, and the white wall that became the white horned bird. . . ."

"Sounds like dream images," Meredyth said. "I use Jungian dream therapy with many of my clients in psychotherapy."

"Visions and dreams are sister states. Each taps in to the subconscious for answers, and the language of each is symbols and careful interpretation of the symbolic," agreed Kim.

"I'm convinced that dreams seek to disclose, teach and embrace truth and not to deceive us at all," Meredyth replied. "If they are interpreted properly."

"Then you'll understand why a psychic vision cannot be taken at face value."

Meredyth nodded. Lucas listened intently to the conversation between the two women, glancing back at them via the rearview mirror. He couldn't see Meredyth's hands, but he got the impression that Meredyth had hold of Kim's hands now.

Meredyth said, "If you can't understand the dream on the level of personal or archetypal association and amplification, you turn to natural and cultural associations."

Kim accepted Meredyth's hands when they covered her own, the women tapping in to one another's energy, and Kim added, "Asking yourself, what do I know about the people, places, animals and other images presented in the dream state? Is the dream speaking in metaphorical, figurative or even spiritual language?"

"Right," added Meredyth. "Is the dream saying something that is a play on words or a pun, for instance."

"Do the symbols make sense at this level of association, or on another level?"

"Does the dream seek to reinforce what your conscious self already knows?"

"Yes, the confirming dream," Kim answered, knowing the terminology of dream interpretation. "Or is the dream compensating, is it a compensatory dream."

"What the hell're you two talking about?" Lucas wondered aloud.

Meredyth tried to explain, saying, "Dreams, visions are multilayered. We know that; it's like peeling away an onion. Some are telling us that we are on the right track, right on target. Others are telling us that we are being foolish, overly exaggerating in our view, so the dream reins us in, informing us that the 'truth'—whatever it is—is at the opposite extreme of the dream, so to speak."

"The onion metaphor is a good way to look at it, Lucas," agreed Kim. "Problem is, which peel to discard, which to treasure. That becomes the question. And it's a real danger to lock down on one interpretation, convincing yourself of a single meaning, and to stubbornly hold on to a wrong interpretation in the light of subsequent levels of understanding and a deeper interpretation."

"I see . . . I think."

Meredyth teased Lucas, adding, "You think?"

Kim gave a half-smile, aware already of the sexual tension between the other two people in the car. "Of course, my visions are often part of a series, and each is reviewed in light of emerging patterns, themes, elements common to the series."

"Like threads in a web, yes," agreed Meredyth. "From a psychological point of view, a recurring trip in a dream can take many forms and shapes, and have differing meanings, Lucas. For instance, you find yourself on a train in one dream, a bus in another, on a busy highway in which everyone is 'driving' plush La-Z-Boy recliners instead of cars. One dream has you on a busy El-train, another a passenger on an airplane. If you see the pattern recurring, it definitely has meaning and should be explored and understood. Same with a theme in which you are constantly finding yourself in a position of being held against your will, trapped and planning an escape for your dream character or characters. Same with a theme of saving a little child, say a little girl or boy you find also trapped or being held against her or his will, you see?"

"Yeah, I've had that dream, about the little girl," Lucas admitted. "But how did you know?"

"It's more common than men want to admit, because the little girl is the child within oneself, pleading to be released, and few of you macho types want to admit to having a little child, much less a little girl, trapped inside you. Maybe if you'd let your inner child come out and play a bit more, Lucas, you'd be a more attractive man. Give it some thought."

Screw you, Doctor, Lucas wanted to say, but not in front of Desinor. "Sounds like the sort of mumbo jumbo dispensed around a Cherokee campfire by the shaman, Doctor," he said instead.

"Well, Lucas, people all over the globe not only interpret dreams, but base their actions and lives on them."

"Yes, I know all about the dream-catchers." Despite his annoyed tone, Lucas felt a sense of pleasure in seeing the two women getting along so well. He had expected some friction, but there seemed not a trace. From the front seat, Lucas continued, "You two are talking about something aboriginal peoples have known since the beginning of time."

"The importance of dream time to the soul," added Meredyth.

Kim solemnly agreed, saying, "We touch the true self, the divine within us, through the unconscious; and the voice of the unconscious, the divine voice, is the voice of dream. When we stop paying attention to that inner voice, we stop living as whole beings."

Lucas quickly replied, "The Native American Nez Percé

prophet, Smohalla, summed it up simply enough. He said, 'Wisdom comes to us in dreams.'"

Kim said, "I'm pleased, Dr. Sanger, that you weren't too scientifically and rationally enlightened to automatically dismiss this realm of self-discovery and knowledge."

"Thanks to Jung and his followers, psychotherapy has returned to ancient truths about mankind and the mind."

"Just as in dream therapy, I must be exacting and demanding of how I interpret any vision I intend to pursue," continued Kim. "I have four criteria I ask of my vision. One, does the interpretation click. Does it feel right? Two, does it act? Does it create a feeling of vitality? Does it flow? Three, is the vision confirmed or overturned by subsequent visions? And finally, do the events, anticipated by the vision interpretation, occur in waking life? Are they subsequently verifiable in *this* reality?"

"Excellent criteria," agreed Meredyth.

"Not too mystical for you, Dr. Sanger?" Lucas asked over his shoulder, then swerved to miss a huge Lincoln Town Car that appeared from out of nowhere. Lucas blared his horn at the other driver and swore, but the driver moved on, oblivious.

Their first stop was the 31st Precinct, where Lucas arranged for Dr. Desinor to meet with the Houston PD's equivalent of Aaron Spelling, the HPD Public Relations officer in charge on the graveyard shift, Dick Chaney. Chaney was floored when given the information on the killer to be released to the press. Dr. Desinor took full responsibility, flashing her credentials and telling Chaney that she represented the FBI.

Chaney asked, "Then why aren't you giving this to the FBI PR people?"

"Because I'm working with Detective Lucas Stonecoat and Dr. Meredyth Sanger through the HPD as a special task force."

Chaney replied dubiously, "I see. . . ."

"Besides, the local FBI branch has its collective hands full. Does that answer?"

"Yes, ma'am, ahhh, Doctor. I suppose so."

Chaney shuffled off with the revamped killer profile, which would see print in the morning papers.

"I have something I'd like to share with you as I have with Lucas, Dr. Sanger," Kim then told Meredyth, as they stood in the near-empty squad room. She reached into a pocket and pulled forth the two typed transcripts, the psychic dialogues she'd engaged in with Lamar Coleson. She explained, "I want your interpretations and free association regarding the images of my visions. This will lend credence to my approach, and something of a scientific platform, which while not unimpeachable, at least has the benefit of not showing any bias or conflict of interest, you see?"

Meredyth felt Kim Desinor had thoroughly thought this through, and she knew that Kim's interest in gaining Lucas's investigative know-how had been based, from the beginning, on her desire to gain access to Meredyth Sanger. Somehow none of these usually infuriating female machinations mattered. Meredyth instinctively trusted the psychic, believing that, Lucas Stonecoat notwithstanding, Dr. Kim Faith Desinor was Lamar Coleson's best prayer. "I will do all I can to help you, Dr. Desinor. You may count on that."

"Please, call me Kim."

Meredyth smiled. "I've heard that your closest friends call you Dr. Faith. I hope to one day be among those who do. As for me, call me Meredyth."

Kim smiled in response. "Thank you, Meredyth. Perhaps when all this is over, we can call each other friend."

Meredyth found black coffee and sat down at a waiting room table, where she began devouring Dr. Desinor's visions. Lucas looked over her shoulder, revisiting the scenario created by the psychic detective. The pages read like dialogue in a movie script. They clicked, they acted, they flowed with a sense of realism.

After reading halfway down the page, Meredyth asked, "From where . . . how did you get this . . . this kind of . . . detail?"

"From here," Kim replied, pointing to her head.

Meredyth read on, then she looked up from the page again to

ask, "Just how accurate is . . . do you believe this scenario to be?"

"I'm always skeptical of first interpretations, always cautious, Meredyth. That's why I need your help. Much of what I see must be translated into a symbolic code to make any sense. The boy's image of the killer may be distorted, and I may be too close to the trees to see the forest, as they say."

"Perhaps, then, the boy's idea of the size and even the age of the old man could be skewed. It could simply be symbolic, that all adults are enormous and old and scary and carry canes, to the boy's way of thinking, and if you step into the head of the boy and become the boy, you see reality differently."

"Precisely. And now that he's in the monster's control, this Uncle Buck, or whoever he is—"

"The names may've been supplied from the boy's or your own 'filling in'," Meredyth interrupted.

"—whoever he is, in the boy's eyes, he has got to be enormous and ugly as hell, you see? As for the man's skin color, again, the boy could be seeing what he *wants* to see, hearing what he *wants* to hear. The killer may well have played to these expectations as well. Our profile places him in his early thirties, late twenties. The image the boy has is of a decrepit old man, but this could just as well be a recurring nightmare from inside Lamar's psyche—*what the bogeyman looks like*."

"Yes, or a disguise the killer wears."

"Another interpretation," began Kim, pacing now as the other two looked on, "is that the boy simply *wanted* to see a frail old harmless black Uncle Buck whom he might take advantage of. Later, he sees the truth, that the monster is not so old and frail and helpless after all. Later, the monster has an animal ferocity, and he's not so black and he's nobody's friendly uncle."

Meredyth protested, "But he sounds so black in this transcript. His language, his dialect, it's . . . it's pure Ebonics."

"Yes, he has the black vernacular down," Kim agreed, "but that proves nothing. He could be a figment of *my* imagination, something out of my Creole New Orleans background, something I brought to the table. My Uncle Remus memories."

"Hell," added Lucas, "he could as well be an actor, capable of playing an aged black man. Is that what you're saying?"

"An actor playing to an audience of one, his victim," Kim entertained the thought aloud, her right hand pulling at her chin. "Sure, sure . . . anything's possible, and my vision is open to interpretation, as I said. It's up to us to interpret it creatively, imaginatively."

"I still gotta ask: Why are you so certain the man isn't black?" pressed Lucas, coming around to face Kim, to search her eyes.

"I see and I feel the whiteness," she stated simply.

"So that's why you didn't turn over these transcripts to Chaney. You don't want to declare him a black man preying on black children."

"No, no! That could be devastating. These scenes are psychic reenactments that have to be studied, read and reread, interpreted as I've asked you to do, Meredyth. That must be done by a trained professional, like yourself, not the general public."

"We can't just ignore this Roosevelt B. Cassell character, this Uncle Buck, can we?" Lucas asked.

Kim vigorously pounded the table and shook her head. "No! Vorel's people have brought in six men who go by the name, and another twenty-nine the computer kicked out as similar-sounding names. They're all being looked at by the FBI field office. Buck could be symbolic. His name could be Dollar or Stag or some form of Deer, say Deer with an *e* at the end. Cassell could be Castle or Palace or Palance. We can't take these gems at face value. It's not likely that Lamar could send exact and clear signals to me."

Lucas persisted, asking, "What about the eyewitness you make mention of, the kid in the shadows of a doorway?"

"Hasn't been found. Again, he could be a product of wishful thinking, or a symbol. As I said, every detail in the scenario needs to be interpreted, translated from every possible angle and conceivable association. If I do it, and if Meredyth does it, and we compare notes, maybe we'll get lucky."

"I believe in making my own luck. I say we canvass again for this supposed witness."

"The witness could have been a shadowy reflection of me, the observer, looking on, or it could be Lamar's wishful thinking, or what Lamar knew of the earlier victims."

Meredyth interjected, speaking directly to Lucas. "Don't you see, Cassell could actually refer to Castle—a name or a place? Anyone's guess. Uncle Buck could refer to a male deer, a dollar bill, a greenback, you see?"

Lucas grunted, nodding, frowning. "I got that."

"Sounds like you've given your visions a great deal of thought already, Doctor," replied Meredyth.

"Will you take the study further?"

"I will."

"On the third visit with Lamar, I saw only this blanketlike white . . . blankness, a cold emptiness. Only in these early instances does the killer appear as a black man, and if you read with care, you will see it's something of a *caricature.* Almost a staged image. It could be due to my preconditioned notions about the case, my bias working in. I read the M.E.'s reports, and I read the case files before going under, and I know what crime statistics say about same-race murder, white on white, black on black."

"Meanwhile, as we argue the fine points, the kid's suffering," complained Lucas.

"What do you propose we do next?" asked Meredyth.

"Let's get out of here, for one thing," suggested Lucas. "The shit's going to hit the fan in a big way in this city come daylight, from here to the FBI building."

"Quantico will have smoothed matters over by then, Lucas."

Lucas looked at Kim, his eyes narrowing. "You mean you already cleared this for me?"

"I spoke to my boss, Eriq Santiva, before you showed up at my hotel tonight. As for Meredyth, well, I'll call him back.

He's Chief of Division Four, the Behavioral Science Unit at Quantico, Virginia. Has a lot of pull and clout. He'll grease the boards for us."

"I hope so. It's going to take a hell of a lotta grease."

☡EN

Horse: travel

From Precinct #31, Lucas drove them to the scene of the Coleson abduction, where Dr. Desinor received only a cold reading, seeing an aged black man walking off across the street, a cane in hand, with Lamar trailing after him—Lamar's hands roped and tugged at as if he were a pack animal, the boy looking back toward Kim, his large eyes pleading. The old man looked to be a grandfatherly figure, an Uncle Remus with a light dusting of a white beard. He looked back at Kim and smiled the sweetest smile she'd ever seen, sending a little salute her way when he lifted the cane to his forehead. She couldn't make out the head and eyes on the cane, and her taking a step closer made the old man's shadowy image fade and disappear as if she'd thrown a scare into him.

"Damn," she muttered, making the others stare in the direction she stared in.

Uncle Buck had once stood in this exact location, and so she went to stand at the precise spot where he and Lamar had stood before Lamar climbed into the van. Lamar already had ropes on, because figuratively speaking, the old man, the moment Lamar climbed into his van, had control of the boy. The old man's image, like a photo negative, had remained behind for her to see. But he'd left nothing else, no scattered pieces of paper, no discarded items, nothing to fingerprint or send to a lab.

Meredyth stood beside Kim now, asking, "What is it? Are you all right?"

"Yes, it's just . . . well, I saw him, the old black man and the boy."

"Do you think that the old man might be procuring the boys for the killer? A kind of front man who gets paid so much a head?" asked Lucas, joining them.

"I don't know, but they stood right here. The boy got into his van right here. I can't believe no one saw him climb into the van."

"There're hundreds, thousands of vans in the city, and if you're right about this guy's appearance," commented Lucas as he searched his pockets for a breath mint, "he'd fit into the neighborhood like . . . like that trash Dumpster over there. Who notices a chameleon?"

"I've developed questions about the killer that no one's thought of, or bothered asking about, Lucas. We need to ask the relatives of the dead children about castles and Cassell, about bucks, greenbacks and deer, uncles and aunts, and anything else Meredyth reads into the visions."

"She's absolutely correct, Lucas," added Meredyth.

"Well, I won't lie to you. I have wanted to ask some questions of the relatives myself, but not being officially on the case . . ."

"Then what're we waiting for?" asked Meredyth.

"Since we're in the neighborhood," added Kim, "can we talk to Lamar's mother?"

Lucas shrugged, replying, "We're actually not so far from Theodore Ainsworth's and Raule deJesus Milton's neighborhoods, the earlier victims." Lucas's thoughts ran to a list of reservations, beginning with having to face Gordon Lincoln, and possibly Harrison Vorel, later in the morning; but with what they'd released to the press already, a few questions to relatives of the deceased seemed a harmless addition. "Later, we can drive across to the other neighborhood. I've got the addresses, so sure, let's do it."

The three of them turned where they stood beneath the orange glow of the vapor lights, and Kim, knowing nothing of the area, pointed out the building where Lamar had lived in relative peace with his mother and siblings. She recognized it from her vision. Lucas and Meredyth were again impressed.

They spoke briefly with Lamar's exhausted mother, the woman on the verge of a breakdown, her sleepy-eyed tears like crystal pearls against her black cheeks. Her crying awakened her four other children, who looked on, wide-eyed, from the doorway of a single back bedroom. Meredyth tried to assure the woman that they would somehow find Lamar and return him safely to her. Lucas glared across at her, for the promise might be, within days, made a terrible lie.

"Then . . . then Lamar is alive?" pleaded the mother.

Kim took the woman's hands in her own, assuring her, "Yes, we are certain that Lamar is, in fact, alive at this time."

"Oh, God! Heavenly father!" she exploded.

"He's being held against his will, but he is alive," Kim further assured the mother.

"Is he . . . is he suffering?"

Kim now looked from Lucas to Meredyth and back to Mrs. Coleson, saying, "He's a brave, strong young man."

"Do you know of anyone in the neighborhood who calls himself Uncle Buck?" asked Lucas.

"Buck, Buck? No, nobody but the fella runs that damned gun store, Buck's Gun Shop, on Madison."

"What about you children?" asked Lucas. "You know anybody lives around here named Uncle Buck?"

The children looked at one another, eyes wide, filled with curiosity.

"Did any of you see your brother Lamar leave with a stranger?" pressed Meredyth. "Did any of you see him get into a van?"

"No . . . no . . . no," came a chorus from the children.

"Did any of your friends see him go?" asked Kim of the children.

The chorus of *noes* repeated itself, all of the big-eyed children shaking their heads in unison.

"What do you know about this gun shop guy?" pressed Lucas, returning to the mother.

"Whatchu mean?" asked Mrs. Coleson.

"How old is he, about?"

"Forty, maybe fifty? How should I know?"

"White man, black man, nice man, bad man?"

"Black man, but I never heard him called Uncle nothing."

"We'll check it out when his store opens," Lucas promised her.

Through clenched teeth, the mother asked, "What's this Buck person got to do with it?"

"Probably nothing. We just want to ask a few questions," Kim assured the woman.

They pursued other avenues that Kim and Meredyth had agreed upon. Gaining no useful information from the Coleson household, the detective and the psychiatrists left.

The threesome drove in silence past littered and abandoned parking lots, dumpy hotels, neighborhood taverns and tenements, retracing the path of the abductions made by the killer, Lucas pointing out each in turn for Dr. Desinor.

As they moved about the cityscape, Lucas glared at every van he passed, and when he fell in behind one, he roared around the big white vehicle and found an on-ramp for Interstate 610. It was a short trip now to the Bellaire District where other disappearances were credited to the Snatcher. Lucas soon found the exit he wanted, and they were barreling down the off-ramp.

The Ainsworths proved much better off financially than the Colesons, and Theodore Ainsworth had only one brother and one sister. But the visit to Theodore Ainsworth's parents' duplex and a repeat of the array of questions asked by Lucas, Meredyth and Kim yielded nothing new. And once again, the detectives faced grieving, bitter and angry people who deep inside felt an instinctive distrust of the white police establishment—even if Lucas was red. Underlying the victim's parents' beliefs lay a bedrock of suspicion and doubt that remained sadly unshakable, stony, making the interview far more difficult for all involved and gaining little.

Searching for the home of Raule deJesus Milton, who'd also lost his life to the Snatcher, the trio of psychic, criminal psychiatrist and Cherokee cop fell into a dejected silence as the car moved amid Houston's squalor. Creating its own cold core, which seeped in through the cracks and crevices along with the chilled air, Houston's underbelly, with its blackened cityscape, pervaded the mind and the car. It crept catlike—this cold night—into the cab of the car to sit alongside them, a heinous, hunched gargoyle, patiently awaiting their next move.

Kim broke the silence, saying, "We may be just getting these poor people's hopes up, waking them at this hour, but there's so little time left for Lamar. What else can we do?"

"It looks hopeless. This freak must be a shadow or about as noticeable as . . . as that trash can on the corner," Meredyth lamented, pointing out the window.

Lucas pulled to a stop, trying to find the street number. Another frustrated silence had settled in over them when Kim suddenly asked, "You hear about the fucking dwarf that Vorel hired to snare the Snatcher?"

"No, what fucking dwarf?" Lucas went along, thinking it a joke, a mite surprised to hear Dr. Faith swear like a sailor.

"Vertically challenged," corrected Meredyth.

Kim filled them in, explaining, "Word was going around that Vorel's people, in their infinite wisdom, had contracted with a sideshow midget, a *vertically challenged* black male, to act as a decoy in an attempt to lure the killer near enough for cameras and microphones to learn something of the Snatcher."

"Okay," replied Lucas. "I'm with you so far."

Kim continued, a giggle intermittently interrupting her. "It was a pretty good bet that neither the FBI nor the HPD was going to get clearance to use real children to attract the Snatcher, so Harrison Vorel cooked this little scheme up. . . ."

"So, what happened?"

"The dwarf was mugged by a bag lady, a street person."

The three of them laughed heartily at Vorel's expense. The laughter warmed the inside of the car, sending the gargoyle back out into the night.

"When you called, I was wide-awake," confessed Meredyth to Lucas. "Couldn't sleep tonight. The thought of the Coleson boy at this very moment . . . what he must be feeling . . ."

"Yeah, I've felt some of those same feelings," Kim responded, "literally."

Lucas told Meredyth what he had witnessed in Vorel's office the day before. The retelling shook Lucas, making him tremble. "Wish the God of us all would grant me some sort of psychic power, some form of the third eye to see into the heart of this mad killer, so I could walk up to his door, take him by the throat and . . ."

"You may've already gotten your wish, Lucas," said Meredyth. "Whataya think Dr. Desinor is?"

"How's that? Oh, oh, yeah . . ."

"We'd heard the FBI had called in a psychic," Meredyth said to Kim, "but no one expected a psychic of your caliber, Doctor."

"Afraid most people think I'm here as a kind of sideshow, to play to the press."

"I think the Milton place is right up ahead here," Lucas suggested, revving up the car and driving alongside the curb, involved now in his address search. "What does your psychic power tell you, Dr. Desinor? Are we hot, cold, warm on this address?" he joked.

"I have every confidence that you will find it," Kim replied in a stentorian tone, signifying a mock psychic energy flow. "However, you may be blocked by a detour ahead. You may have to go around a barricade of some sort. Try the next block over."

Lucas suddenly halted the car, faced with a dead end to the street ahead. Out the front windshield, the threesome stared at a solid brick wall in their path. The street numbers had literally stopped short of the Milton address.

So far as Lucas Stonecoat was concerned, Houston stood out as a brawling, kicking, hollering *he*, not a cat-fighting *she,* city. The neon cowboy's city breathed and pulsated with an electrical power that coursed through its concrete towers, bridges, highways and all-night businesses while the prostitutes plied their trade.

The city was lit against the encroaching desert surrounding it, and on its weary shoulders rested the illusion of great beauty and absolute eternity, the Christmas tree–like office buildings of downtown spiraling skyward, while mediocre decorations of a far cheaper nature adorned the major arteries that had led Lucas and the others to the Bellaire District, where several of the abducted Snatcher victims had last been seen alive. People who placed the abducted at or near these sites before the disappearances had done so from their own windows, or from the nearby parks and playgrounds and alleyways. Some people who'd watched too many *X-Files* episodes on TV had the killer rising from manholes and dragging his young victims into the sewers. Lucas didn't think so.

Lucas, catching a glimpse of his hard-edged features in the rearview mirror, now wondered if perhaps they weren't simply being foolish, going out into the night this way without a well-ordered plan, but here they were, searching for a street address Lucas must locate tonight, now.

Lucas's bloodshot eyes worked to focus on the list of victim addresses Randy had given him, but city streets didn't always follow through, and they'd run into a dead end where the train tracks cut off the small street. Dr. Desinor had been correct. He needed to drive out to the main drag, go under the train trestle there, and then return to where the street resumed on the other side of the tracks.

"And you say you've never been to Houston before?" Lucas asked, knowing the answer.

"No, not physically . . . no," replied Kim.

Lucas wanted desperately to talk to the family of the first Snatcher victim, Raule deJesus Milton, to see the home of the first known victim of this ugliness.

As they eased along St. Croix Street, Lucas explained to Meredyth and Kim Desinor, "I really rather doubt this is the Snatcher's first go-round with murdering innocent children."

Meredyth readily agreed, but commented, "No search of the computer files turned up anything similar since Atlanta, and Wayne Williams is still very much in custody."

"And Wayne Williams still maintains his innocence," added Kim.

"So, you're saying this guy's the real Atlanta child murderer? That he has somehow controlled his needs all these years, since what, '79? I don't think so," said Lucas, annoyed at the suggestion. "I don't think so. . . ." he repeated.

"He may not be the Atlanta child murderer, but just the same he may've done one here, two there, moved on, landing here only recently. We don't know, now, do we?" Meredyth defended Dr. Desinor.

"You Anglos, you have to have a label for everything, so everything is put in a neat, tidy place. It's why the press has to give cute little names to serial killers: the Shadow, the Punisher, the Painkiller, the Snatcher in this case, but you know what?"

"No, Lucas, what?" Meredyth clearly displayed her irritation now.

"The sky over the desert is and isn't the same sky as overhead here," Lucas said, pointing upward through the windshield. "The desert sky is unpredictable, one night littered with cold, blinking stars, a stillness like a stone wind and a waning moon that doesn't care about us and our petty problems, while on another night everything is raging, the sky filled with churning twisters and thunderbolts, preparing to spread death. But here in Houston, the entire dark firmament of the galaxy is blurred by the city lights. Just the same, just because we can't see the sky from here, that doesn't mean the chaos isn't out there, beyond our limited vision."

"I simply saw some similarities with the Atlanta case, Lucas," Kim now replied. "As I'm sure you have. Still, you're right about white men and chaos. They like their chaos in controlled dosages only, the way people like to watch a battlefield skirmish from a safe distance."

A dull orange glow filtered down from city lampposts, the vapor lights creating a mediocre substitute for moonlight over a playground, a churchyard and adjacent cemetery, a grocery store and a line of storefronts here in the Bellaire District.

"Here it is . . . here's the address," said Lucas, pulling the car to the curb. He got out and opened the door for Meredyth, helping her out, taking the opportunity to hold her hand, holding it a bit too long, squeezing her hand before she pulled away.

"Hey, we're on serious business, Cherokee," she murmured with a half-smile.

"My feelings for you are serious business, Meredyth."

She shook her head. "Lucas, we've been through this. We'd never work out twenty-four hours a day, seven days a week."

"I've never asked for that kind of commitment."

She frowned. "But I need it, and there's the rub."

"So, you're determined to play life safely, to marry that . . . marshmallow McThuen?"

"Let it be, Lucas." She said it with a touch of breathlessness, reaching out and taking his hand in hers now, giving his hand a squeeze. "We'd only poison each other."

"Can't you stop being a shrink long enough to quit analyzing every damned thing in sight?"

"See what I mean?"

"Grrrrrrrrr," he growled wolflike.

She laughed in response, before saying, "Don't you ever ask questions of yourself before jumping off a cliff? Don't you ever reflect on your words, your actions, where you put your hands before you put them?"

"At the moment, I've got a head full of questions for the parents, or more likely parent, of a fourteen-year-old named Raule deJesus Milton." He snatched his hand from hers.

She searched his immutable eyes, unable to read his stony countenance. "Don't get ugly on me, Lucas. But I agree, at the moment, all either of us has time for is Lamar Coleson."

Lucas's police band, installed in his private vehicle, crackled to life, a call about a burglary on the other side of the city. He unnecessarily translated the garbled numbers and their meanings for the two women.

"I think I know what an 11-8 is, Lucas, but thanks anyway," said Kim, who'd climbed from the car on the street side, allowing the other two a bit of room in which to conduct their little flirtation.

Meanwhile, a feeling of frustration crawled up from Lucas's groin and into his lower abdomen, rising to his chest and heart before welling up in his throat. He turned to Kim Desinor and asked, "She's never going to go to bed with me, is she? Come on, tell me my fortune, Dr. Desinor."

"At this rate, I'd say forget it. . . ." Kim's cutting grin fit perfectly with the toss of her shoulder-length hair.

When Lucas knocked on the door in the tenement that was once home to Raule deJesus Milton, he was instantly sorry, and he turned to Meredyth and said, "Maybe this isn't such a hot idea."

It was still well before dawn, but the door was quickly answered by a young black uniformed cop, surprising them all. The cop, an indignant look on his face, ferociously snarled at Lucas, "Whataya want?"

Lucas flashed his badge and said, "Detective, HPD. I'd like to talk to the mother of Raule deJesus Milton."

"He was my brother. Whataya want?"

Lucas saw that the man's nameplate identified him as Darius Milton. "Looking for some answers."

"Questions?" he asked, confused. "This late, after all this time?" Raule's big brother had obviously happened by while on graveyard shift, to look in on his mother, Lucas supposed.

A female voice from within called out, "All the questions done been asked over and over." The sound of his mother's voice made the young cop turn and shake his head.

"Oh, Mama," he said, "go on back to bed. I'll take care a dis." He turned back to Lucas, Meredyth and Kim. "Can't you people talk to one another?"

Meredyth stepped closer, saying, "We're new on the case. I'm Dr. Meredyth Sanger, crime psychiatry, and this is—"

"I thought the FBI was taking over."

"We're working closely with the Feds, and so is Dr. Desinor, here. She's the psychic FBI agent who's been put in charge," explained Lucas.

"Yeah, the psychic I read about?" The young man's eyes widened almost imperceptibly. He was jaded, cold to the idea that anyone might ever end his family's misery. "I see . . ." he finally added. "All right, I'll tell you what I know, but don't 'spect nothing outta Mama."

As Lucas and his two female partners entered the small apartment, Lucas said, "I'm sorry about your baby brother."

"Raule was the baby, all right."

"How many in the family?"

"Eleven of us."

"You the oldest?" asked Meredyth.

"Father to 'em all. You got that right."

Kim asked, "The others all living here still?"

"Some, not all. Some of us got our own places now. I come sit with Mama nights, you know, after my shift, usually. Tonight, she's in a bad way. Some nights she's bad, some nights worse than bad. . . . You people aren't going to report me, are you?"

"Relax, Officer Milton," Lucas assured the man. "Do we look like Internal Affairs?"

"Matta-a-fact, you do, all buttoned up in your trench coats."

Lucas emitted a brief, staccato laugh. "IAD would be insulted to hear it, Milton." Lucas saw the young cop relax now, and Lucas sensed in him a core of strength, courage and resilience; he seemed a solid, firm-minded young man, caring and angry.

Meredyth said, "We just have some questions hanging that we'd like cleared up."

Lucas noticed the bedroom door down the hallway ajar. The mother listened in.

The young man insolently asked, "When the fuck's division going to catch the motherfucker that tortured little Raule to death, anyway?"

Meredyth's reply came out in a consoling melody of warmth and words. "Officer, we have everyone on it, I assure you."

"He got hold of another one the other day. You think for one moment this city'd put up with little white boys being snatched off the streets and returned all bruised and burned and cut up like . . . like sausages?"

The same complaint, making the rounds of every neighborhood of color in Houston, had been sounded by every black activist in the city and beyond, all the way to Chicago's Jesse Jackson, who'd held a news conference on the "dreadful lack of progress" in the case. The NAACP leadership echoed Jackson's acrimonious tone, and race relations in Houston now stood as torn and frayed as when the O. J. Simpson criminal trial verdict had split the nation.

Lucas's hands were in the air now, and he said, "Unfortunately, this sort of ugliness happens to little boys of every color, every day, Officer Milton. Even little Indian boys."

"That what you are? Indian?"

"About those questions . . ."

"Go ahead. Tell you what I know. That's all I can do."

"Anyone you know in the area, or anyone the kids know in the area, who drives a van and answers to the name Uncle Buck?"

He gave it a moment's thought, indicating that the intruders should sit. Finally, he said, "Well, no, can't say as I know of anyone calls himself Uncle Buck, but sure, there's all kinds of vans up and down the block here."

"Anyone who drives a van and works construction who might've given Raule gifts of any kind?"

Officer Milton's face twitched, but he shook his head as if to answer no.

"You're sure?"

"What'd I just say?"

"What about Toombs?" asked his mother, barreling down the hallway. "And Davey Dulfour, Melvin Sims? They all drives vans and they all works in the construction trade!"

"Mrs. Milton, hello," said Meredyth, introducing herself, Lucas and Kim.

"You a psychic, too, lady? You both psychics?" asked Mrs. Milton, an emaciated woman with red eyes, swollen from drink as much as from tears.

Meredyth displayed her credentials. "I'm a psychiatrist."

"Psychiatrist?" asked Officer Milton, looking to Stonecoat for further explanation.

"Division thought it a good idea to team me with a psychiatrist, yeah," lied Lucas. "So, all right, any of these guys you know working construction and driving vans, any of them done time?"

"No, can't say they have done any serious time, no," replied Officer Milton. "Not to my knowledge."

"Toombs, maybe," muttered the mother.

"I see." Lucas wrote this down. "Does this Toombs have a first name?"

"Obediah . . . Obediah Toombs," she said, shaking a fist. "Told the other cops all about him. You think he coulda done something like that to my baby? He acted de boy's uncle."

"Now, I done told you, Mama, that's just crazy," countered Officer Milton.

Lucas calmly asked, "Lives nearby, does he?"

"You think Toombs got something to do with the murders?" asked Mrs. Milton, her watery eyes pleading more for retaliation and retribution than for an end to her suffering.

"Just checking hunches, ma'am, nothing more. Don't read anything into my questions, and whatever you do, don't approach Toombs on this. Do you understand?"

She nodded, clearly frightened.

Lucas turned to her son, Darius, and again asked, "Do you both understand?"

Officer Milton bit his lip and said, "Following hunches, hell. You never heard of Toombs till tonight."

"Sometimes the least likely suspect, the one who's beneath your very nose, Officer, turns out to be a killer," Kim told the man.

"If that old bastard did anything to Raule, I'll kill that son of a—"

Lucas shot out a powerful hand and grabbed Milton by the arm. "No. You don't go near anyone! Got that?"

"What's going on here? You got something on this man, Toombs, but you ain't going to do nothing 'bout it?" It was the mother, fully awake now, her eyes glaring hatred. "You know how long we been suffering in this house here since . . . since . . ." She broke into a full-blown flood of tears, her bony knees giving way, her eldest son catching her and easing her onto the sofa.

Her son gave her a box of Kleenex and chanted what must by now be their liturgy: "It's goin' to be all right, Mama. Goin' to be all right." He then stood and faced Lucas, his nostrils flaring like a winded horse. He spoke loudly, his words directed at his mother, but he stared at Lucas the entire time he spoke, saying, "Toombs is a bad man, but I don't see him torturing and killing kids, Mama, no. These . . . the detectives here, they're just following up every possible lead. They likely found Toombs got a record for exposing himself on the street some time back. Isn't that right, Detectives?"

"Yes, Mrs. Milton, that's exactly right," said Meredyth, stepping closer, assuring the mother of the murdered child.

"How old is Toombs?" asked Lucas.

"Thirty, thirty-five maybe."

"Sounds about right," agreed the mother.

"Do you know what he served time for?" asked Kim.

"Didn't say he did, and if he did, we don't know. Do you?" asked Officer Milton, his nostrils still flaring, his eyes hinting at flame.

"Anyone else you know who lives in the area, works

construction sites, has had previous trouble with the law?" asked Lucas.

"That could be half the damned neighborhood," complained the mother.

Lucas kneeled before the woman and asked, "Could you make a list for me?"

"I don't know. . . ."

"It could be very important."

"Will it lead to an arrest?" she asked.

"It could help."

"They put out a reward now. I saw it on that *Unsolved* show. My other children could use that money."

"Ten thousand dollars, yes, ma'am," Lucas replied. He'd heard that the reward had generated hundreds of useless calls so far.

"All right, I make the list, but I ain't thinking too clear. Let me make some coffee."

"Sounds good," agreed Lucas.

The mother rose from the couch, a clear mission now in mind, going for the kitchen.

"Does Toombs smoke?" asked Meredyth of Milton, recalling that on every murdered child's body there'd been cigarette burns.

Milton thought for a moment, then nodded. "Some . . . Whataya got on ol' Toombs, anyway?"

"Not much, yet," she replied.

"Not enough for a warrant, you mean."

"Tell me, Milton, does Toombs live alone or with someone?"

"Think he's married."

"What's the man's address?" Meredyth asked.

"Don't know, but I can point it out to you."

Lucas nodded and said, "You do that, and you leave it to us, understand, Officer Milton?"

"If I truly believed Toombs was responsible for what was done to my little baby brother, no man—not even the Pope— could keep me from putting a 9mm. hole through that mudder-fucker's heart."

"Quit all that swearing, Darius, now!" the mother called out to him from the kitchen. She hadn't missed a word. She stepped back in with four instant coffees, creamer and sugar packets all on an ancient tray. As she acted the hostess in her nightgown, she said, "Toombs is married to a quiet woman he took up with who hails from St. Louis who I can't believe stays with the man, and I can't believe she'd let him do such things to children in her house. . . . Can't believe it."

"Have you ever been to the house, Mrs. Milton?" asked Kim.

"Once or twice, but only for short stays. They don't have no children, you see, and they took a shine to Raule, both of them."

"Took a shine to him?" asked a suspicious Kim Desinor.

Lucas asked, "What kind of carpet is on the floor?"

"Sears special, I 'spose."

"What color?"

"Blue, gray maybe. Why?"

"Ever see any red carpet in the house?" Lucas pursued, knowing about the red rug fibers found on all the victims to date.

"No . . . never did."

"Bathroom throw rug?"

"Never got that far inside. Raule stayed over with them one night. He never come home with any complaints about the Toombses, though, never."

"You're doing just great, Mrs. Milton," counseled Lucas. "Can you write up that list of other people you know who live in the area and who drive pickups or vans and had contact with Raule? Any contact at all."

"There's the janitor down at the school."

"Good, start with him."

"Don't know his name."

"That's all right," coached Lucas. "Put him down anyway."

ELEVEN

Thunderbird track: bright prospect

They left with the short list of names and addresses, numbering five possible Uncle Bucks or Roosevelt Cassells. The list guided them to the doorstep of one Obediah Toombs. In the driveway a rattletrap old van waited like a water buffalo, the color a purple-blue in the shadows cast by the house and the closest street lamp, which fashioned an orange tapestry like a giant spider's web of black and orange from its vaporous glow; the strange mix of light and shadow spread from fenced yard to front sidewalk of the run-down place.

"Wonder if there's carpeting in the van. Sure would like to get a few fibers out of that van," Lucas mused aloud. They stood on the curb beside Lucas's car, Kim Desinor showing signs of fatigue, leaning against the red Dodge.

"We need time to check him out, Lucas," warned Meredyth. "If he is connected with these hideous murders, then we have to proceed with all due caution. By the book."

"By the book could get Lamar Coleson dead," replied Lucas.

"Lucas, it's the only way to nail his bestial ass properly, so he sees the death penalty."

"By the book," Lucas angrily muttered. "We take him in to stand trial, so some civil libertarian can fawn over his rights. But for right now, Meredyth, we've got to consider the kid's

right to life. What if this sick bastard's got Lamar Coleson
inside there? Or at some other location, as we speak? We've got
to act now. And if we have probable cause in the case of a child
in danger, we can kick down the door."

"Agreed," replied Kim. "We've got to secure Lamar Coleson's safety above all other considerations, including due
process."

"Reason enough to kick the fucking door down," bawled
Lucas. "What's your plan, Meredyth? Bring the bastard in for
psychiatric treatment at the taxpayer's expense? To study the
criminal mind? To find out who or what warped him? And
why? So you shrinks can earn your keep and have fun in the
bargain?"

"Take it easy, Lucas," Kim shouted. "Calm down."

"I know he doesn't mean a word of what he's said, Dr.
Desinor," Meredyth interjected. "He's just had a bad experience with a psychologist in the past, haven't you, Lucas?"

Now she was patronizing him. Lucas stepped away, his eyes
going to the dark house across the street. He surveyed the junk
all around Toombs's place: an errant gas oven, a gray cement
mixer drum so well used it looked itself to be constructed of
uneven cement drippings, an old tire amid the weeds, loose
sections of pipe carelessly strewn about. If Toombs *was* the
killer, why hadn't he cemented up the bodies to discard them in
the nearby bayou that ran through this section of the city?
Lucas wondered.

Kim calmed Meredyth with a few words before coming to
stand alongside Lucas. Lucas saw that Meredyth now paced in
a tight little circle—catlike—in front of the car.

Kim calmly assured Lucas, saying, "We all want to see the
bastard responsible fry, Lucas, believe me."

"I guess I know that," he confessed, taking in a deep breath
of the cold night air, everyone's breath creating an airy smoke.

Meredyth tried now to patch things up, coming to join them
and whispering, "We don't know that it is Toombs, Lucas.
We're just out here grasping at straws. Even that kid officer,
Milton, sensed as much."

"What do you propose we do, Mere? Sit on our asses like Vorel and the rest of Houston?"

She marched him away from Kim. "Now you listen to me, Lucas Stonecoat. None of us are working at a hundred percent out here at dawn, and if you go cowboying around, and they test you for drugs, Lucas, what're they going to find?"

There it was again: Meredyth's complete knowledge of him and his habits. She stared a searing laser beam through him. Finally, Lucas replied, "It's just so damned frustrating, Mere."

"We're all frustrated, Lucas. The whole damned city is frustrated."

"Somehow, that doesn't help."

"I know you want to rush right into this Toombs's place and put one in his brain, and believe me, part of me wants just that, to get near enough to put a bullet through the Snatcher's head. But we aren't even close here. This is all *conjecture*. Toombs may not be our man. So, I want you to keep calm and stay away from Toombs until we get more facts."

Lucas clenched his fists and teeth, saying nothing.

"Can you do that, Lucas? Can you?"

"I 'spose I can . . . for now, but I'm going to stake this place out, see what happens when the lights come on, all that, Mere, so why don't you take my car, take Dr. Desinor back to her hotel." He extended his car keys.

"No way we're leaving you here alone, Indian man, tracker-hunter man, no way!" She smiled, forcing a smile from him. "If you're staking this place out, Lucas, then we're on stakeout with you. No arguments, Lucas."

Lucas let out a long, exasperated, pent-up breath of air before climbing back into his car and adjusting his seat back and down. He got comfortable, resting his head and closing his eyes, concentrating now on complete relaxation and going into a meditative state, which effectively removed the two women from his sphere for a time while he gathered about himself his scattered energies.

Before the stakeout became a complete bore, Lucas had fished out the amulet that supposedly once belonged to Minerva

Roundpoint, the one that Zachary Roundpoint had said Father
Avi got from the police along with her other belongings at the
murder scene. He explained to Dr. Desinor that the necklace
and amulet could be important in another, separate investigation, and he asked if she would do a psychometric reading of it.

Kim Desinor agreed without hesitation, and after several
long minutes of meditation over the amulet, she took a deep
breath and declared, "Useless."

"Useless?"

"Sorry, but they seem . . . well, to have no history whatsoever, as if they were recently made. There are no images
coming off the amulet or the necklace, nothing useful. Sorry."

"What crime are they supposedly connected with, Lucas?"
asked Meredyth, pretending not to know, he guessed.

"Never mind. It's just one of the Cold Room files I've been
looking into."

"Really. Perhaps you could tell us about it? It might help
pass the time more quickly."

"Maybe when I get back," he hedged.

"Back from where?" she asked.

"I'm going in for a closer look, scout out that van, see what's
behind door number one," Lucas told the other two.

"What? Wait a minute, Lucas," complained Meredyth, her
eyes heavy with exhaustion.

"Just a peek at the damn van, that's all."

"Without a warrant? You're going to violate the man's
property without a warrant, without probable cause, with zip?"
Meredyth's eyes were incredulous, her hands flying amid the
small space of the car.

"It's a Catch-22. No evidence, no warrant; no warrant, no
evidence. Goddamn the civil rights of murderers and rapists."
He tore open the car door, leapt out and said, "You two just stay
put. This'll only take a moment or two."

"Detective Stonecoat," began Kim, "I've done everything I
can to psychically read that house, and I'm getting nothing, no
sign of Lamar. Nothing whatever to do with the monster I've
been sensing in visions, nothing. I wish I could say otherwise,

but I have to agree with Dr. Sanger. You've got no probable cause here, not even psychically perceived probable cause."

Lucas looked away from the ominous, dirty little house and into Kim Desinor's eyes. He held her stare for a long moment.

"I'm sure," she finally said, as if he'd asked a question.

"But if your signals *have* been emanating from Lamar, and if he's asleep or unconscious, you're not likely to receive any help from him. And if we believe a child's life's in danger behind those walls, that's enough warrant for any cop in the city, isn't that right?"

Kim breathed deeply, nodding. "That's the law, yes, but—"

Meredyth shook her head. "I'm not sure a judge and jury would interpret the word *believe* in the same way as you, Lucas, not in a brightly lit courtroom."

Kim quickly added, "There has to be a sincere conviction behind the belief to make it legal, and we just don't have enough to go on."

"Oh, I've got plenty of sincere conviction, enough for all of us."

"Lucas!" moaned Meredyth.

"I can't walk away from this. Suppose Lamar Coleson *is* in this guy's basement right now, dying of his wounds, and we walk away today like the cops who walked away from Jeffrey Dahmer's place and left his last victim in that cannibal's hands? I couldn't live with myself after that, could you?"

"What're you going to do? Knock on the door?" Meredyth seethed, her teeth clenched.

"How did you two ever work together on the Helsinger case?" asked Kim, making both Lucas and Meredyth stop to stare at her.

Finally, Lucas calmly said, "Suppose Mr. Toombs is burglarized this morning?"

"No, no . . . Lucas, it's too risky."

"I don't see any great evidence of protection on the house, but have you noticed the basement windows?" he countered.

"What about them?" asked Kim.

It was not easy to make out, but the basement windows were

thickly painted over with a gray or green color. It was
impossible to discern the exact color, given the low light. But
the message seemed loud and clear: Mr. Toombs wanted no one
spying whatever he had in his basement.

"I'm going to have a closer look. Start the car and keep the
motor running for a fast exit, should we need it. This guy never
has to know we're police."

Meredyth gritted her teeth, controlling herself. "This is
crazy, Lucas. *You* are crazy, you know that?"

"I have to agree with Meredyth," added Kim. "You are
acting rashly."

"Indians are supposed to be crazy, remember?" Without
skipping a beat, he added, "There's a flashlight in the glove
compartment. Hand it to me."

Kim reached over the seat, grabbed the light and handed it to
Lucas.

"Aiding and abetting," Meredyth said to Kim.

Flashlight in hand, Lucas dashed for the driveway where the
van waited like a hunched rhino, parked between Toombs's
place and the house on the right. Lucas stood below the
windows for a moment before leaping up on the van's back
bumper. He now stared into the dark interior through the filthy
glaze of dirt and oil smearing the windows. Unable to see a
thing and knowing the flash would only add to the glare, Lucas
reached into his pocket for his burglar's key, a long, slim piece
of steel designed to pick any lock. He struggled with the old
lock at the back of the van for a few minutes before it popped
open with a sudden click. Carefully he opened the squeaky
door and flashed his light over the interior. There was no
carpet, merely a rust-red floor. The backseats had been removed to accommodate the man's arsenal of tools and tool-
boxes. Lucas saw no restraints or anything else that smacked of
the work of the Snatcher, save the rolls of duct tape and the
loose wire and electrical cords. The place was a veritable
storeroom of such materials. He looked for anything resembling a cane—nothing.

No fibers here to compare, since there was no carpeting, but he cut a section of the tape and electrical cord used by Toombs just the same. Pocketing these items, he doused the light and quietly eased the door closed, but it groaned in the cold air like one of those distressed sedated lions one saw on PBS programs.

Lucas quickly relocked the door using his steel rod.

Perhaps he ought to call it a night, go back to Meredyth and Kim with what little he had, admit defeat. It had been a wild-card attempt at best anyway. But the painted basement windows nagged at Lucas's curiosity.

He moved from the van to the side of the house, his enormous, serpentine shadow snaking alongside him. Once there, he pulled himself up to the sill to stare into the darkness of a grubby-looking living room. Leftovers, scattered clothing and shoes, rugs and blankets were tossed pell-mell everywhere amid the rubble of the household. Nothing moving; no one there. No lights on in the place.

He dropped to the pavement once more, again his shadow taunting him, telling him it would give him away. Ignoring his shadow, and using his jacketed elbow and a quick in-out jerk, Lucas smashed a basement window. The noise was like a gunshot to his ears, but a look in Meredyth and Kim's direction told him they hadn't heard a thing.

He flashed his light down through the hole he'd created and all that returned to him was emptiness and darkness. The pit, he thought, until his eyes adjusted to the range of the flashlight, which reported back the facts: The basement was a collection of junk from old beds to stacks of wallboard, frames, joists, ceiling fans, baseboards, paneling, kitchen cabinets, stainless steel sinks, countertops with huge holes in them. Stolen goods from a hundred-odd construction sites, Lucas guessed, but no sign of torture instruments or dangling lost children.

It was just as Kim Desinor's cunning mind had surmised: If Toombs was the Snatcher, he wasn't using this place as his torture chamber, and Lucas doubted he used the nearby van, either, but he could be using *another* vehicle, and he could be using *another* site as his killing ground. This final thought, like a flimsy straw in the wind, held little firmness or shape, yet Lucas grasped at it.

Lucas quietly made his way back to the car where Meredyth surprised him simply because she had remained put.

He immediately confessed, "I think we may be on a wrong path here with this Toombs character."

Kim shrugged. "Had to be checked out. He did fit the profile on most counts. Still, we've got other names from Mrs. Milton to follow up on."

He nodded. "Yeah, we do, but time's running out."

Disappointment swept over the trio. Toombs had looked so good. "Maybe we ought to have a talk with Toombs just the same," suggested Kim. "See if we can jar any thoughts on the subject from him. If the killer is in the trade, and if the killer lives or works in this same area, there's a chance Toombs could know the Snatcher and not even know he knows."

"We'll come back later, then," suggested Meredyth.

"No, we wait here," countered Lucas. "He's in construction and he's been a busy beaver. He'll be up and out shortly."

"How do you mean, busy beaver?" asked Kim.

"Much pilfering going on, obviously. Looks like a Home Depot working out of his basement. At any rate, if he's working all these job sites, and apparently he is, he'll soon be up for breakfast. I want him when he wakes up."

"Again, I remind you, we have no authorization here, Lucas," Meredyth said, a groan escaping her.

"For now, Toombs's basement full of goodies is all we need for probable cause, Doctor," Lucas corrected her. "Maybe not for murder, but definitely for robbery."

"And how are you going to explain finding the stolen goods?"

"An anonymous source called it in."

"Sure."

"Said they heard a break-in at Toombs's residence. We checked out the broken window and found the goods. Simple as that."

"And nothing on tape?"

"Won't need the tape or the story much beyond today, when we greet Toombs with it. I'd bet my badge on it."

Meredyth shook her head and as much as admitted defeat by saying, "All right, but he's not all we've got. What about the other names on Mrs. Milton's list?" she reminded him.

"We'll phone them in to Randy in a little while. He can run checks on 'em a lot faster than we can. I say we stay on Toombs."

"All right. One on, two off?" she asked of the arrangement.

"You take the first watch," he agreed. "Wake me and Kim in an hour."

Meredyth muttered, "I sure hope this is worth it. . . ."

The only reply came from the blinking Christmas lights decorating every second or third two-story along the street.

It seemed like mere minutes later that the lights went on in Toombs's house, and Lucas and Meredyth were whispered at and pushed awake by Kim Desinor, who, taking second watch, had found Lucas's crime scene photos of the murder of Minerva Roundpoint, and to pass time, had viewed them with interest, guessing that the 1948 stamp on the photos and on the envelope meant this was the same case that went with the amulet. She told Lucas, "Appears that Toombs is moving around in there. And by the way, these photos of the dead woman in '48, something peculiar about them."

"What's that?" Lucas asked, grabbing them and stuffing them back into the envelope.

"Well, you said the amulet came from the victim, but it's not in any of the crime scene photos. It's not on her neck, that's for sure, but neither is it photographed anywhere about the body, so—"

"So, maybe it was never there to begin with," finished Lucas, recalling all that Roundpoint had fed him about the "mysterious" amulet, and wondering what he meant when he said the amulet had been collected by Father Avi along with all of Minerva's things at the police lockup. He searched his memory for anything in the manifest that he'd read about a necklace and amulet, and certain there had been nothing, he wondered why Roundpoint would lie about this piece of jewelry. Or had the lie been Father Avi's?

Lucas yawned and rubbed his eyes with the palms of his hands, using enough force to conjure a relaxing darkness behind his eyelids. "Yeah, you're right about the photos and the amulet."

"I would have thought you'd seen enough at FBI headquarters, Lucas. I didn't expect you to be testing me like this, to see if I'd go off on that amulet."

"Really, it wasn't a test."

"Oh, then what the hell was it?" asked Meredyth, who then began to apologize for Lucas.

"That's quite all right, Meredyth. I'm used to skepticism in all its . . . permutations. Really, I am." Kim then abruptly changed the subject, asking Lucas, "How long before Toombs learns we—you, rather—broke his window?"

"Shouldn't be long," replied Lucas, his eyes still closed, his head leaning back against the leather-covered headrest, feeling his footing with both this Coleson case and the Roundpoint case slipping as if he were standing in a flooded ravine. "In the meantime, maybe Toombs'll make a pot of coffee, and we can all sit down to discuss our mutual needs." At the same time, Lucas's mind busily worked over the confusing business of the origins of the amulet.

"It may be of some interest to you, Detective Stonecoat, that I felt something on holding the photos of the 1948 murder victim."

"What did you feel?"

"Extreme betrayal. She felt extreme betrayal. That thing she did with her hands even in death, some sort of sign she left behind for you to see, Lucas. Don't dismiss it."

"I haven't. Believe me, I haven't."

Kim smiled at this, a smile verging on contentment. She had, in fact, passed his test, with flying colors. "You think like a criminal," she said to him. "That's why you're such a good tracker, a born hunter."

"It's the only way to survive out here. Watch this mole
Toombs," suggested Lucas. "I'm going to catch some more
z's."

Meredyth saw the man exiting his house from the rear,
carrying something heavy. It looked like a canvas-covered
body, and for a moment, she believed Toombs was the Snatcher
after all, until Lucas ruined the illusion by saying, "It's the guts
out of a heating unit, I think. Come on, let's go pay Mr. Toombs
a call."

They saw Toombs suddenly freeze in his tracks, staring now
at the busted window near his feet. He quickly glanced about
for any sign of movement or other disturbance, and the first
thing his eyes trained on was Lucas Stonecoat, who was out of
the car and coming at him.

The two doctors exited the vehicle and tried catching up to
Lucas, all three now making for Toombs, whose mouth had
gone slack and whose eyes had gone wide. He knew he'd been
found out. The oversized black man pursed his lips and shook
his head as if listening to a sad blues song. They could hear his
muttering of curse words in the frigid, silent air. "Damn me for
a fool, goddamn me over again. Fuck me."

The light from a kitchen window spilled out over Toombs's
features. He was a graying, balding black man some six feet
two inches tall; his hands were those of a giant. His window
light represented the only warmth along the entire length of the
block. No one else was getting out so early. At least he was an
industrious man, Lucas thought.

It was 6:45 A.M., and from where they stood identifying
themselves to Toombs, they could smell the coffee brewing in
the coffeemaker inside the house—it was likely a stolen item,
as well.

"We'd like a word with you, Mr. Toombs, inside, if you
will," suggested Lucas.

Toombs, the hefty heater intestines still in his hands, only
breathed in deeply and nodded. "Jus' let me put dis down to de
ground. Did you all have to bust out my winder?"

"Window?" asked Meredyth. "What window?" Looking around, she saw the broken window and acted surprised.

"We don't know anything about your window, Mr. Toombs, but we do know about your illegal activities," Lucas assured him.

"Who ratted me out?" he asked when he straightened up from the ground. "It was Bubba Wright, wasn't it? Son of a—"

Lucas smoothly replied, "No, sir. . . . Your employers have suspected you for some time. They called us in, but frankly, Mr. Toombs, we've been looking at you for another reason. Ever hear of a little boy named Lamar Coleson or Raule deJesus Milton?"

"'Course I have. Whole damned state knows 'bout those boys being snatched and beat to death and th'owed out like garbage. Hell, I come close to finding one of the bodies myself."

"Really? Then you know why we're here, aside from the stolen goods."

"Hey, now, I ain't got nothing to do wid murder, no way. I liked little Raule. Had him in my house, but I never hurt the boy, not once."

"Let's talk about it inside, shall we?"

"You wanna search my house? You go right 'head. I got nothin' to hide on them murders."

Lucas and Meredyth exchanged a glance. They'd just been given permission to do a complete house search by the owner. "Maybe so, but we've got to do our job, too," Meredyth casually replied.

"I understand that. You got to do what you got to do. Well, come on inside. Just try not to upset my old woman too much, will yous?"

"We'll try," Meredyth replied with a smile and a thumbs-up behind the man's back.

Inside, an examination of the house revealed no evidence that any child was being held against his will, and Kim received no bad vibes, either. There were no hidden rooms or soundproof boxes, and another cursory glance at the basement revealed only what was there—the stolen goods, stacked and arranged in rows for browsing and easy access, a regular supermarket of building materials.

"We want your cooperation, Mr. Toombs," said Lucas, leading the discussion at the breakfast table over coffee.

"What kind of cooperation?"

"Show him the list," he told Meredyth, who placed Mrs. Milton's list before Toombs's bulging eyes.

"You know any of these men?"

"They all brothers, and my name's at the top of the list, but no . . . I don't know all the names. What's this all about?" he asked, turning in his chair, his eyes going from one to the other of his interrogators.

Lucas, spinning out his tale, said, "We developed this list from a computer, very high-tech, Mr. Toombs. And our computers don't lie. And Dr. Desinor here is a psychic and psychics don't lie. Both the computer and the psychic tell us you were once in trouble with the law over something to do with a minor. Isn't that right?"

"I done paid my time for *that* years ago. Never done nothing like that again, ever!"

"Not even with the Milton boy?"

"I treated that boy like he was my own. When we heard he was killed, my wife, Ravinia, and me, we was more broke up than his own mother. We loved that boy, too."

"If that's true, Mr. Toombs, then you have even more reason to want to help us locate Raule's murderer."

"How can I help? I can't do nothing about what's done done."

"But you can. . . ."

"How?"

"Do you own any other vehicles, Mr. Toombs?" asked Lucas. "And don't lie. One call to the DMV and we'll know."

"Got a broke-down little Escort, but it's in the shop."

"Any other vans or a pickup?"

"No, looking to buy a new one, but no."

"Tell us what you know about the comings and goings of the

rest of the men on this list," said Meredyth. "We believe the killer either works or lives in this area, Mr. Toombs."

His eyes widened anew over his coffee cup.

Meredyth added, "And if that's the case, you might well have come into contact with him on a daily basis, since we also believe he works in the construction trade."

Toombs breathed in deeply and shook his head.

Kim asked, "Do you know other people like yourself, pedophiles, Mr. Toombs, who live in the area?"

"Ped-a-phile . . . God, I hate that word. Label a man with that just once and there ain't no 'scaping it, mistake or not, paid for or not. . . ."

"Do you know anyone who likes young boys too much!" Lucas's voice woke the wife.

"Damn," muttered Toombs.

"Do you, damn it?"

"No, not in that way, no. I don't associate with men like 'at."

"That you know of," Meredyth returned. "Think, has anyone ever struck you as different, odd or peculiar in any way?"

"Franklin, maybe."

"Don't tell us what you think we want to hear, Mr. Toombs," Meredyth countered. "Don't lead us down any wrong avenues."

"We don't have time for wrong ways," added Kim. "The Coleson boy has very little time left, sir."

Meredyth pointed and said, "Tell us what you know."

"Take a closer look at . . . at Franklin Hobbs."

"Hobbs. He's not on the list," Kim replied.

"None of those boys on your list is strange like Hobbs is strange."

Lucas asked, "How is Hobbs strange?"

"He don't let nobody get near him or his van; and he don't let nobody use his tools, not in the slightest. He's strange that way, and don't nobody like Franklin Hobbs. Something . . . I don't know, spooky about that man."

"Where can we find this guy, Hobbs?"

"I take you right to the site where he's working, but I don't know where he lives. He don't live 'round here, and he don't want nobody knowing where he lives. That's strange behavior, ain't it?"

"And he's not on our list," repeated Kim.

Toombs looked up at Kim and replied, "He's a young man. Give 'im time."

"How young is he, Mr. Toombs?"

"Late teens, I'd guess, early twenties . . . at most maybe twenty-two or -three. Just a kid, but strange . . . dresses weird, has colored fingernails, earrings and tattoos all over. You don't see that many colored men with tattoos all over, but this one's full up with 'em. He's a biker, too. Goes all the way to Daytona Beach, Florida, every year for Bike Week."

Lucas conferred with the two female doctors. "Too young to fit the profile or your vision, Dr. Desinor. Could be a royal waste of time."

Kim cautioned with, "As I've said, we can't take everything from my vision at face value. It needs to be tested against personal, cultural, natural and archetypal associations."

"She's right," added Meredyth. "Nor can we blindly follow a profile."

Lucas frowned and returned to Toombs, who was now desperately trying to explain to his heavyset, robed wife what was going on in her kitchen this morning. The wife looked sour and hateful, as if she might take a butcher knife to them all at any moment. She said to Toombs in a cutting, abrasive voice, "You got to stop this, Obediah, conducting illegal business in my home. It's going to put us both in jail."

"Shut up, woman."

"Don't you take that tone with me, old man!"

"Your wife's quite right, Mr. Toombs," said Lucas, stepping between the glaring couple. "Let's go to the work site where you can point out this guy Hobbs to us," Lucas further suggested. "We'll soon know where he lives and what he has for breakfast, like we do you, Mr. Toombs." Lucas pointed at the coffee, toast and jam Toombs had consumed. "Now take us to see Mr. Hobbs, and along the way you can tell me more about him."

The wife's mouth gaped open now, realizing the three white faces in the room were the authorities and not new customers. Toombs's face was a mask of despair and hopelessness, the jowls sagging like those of a basset hound. He rocked on his heels, scratched at his arms and neck as if a body rash had come over him.

"You are telling us the truth, aren't you, Mr. Toombs?" asked Kim.

"That I am, but I don't wont to cross Hobbs. He's a *mean* bastard."

"Mean enough to torture little kids?" asked Lucas.

Toombs considered this. "Maybe . . . just maybe."

"What they talkin' about, Obediah?" asked the wife.

"They got some notion I can he'p them find the Snatcher, the one that took Raule."

"We don't know nothin' 'bout that boy's disappearance!" she shouted.

"Mr. Toombs, Mrs. Toombs, stop worrying," Meredyth assured them. "We'll keep your identity out of it until we're sure of Mr. Hobbs, understood?"

"Thank you. It's all I ax," replied Toombs.

As they exited the house, Mrs. Toombs shouted after them, saying, "Obediah, you get done with the po-lice, you get your sorry ass back here, 'cause I ain't half done wid you, mister. You got that? You got that, Obediah?"

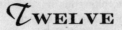

TWELVE

Arrowhead: watchful

Lucas again coached Obediah Toombs on the prearranged signal Toombs would flash when he saw Franklin Hobbs arrive at the construction site that Toombs had brought them to. "As soon as the signal is given," Lucas told Toombs, "make yourself scarce. Now, Obediah, what's the signal?"

"I grab my head in two hands and complain of the worst headache I ever got."

"Then you go off looking for a goddamn aspirin, got it?"

"I got it."

"Okay, we've got a deal now. We don't touch you on your little neighborhood operation if you give us Hobbs, understood?"

"I got it."

"Then get going."

They had come in two vehicles, Lucas riding with Toombs in his van, which reeked of oil, gas fumes, tobacco and alcohol. Lucas clambered out of the van when they pulled into the construction site. Obediah Toombs came around and led him to the foreman on the work site, introducing Lucas as a man in need of a job. "He's an Injun," said Toombs. "That means he can do your high-wire act better'n most."

The foreman didn't take Lucas's hand, but rather studied him from sole to crown, biting his lip, and finally asking, "You dress pretty well for a man out of work."

"I ain't been out of work long."

"What you do before now?"

"Blackjack at a casino."

"Ahh, no wonder your hands are clean. Like to gamble, huh?"

"Not on a construction site, sir."

"Good, a smart Indian. You ever walk the rails before?" He indicated the high steel beams of the giant erector set overhead.

"Did a lot of construction work a few years back, yes, sir."

"What outfit? And don't lie to me. I can check it with a single fax or phone call, son."

"Rough Diamond Construction Company. I was with them two and a half years, but they're no longer in business."

"That was some time ago. You sure you can handle yourself up there?"

"I'm sure."

"All right. I'll give you a chance, a probation period. Thanks, Toombs. You got work to do?"

"Yes, sir."

From across the street, in a convenience store parking lot, Meredyth and Kim watched as Lucas infiltrated the construction site where they hoped to find Hobbs. Meredyth telephoned Randy Oglesby, telling him she needed a list of names run through the crime files. She added Franklin Hobbs to the list given them by the Miltons.

"Now what?" Meredyth asked Kim.

"We wait for Toombs to indicate which one is Hobbs."

"Then what?"

"We keep a close eye on Hobbs."

Just as Lucas began ascending the skeleton of the high-rise via an open-sided elevator lift, a black-clad African-American on a Harley-Davidson blew on to the construction site, sending sand and gravel up in all directions as he screeched to a halt.

From the rising elevator, Lucas watched as Toombs approached the cyclist, and from the car in the lot across the street, Kim and Meredyth also watched. Toombs struck up a conversation with the cyclist, whose biceps bulged with an array of variegated colors—tattoos.

"Who needs a signal?" asked Meredyth, amused now.

"Toombs didn't say Hobbs'd be driving a motorcycle to work, or wearing a leather vest and no shirt . . . in this weather. The man must be mad, all right. . . ."

"Yeah, Toombs isn't very bright. He left a lot unsaid."

Toombs now reached for his head and, dramatically overdoing it, signaled his bogus headache, indicating that he was speaking to Franklin Hobbs. Toombs then quickly moved off.

"You getting any sort of read on this guy, Hobbs?" asked Meredyth of Dr. Desinor. "Any psychic feelings about the man at all?"

"Absolutely, sure, yes, but nothing tying him to Lamar Coleson, not yet."

Meredyth saw that Lucas was waving them off. She realized that Hobbs now stared curiously across to the parking lot and the red Intrepid sitting idle there. Meredyth revved up the motor and shot out into traffic, not looking at the man.

"Where are we going?" asked Kim.

"Down the block. We'll circle."

Lucas changed the direction of the elevator, taking it down. He carefully shadowed Hobbs, who now busily employed himself with pipe and metal-cutting tools. He'd set to work on plumbing pipework at the site. Lucas remembered one of the coroner's reports on one of the deaths spoke of marks on the body made by slim, tubular pipes, one-quarter- and two-quarter-inch pipe, the sort used in plumbing. Some of the welts held minute copper particles embedded in the skin from the force of the blows.

Was Hobbs the bastard? Lucas had to know.

He watched hawklike as Franklin Hobbs labored over a complex set of pipes that littered an entire area of some ten by twelve feet, the copper pipes beginning to reflect the morning sun. Lucas went for Toombs, and locating the big black man, he pushed him behind a wall so they could talk with some semblance of privacy.

"Whatchu want now? I pointed the man out to you!"

"He's got no van! You said he had a fucking van. Where is it?"

"He come in on his bike today. Had his tools strapped to the back."

"I need to investigate the van. Where does he live?"

"I tell you, I don't know where he live! Now let me go!"

Lucas hadn't realized that he had Toombs pinned against a concrete wall. He let the other man go. "All right, get out of here. You're useless, anyway! Go!"

Lucas went for the trailer where the foreman would be sitting with a cup of coffee and a doughnut, likely on the phone to some contractor in an attempt to save money. If he could just get to the man's payroll records, he'd have an address on Hobbs. He'd have to blow his cover, flash his badge and pray the foreman might understand and cooperate.

"You?" asked the foreman, dropping his feet from his desk and asking the man at the other end of the phone line to call him back. "What're you doing here? I sent you to the top." He dropped the phone onto its cradle.

Lucas produced his badge. "I'm working the Snatcher case, and I have reason to believe that one of your employees might have information useful to the case."

"You came in with Toombs."

"Just to get a look at this guy, Franklin Hobbs. I'd like his home address."

"Hobbs? You think Hobbs might be this bastard monster who's killing those kids?"

"I don't know that, no, and I can't know it until I have a look around his place, but I can't find his place without your help."

"Oh, I'll help you all right." The foreman, a thick mane of sandy hair in his eyes, searched through his computer files for the address, and he jotted it down for Stonecoat. "Nail the bastard. Nail 'im for all of us."

"Like I said, he's just a suspect for the time being. We're just

looking in to possibilities, here. May prove to have nothing whatever to do with these crimes, so please, don't let
on . . . Don't treat him any differently, and for God's sake
don't accuse him of anything. We don't want him fleeing the
area."

"I knew when I saw you with Toombs something was up,
that something was funny."

"Promise me you won't go near this guy Hobbs. Let us
handle it, all right"—Lucas searched for the name on the
nameplate on the man's desk—"Harold?"

"Got it."

Lucas left the trailer office and went searching for Meredyth
and Kim. They needed to call in a surveillance team, keep a
close eye on Hobbs while he looked over the man's van. In a
moment, Lucas saw his car, with Meredyth at the wheel, come
cruising toward him. He got into the rear seat and told
Meredyth to keep driving.

Lucas did everything by the book: surveillance team in a
telephone repair truck, all the necessary paperwork turned in,
thanks to Randy Oglesby. A warrant, signed and legal, had been
obtained from a "soft" judge. All else, once again, waited on
time and patience, both of which proved in short supply.

And BellSouth Houston wanted their van back.

Lucas returned to the construction site while the cameras
zoomed in from across the street. Immediately on arriving,
he sensed an unusual tension in the air, as if the men had been
shouted at by the boss about some looming deadline. Everyone
seemed sullen, silent and brooding, and several small cliques of
men huddled about in private whispering groups. Lucas, so as
to look less conspicuous, climbed aboard the crane elevator and
gave the operator the sign to pull him skyward, where he could
appear to be at work riveting on the high beams. It was getting
near quitting time, and the van had orders to shadow Mr. Hobbs
off the work site and to wherever he might go after work to
"unwind"—possibly on Lamar Coleson.

Lucas's thoughts returned to his meeting with Captain

Lincoln, who didn't approve of the "bullshit FBI tactics"—as he put it to Kim Desinor—"of having some bastard in Washington, D.C., tell me how to deploy my men."

"But it was at my request, Captain," said Dr. Desinor, trying to soothe the man's ruffled feathers. "And you're absolutely right. I should have come directly to you and not gone behind your back, but time has been of the essence, and you were rather busy last night at that black-tie affair, something to do with the governor's reelection campaign, I was told. . . ."

Lincoln's entire face tightened and then softened all in a flash of realization that he could not keep any aspect of his life a secret, not since these child deaths began here in Houston. He knew he must be involved in the resolution of this case, and if not, then he must totally wash his hands of it, pass it off to another agency. He thought he *had* turned it over to the FBI, but obviously not. Lucas saw the confusion working its way through the labyrinths of Lincoln's agitated brain.

"All right . . . all right, Stonecoat's on the case, assisting you, along with Dr. Sanger, here, who obviously has an insatiable appetite for the criminal psychology aspects of such a case. But hear me now, all of you," he roared, getting to his feet to appear the imposing bear that he was, "I don't want this all over the newsstands again—that we look like we're running a dog and pony show here. I want your investigation, Lucas, kept quiet and low-key. As it is, Vorel is foaming at the mouth."

"He left me messages at the hotel," replied Kim. "I know he's a bit peeved."

"Peeved, madam? You are the soul of understatement. Do you know that?" replied Lincoln. "Pissed is the word—truly, absolutely pissed. And it jeopardizes COMIT, Lucas. I hope you realize the enormity of this decision."

"I do, sir."

"All right, but keep it hush-hush until or unless you solve the damned case, at which time we can hold a goddamn press conference both here and in D.C. for all the cooperating agencies to take part in, understood?"

"Yes, sir."

"Meantime, I'll put someone on the Cold Room to spell you."

"Thank you, sir."

And so it had gone, earlier that day. Lucas meant to keep as far away from the press on this matter as was humanly possible.

Almost as soon as the elevator platform he was standing on began lifting, Lucas saw workmen on all sides brandishing pipes and power tools, and those who had been speaking in small groups had suddenly become larger groups and these groups, as in a prison riot, joined suddenly to form a single, living creature called a mob that came tearing down the midway of the construction site. The mob monster held vengeance in its heart, murder on its one-track mind, and blood in its single eye, and every man in the mob with some small bit of information about a possible relationship between Hobbs and the dead children had turned over his soul to the creature's will and cause, the end result of which would be Hobbs's bones crushed, his blood running out over the sand.

Lucas uselessly shouted and waved at the crane operator to lower him, but the man was busy with coffee and a doughnut at his station. Lucas couldn't be heard over the roar of the machinery, so he threw the emergency switch, which effectively stopped the upward movement of the car he stood in. The sudden stop threw him to the metal mesh floor. He could see the mob growing larger below him.

Lucas realized that Hobbs could be murdered or put into a coma by the fanatics whose imaginations had been fanned by the foreman or by Toombs's big mouth, and that Hobbs dead or unconscious meant no help in finding Lamar Coleson. "What the hell are those guys in the van doing?" he shouted loudly, got to his feet and signaled the crane operator to lower him immediately, indicating the emergency below. The operator quickly reversed the elevator's movement, and Lucas was on his way back to the ground.

It appeared that every man working the job site—a job site where one of the bodies of the victims had been discovered in a Dumpster—wanted a shot at Hobbs, who, taken by surprise, looked up from a welding job requiring his full attention to see the mob bearing down on him.

"What the fuck!" he shouted as the mob moved closer, calling for his blood.

Some men in the crowd shouted obscenities at Hobbs, while others informed him that they knew his dirty little secret, that he was the Snatcher. Hobbs rose to his feet, a welding torch held ahead of him, threatening anyone who came close. The crowd began an age-old ritual, circling its prey.

The mob closed in on Hobbs, whose single blowtorch kept the crowd at bay. He pleaded to know why they wanted to bash his skull in. Lucas could not make out the man's words over the din of the crane and the taunts of the single-minded monster about to devour Hobbs. Suddenly the arm of the mob reached out, knocking Hobbs's puny defense aside, and they were on him like jackals, many swiping at and hitting their own in the bargain in an attempt to get at the supposed child molester and murderer. A huge dust devil rose around the mob.

Lucas leapt the five or so remaining feet from the crane elevator and pushed through the mob, firing his gun into the air until finally he stood between Hobbs's bleeding and broken prone body and the murderous mob. Lucas's cover was totally blown.

"We've had this man under surveillance," Lucas informed the outraged mob, holding his badge high for all to see. "And I'm taking him into custody."

"The hell you are!"

"We'll see he gives up the missing kid! Can you promise the same?" came the taunts.

"Fucking cops can't catch a cold, much less a child killer."

"Get out of the way!" Lucas warned the single-eyed snake before him.

When the mob heaved forward, Lucas fired off another round from his 9mm. Glock in a show of power, stopping everyone's mad rush. "Do I have to point out to you morons that you're all on camera? That if you kill this man, and he's *not* the Snatcher, then you'll all serve time for murder?"

"Even if he *is* the Snatcher," shouted Captain Joseph Rollins, a huge black man with penetrating eyes, "you'll serve time for manslaughter if you kill Hobbs." Rollins and his surveillance team now stood like guards at a rock concert alongside Lucas, all to protect the likes of the sorry and miserable Hobbs. Lucas had studied the man's rap sheet, and Hobbs had in fact done time for sexual attacks on minors, among other crimes.

"You're going to protect this scum?" shouted the leader of the mob, the foreman who had promised to keep the information quiet. Toombs was nowhere to be seen, likely in a John-Boy by now.

"Break it up!" shouted Lucas, again brandishing his weapon in the air. The other cops followed suit.

Rollins cried out, "Go about your business! Now!"

The crowd's mood changed, at first imperceptibly; then weighing their cowardly options and deciding to slink off like a wild cougar that's been bested, the workers lowered their tools and weapons and returned to a semblance of rational thought as reality seeped back into their heads. Lucas saw the relaxed position of the hammers and tile cutters and lead pipes, and he saw the fringes of the crowd breaking off, moving back to pick up jobs that had been laid aside and the individual minds moving back to their lives.

Joe Rollins, the surveillance team captain, congratulated Lucas on his bravery. "Don't know that I'd have had the guts to step between Hobbs and that bunch alone the way you did, Chief. They might've gone right through you."

Lucas didn't mind Rollins's easy familiarity, calling him Chief not because of any perceived rank but due to his skin tone. "Would've made a hell of a show for the six o'clock news, huh? Men rip apart child killer, caught on police tape," Lucas replied before turning to Hobbs and saying, "Okay, Mr. Hobbs, you have the government-given, inalienable right to remain silent, but if you give up that right, anything you say can and will be used against you. You have a right to a

lawyer . . ." He read the Miranda proceedings in the voice of
a cop tired of the litany that'd become a slogan for the civil
rights of the criminal.

Meanwhile, Rollins cuffed a protesting Hobbs, who shouted,
"What's this shit about me being the Snatcher? I'm no child
molester and killer! I did my time; served and released! You
people . . . you hound a man till the fucking grave, don'tcha,
and you enjoy it, don'tcha?" All this venom spewed forth from
Hobbs as blood rivulets ran from head wounds into his eyes
and mouth. "Wait a minute!" he continued, protesting as they
led him toward the surveillance van. "What about my tools?
And what about my bike? I leave my bike and those bastard
toads'll destroy the fuck out of it! What about my stuff, man?"

"It'll be impounded, Hobbs, right along with everything you
possess if necessary," Lucas assured him, waving the open
warrant in his face.

"Whataya mean, everything I own?"

"We're searching your apartment when we're done here, and
we're going to find the evidence to put you on Death Row,
asshole."

"But I ain't killed no kids! I love kids!"

"Yeah, your spotless record tells us all about your love for
kids, Hobbs. Get into the van, now!" Losing control, Lucas
rammed the man's already bleeding head into the doorjamb,
instantly apologizing for the accident.

"Run him by St. Luke's for stitches and a cleanup and then
down to the Thirty-first Precinct where we'll talk, right, Brother
Hobbs?"

Hobbs only moaned in reply from where he lay bleeding on
the carpeted van floor. Then he piped up and said, "I want an
ambulance, man! Get me an ambulance or I cry police brutality."

"You want to see police brutality up close?" shouted Lucas,
grabbing Hobbs by his shirt and snatching him into a sitting
position, jamming his gun into the other man's crotch. "I
should just blow all your equipment right off, you bastard!"

Rollins grabbed Lucas, shaking him, telling him to calm

down. All the other police officers looked on as if they were
staring at a madman.

Lucas let go of the suspect and let him flop back down to the
floor where his blood continued to discolor the carpet. Rollins
pulled Lucas away while other cops got the suspect fully into
the vehicle and whisked off toward the hospital. Rollins's car
was driven up, and he offered Lucas a ride back to the 31st.

Inside the car, Rollins cautioned Lucas about getting rough
with prisoners and suspects these days. "Too many cameras
watching our every move from too many rooftops and windows. Trust me."

"Sorry, I lost it with the creep."

"Hey, don't apologize to me. I'd have whacked him myself,
but not out there on the street, not anymore. I've had two
disciplines against me already, and Dr. Sanger's recommended
an extended leave so I can get in touch with my inner feelings."
Rollins laughed heartily at this, as if he'd told a joke. "With
what we see every day, it's a wonder more of us don't lose it
more often than we do. We're none of us fucking machines,
now, are we, Chief?"

Lincoln greeted them at the door, excited at the prospect they
had a suspect everyone could "like" as the Snatcher, one that fit
the profile, one that had slipped through when the usual
suspects had been amassed because he'd been paroled in
another state and had chosen Houston as his destination after
serving time because he knew the territory so well. He'd grown
up on the very streets from which the victims had disappeared,
and he worked at a job site where one of the victim's bodies
had been discovered, proving the old theorem: Killers and
criminals shit where they eat. Over a period of time, the act
becomes so familiar and easy for them that they become bolder,
and in being more emboldened, they commit the crime closer
and closer to home. Could this not be the case with Franklin
Leon Hobbs?

However, after long, arduous hours, interrogation of the
suspect proved fruitless and frustrating, and while the search of

his apartment turned up duct tape and carpentry tools, Hobbs was, after all, a working carpenter and pipe fitter, so there remained nothing whatever to directly link him to any of the dead children or the disappearances and killings. Still, hair and fiber samples, taken at Hobbs's place and from his van parked just outside, must, Lucas believed, turn up something at the microscopic level that they could use as a key to unlock his filthy, cold heart.

During interrogation Captain Lincoln interrupted Lucas, ordering him out and into his office immediately. Lucas sensed that something had gone wrong, but he hadn't a clue as to what. Lincoln told him to sit, and Lucas obeyed. Lincoln, using his remote, then turned on the television set atop his credenza, and Lucas watched, stunned, as a blue-eyed blond in stage makeup spoke over the sights and sounds of Franklin Leon Hobbs's ordeal at the hands of the mob, the reporter narrating events, naming names, including Lucas's and Rollins's. The reporter finished with the sordid detail that police might have set Franklin up for the attack in order to frighten him in a witch-hunt that—as she put it—had turned up absolutely nothing save what the killer wanted them to have—namely, the brutalized bodies of the wretched children. The reporter made quick mention of the "so-called" progress in the case, citing the profile given members of the press by HPD's public relations department.

The images of Hobbs being brutalized by the mob, and the idea the police set him up for such brutalization, perhaps in order that their own marks on Hobbs would not show, seemed all that mattered now. Despite this, Lucas foolishly asked, "How did the TV people get hold of the surveillance tape?"

"I made a deal with this woman a long time ago, Lucas, that all our tapes are open for view, that we don't have a fucking thing to hide! Why didn't you tell me about the attack? Did you set Hobbs up?"

"I absolutely did not, sir, no."

"Then what about Rollins, his men?"

"No, sir. They acted properly every step of the way." Lucas

didn't believe this one hundred percent, but he knew he'd have to work with Rollins and the others again on many a case, and he didn't wish to lose what few friends he'd managed to make on the force. Besides, he wasn't about to rat out on anyone.

"So everything this reporter is implying is nonsense, conjecture, half-truth, what?"

"All of the above . . ."

"You promised me you'd keep a low profile on this, Lucas."

"Shit happens, sir. I responded as fast as I could have. I was on an ascending crane elevator when I realized what was happening on the ground, and I—"

"Enough, Lucas! I don't want to hear excuses from you or Rollins."

"Then you've talked to Rollins?"

"I have."

Typical departmental bullshit, Lucas thought. Treat your own force no better than the street scum like Hobbs. Divide the suspects and conquer; keep them in separate rooms; get one to rat out the other.

"All police personnel at the scene, sir, acted courageously and with all due speed, sir, once it became apparent what was going down, and that's all I have to say about it, sir."

"All right, so get back in there and get a confession out of this creep and tell me we've got a location on the Coleson boy, go!"

"Yes, sir."

But further interrogation of Hobbs only solidified his stubborn resolve that he was not the Snatcher and knew nothing of the killings or Lamar Coleson. Nightfall came, and still Hobbs stuck to his plea of innocence, by then with his court-appointed lawyer at his side. The lawyer, a bright, thin young woman, having seen the latest news reports, was now threatening a lawsuit against the HPD on behalf of her client.

"Lady," Lucas finally exploded, "we saved your client's sorry ass from being murdered by that mob."

"If you set him up, you're accomplices to attempted murder."

"Damn it, woman—counselor—nobody set your client up!"

"Maybe not for murder, but to throw a scare into him before you had to Mirandize him?"

"You get your facts from the ramblings of a bad TV reporter and you try to make a case around misinformation. What does that make you?" Lucas stormed out, leaving the final booking to Rollins, who stared at the lady lawyer with eyes that could kill.

Meredyth Sanger and Kim Desinor caught Lucas on his way from the interrogation room; they'd been on the other side of the two-way mirror, listening in, and each felt Lucas's frustration.

Meredyth described her feelings toward Hobbs, saying, "From a psychological viewpoint, I'd say Hobbs is a pathological liar, but—"

"Exactly right."

"But this time, Lucas, he may be telling the truth."

"His body language tell you that?" he snidely replied, tired and upset with the way things had gone. It was almost ten P.M. The interrogation had gone on for the entire day—four more hours Lamar Coleson could not regain.

Meredyth frowned, bit her lip and continued, saying, "In effect, yes. You can tell a great deal from body language. I read yours all the time. And in Hobbs's case, he's as frustrated as we are, and he's afraid. He thinks he's going down for this because the police have to have somebody to hold up to public rage, someone to punish. In effect, Hobbs is demonstrating normal behavior in there for an innocent scapegoat."

Lucas began to protest, but she stopped him with a finger on his lips, saying, "The man didn't cave in or doze off to sleep when he was left alone in the room; it all points to an innocent man."

"Innocent, bull. He's guilty of something."

"Something, sure, but not this. Not multiple murder and mutilation of children, no. He's not the Snatcher, as much as we'd all like him to be."

Lucas countered, asking, "You mean as much as Lincoln would like him to be?"

"No, Lucas, I mean you, me, Kim, Rollins—all of us, including Lincoln. The captain showed me the story they ran on Channel 6. You could've been killed, Lucas."

"Thanks for making no half-assed assumptions." Lucas had detected the sincere note of concern in her voice, and his eyes met hers. "Thanks for your confidence and your interest, Doctor." Lucas knew that Lincoln had undoubtedly solicited from Sanger sanction of Lucas as both a sane and good cop, that he wasn't out of control. He trusted she'd told his captain the right thing. With Rollins, he couldn't be nearly so sure.

Kim asked if she should leave the room, allow them a moment alone, her tone half kidding. "Or do you two want to get a room of your own?"

"Never mind," Lucas countered.

"I did a psychometric reading of Hobbs's things, just as I did of his van at the house during the search, and I'm sorry, Lucas, but nothing . . . no images, no visions, not a scintilla of feeling that Franklin Leon Hobbs is our guy, despite the similarities to the profile."

"Great. We've got no physical evidence on the guy, and now you tell me there's no mental evidence either."

She confessed, "I got about as much from the man's house and van as your forensic team carried away, I'm afraid."

"So you got absolutely nothing from reading Hobbs's things?" Lucas stepped to a nearby coffee machine and dropped two quarters and a nickel in for the hot, black caffeine hit.

"Hobbs is an angry man . . . feels a deep sense of hatred, resentment and sadness for having been abused as a child by either an alcoholic or a religiously fanatical parent or parents, and one day he may again take out his anger on society—some young person, I should say—but I get no sense of his having taken Lamar or anyone else hostage in that black van of his, no."

"So, what you're saying, Dr. Desinor, is that while you're

psychically positive that this creep's going to harm someone in the future, we don't have anything to hold him on now?"

"'Fraid so."

"Damn, I hate to see this guy walk; and if he does walk, and later he turns up as the Snatcher, we're going to look damned foolish."

"If hair and fiber have turned up nothing, what can you hold him on?"

"General indecency? I don't know. . . ."

Lucas thought about the total lack of physical evidence against Hobbs. He'd rushed the M.E.'s department for answers; perhaps they'd made mistakes. It was hardly out of the question; still, why'd it feel like he was grasping at straws here? Earlier, Lucas had taken his high-profile, high-incident case before the coroner, telling him to put it atop his to-do list. Captain Lincoln had given his sanction, but maybe they'd only pissed off the inscrutable Dr. Chang by ordering the little man around. Chang felt that his domain should be inviolable, untouchable, and of course, he didn't want criticism leveled at his office any more than Lincoln wanted it directed at the 31st Precinct. Chang's stance was exactly what it had to be for a medical examiner—nonpartisan and incorruptible. Lucas normally wouldn't have it any other way; but in this case, involving dead and dying children, Lucas wanted to break Chang's inscrutable face along with Chang's incorruptible rules.

Just then the sharp-tongued lawyer for the degenerate Hobbs rapped her knuckles against the glass, causing a staccato alarm. Counselor and client had grown bored with one another, Lucas guessed. Through the glass, the tough lawyer shouted, "Either formally charge my client or open the f-ing door, gentlemen!"

Lucas snatched open the door and let it bang against a wall, shouting, "You're free to go, Hobbs, but know this—every cop in this city's going to have his eye on you from here on out."

"I . . . I can go?"

"We're kickin' your sorry ass out, so get moving!" shouted Lucas. "Both of you. You're stinkin' up the place."

Franklin Hobbs needed no third telling. He got up and sauntered out ahead of his bitch lawyer, eyeballing Meredyth Sanger as he went, while his lawyer stopped at the door and stared into Lucas's eyes and said, "Everyone, including a man like Hobbs, has the right to counsel, Detective. Surely you know that, and while we might all wish to throw the Hobbses of the world into a pit of fire without due process, you can imagine the far-reaching ramifications for all citizens of these—"

"Save it for your cocktail party friends, Counselor."

"This isn't medieval England, Detective. People have rights in America, even the accused."

"I've heard all the excuses for violent criminals, for early parole and time served, Counselor, much of which nonsense was created by liberal bleeding hearts who have never lost a loved one to the cowardly, ignorant and driven killers among us. But who am I? I don't write political commentary, and I don't have your expertise with the law, so all I can do is give you fair warning. . . ."

"Warning?" she asked.

"Just don't go anywhere alone with that creep Hobbs."

"Are you worried about my safety, Detective?"

"I don't want to be doing a sketch of your silhouette on a carpet or sidewalk somewhere, Counselor."

"I'll take all due precautions. See you in court."

"The man's being released. What court?"

"We'll see what a judge has to say about my client's battered condition."

"Which occurred on the street, at the work site."

"He says you worked him over pretty good afterward, in this interrogation room."

"That's bullshit and you know it."

"Like I said, Detective . . . see you in court."

"Go ahead, serve your damned papers. Make an ass of yourself, lady!" he called after the lawyer, who walked swiftly away.

Meredyth placed a hand on his shoulder, soothing Lucas as

she might an angry child. He responded by pulling away and saying, "I'm going upstairs to see Randy. See if he's got anything for us." Lucas, his shoulders hunched forward from fatigue, marched from the interrogation area, leaving Kim and Meredyth to contemplate their failure and time lost.

$\mathcal{T}$HIRTEEN

—○—●—○—●—○—●—

Days & nights: time

Time lost, thought Lucas . . . Lost time sat perched like an annoying crow on Lucas's shoulder, a constant reminder of Lamar Coleson's distress out there somewhere. But the dark crow also reminded Lucas of the Roundpoint case, which he had shelved. He must visit trustworthy Randy Oglesby for help, asking him to locate anything on the computer involving the 1948 case.

Lucas found Randy leaning in over his computer screen, working diligently at beating some remote opponent at a chess match. Lucas placed his hand over the screen to get Randy's attention, and over Randy's protests, he quietly said, "Put away your games for the moment. I need your help on one of the Cold Room files dating back to 1948. I sent up the file to be placed on the COMIT program, remember?"

"Sure I remember it."

"So, what's become of it?"

"Did you really expect to find anything on a case that old, Lucas?"

"I don't know. You tell me."

"To be honest, I've not gotten to it, but I figured with you busting your butt on the Snatcher thing, well, there seemed no hurry."

"Why don't you cross-reference the Houston newspaper files that go back beyond the late forties, Randy?"

"Yeah, good idea." Randy promised to do what he could with what little he had to work with, asking, "Just how important is this '48 business, Lucas?"

"It may lead nowhere, but it might prove the test case for COMIT, so . . ." Lucas shrugged his shoulders.

"I'll see what I can do, but you'll have to let Dr. Sanger know I'm doing the work for you. She's been on my case about spreading myself too thin as it is, so—"

"I've already talked to her about it, and she's got no problem with it," Lucas lied. "Just get on it, and anything you learn, let me know as soon as you know. Got that?"

"Got it."

"Call you later, then."

Randy waved off the big Indian detective, but Lucas, never one for formalities of the "white" kind, had already rushed away.

Lucas found the elevator, made his way to the basement where he checked his messages in the Cold Room and from there made arrangements for an unmarked, battered undercover car to be at his disposal that afternoon and evening.

Regardless of the lack of evidence, Lucas stubbornly stayed on Hobbs, staking out the man's place for any movement, hoping he might give himself away by going to the location where Lamar Coleson was being held hostage. After two hours of nothing, no sign of Hobbs, and with Lucas growing restless under the black Texas sky, suddenly someone snatched open the passenger side door and presented a gun to Lucas's face as he climbed into the car. "Damn, it's you," Lucas said, realizing that Roundpoint had caught up to him. "What the hell're you pointing that thing at me for?"

"You've done nothing to pursue leads in my mother's murder case, and I'm duly pissed off."

Lucas raised his hands in a gesture of defeat. "You see me working here?"

"You're sitting on your ass here."

"I'm working a case here."

"You're wasting your time here," disagreed Roundpoint. "Hobbs isn't your man. You're overtired maybe, maybe not thinking straight. Go home, get some rest, and get started on my mother's killer."

"Don't tell me what to do, Roundpoint."

Roundpoint gritted his teeth even as he put his weapon into some deep pocket. "You've done nothing with Minerva's case."

"That's just not so! I'm running a computer search for information leading to the circumstances surrounding her death as we speak. I don't know who your mole in the department is, but his information stinks."

Roundpoint, mollified for the moment, relented, his body language speaking for him. Relaxing now, Roundpoint suddenly found the muzzle of Lucas's 9mm. resting on his forehead, just between the eyes. "If you fucking ever put a gun in my face again, Roundpoint, then you'd better goddamn use it. You got that?"

"All right, take it easy. I've brought you something that might help in your investigation of my mother's case."

"Oh, and what's that?"

"You can put away the gun."

Lucas frowned and holstered the gun. "So, what've you got, Roundpoint?"

"This." He held out something that looked like rosary beads under the orange glow of the streetlights.

Lucas, angry, exploded at the assassin, saying, "What's this, another useless necklace and amulet stripped from your mother's body by the killer and left for you to find? Give me a break, all right? I've already gone the rounds with that other piece of crap you handed me."

"Look, I'm sorry about giving you a copy of the amulet before, but it's quite valuable to me, sentimentally speaking, so I had a copy made. Besides, it would've just led you back to the reservation where you'd have wasted your time; but this is the real amulet, and you see, it was left at the altar, Father Avi's altar, or so he told me, after my mother's death. And now, since you've got the ear of that psychic, you can have her give you a reading of the genuine article. I read where she does that sort of thing, and that she's very good at it. What can it hurt?"

"What can it hurt? I already had her read the junk once, and she told me it had nothing, absolutely nothing to do with anyone's murder, that it felt, in her words, to have no 'history' of its own."

"Then she was right. Her psychic powers are good."

Lucas took a moment to study the necklace. "The necklace and amulet don't show up in any of the crime scene photos and are not in the death manifest, so it wasn't on her when the body was discovered. So, she must not have been wearing it that night, or her killer took it off her."

"She always wore it, or so I was told, but it's true the amulet wasn't on her the night she was murdered."

"Unless the killer took it and returned it to Father Avi's altar, which means the killer responded to the amulet and felt something for your mother. Damn you for withholding this information, Roundpoint."

"I knew you'd go suspecting Father Avi, and that'd be a waste of time. Father Avi was incapable of harming any living thing, much less my mother."

"You're sure of that, are you?"

"As sure as I am when I put a bullet in someone, yes."

Lucas felt the hard ice in his tone. "When the amulet showed up at the reservation, draped over the altar for Father Avi to find, rumors began to circulate, no doubt, that your father had killed her. Is that right?"

"That is what I was told, yes."

"And out of some sense of remorse, your father laid the amulet on the altar? Correct me if I'm wrong," Lucas continued.

"Even Father Avi thought my father must have done it."

"But you never accepted that?"

"Never."

"How, then, did the amulet come into your possession? And this time, no lies."

"Father Avi, as I've said. He told me that it was hanging in the church at the reservation, mysteriously left there. . . ."

Immediately, Lucas knew that this amulet could well be the key to solving Minerva Roundpoint's murder. "Left there when and by whom appears to be the sixty-four-thousand-dollar question, heh?"

"No one is sure who left it there or how it got there."

"And you got it from the priest?"

"Avi, on his deathbed. He gave it to me."

More with the deathbed priest and his confessions, thought Lucas.

Roundpoint continued, saying, "He told me the whole story. How my mother was murdered, and how the amulet—"

"Yeah, I know, mysteriously showed up on his altar one morning in 1948."

"The day *after* Father Avi learned of the murder."

"And what was that, a week later, two?"

"Six days."

"What else did the priest tell you?"

"He said whoever left it, must . . . had to have taken it forcefully from her and must have been her killer."

"He told you that?"

"And he believed her killer to be my father. He even confronted my father with it, asking him to confess and turn himself in. According to Father Avi, my father denied having killed her, yet he couldn't look at the amulet, Father Avi said."

"And less than a week later your father died drunk in a pool of water?"

"Not three feet deep, not far from our home."

Lucas knew no autopsy would have been performed on yet another drunken Indian drowned out at the reservation. "Did Father Avi give you any history about the amulet?" asked Lucas, looking at the sparkle of the thing in the dim light. "How she came to own it, all that?"

"He said it was given to her by her mother."

"Did he have any *other* theories about who might've killed your mother and placed her amulet on his altar?"

"I pressed him, and he suggested that it must have been my father, that this is why my father committed suicide. But my father was always a drunk, and he hardly cared about her leaving him, so long as he had drink. He drowned. He did not drink heavily or commit suicide over some remorse he suddenly had over my mother. I don't believe it . . . never have. Call it instinct, if you like."

"Have you ever considered the possibility he was murdered to make it appear that he died remorseful and broken by his act of killing her?"

"The thought has passed through my mind often, yes."

"Anything more about the amulet that you can tell me?"

Roundpoint scratched the back of his head and replied, "No, nothing more." Lucas thought there might well be a connection. Roundpoint's father chases after her, kills her in a fit of rage, returns to the res and the bottle, dying himself in a fit of despair and fugue, but not before he romantically returns the amulet to the altar, a sign to . . . to Father Avi, perhaps, a clear confession? What a cover for the true murderer, if in fact a cover-up had been accomplished.

Roundpoint looked into Lucas's eyes and shook his head as if he'd read Lucas's mind, saying, "Look, whoever killed her in Houston in 1948 returned to Kansas and placed her most prized possession on Father Michael Avi's altar a week later. No one paid much attention to the comings and goings of my father, but he hadn't the wherewithal to make a round-trip like that in a matter of days. He hardly knew from day to day what fucking day of the week or month it was. Believe me, I'd know."

"Sounds like you've stored up a lot of anger for him."

"And why not."

"Hopefully, Dr. Sanger's helping you with that."

"She is. We don't need to go there."

Roundpoint quietly slid from the car and leaned back in to say, "If you fail to find Minerva's killer, then you will pay a high price."

"What are you, one of those death-wish guys? Just keep threatening me, prick, and maybe this"—Lucas tapped his gun where it rested below his coat—"goes off in your face right here and now."

"You drop this obsession with Hobbs and this Snatcher thing. The FBI's got it. There're a thousand cops on it. You're not needed on it." His tone of voice left a clear message in its wake.

"You'll find I don't respond well to threats, Roundpoint."

But Roundpoint had closed the door with a thud and had disappeared. Now, once again, Lucas sat alone, staring across at Franklin Hobbs's hovel of a home. Maybe everyone was right, from the coroner to Dr. Faith to the Fox assassin; maybe Lucas was on the wrong track.

Lucas gave thought to Roundpoint, the coyote, slinking off into the darkness, disappearing back into the shadows from which he'd come, a dangerous man indeed. But now that Roundpoint had left Lucas once again in solitude, he began thinking deeply on the kind of night Lamar Coleson must currently be enduring. Lucas finally saw Hobbs's living room light go on. The bastard had obviously been enjoying a good sleep this whole time. Lucas clambered from the car, his body like lead, his mind dazed from lack of sleep, and he found himself standing outside Hobbs's window.

Lucas felt a surge of raw anger rise from the pit of his being, a vigilante's hatred like that displayed at the construction site today. Lucas wanted to burst into the bastard's bungalow and beat him to within an inch of his life as the mob had tried to do.

Instead, Lucas checked the impulsive desire. His nostrils flared at the stench of Hobbs's seedy neighborhood. The man lived not five blocks from where Lamar Coleson had disappeared. Lucas moved in to investigate more closely, a small fraction of his brain clear and shouting, *Don't do anything stupid!*

Lucas peered in at the living room from the front window through broken and twisted blinds. He saw Hobbs stripped to his waist, in his boxer shorts, having a beer and a sandwich of cold cuts, his TV blaring the late-late news. In fact, he'd obviously taped a news segment, Lucas realized when the man, using the remote, replayed the incident of his own attack at the construction site. The second run-through finished, the tape now displayed images of a pleading black woman—Lamar's mother—a tape that had been playing now for two days on every major station.

Lucas watched as Hobbs shook with laughter over the woman's pleas. Hobbs, a black man who fit the profile in all but age, remained a long shot even in that rational sector of Lucas's sleepy brain, but here he was raising his beer in toast to Lamar's mother's pitiful image. Lucas decided to watch him longer. Should he make a move for some other location, Lucas would be on him in a heartbeat.

Tangled and dangled, tortured and brutalized, Lamar Coleson fears his head will explode before his caregiver and butcher returns; each time he sees around the edges of the tape covering his eyes, the big white wall that hovers over him, lets the net-sack-rope contraption down from the ceiling where it dangles by a hook. Lamar fears he will not come again, to ease the weight and blood rushing to his head. He fears the monster will not return in time to keep him alive, and at the same time he prays the monster will let him die, and it has all become one and the same and none of it matters now, since all that matters is an end to the pain. To end the pain, the big white monster's got to come back and end it, but before he will end it, he will think of more torture-games to play out on Lamar's already bruised and suffering body.

Lamar never imagined he could become the victim of someone like the Snatcher. That kind of victimization was for losers, fools, cripples, shit like that; but now he felt the loser, the fool, the cripple.

His nostrils fought back the disgusting odors surrounding him, from his own feces, caked now on his body, on the rope net, on the floor below him like bat droppings in a cave, to the foul odor in his mouth, left dry and disgusting by the awful stuff forced down his throat by the Snatcher, something tasting like dead fish. Previously, before the decaying odors of his own body had begun to take a toll, Lamar had smelled concrete dust, freshly cut wood, the odors of construction and building. It was the odor of the large coffin built here for Lamar, the coffin of this cubicle room with cinder-block walls all around and a single door through which stepped only one being, the monster that pleased itself with Lamar's cries of pain.

Lamar Coleson . . . I am Lamar Coleson. He kept sending the signal out there, using what little remained of his faculties. At first he'd put the message out for himself, to hold on to his sanity. It was only later that he caught some glimpse of a woman reaching out to him, a beautiful angel woman who kept appearing, reaching toward him, telling him that she was searching for him, that she would find him—saying all this without moving her lips or speaking. So he redoubled his efforts to communicate with the vision, and it'd kept him alive. What he smells, hears, sees, feels, and the taste in his mouth he now communicates to the floating, angelic woman. . . .

Was she real or imaginary, an afterthought to the pain? "When we awake from the nightmare," Lamar asked aloud but with so dry and gritty a throat as to be unable to form coherent words, "will we be in heaven?"

Kim Desinor did awake, as if on cue. Staring out into the darkness of the empty space above her bed, she felt an overwhelming sense of failure and the sensation that time had already run out for Lamar unless the boy's spirit remained as strong and indomitable as it had appeared to be in her early visions of him. But it seemed to be otherwise now; the white wall of the torturing chamber had all but claimed Lamar's will and drained him of resistance, including mental resistance.

A tear welled up from deep within Kim, rising out over the swell and valley of her eye and cheek and stopping to rest on her upper lip, where the saltiness tasted good. She sent Lamar a message of hope, a taste of her tears, pleading that he hold on a little longer. . . . Like some strange, otherworldly E-mail, her message flew from her along a channel just as mysterious and more complex than silicon chips and miniature circuitry, flapping white wings like some ethereal homing pigeon, the message on its way to Lamar.

They'd made a cosmic connection, a rare occurrence even in Kim Desinor's realm of experience. Still, Lamar didn't have the strength or know-how to send stronger messages laden with useful clues; she must work with just a few clues that had been added to the complex puzzle that needed filling in before Lamar's life became forfeit.

Once again she desperately attempted to make the connection with Lamar, but this time she saw two huge white hands reaching right out of the darkness toward her. Crawling all over the hands: spiders, roaches, ants, night crawlers and other insects. She felt these creatures crawling about open sores on her body—Lamar's body. The shock and disgust she felt sent her reeling back to her room in downtown Houston—her quiet, safe place. She cried for Lamar and cursed her own cowardice. Her single most abiding phobia was of being buried alive and having insects, and spiders in particular, crawling about her while she lay helpless, unable to get them off.

Once again convinced by Lamar's keen perception of things, convinced that Lamar himself was using psychokinetic and telepathic powers brought on by his intense and unrelenting stress, Kim believed the "black man" was actually a "white man" who disguised himself as a harmless old neighborhood bum. *Lamar can't be so wrong about the color of the monster's skin*, she told herself now.

Shaken by her latest contact with the suffering child, Kim climbed from her bed and went into the bathroom where she splashed water over her face and neck from the tap, desperately trying to feel again and to think clearly. She returned to her bedside notepad and jotted down everything she had seen, heard, felt, smelt and tasted while in Lamar's present world. Aside from the "facts" as reported by Lamar, Kim added her own "beliefs"—that the killer was in fact a white man, possibly with a deep-seated hatred for blacks, just raw enough of an image to start a race-relations riot here in Houston should the press get hold of the notion. She also added that perhaps their killer might be an accomplished actor with the skills of a Hollywood makeup artist, as well as a keeper of animals and a construction worker.

She dialed Lucas's number and got his answering machine, cursed and hung up. She dialed Meredyth Sanger. She needed someone to talk to.

As soon as Meredyth came on and was lucid enough to ask the hour, Kim said, "We should be able to narrow this man's identity down to a handful of individuals working and living in the geographic location of the killings, Meredyth."

"Really, and how do we do that?"

"Think of it. . . . A construction worker, or former construction worker, who has a household of pets, likely lives alone or with an estranged wife or parents, a white man who knows something about makeup and disguises himself so well he can pass for black . . ."

"So you're sticking with the theory he's white?"

"I am more convinced of it than ever."

"Disguise, huh? Sounds like the clown killer of young boys in Des Plaines, Illinois, a decade or more ago, John Wayne Gacy—construction worker/employer, drywall, I think, hired young boys who kept disappearing, and on weekends he entertained at children's parties by dressing up as a clown, and neighbors said he loved children and animals, and friends said he was tops in the local Jaycees."

Kim agreed, saying, "Gacy was a white man who tortured and killed young boys after forcing sex on them, and he wasn't choosy about the color of their skin. Most of his victims wound up under his floor in concrete. But this guy wants his victims found in humiliating circumstances, tossed out like garbage. He doesn't want to hide the results of his . . . his labor."

"We'll have to convince Lucas. He still believes the killer is a black man. In fact, he still believes it's Hobbs."

Kim snorted derisively into the phone. "Franklin Hobbs may be guilty of a good deal of crime, like our friend Toombs of the other night, but Hobbs isn't the Snatcher."

"Lucas is a born hunter, a Cherokee tracker, and once on a

scent . . . well, let's just say he can be stubborn and tenacious and persistent as a . . . any predator, and like most of us, his best qualities, the qualities that make him who he is, can and often do become his worst qualities."

"Gotcha. But with both of us working on him, maybe we can convince him to start on another set of tracks. We'll begin tomorrow. Sorry I disturbed you. Needed someone to talk to, bounce ideas offa."

"Don't mention it. Glad I could help. Any time, night or day. This case has me twisted up inside, too."

"I called Lucas's place before you."

"And?"

"He's out."

"Damn fool's likely staking out Hobbs's place."

"Could be. Well, see you in a few hours at your office?"

"Right, and Dr. Desinor . . ." began Meredyth.

"Kim."

"Kim, get some rest yourself. You're going to need it."

"Thanks, I will."

"I admire your work so much," Meredyth finished, about to hang up the phone when Kim stopped her.

"Don't admire me. I've done precious little to help the Coleson boy."

"Nonsense, you've made a greater contribution than any—"

"Just don't let your admiration of me get in the way of doing your job," Kim replied. "Look, do you think . . . I mean, is there any way to get in touch with Stonecoat tonight?"

"Tonight as in now?"

"Yes."

"I think there's a way, yes, through Dispatch."

"Good. I want to kick some of this new information around with Lucas. Get his opinion, any insights."

"Just remember one thing."

"And that is?"

"He's bullheaded stubborn, like I said."

"That's actually an admirable quality in a homicide detective."

Meredyth relented. "True, so long as he's man enough to admit when he's wrong. Problem is, he's too macho for his own good."

"Get in touch, and tell him we need to get back on track as a team, together, tonight," Kim finished. "And call me back when you have a rendezvous point."

"Tonight?"

"Yes, tonight."

Lucas, frustrated and angry, returned to his car, disappointed with Hobbs, who was now watching *Baywatch* reruns and masturbating to images of Pamela Anderson's heaving breasts as the actress streaked down the beach right there in his living room. The police radio installed in Lucas's undercover car crackled into life, the dispatcher hailing Lucas, wishing to patch a call through to him.

Lucas responded, speaking into the mike, saying, "Go ahead, headquarters."

He went on alert upon hearing Meredyth's voice repeating his name. "Lucas? Lucas, are you there, Lucas?"

"What's up, Mere? Why're you calling at such a godforsaken hour?" A glance at his watch told Lucas it was nearing 2:45 A.M. He hadn't slept in a bed for forty-eight hours.

"I just got a call from Kim Desinor and—"

"And?" he mimicked, hurrying her along.

"And, damn it, she wants to meet, the three of us, tonight, now. She's had another vision, it seems, and wants to share the details. See if anything shakes out. Will you meet with us?"

"Your place? Isn't what's-his-face going to be, you know, put out?"

"Conrad is sleeping at his own place tonight."

"Ahhh, sounds like there's hope for you yet, Mere."

"Never mind that. Will you come?"

Lucas took a deep, long sigh before answering. "I might fall out on your couch. That going to be okay with McThuen?"

"Kim has some additional ideas about the Snatcher case, the killer and, I think, Lamar."

Lucas ignored this, asking, "Your fridge well-stocked? I'm starving."

"Yes, damn it, plenty of food and drink."

Lucas finally agreed, wondering if she knew how much he enjoyed making her work for it.

He replaced the receiver on its cradle, thinking how inexorably the movement of time actually was in the face of puny mankind. Death was approaching, riding high on a swift, pale horse of ethereal skin and bone. Death was a soft-skinned woman rider who straddled no truer a horse than that intended for Lamar Coleson. Death and time conspired against a child as a fourth day wound down since Lamar Coleson's disappearance. The clock's unstoppable tick-tock, tick-tock, tick-tock grew faster and faster.

"Meet with Sanger and Desinor," he reminded his now soft mind. "What else you got?"

Lucas loved Meredyth's place, the clean, elegant, white and gray furniture, the white carpeting, the glass all around, the huge wraparound balcony, only the best, and a far cry from his low-rent district. Sometimes he teased her about making her personal fortune on the frailties, weaknesses and suffering of others. She didn't care for that line of teasing, but he did it anyway.

The women plied Lucas with coffee and a Healthy Choice frozen gourmet meal, and while Lucas thought it an oxymoron to say frozen gourmet meal, getting an image of a corpse at the morgue in the freezer when he thought of *frozen gourmet*, he found that the meal wasn't half bad. "I must really be hungry," he told Meredyth, his hostess.

"Thanks, I think," she replied.

After eating, Lucas became more alert, and he listened attentively to Kim Desinor, who read from her latest notes created after Lamar's most recent contact with her. But he again balked at the mention of their prey as being white and not black.

"Wait a minute. For all you know, this could be symbolic,

say, like the killer drives a white Cadillac, a white man's car, or he's white in his politics."

Kim shook her head. "No, I believe the man is white. Lamar sees him now as a white man, and not the black man he presented himself to be on the street during the abduction. It's almost as if there are two men, working in tandem."

"Two men? One lures them in, the other tortures them? The killer has a pimp, a procurer? Is that what you mean?"

"Perhaps, or perhaps the killer is a master at disguise and deception."

"Either way, he's a black man and not a white man. We know that serial killers generally kill within their own race."

"We know that, yes—generally, but not always or exclusively. Gacy did some Spanish and black kids, although most of his victims were same race."

"And there've been others like Gacy," added Meredyth.

Kim lifted the late-edition newspaper she'd found at a nearby newsstand, and she laid the bold front-page headlines across Lucas's lap. "Take a look. We made front-page news."

Lucas scanned the story. He suddenly stopped and shouted, "Wait, hold on, what's this shit about the killer being a black man in his mid-thirties? Who gave them this? Damn it, Doctor, thanks to you, the city could erupt in a war zone tomorrow. I thought we agreed to keep the racial makeup of the killer out of the story."

"It's a good story, and it'll have the effect we want on the killer. He'll get cocky, tell someone something strange, like 'If I did these killings, I'd feel good how I make fools of the cops every day,' or some such remark."

"A good story?" Lucas disagreed.

"Newspapers and wire services are now carrying the profile of the killer alongside stories featuring his victims, their families, the ugliness of it all, and the profile hints at the killer as most likely a black male, possibly in his late teens to early thirties, so—"

"Just hold on, Dr. Desinor. We had an understanding, I thought, regarding the racial thing being put out there."

"No, you hold on, Lucas!" Kim got to her feet and pointed a finger at him. "I said nothing to the press about the racial makeup of the killer."

"Well, neither did I."

"It's just leaked out that way, probably because the usual statistics support the supposition," countered Meredyth.

Both Lucas and Desinor turned their stares on her. "You spoke to the press?" Lucas asked Meredyth.

"It was you who told them the killer was most likely a black male?" asked Kim.

"It was before either of you became involved in the case, days ago, a reporter from the *Sun*, the black community newspaper, or so she said," confessed Meredyth.

Kim fell back into a chair, saying, "I knew I never told the press that."

"Same here," replied Lucas, exasperated. "You have any idea how divisive this information could be on whole segments of people in this city?"

"I simply stated what the profilers in D.C. sent us."

"So, what do we do now, Dr. Desinor?" asked Lucas. "Set the record straight, or rather balance it, by putting your theory of its being a white man doing the killing out there? We put that out and maybe it'll confuse everyone enough that no one'll do anything stupid like they did on the construction site today."

"Boy, Lucas, you sure don't have much faith in human nature, do you?"

"Faith in human nature? Sure, I have faith in human nature; I faithfully believe that human nature is rotten to the core, with a few notable exceptions."

"Oh, great answer, for a juvenile's junior high debut, maybe."

"You want to know what the so-called good guys—the religious right—are saying now about the future of human-kind, and I include all the Holy Rollers and metaphysical lunatics out there who see some cosmic karma descending on planet earth at the millennium?"

Meredyth took the bait, saying, "Really, what are you going on about?"

"Do you hear what they're saying? They're projecting like so many science fiction writers that the human race will reach a state of bliss, total harmony and nonviolence, that we will communicate through pure energy, pure thoughts, and those pure thoughts will be *pure*. But to get to that level of human social evolution in which one sex, one race, one creed, one color and one 'thought language' will prevail, those evolutionary misfits and irregular fits—people like me, I suppose—must all die off or be obliterated by storm, flood, earthquake, hurricane, volcanic eruption, meteor showers, alien abduction—since the good guys become bad if they themselves exterminate the evil seed—and a general cleansing of the earth not seen since Noah's flood will prevail."

Meredyth laughed and Kim stared across at Lucas.

"Mock me if you like, but these people are brutally serious, and they honestly believe that out of natural catastrophes, out of the devastation and vast destruction in which somehow tornadoes know just who to kill and who to bypass, clearly understanding the difference between a Jerry Falwell and a Larry Flynt, for storms are not the works of the devil, nay, but the works of God, as the insurance companies say—acts of God, so that those struck by lightning and drowned by flood only get what they freaking deserve, just like victims of disease and plagues."

"That's absurd," said Meredyth.

"But it's being put out there," added Kim. "I've been the victim of it myself on more than one occasion due to my being a psychic."

Lucas continued without interruption. "Exactly. These small-brained pea heads *would* attack a fine person like you, Dr. Desinor. That's the kind of brainless drivel that's being preached on the Internet across this country, by TV evangelists, shows on Religion Rules Radio, and in countless houses of worshipping minions, from the lowliest fundamentalist pulpit in Pocatello, Idaho, to the Pope and his bishops in Rome. So, you tell me . . . is it me or the rest of the g'damn world's gone freaking paranoid crazy? I mean, imagine a utopia founded on the blood of the degenerate among us, founded on the blood of flood victims, hurricane victims, meteor shower victims who were selected to be weeded out so that once more the 'chosen people' might be left alone to tend to sheep on hillsides dotted in clover."

Kim clapped wildly at Lucas's tirade, shouting, "Bravo! Bravo! I also hate the kind of superficial, bargain-basement piety one can only get from people who read the Bible so literally that they see no beauty or literature or story in the very pages of the prophets who penned the words. These same people live their lives thinking that they can cloak cult-thinking of that sort, and to think that AIDS or an earthquake is justice deserved by those among us who have wronged God in some way. . . . Well, if Jesus were here to defend himself . . ."

Meredyth interjected, "Never talk religion with people. It'll only get you in trouble."

Lucas looked into Kim's eyes, saying, "I'm glad we agree on the one issue, but I can't agree with you on the matter of the killer's race. I think—no, I *know* he's black. I know it in my bones."

"And I know it in my heart that he is white."

"Based on the flimsy images you relate here?" he asked, having glanced over the notes she'd taken earlier.

"Hobbs and Toombs, all a wild-goose chase, right?"

"Ouch!" added Meredyth.

"Well, weren't they?" persisted Kim. "I wouldn't be so pushy under normal circumstances, Lucas, but the Coleson boy's time is growing shorter every hour."

"Don't you think I know that?"

"Yes, I believe so, yes," replied Kim.

Meredyth attempted to referee, saying, "White or black, no matter, the victims felt comfortable around this man, making his abductions as easy as walking off to a candy store down the street. Toombs, Hobbs, the victims, the victims' families, they could all know this man, could all have come into contact with him. White or black, he lives and/or works in the neighbor-hood, and he's still most likely a tradesman or construction worker."

There came a long pause and silence among them then, until Lucas asked Kim, "Are you sure the signals you're getting aren't confused? Mixed-up? I mean, if you think he's an actor, perhaps you're confusing his act?"

"Confusion is part of any vision, but this . . . this recalls the Queen of Hearts killer in New Orleans. There I was blocked by the killer's own sense of confusion. There the killer was confused about her sexual identity. This . . . this monster is somehow different, yet similar."

"Exactly how is he like the other?" pressed Lucas, genuinely interested in the answer.

"He also has deep confusion about his . . . his identity."

"I don't follow you. Is it an emotional crisis? Some other sort of confusion?"

"Meredyth," asked Kim, "what do you think? You're the psychiatrist."

"I see him as angry."

"Just angry?" Kim pursued the question.

"He's filled with hatred, not only toward those he captures and tortures, but toward the world, perhaps—more specifically and unconsciously, perhaps toward himself. He's actually torturing himself."

Lucas snorted and said, "Only wish it were so, then it might be harmless enough."

"But if he's symbolically torturing himself when he tortures Lamar Coleson, then doesn't that point to his being black?" argued Meredyth.

Kim breathed deeply, poured herself a second cup of coffee and replied, "He looks on his victims as if they are the self he wants to excise, I think. . . ."

"You think?" repeated Lucas, upset.

"I think, yes."

"She's on to something here, Lucas," Meredyth said, and

then turned to Kim, asking, "Can you tell us more about your last vision, Kim—everything."

"I've supplied you with the written record of it. It's as complete as I can make it," she explained as Lucas finished reading the report, Meredyth now hunched beside him, looking over his shoulder. Kim saw Lucas appreciatively inhale a whiff of Meredyth's perfume.

"But there're things you can't fully recall, some fuzzy items, right?" asked Meredyth.

"Yes, little scurrying bits of information, images moving away from me like frightened creatures, yes, but there always are."

"Perhaps you might recall more clearly under hypnosis?" Meredyth suggested.

"I have been known to do so, not always, but sometimes, yes."

Meredyth smiled wide. "Allow me to hypnotize you, to dig deeper."

"Time is running short. I'll do it."

"My apartment is equipped with everything we'll need. We'll tape the entire session. Lucas, you can run the video camera."

Lucas agreed, realizing that without Hobbs, they had nothing else to go on.

FOURTEEN

Medicine man's eye: vigilant, wise

Lucas focused the camera and stared through the viewfinder, somewhat amazed at Meredyth Sanger's uncanny ability to so thoroughly put Dr. Kim Faith Desinor under hypnosis; perhaps the ease with which the psychic went under had to do with her being the empathic individual she was, he guessed. Still, he couldn't help but wonder how quickly and efficiently Mere might be capable of putting him under her spell. Just another reason, he told himself, to steer clear of her.

Meredyth had been counting backward, taking Kim to revisit Lamar Coleson and the environment the Snatcher had created for the abducted boy. "Seventy-nine, seventy-eight, seventy-seven," Meredyth now chanted the numbers. "Looking around at your surroundings as Lamar Coleson, recalling exactly every detail when he contacted you, seventy-six, seventy-five, seventy-four, three, two, one—"

"Ahhhh, God . . . the humiliation, the pain . . . pain beyond all feeling . . ." Kim said, her voice a guttural, torturous whine, that of a wounded animal.

Lucas held the camera steady, although he felt his nerves rubbed raw. He, too, felt Lamar's palpable pain and presence somehow through Dr. Desinor's tortured and desperate eyes, which looked blankly past the present moment and place and into another dimension.

"Life not life here . . . as a hostage in the Snatcher's straitjacket. . . ."

"Straitjacket? Tell me about the straitjacket, Lamar. You are Lamar, aren't you?"

"Yes . . . but not a straitjacket . . . more like a jungle net, kind that caught Luke Skywalker and Han Solo and the Wookie in *Return of the Jedi*. Bastard has me all balled up inside it; can't fight back. Woke up inside this rope prison inside this concrete room."

"Do you know where you are, Lamar?"

"No, no."

"What does your jailer look like?"

"Old black man turned white. Can't see him clearly. He keeps my eyes taped."

"Is he white or black, Lamar?"

"He's both, I think. He's a changeling, like in science fiction books and movies."

Lucas looked around the camera at Meredyth, whose shoulders raised at this.

"What do you sense about your surroundings? Anything special about it?"

"It's a big coffin built for me. Cold, damp, dark place."

"Any unusual smells?"

"Animal smells, urine, and every time the monster comes to beat me, I hear animals outside the door trying to get in. I think he's going to let them come in someday and chew me to little pieces. He burns me and beats me and curses at me."

"Dr. Faith, do you detect any subtle items from sounds to smells that are taking on more vividness and resolution?" asked Meredyth.

Kim slowly nodded, her blank expression showing no emotion as she said, "It appears that the killer maintains some sort of animal menagerie. Since Lamar's eyes are covered in a blinding white mask of tape, he *perceives* his tormentor as white. The other possible explanation is that while he is genetically a black man, the killer passes for white, or so the 'vision' tells me."

Meredyth suddenly took the hypnosis from abstract feelings to a more concrete stage of questioning. "How did you get to this place? What street signs do you recall?"

Lamar, speaking through Kim, replied, "A giant cowboy or horseman, a railroad crossing, a burned-out war zone, a magician with a lamp riding a magic carpet, a lost cat in a corridor or castle, a dungeon-filled castle built of enormous cement blocks."

Without warning, Kim shrieked the way one imagines a dying banshee wails, and in an instant her skin became spotted with welts, cigarette burns and small cuts. She began whimpering and crying like an infant.

Lucas turned off the camera while Meredyth brought Kim out of hypnosis. She was sweating and panting from her ordeal, spectral wounds to her wrists, arms, legs and along her bare neck having slowly relented, disappearing like a fading tide under her skin now.

Meredyth had become thoroughly entranced by the wounds, which quickly healed and disappeared altogether. Lucas had caught the welts and blood on her arms and along her neck on camera, but he rather doubted that they would show up on film. He wondered this even as he watched the bruises, welts, tears and burns fade from Kim's skin, tiny droplets of blood staining Meredyth's white carpet, all too real, drying as the only visible evidence that anything awry had happened here.

Meredyth looked deeply into Lucas's eyes for answers, but she found only a mysteriously resigned look on his part at the supernatural stigmata displayed by Kim Faith Desinor. "You won't find answers to this in your textbooks," Lucas guaranteed Meredyth.

"Get it on film," she told him.

"What?"

"The blood. Get it on the tape. I want it on film."

Lucas frowned and replied, "What's the point? None of your snobby colleagues are going to believe it anyway. They'll say it was all a hoax."

"Just do it before it disappears with the rest."

Lucas smiled and made the shots, saying, "Does this mean you're going to quit your day job, take to the desert and the mountains in search of all the metaphysical truths that have eluded you all your life?"

"Shut up and film!"

Kim Desinor, coming back to the present and the geographical center of her being, pleaded, "No more . . . I can't take the pain anymore. . . ."

Lamar Coleson's body temperature went from cold to cold sweat to hot and fevered. Somewhere deep in his brain he recalled sick fevers and illnesses that ran his temperature up and down, but this cold sweat, it was something new and strange and alluring. It was death extending its hand.

Lamar's eyes were taped shut while his mouth and nostrils were left unencumbered so that the monster could hear him squeal and squawk and make horrible noises in response to the torture. He stuffed all manner of crud down Lamar's throat whenever he howled too loudly, making the boy gag on whatever foul and gross matter was pushed down his gullet. Whatever it was, it smelled awful and it tasted worse.

The nightmare of this existence was its pure insanity. On the one hand the monster wanted him to scream, but he punished him for screaming, too—a vicious circle of the monster's making. And Lamar wanted out of the circle, off the madman's spindle, out of reach of pain and feeling and utter despair.

The only reason he hadn't completely shut down was the possibility of sending another clue to his imaginary friend, an angel who this moment searched for him. When she found him, then and only then could he die—then and only then could he go to heaven.

He had felt her—his guardian angel—for some time now. He carefully hid her away from his captor, though, for fear the monster read his mind.

A sudden clattering of locks told him the bastard named Cassell was back for more of his perverted, twisted games—played out on Lamar's body and nerve endings. His captor enjoyed peeling back the eye tape just enough from one eye to show him the latest instrument of torture he intended using on Lamar. Lamar smelled disinfectant and soap on the man, but he also caught traces of animal odors, dog and cat odors, and when the door had swung open, Lamar heard the cackle of birds from somewhere beyond.

Lamar, for the first time, catches a quickly lost glimpse of the monster's hands without his makeup. They are white palms, somewhat young. He is no black man. And tonight's instrument is an electric cattle prod.

Lamar's scream is halfhearted. He no longer has the strength or will to scream as before. He's fast becoming so numb that the monster will kill him, he knows, since he can no longer derive any pleasure from Lamar, because Lamar's body has shut down and is no longer an entertainment for the bastard.

Another shock and Lamar's body reacts involuntarily, going into a spasm, but his throat's tortured scream only comes out as a frog's croak.

At this point the madman opens a bag he has brought into the concrete-walled coffin with him, and he holds the bag up to the rope net and pours its contents over Lamar. It's frogs, a bag of small tree frogs, green and big-eyed. They'll seek out and destroy all the insects and spiders already living in and around Lamar and the net. From another bag the monster pulls forth a writhing snake, telling Lamar, as he had with the frogs, what's coming to live with him in his net. "Don't worry. She's not poisonous, but she'll hunt down the frogs that creep about you and keep you company, Lamar. How's that, huh? Fun, huh?"

Getting no answer, the psycho grunts and pushes the net into a swing, frogs, insects, spiders, snake and Lamar all dangling in a bizarre ecosystem in which the surface of Lamar's skin forms the base.

Lamar hadn't asked the killer why for two days now, but he recalled asking why the madman was doing this to him, and the madman's simple reply had been, "I hate you niggers! I really hate a true, dirty little nigger boy."

Lamar concentrated hard on this memory and the venom in

the killer's voice, even down to the timbre of his voice—a
black voice, he'd thought at the time. He concentrated on this
detail in order to stop feeling the frogs and the snake squirming
about his body and his space. But mostly, he concentrated on
the killer's voice and words in order to send them to his
searching angel. Perhaps the information might help her to
locate him more quickly.

His mind pleaded for her to come again.

It was well past four A.M. now, and well into day four of
Lamar's ordeal.

Meredyth poured them all some more coffee while Lucas
located some Jack Daniels in her liquor cabinet, adding dollops
to his black coffee, offering the whiskey to the others. Kim
thankfully accepted; Meredyth did not.

"I'm ready. I want to see the film," Kim told them.

Lucas quickly took the cassette from the camcorder and
placed it into Meredyth's VCR. Through the TV screen, they
were treated to a clear moving picture of Kim while under
hypnosis. The tape clarified a great deal for them all, especially
Kim, and especially the section of tape that referred to the
details that Lamar may or may not have sent her telepathically.

Using the remote, she stopped the tape at one point to
caution the other two, saying, "These images I see through
Lamar's eyes might well be the wild and useless scatter info
surrounding the case that may be coming from any energy
source, any highly charged, emotionally invested individual or
individuals, maybe even spark thoughts coming off you, Lucas,
or you, Meredyth, perhaps even the random clutter of my own
inner thoughts."

"So such things as a lost cat in a castle may be meaning-
less?" asked Lucas.

"I'm not at all sure, one way or the other—not always."

"*Nothing's* absolutely one hundred percent," said Meredyth,
as if compelled to justify Kim's doubts.

"So, you're not at all sure about any of these fresh images?"
asked Lucas, his frustration coloring his tone. "Not the giant

cowboy, the railroad crossing, the burned-out war zone, the magician with a lamp, riding a magic carpet, the lost cat in the castle, a dungeon-filled castle built of enormous cement blocks."

"Like I said, could be scatter information."

"Scatter? Scatter like airwaves' scatter?"

"Yes, much like airwave debris."

"What kinda psychic is it who won't stand by her own visions or impressions?"

"An honest one, perhaps?" interjected Meredyth. "Leave her alone, Lucas. She's exhausted, and she's been through enough here. She doesn't need your third degree tactics."

Lucas replied apologetically, "Forgive me, but I'm exhausted, too. All the same, I suggest we take your new list of images at face value for the moment and go looking for this animal menagerie or zoo or whatever it is, and we do a scavenger hunt for the other items on the list as well."

"This time of night—morning—and you're going in search of smoke?" asked Meredyth.

"Clues, not smoke," countered Kim. "Psychic hits if we match up this smoke with something real and of this dimension, Dr. Sanger. And for each hit, we come that much closer to locating Lamar. I fear he hasn't even the small amount of time we have assumed left him. I fear he is giving in, preparing himself for death, willing it his way."

"You got that from your hypnosis session?" asked Lucas.

"It's nothing I could pin down, but yes, an overwhelming feeling of wanting to let go, to end it."

Lucas bit his lower lip and replied, "Then we can't assume that Lamar has another day, much less the rest of the week. We've got to find the boy, somehow, today."

"So, the scavenger hunt begins," Meredyth said, twirling her keys. "Your car or mine?"

"Mine," replied Lucas. "I've got the radio should we need it."

"Let's get out there, then, find that cowboy and that cat and the rest. I've transcribed what we're looking for from the tape."

She lifted a yellow legal pad and ripped off the single sheet she'd used to record the salient points in Kim's hypnosis session.

Lucas rose wearily from the comfort of the couch, put down his empty coffee cup and led the way through the door and out into the night.

The all-nighter took its toll on Lucas and the others, and it appeared all for naught, a royal bust. They had again canvassed the two areas that the killer had made his hunting ground in an attempt to follow his footsteps and to seek out signs of the psychic clues Dr. Desinor believed to be coming from Lamar Coleson.

Meanwhile, other FBI and HPD personnel, according to the police band, were on alert to "watch the dump sites"— construction sites—across the city, but in the two suspect neighborhoods in particular. Vorel and others had taken a lie-in-wait approach, which assumed a horrid death for young Lamar Coleson.

Driving through the rough streets of the Jacinto City area, Lucas thought about the sort of mind-set that allowed a man like Vorel to sleep nights. Vorel worked on the law of averages, liked statistical analysis, medians and means. True, it was just this kind of thinking that finally caught the Atlanta child murderer, but this sort of thinking also meant taking a seat and waiting for Lamar Coleson's body to be disposed of by the killer. Fortunately, so far, those working the case had kept this so-called plan under wraps.

Like so many in law enforcement, Lucas believed that once the black community got wind of this policy being followed in the Lamar Coleson case, the lid would blow. At the same time, once the press got hold of it, and the killer read of it, he might well change course, dispose of the body in a wholly different manner, and so remain as anonymous as ever.

"Are we warm? Can you tell us that much?" Lucas angrily asked Kim while they canvassed the last block of the last neighborhood where they thought the killer might be in residence.

"It's not coming to me. I'm sorry, but if I had to say so, I'd say we're cold, very cold."

"And Lamar Coleson? How damned cold is he by now?"

Meredyth shouted, "Lucas! Dr. Desinor is doing all she can."

"If he's a white man, he might not live in this neighborhood," replied Kim, undaunted by Lucas's display of emotion, quite capable of defending herself.

"Maybe then he only works in this or the other neighborhood he's plucked his prey from?" suggested Meredyth.

"I still say he's a black man," Lucas said, taking a final right onto Osborne. "It's black-on-black crime. We know from experience and the numbers that white serial killers kill within their own race and black serial killers kill within their own race, taking the occasional other race as victim only when it's expedient to do so."

"There's always the exception," Meredyth disagreed. "For one minute, think of the killer as a white man, Lucas, and what does that do for you?"

"White man. Doesn't live in the area, then . . . possibly just works in the area as a construction worker?"

"Construction worker, plumber, whatever . . . Go on," she guided.

"Maybe he's a merchant? Runs a grocery, tavern or other business in the area? Does construction on the side? Doesn't live in the area, but he may've grown up in the area when it was predominantly white, moved out? Now he's come back to clean the streets of what he considers scum?"

"All right, so he's a street cleaner? Maybe works for the city? Or maybe he just maintains a business here?"

"The business district. We need to focus on the business district."

"Bingo! What's to say he's not keeping the boy in the basement of a business establishment? We've been focusing on the killer's home, but what about his place of work?"

"We've been assuming that he's in the construction trade

only because he dumps the bodies at job sites, and some of the microscopic evidence has pointed to construction dust and construction tools being used to torture the boys, but there's maybe another reason for the tie. Maybe he's a job supplier, a contractor's supplier, something like that. . . ."

"A vendor of some sort, maybe," suggested Lucas, his eyes alight with a renewed fire.

As they made their way toward the sixteen-block strip that made up the Jacinto business district, Meredyth pointed and called out, stuttering, "Th-the-there's a horseman! Look!"

It was a neighborhood tavern, sporting a large horse and rider as its logo overhead. The establishment was called The Fifth Horseman.

Lucas stared at the sign of a shadowy, dark-cloaked figure on horseback—the very image of death—filling the tavern's overhead hanging sign.

Meredyth said, "It's tattered, beaten, aged, but it's there, just as Kim predicted. Do you feel any warmer now?" Meredyth kiddingly asked Kim.

"No, but let's keep our eyes open for any other signs, shall we?" suggested Kim. "This could be a fluke, a coincidence without meaning. I may even have seen it before on our earlier patrols, and it stayed in my subconscious."

"Read the list of things to be on the lookout for again," replied Lucas.

Meredyth lifted the list and did the honors, reading aloud, "A giant cowboy or horseman, which we've got, a railroad crossing, a burned-out war zone, a magician with a lamp riding a magic carpet, a lost cat in a corridor or castle, a dungeon-filled castle built of enormous cement blocks."

Lucas felt a sense of hopelessness wash over him. Even so, he drove on in earnest toward the center of the city, hoping against hope to find the menagerie of Dr. Desinor's psychic vision.

Just before entering the business district, they had to cross a railroad track, but no one saw anything of a burned-out war zone. Along the business strip here, they hoped to locate additional puzzle pieces, but the pieces were either woefully lacking or the three of them were too tired to be effective. Lucas's head felt like dense granite. His frustration level rose incrementally with the passing of each storefront and street corner without any sign of genies on magic carpets, war zones or cats in corridors. Sunrise began to bathe the gray streets in light, displacing the artificial street light.

"There's still another business area to look into," suggested Meredyth, "in the Bellaire District."

However, the others were not only bedraggled and beat, but without hope, so deep was their disappointment after seeing only the horseman on the tavern sign. Lucas was hardly capable of holding his eyes open any longer. Each of them had been up all night once again; they had to call a halt to the psychic scavenger hunt.

At that point, Lucas drove the two women back to their respective homes and raced away to his own place to catch a nap.

Lucas stumbled the last few yards to his doorstep, found his keys and unlocked the outer so-called security gate, found the elevator and rode up to his room without knowing where he was. Just outside his door someone had left a UPS package. He made his way into his apartment, the parcel in hand. Tired but curious about the package, he cautiously began to unwrap it, not altogether certain that Roundpoint wouldn't put a bomb in his mail.

But as the wrapping safely fell away, Lucas found a computer-generated stack of news clippings inside. From Randy, he decided. Each clipping was dated, ancient, having to do with the "prostitute" murder of Minerva Roundpoint.

Lucas now saw that the green light on his answering machine was blinking, a message or messages to check; he'd been away for some time. He pressed the button to retrieve his messages. The first one had to do with some land he'd been looking into buying near Jackson Hole, Wyoming. The second message came from a friend named Joe Laughing Bear, a reservation cop in Kansas, whose deep, guttural voice on the tape filled Lucas's apartment. "Hey, you old white dog! Why is it I only hear from you when you need a favor? When will you be coming through Kansas territory? I've got some sheep now I raise, and they make great lamb chops. Anyway, ol' buddy, about your inquiry here. Seems Roundpoint's great-grandfather Osheeniwah ran with my great-grandfather, you know, the famous Albert Two Horses, and Albert says he interviewed the old man on my behalf. You ever wonder why the white man doesn't learn what keeps the red man alive to such old age? You'd think they'd get some Harvard genius on that one. Anyway, Albert's message is a long apology for having learned very little, but in his message, there is maybe something you can use, if you're half the tracker they say you are." Laughing Bear paused for effect. "The old man said she—his grand-daughter—went to Houston to escape."

The word *escape* gave Lucas pause.

"Escape reservation life? Albert asked. No, his old friend confided, to escape shame, said the old man. She was pregnant out of wedlock."

"Addled old men talking to one another about perhaps the wrong granddaughter," Lucas told himself and the room. "Minerva was married," he said directly to Laughing Bear's recorded voice, "and nothing was mentioned of a child in the autopsy."

Bear's recorded reply made it seem he was on the line instead of caught in the machine: "And when the body was claimed, mother and child were buried together. You want to know more about the stories told about Minerva and her son, call me. There's much to tell."

Not an uncommon practice among Native Americans when mother and child died together in childbirth to have them share a common grave.

The answering machine beeped three times and went dead, no more messages. How could the autopsy have been so botched that the cutter could miss a child, if it were so? And if it were so, did a shitload of money pass hands to keep the autopsy of the so-called street whore and her murdered child an official secret? That amount of secrecy cost big bucks, Lucas knew. So whoever this Roundpoint character was, he either knew about his stillborn—or rather, murdered—half brother, or not; but either way, he had a lot of hatred stored up for someone.

But then Lucas began to consider the remote possibility that some juiced-up pathologist, who didn't know a hell of a lot back in 1948, may simply have made a shambles of the autopsy. After all, she was just another streetwalker come off the prairie grass.

Lucas spread the packet of news clippings out across his dining room table, then went about peeling off the long day's clothing. As he moved about the apartment, he thought of the possibility that Minerva Roundpoint had lived the last minutes of her life understanding, perhaps for the first time, the enormity of the dilemma she found herself embroiled in, and Lucas wondered if it had anything, nothing or everything to do with her "escape" from the reservation. He knew that if Laughing Bear had anything more than the usual tribal gossip regarding Minerva, he'd call back. No way would he wake up Bear at this hour. Besides, Lucas believed that he had gleaned enough information about Minerva to put the picture into somewhat sharper focus than before: Unable to take care of herself, she left her young son in the care of a drunken husband, pleading for Father Michael Avi to look in on her son, a boy named Zachary, from time to time. Father Avi obviously did a sterling job, Lucas thought facetiously. But Minerva's escape hadn't lasted long before someone caught up with her and recaptured her. Or had her prison been one of her own making? Hard to say from such a distance.

No one save for a handful of people back in Kansas on the reservation would ever know about the child, especially if enough hands were greased. The black robes of graft hid more truth and history than any Anglo textbook.

Whoever murdered Minerva may well have loved her, but he'd also felt vulnerable to attack from her, threatened by her, not unlike the shaky relationship Lucas had with psychiatrist Meredyth Sanger only tenfold, perhaps a hundredfold, given the times. Father Avi? It came to Lucas in a flash. If the good priest had sired a child with a parishioner, he might well have felt threatened by her. But threatened enough to kill?

Consider the times, he told himself. Motive, means, opportunity . . . the old formula rushed to Lucas's mind. If Father Avi's story about how the amulet had magically returned to his altar had been fabricated, then the faithful priest might well have murdered his love to keep the secret of his lust concealed. When she had "escaped" his influence, she may well have felt safe, even that her son was safe, but the priest may have felt betrayed and vulnerable, and sometimes vulnerable people who might otherwise be peaceful, even God-fearing, acted out in dangerous ways.

While it remained pure conjecture, Lucas knew that Avi's guilt or innocence—now taken to the grave with him— depended entirely on the dead man's character. Lucas knew he had to look into Avi's background.

Instead, without knowing it, Lucas fell asleep on the couch, exhaustion and fatigue taking over his body.

Two hours later, the sunlight through the recently barred windows creating a pattern of lines of shadow and light on Lucas's face, he came awake. After a shower, a shave, a change of clothes and coffee, Lucas called Laughing Bear back, asking him to return to Albert and his friend, to push Osheeniwah for more than riddles, to ask him directly about Father Michael Avi and whether or not it was possible that young Minerva could have been carrying the priest's baby at the time of her death.

"Damn, Lucas, but that's a stretch. Father Michael was and still is thought of as some sort of saint among the people. I could get people pulling knives and guns on me for just suggesting he did anything wrong his whole damned life, regardless of the fact he was a man."

"Go lightly, but look into it, will you, Bear?"

"For you . . . no! For Minerva, yes."

"You talk as if you knew her, Bear."

"Every child of the nation deserves our love, Lucas."

"Of course."

Lucas still had the packet of news clippings left him. He'd been too tired to do anything but ignore them earlier, but now he looked closely at the return address. They were indeed from Randy Oglesby, whose cryptic little note covering them said in part, "When're you going to get equipped with E-mail so you can download this sort of shit yourself?"

Lucas stared down at Randy's findings on the Minerva Roundpoint case of 1948: primarily news stories dealing with the gruesome death of the so-called prostitute. Many of the stories were written by one man who appeared to have dug more deeply than others, giving Lucas more details about Minerva, such as where she worked—Pat's All Night Diner— her age—twenty-three (incorrect, as with so much else surrounding the official record)—condition of the body— mutilated but nothing severed.

Lucas, tiring again, carried the remaining news clippings to his bed, where he lay them beside him, taking them up one at a time, reading them as he lay on his back. From the remaining more recent clippings, Lucas learned that the two detectives working the case were both dead. He wondered if the reporter for the defunct *Houston Sun-Sentinel* was alive or dead.

Lucas skimmed all the other stories and learned nothing new before he again fell off to sleep, with the news items still spread across his bed.

FIFTEEN

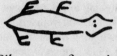

Gila monster: desert sign

Like Lucas Stonecoat, Dr. Kim Desinor also awakes to the light streaming in through her hotel window, but her awakening is to a primordial scream and the pain of the ages. She feels the pain and suffering in breast, genitals and backside. She is awakened to the searing smell of her own flesh burning. And she is awakened to the realization that her pain must be due to the scars of the night inflicted on young Lamar Coleson.

She knows certain facts to be incontestable: Lamar has been burned with some stingingly cold instrument, and that the burns showing up on her own skin are identical. She surmises they are electrical burns from the pattern made against the skin, something she once learned from FBI Medical Examiner Jessica Coran.

Kim struggles now with her suitcase, desperately seeking her Polaroid camera, desperately wishing to get photos of the burns exhibiting themselves on her arms and legs; but like the earlier stigmata, these ghostly marks fade quickly, before she can get them into her viewfinder.

She knows Lamar is hungry, tired, beaten and preparing now to die, to give in to death, and she further knows that he can no longer "send" messages, that he is too weak and brutalized. He shrieks now more for his captor's benefit than his own, as he no longer feels anything.

She knows they must find Lamar *now*—within twenty-four hours—for he has given up all hope, and he is letting go now, dying now. She also knows that if he does not react to the beatings, to the pain, to the burning, then the killer, growing bored with Lamar's lack of response, will in anger kill the boy outright.

He leaves her now, perhaps for the last time sending out his call to his angel of mercy. He's gone now; she knows this.

Tearfully, Kim showers, dresses and readies herself for another day of battle.

"Why so late this morning?" Randy Oglesby asked Dr. Meredyth Sanger from behind his computer screen. *You look like hell*, he wanted to say, *but even at your worst, you're a beautiful woman*, he wanted to add, but instead he asked, "Rough night?" He wondered about her sex life, what she saw in the preppy McThuen, and if she liked rough sex. He seriously doubted she'd had any experience of it since she was with McThuen, but he dared not directly ask her any such questions, allowing them to simply play in the recesses of his overeager mind. She looked a bit shopworn this morning, her hair somewhat unkempt, her usual just-so-immaculate clothing not a perfect match with shoes and purse today. Why was she so *off* today?

"Been a rough night . . . long night," she told Randy, turning his screen on its swivel base to see what he had been working on, only to find him busy at a game of solitaire.

Randy had always had a crush on his boss, and once, faced with the prospect of dying in a ditch alongside her, with only moments of life to cling to during the Helsinger's Pit case, he'd pulled out all the stops and had attempted to make love to her then and there, to feel her body close against his. But that night he learned exactly how strong-willed and how physically strong she was when she firmly rejected both the prospect of death and the prospect of making love to him. She'd thrown him off her and yelled at him and told him—ordered him—to run for help while she ran off in the opposite direction, toward

certain death, in an effort to assist Lucas Stonecoat, who had
lured the killers away from them.

She glared down at him as if he were a child caught in the
act of playing doctor with the neighbor's little girl as patient.
Meredyth reached over the screen and brought up what was
behind the solitaire—the FBI Web site. Meredyth's sharp eyes,
like daggers pointed in his direction, badgered him for an
explanation when the screen showed that Randy had been in
the midst of a search for what, if anything, local FBI officials
had done in the murder case of one Minerva Roundpoint in
1948. The computer showed no FBI involvement whatsoever.
They had no file on her.

Randy swallowed hard as he watched Meredyth's eyes
narrow over the information on the computer screen. "I want
your log-on information up now, Mr. Oglesby. Now!" she
nearly shouted.

The extracurricular computer digging he'd been doing for
Lucas Stonecoat on a fifty-year-old case involving a murdered
prostitute named Minerva Roundpoint must now come to light.
He'd earlier wanted to tell her about Stonecoat's request, how
much he'd involved Randy in the ancient case, but instead he
had kept it from her this long—longer than he ought to have,
he supposed.

"I had every intention of telling you what's been going on
with this, Dr. Sanger, but—"

"When did he make his initial request of you?"

"Day after he asked for the Snatcher files, but this stuff on
Roundpoint was buried. I had to do an advanced search.
Believe me, Stonecoat just got these news clippings late
yesterday."

"I see. . . ."

Randy continued a feeble attempt to soothe her, saying,
"Stonecoat could not have located the news clippings in any
other way—in the usual fashion, that is, since the newspaper in
question went bankrupt in 1959."

"Bankrupt . . . '59," she repeated, her thoughts elsewhere.

"Yeah, the records had gone to microfiche files, but they

were only recently placed into HPD computer files, recent by today's standard, 1987, and the microfiche was then destroyed, but finding the password proved a hell of a problem. It's almost as if someone didn't want the newspaper to ever rise again. But then . . . well, call me Mr. Paranoia since . . . well, since Mother-Brother's been installed . . ."

Randy stopped in his prattle long enough to stare at her, realizing that she'd stopped listening some time back, that she was lost in thought.

Curious, Randy asked, "Everything all right, Dr. Sanger? Dr. Sanger?"

She came out of her reverie, which had been induced by the strangely quaint murder photos and news clippings from the 1948 newspaper. Roundpoint had said that his mother had been the victim of murder, but she had had no idea the brutality involved until now.

Randy asked point-blank, "Dr. Sanger, just how'd you find out about the Roundpoint thing? I installed the Big Prick . . . ahhh . . . Mothership Down, Big Brother system myself, specifically telling it to bypass my terminal under my log-in handle, so—"

"The program is designed to weed out special requests, Randy—even those of Dr. Meredyth Sanger and Mr. Squee-gee." She had always thought his log-in name was cute. "The program continuously downloads information on users. You can't bypass it. No one can, not even the commissioner of police or the mayor of Houston. Everything by everyone gets recorded and analyzed and evaluated."

"By us! Awesome responsibility."

"Not ours for long. Just until the system is up and running and debugged, and that's where your energies are to go, toward debugging the program so it's foolproof, and not toward trying to fool the damned thing! Got that? In a month or so, it becomes the responsibility of Internal Affairs, and it's out of our hands."

"It still sucks."

"I'm afraid that despite all the warnings as far back as

Aldous Huxley's *Brave New World*, this is what cutting-edge technology's come to, to keep you, me and the fence post honest as a court reporter. Else we're back to Helsinger's Pit and Internet intrigue of every shape and stripe. Now, answer my question."

"Damned Mother-shit program's not right, Dr. Sanger. Few things in this life are sacrosanct anymore, and a man's computer ought to be, you know, sacrosanct."

"Answer!"

Randy gave another moment's thought to the new system that he himself had instructed to make an exception in the case of his computer, a system that Dr. Sanger had been told she must manage as part of her precinct duties, a system that kept tabs on who showed up on-line conducting authentic police business and who might be stealing that most ancient of stolen commodities, office time, squandering it on such things as surfing the Net and computer games. The program, aptly titled Mothership Down, was being called by everyone Big Brother Prick. An electronic monitoring program to cut down on unnecessary and unauthorized on-line traffic, this internal "bugging" came as a reaction to the Internet murder ring discovered using HPD computer information two years before.

Since Meredyth and her computer whiz secretary, Randy Oglesby, were highly instrumental in uncovering the unauthorized use of the lines, Captain Lincoln had ironically proposed that her department be responsible, for the time being, for overseeing the installation of the introspective software meant to keep them all honest.

Randy had thought he'd have time to cover his tracks, but he hadn't counted on Dr. Sanger's early morning insistence on seeing how the system was working. She'd stepped directly to his terminal and asked for an immediate display on-screen of all that had gone on in the system the day before. She had to report today to Lincoln on the matter, and then make further recommendations.

It had been Meredyth's idea to create such a system in the

first place, and with Randy's expertise, she felt it represented a simple and easy task.

In reviewing the previous day's traffic on the HPD computers, Meredyth became curious about Randy's having attempted to bypass the system. Once that failed, he had "admitted" to some Net surfing, but the destinations didn't look right. He was digging through ancient history on a case dating from 1948. Randy had downloaded and printed out newspaper clippings covering the grisly murder of a woman by the name of Roundpoint, who'd been hacked to death by her killer. Meredyth also recognized the name of Roundpoint as one of her private-practice clients, Zachary Roundpoint. She had once told Roundpoint about the Cold Room files and about Lucas Stonecoat, saying that she thought they might have much in common, both being Native Americans.

She had told Roundpoint that she might persuade Lucas Stonecoat to allow him an opportunity to look over his mother's murder book, hoping that it might give the troubled man some sense of closure, but since that day's session, almost a month ago, Zachary Roundpoint had simply stopped coming to see her, and she hadn't heard from him since. He hadn't kept their next appointment, not bothering to call, and when she had telephoned the company he allegedly worked for, she learned that he did not work there.

"You mean he's left?"

"No," said the personnel person to whom Meredyth had finally been turned over. "We have no record of a Mr. Roundpoint ever having worked for us. Sorry."

"Ever?"

"Never, Dr. Sanger."

Then he had lied about his place of business. What other lies had the man told? Meredyth hated to be lied to, but she understood lying and its dynamic better than most, being aware of its psychological roots. Lying was nowadays considered part of the new psychology of evil, in which the patient or client can only be helped if he or she can stop thinking that if you can believe your own lies, no one can touch you. Meredyth believed that this in its ultimate form created a situation such as the O. J. Simpson case, in which a killer lies so thoroughly and well to himself that he truly believes in his own innocence, regardless of the evidence and regardless of reality. It had happened before O. J. in the infamous case that spawned the book and movie *Fatal Vision*. Magical thinking or easy rationalization, some called it.

From what she could gather of Roundpoint, he needed to come to terms with what he considered evil in his parentage, and Meredyth had little doubt that such evil existed. In fact, she saw evil parents at every turn, and while media attention brought this ugly social condition more into the light than ever before, evil parents had existed throughout the ages. They could be found in the Bible and in the earliest tragedies. Hamlet had evil running through his DNA. Roundpoint needed to come to terms with the evil in his heritage. Perhaps it represented the most painful, nearly impossible task in human relations, to accept the fact your father, mother or both were simply evil people. In psychotherapy, Roundpoint was called upon to accept this fact of his birthright, and she had squarely informed him that if he could not face this ugly reality, then he would remain a victim, as apparently he had all his life—the victim of abandonment first by an alcoholic father and then by a mother who left him in the care of others, never to return. The only way Roundpoint might move on with his life now was by putting a name to the evil lavished upon him—child abuse, pure and simple. As his therapist, it was Meredyth's obligation to do all in her power to direct Zachary toward this realization, but he had to make it completely on his own. She'd told him that he must give his "affliction" a name, so that he might begin to heal.

She had thought they were making great progress. Obviously not. He'd been lying to her the entire time. How much could she now believe, and how much must she toss aside as part of his fabrications? If he wasn't a salesman, what was he? Who was he?

Obviously, he'd used her. He'd taken what he wanted from

her, and then decided to work around her. Growing up, so far as she could tell, had been a painful isolation for Zachary, but he'd developed his ego boundaries, storing them up, making them firm in large measure by creating his own lies as a defense against reality and the harshness of others—even the well-meaning. He preserved those ego boundaries by making them huge and excessive and unassailable, as any creative mind must do under the circumstances. As a result, he'd paid the heavy price of alienation and isolation from others.

She wondered now what he really did for a living, as money appeared no object to the man. She wondered what his next step might be. Would he continue to work his own brand of therapy on himself, despite the progress they'd made, or was the core of that progress a mere sham, too? When people lived lies to cover the lies and secrecies surrounding dysfunctional families, they often became walking lies—people of the lie, psychiatrist M. Scott Peck called them in his popular book of the same name. And as often as not, this lifetime of ingrained "evil" won out.

In any case, it appeared that Zachary Roundpoint had decided to take a more direct route to the truth about his mother and the manner in which she had disappeared from him. Lucas Stonecoat, apparently, represented that new route.

Doctor-patient privacy had prevented her from speaking of Zachary Roundpoint's unusual case with Lucas, but now that Lucas had obviously been in contact with Roundpoint, she might at least discuss their mutual acquaintance if Roundpoint himself had disclosed to Lucas that he was seeing her in her professional capacity. Thanks to Mothership Down, and her discovery via Randy's computer log, she now had the perfect foyer from which to step into the subject of the mysterious Mr. Roundpoint with Lucas.

She'd sat at her desk, fidgeting with items atop it, while the handsome Roundpoint explored his inner mind in her presence, and she'd made judgments based on all that he had said. Now every judgment must be suspect. Now she wondered at the depth of the coldness she'd felt in him when they first met. She wondered if she'd even begun to chip away at the inherent evil he represented.

All her medical training had not prepared her for such patients as Roundpoint, nothing could. There was nothing about parental evil—much less radical evil—in the standard *Diagnostic and Statistical Manual* used by every psychiatrist in the U.S. Despite the fact that all good psychotherapy boiled down to an old-fashioned exorcism, such notions as Satan and evil had been left to the battlefield of religion. And in the case of Mr. Roundpoint, perhaps he proved that psychotherapy could never tell where the ugly human shadow left off and the black light of Lucifer, the "Light Bearer" and the Prince of Darkness, began.

Meredyth's thoughts were suddenly interrupted when Randy sullenly asked, "I suppose you're going to have my job now?"

"No, nothing of the sort," she countered.

"Then you'll have me before the disciplinary board, and I'll be pissy and shoot off my mouth and then be fired."

"It's not going to happen."

Randy stared at her. He had expected her to be extremely upset with him, but he found her smiling instead. Surprised by her reaction, he, too, began to relax and smile, asking, "What's cooking in the doctor's laboratory?" Randy pointed to his head as he asked this.

"I want you to continue feeding Detective Stonecoat exactly what he wants, Randy."

"What?"

"Give him all the assistance he requires."

"On the Roundpoint murder of '48?"

"On both the Roundpoint affair and the Coleson boy's case." She knew from his eyes that she had thoroughly confused Randy in this matter, but that he couldn't help but be completely relieved that he had managed to dodge a major blow to his position with the HPD, for as a civilian assistant, his replacement waited in the wings, and little or no help from the union would be forthcoming.

Randy had been prepared to defend his position, citing his

job description: Lend support to law enforcement personnel. He wanted in the worst way to spout it aloud now, but something deep inside his brain—the censor chip—told him to keep his lips firmly closed.

She next told Randy to make copies of the news reports he'd downloaded for Lucas for her. "And keep the facts of this matter between us, Randy, and I promise you there will be no firing and no disciplinary action. Deal?"

"Deal, sure . . ."

"How soon can you have those news clippings and all the other information on the Roundpoint case in my office?" she asked, while drumming a pencil atop his computer screen.

"Fifteen minutes, tops."

"Hmmmm . . . fifteen minutes." She stared at her watch, reading it as now 9:50 A.M.

Looking up at her from his seated position, Randy apologetically replied, "It's the printing takes most of the time."

"Make it so."

"Sure, boss." He knew now that the line between them, boss doctor and civil servant with a computer, would never again be blurred. "How 'bout your morning coffee with that?"

"A little late, but sure . . . yeah, thanks, Randy."

With that she disappeared into her office, he supposed to arrange her desk, as she was obsessive about neatness, and there to await her morning coffee and the reports he'd be duplicating for her. Whatever else, he'd been spared, and Randy breathed a deep, full breath of air into his lungs and set about getting Dr. Sanger what Dr. Sanger wanted. Sure, he told himself now, he could get work anywhere with his computer expertise, and someday he might just go out and start up his own consulting firm with a Web page and everything. But he knew he'd miss the action of this place, the proximity to real crime, real cops, the real-world connection. He feared that without a grounding, he might become, as he had been in his youth, just another computer jock nerd whose total take on the world came via the screen.

•   •   •

Meredyth read up on the 1948 Minerva Roundpoint case, out of
professional curiosity, she told herself, sitting back now,
sipping at the last of her late morning coffee and wondering
what Lucas had made of the skimpy information surrounding
the murder. Suddenly she realized that someone stood over her.
It startled her to realize she was not alone. She gasped with
fright to find Mr. Zachary Roundpoint, his eyes like two
shining black beads, staring back at her.

"I knocked but you didn't answer. You must have been
absorbed in your reading," he said, but she had heard no
knocking at her door.

"Where's Randy, my secretary?" she asked.

"He's not at his desk. Summoned away, I suspect. Listen,
Doctor, I just wanted to express my heartfelt gratitude for all
your help. I believe I'm on the right track now, as you Anglos
say."

"You disappear on me without warning or a word, you leave
me with a phony number to call, you lie to me about your
profession and how your mother *left* you and now you're here
apologizing for . . . for what?"

"I was as honest with you as circumstances allowed."

"That's a nifty, handy little phrase. Next thing, you'll be
telling me that you work for the CIA or you're undercover with
the FBI or DEA or something."

"Let's just say 'something,'" he replied. "Look, I know I
should have called, but I didn't want to involve you any further
in . . . in my problems."

"I'm thoroughly involved now," she replied, slapping open
the file of downloaded news clippings given her by Randy
earlier. "Has Stonecoat shared these with you?"

His eyes widened. He didn't know what to make of the
clippings. "No, he hasn't."

"Take my copies, then. Get all the information on the killing
you can, and when you are sated, come back to me, and we'll
talk it all out. You'll be a better man for it. Perhaps you can

begin living life without feeling you have to lie your way through it."

"I'm sorry I've had to lie to you, and thanks for the information. I've been disappointed with Stonecoat's lack of progress, but I didn't know he'd gotten you involved, as obviously he has."

"He likes working alone. He doesn't ask for help often, and he hasn't actually asked for my help, but I've been shadowing him on the investigation when time allows."

"I see. Well, thanks for the news clippings, and again, I offer my apologies to you."

"Where can I reach you?" she asked.

"I'll find you," he replied, leaving as quietly as he'd come, the clippings in his hand.

It must be bizarre to read news clippings of the murder of your own mother, Meredyth thought, trying desperately to imagine what it must be like, what turmoil must be racing through the outwardly placid Roundpoint. Much of the man reminded her of the sometimes infuriating but always admirable Lucas Stonecoat, something about the stolidness, the solid bedrock. She wondered if it were a uniquely Native American trait. But while there was an air of danger and edginess to Stonecoat, that air of danger in this man Roundpoint felt more threatening.

Mr. Roundpoint, in search of his self-identity, in order to bridge the gap of years, had to understand that his mother had not willingly or wantonly abandoned him in infancy. When Meredyth had first learned of the manner in which his mother had "left" him, and when he learned that she had access to police records, they had mutually agreed that he had every right to the file on his mother's murder, but that it must be handled delicately. She'd told him of the Cold Room files and of Detective Lucas Stonecoat, the man in charge of the dead files, and that she would intercede on his behalf, but she'd not done so since the commotion of the Snatcher case had taken her attention away, and since Roundpoint had disappeared.

Now she had seen firsthand just how anxious Roundpoint

was for any information leading, not to his mother, but to his mother's murderer. He seemed obsessed about learning the identity of his mother's killer.

Meredyth recalled the first time that Roundpoint had walked into her high-rise, high-rent downtown Houston office for therapy. He'd claimed to be in great pain and depression over an immense void in his life, and then he proceeded to tell her the story of how his mother had chosen to abandon him as a child, leaving him to fend for himself on an Indian reservation in Kansas where a dying priest named Avi imparted the information that his mother had been driven by great passion to follow a man to Houston, Texas, where she was murdered.

All information regarding his mother Zachary had gotten secondhand from the priest who, along with the tribal elders, oversaw Zachary's education and upbringing. Meredyth, sympathetic to her patient's needs, suggested she could arrange for him to see and review Minerva's case file there in her private office, but then he suddenly stopped seeing her for therapy. Now, on reading the news stories from 1948, and learning of the heinous nature of the woman's death, Meredyth realized just how double-edged the information was, that it cut both ways for Roundpoint, first as an answer to his mother's forced abandonment of him—*she'd been brutally murdered*—but it also raised the input to a level no child should have to bear. The newspaper stories had been news to Roundpoint, judging from his reaction on seeing them, so they'd obviously not been made a part of the murder book he'd already seen. The news clippings, and no doubt the murder book, raised more questions than either answered. Who might have hated the young mother as to butcher her so? Now the handsome Mr. Roundpoint wanted a solution to the added mystery surrounding his mother, and who better to help him than Lucas Stonecoat?

Meredyth fully understood why the mysterious Roundpoint had elicited Lucas's help, but she was unsure why he hadn't asked for her help, to intervene and smooth things out for him. Perhaps it was part of that Indian machismo: God help the redskin who asks a woman for help and support.

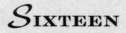

Sixteen

Bear track: good omen

Lucas had sick leave coming, and with the sleep-deprivation hangover dulling his senses, he decided to take the day off, calling in to inform the duty sergeant of his decision. From the newspaper clippings on the Roundpoint murder, Lucas gleaned the whereabouts of the reporter who'd tenaciously stayed with the Minerva Roundpoint story when other newspapermen had long before relegated it to yesterday's trash bin. The reporter whose byline kept coming up in clipping after clipping was a man named Matt Greyson. Lucas at first doubted that the man was still alive, much less in the Houston area, but miraculously, after a few phone calls to targeted individuals, people who would have an interest, such as the DMV and the IRS, Lucas had an address on Mr. Greyson. While the IRS gave out information reluctantly, Lucas was easily able to get Greyson's Social Security number from the DMV when he read off his badge number for the lady at the other end of the phone. Lucas praised once more the modern age of the computer, for it was through the Internet search of Social Security records that Greyson was located, since he no longer drove a vehicle. His current address read: 1218 Hanover Street.

When Lucas arrived, he found a renovated tenement posing as a retirement home. The place, gated against intruders, sported a huge sign reading PLEASANT MOMENTS RETIREMENT CONDOMINIUM, ESTABLISHED 1969.

Lucas gritted his teeth, bit his lip, hoped against hope that Greyson hadn't died yesterday and rang the bell at the security gate. When a cooing, overly friendly female voice answered, asking him to state his business, he said that he was a visitor for Greyson, and without delay, the gate went up, and he drove through to a spacious but nearly empty parking lot. Surrounded by trees now, Lucas found himself looking directly into the guest rooms on this side of the old building, a stucco gray gone green with age and crawling ivy vines.

Lucas found the place strangely quiet and set apart from the bustling city surrounding it, as if noise and dirt and pollution were kept at bay by an invisible shield or cloaking device of some sort. Around the grounds, stone benches and tables of ancient vintage, some with gargoyle images, sat empty and waiting amid hanging willows.

Inside, Lucas found himself being led by a nurse up a flight of stairs, down a winding corridor to Greyson's semidarkened room; Lucas thought the corridors and rooms here were decorated in a depressing manner, much like an old hotel out of the historical Southwest, far too dark and dingy to inspire hope or so much as a smile.

Greyson glowered at Lucas when he entered and as the nurse, in a Pollyanna fashion, informed him of his visitor. "I don't know you. I don't know this man. Who are you? Whataya want?"

"I'm a detective with the Houston Police Department, and I've come to talk to you, sir, about a murder case that you covered as a reporter in—"

"Hell's bells, man! You have any idea how many murder investigations I covered in my lifetime? Be specific!"

"It was 1948. Mutilation murder of a young Indian woman."

"Girl."

"What?"

"She was hardly more'n a girl."

"Name of—"

"Roundpoint. Remember it like it happened yesterday. 'Course, it did happen yesterday in the larger sense, right, Mr. Detective ahhh . . ."

"Stonecoat, Lucas Stonecoat." Lucas indicated the chair beside the old man's bed, and asked, "May I sit?" Lucas's hip and back were both killing him at present. Stakeouts were for the young.

"Sit," replied Greyson. "And tell me what's on your mind."

"Minerva Roundpoint's on my mind. You wrote these articles about her death."

"Death's too nice a word for what happened to that young woman and her child."

"You knew she was pregnant?"

"Not at first, no. It was hushed up."

"I knew it. Payoff, right?"

"Don't get on your uppity high horse, Detective. It was hushed up because in those times you didn't print the grisly details that you now *see* on TV every night. We knew about the child through the coroner's office, but officialdom, and in those days that included the press far more so than today, we had a pact not to discuss the mutilation of the child."

"The child was mutilated, too?"

"Wasn't printed anywhere, but the child had taken seven or eight knife thrusts, directed at it, yeah."

"But there's no mention of it whatsoever in the medical examiner's report."

"Coroner at the time was a know-nothing, low-ranking pathologist on loan from Houston General. He did what he was told."

"And no graft involved?"

"Wasn't necessary in those days. The commissioner and chief tell you to do a thing, you just did it. It was part and parcel of the mentality of the people then; quite another story today, quite."

"But you're saying the PC and the chief of police of Houston both saw to it that a cover-up—"

"Yeah, they were all in on it, and they knew I was being threatened and they did nothing about it."

"Threatened?"

"I could tell you some stories."

"About this case? Go right ahead."

Lucas settled in, studying the aged man before him, tufts of gray hair clinging seaweedlike to his scalp, the patches of bald pate covered in age spots, his skin like crinkled leather, but his eyes a colorful, clear blue and as sharp as two pins. Using his ancient news stories as memory prompters, Greyson again said he clearly recalled the case. But he remained suspicious of Lucas's motives. Wary like an old fox, he asked Lucas outright, "Why are you looking into it fifty years too damned late? At the time, no one gave a damn."

"Not exactly. Someone was extremely interested," replied Lucas, who gave Greyson an explanation of the COMIT program, telling him about the infusion of funds, manpower, machinery, FBI personnel, all of it. He also told the aged reporter that Minerva's case represented a "test case" for COMIT, and to some degree, Lucas felt this to be true.

Greyson studied Lucas again as if seeing him for the first time. He finally began to shake his head and to laugh.

Lucas asked, "Why did you pursue the Roundpoint investigation so doggedly?"

"I . . . I knew . . . I had known her."

"Really?"

"Really."

"In the biblical sense, as they say, or—"

"Don't you dirty her memory, you bastard. They did enough of that in '48."

He's got the year right. "Then to know her was to love her?"

"Something like that. She was a beautiful person, glowing, full of life."

"Did you know she was pregnant before the incident?"

"Hmmmph, incident, another nice euphemism for child murder. Goddamn it, Indian man, it was my child. Of course I knew it."

"Your child? You're sure?"

"She told me it was my child, and she told me that someone else, a guy in the Indian underground, wanted to kill her for having a child with an Anglo."

Lucas wondered how much to believe and how much the old man was fabricating in order to break the monotony of his day and his story.

"I always contended it was some guy from her past, her own people, who killed her, but the cops hauled me in for questioning, thinking I might've killed her since it was no secret I spent a lot of time with Minerva. When I learned about her and the child, how they died, it sickened me. The whole affair sickened me. Ever work a case, Detective, where the corpse had a familiar face?"

"Yeah, matter of fact, I have."

"Then you know how determined you can get on a case when you have a personal stake in the matter. Anyway, Minerva was just a kid herself. I met her at a dive where she'd been working for a few weeks, a place called Johnny Diamond's Cowboy Bar and Grill, or some such shit as that. Anyway, she wasn't any whore like the authorities wanted her to be. Easy to close the case file on a streetwalker in those days, particularly if she was an 'Injun,' don't you know. Cops called it gutter-cleaning."

"Yeah, I got some sense of that from the case file."

"Lack of enthusiasm on a case usually points to greased fingers, graft, so I went at it that way, too."

"Lack of respect for the dead can be accounted for in dollars and cents, you mean?"

Greyson nodded, still a shrewd newsman's mind behind the craggy brow. He studied Lucas's features for a moment before adding, "Any rate, she told me she had a kid somewhere back home, that she was trying to get together enough scratch to send for the boy, and she intimated that she might have a story for me, something *big*."

"Is that right? What else did she tell you?"

"She couldn't talk about it over the phone; said she'd meet

me later that night. Scratched her new address—she'd just moved—on the back of a matchbook, but when I got there, she wasn't home. It was the matchbook that got me in pretty hot with the cops. They were sure I did it, but there was no evidence and I had good alibis. Anyway, when I went to meet her, I waited around for forty, forty-five minutes before I gave up the ghost, as they say. Next thing I hear on the police band at the office the next day is the discovery of a woman's body, that she's Native, and she's sliced up like a tarpon on a Galveston wharf. I raced down there to get the story, and there she was, dead."

"You have any idea what she wanted to share with you?"

"No, but it was an election year, and she said it'd have an impact on the city fathers, if you get my drift. She'd stumbled into something people were willing to kill for, that much I knew, but the cops wouldn't give me the time of day on it, like they were part of a big cover-up, and maybe they were. I was just a kid myself at the time. . . . Miss those wild days . . ."

"Then earlier when you said there was no graft or cover-up, you were what? Testing me and my information? Or were you just being facetious?"

"A little of both." The old man roared with a laughter that escaped the room and roamed the dark corridors of this place.

"How far did you pursue the story before you no longer gave a damn?" Lucas asked.

Greyson righted himself in bed, grumbling about the condition of the place, his sheets, the "bloody" pillows, his own condition—old age and a failing renal system. "You want to hear about the renal system? I've had to become an expert. Funny how a word means nothing until it applies to you. Seriously, I could tell you all about renal arteries, renal biopsy, renal cortex, renal diet, renal cell carcinoma. . . ."

Lucas, unsure what to say to the obviously once rugged, handsome old man, stuttered and fell back on cliché, saying, "And I thought I had troubles."

The old man laughed at Lucas's words and the way he said them. "You? Troubles? Wait a minute, hold on there. You . . .

are you that cop they knighted for having brought Judge Charles Mootry's murderers to justice?"

"I killed all of them, if that's what you mean."

"Better justice than sitting them behind bars for twelve or so years and then releasing them for being good boys and girls, like they're doing today. My day, once a killer was taken off the streets, he stayed off the streets."

"What about my question, sir?"

Finally, he again looked into Stonecoat's level eyes and said, "I stopped working on Minerva's case when first my city desk editor suggested I do so, having had a call from the police commissioner, and secondly when I was put in the hospital for continuing to sniff out the real story."

"Then you were actually warned off? By police personnel? Are you sure the commissioner of police was involved?"

"Warner Solby, a Texas good ol' boy," reminisced Greyson, "a politician's politician. Hardly clean. I don't know. Maybe he was, maybe he wasn't, but somebody ordered someone to run me off the road and someone ordered the attack on me."

"Attacked? Run off the road?"

"A broken arm, broken ribs, damned near hobbled me for good."

"Who did it to you?"

"Cops . . . maybe . . ."

"The guys working the case?"

"Maybe . . . I kept embarrassing their asses in the press. Yeah, they were fired up enough to take me down, but I never had a chance to see any faces. They caught me in a dark place, a setup. Ran me off the road. My head was bleeding all over the steering wheel. . . . I was dazed. Call from an informant said he knew why Minerva Roundpoint had to die, and I was on my way to meet the informant, but there was no informant, I figure."

This was all far more than Lucas had bargained for. He had previously viewed Minerva's wounds as inflicted by a jealous, perhaps outraged lover, but now this nasty little political angle grew tentacles. "But you aren't a hundred percent sure it was cops who put you out of commission?"

"Could've been some wharf rats hired by the party or parties who had paid so much green to keep the heat on me to drop the story. Fact is, if they were cops, they were native to the area. All of 'em spoke Spanish to one another with a few Native Indian words interspersed. One of them spoke like he had a knife lodged in his throat, real gravelly, coarse-sounding. Remember the voice like it was yesterday. Says in my ear real coldlike and spitting, while I laid there in my own goddamn blood, says in English, 'You a damn good newsboy, man, and I admire your style. You got guts. You got the gift of gab, but you ain't going to gab about Minerva no more. *Let sleepy dogs sleep.*' That's what the bastard said. So then I get this theory—"

"Theory? What theory?"

"That Minerva paid one hell of a price, that of our child, the only child I ever had before or since, for whatever it was she knew. She certainly scared hell out of whoever killed her."

"So you believe Minerva was killed due to some information she had on someone in high office?"

"High office, right. Someone in a position to control the police, so naturally Warner Solby was in the middle of it, yeah."

"So they wash away anything to do with the murder of the fetus because they want the official reports of the autopsy about a child in the womb to stay out of the newspapers, and you obliged them. You said nothing about it in your newspaper."

"Covered up. Too gruesome, the city editor said. So, as for the coroner's office, at the time it was an elected office. The guy was no Quincy. He wasn't even an M.E., like I said, just a hospital-certified pathologist, making twelve grand a year, and his office was an extension of the Houston Police Department, pal, not independent like it is today."

"So, we're back to graft." Lucas considered all the ramifications of what Greyson had to say.

"It's all I know, except for this one shady operator who ran the Spanish and Native American Mafia at the time. Name was Noussaint, Alvarez Noussaint, as I recall, a dangerous thug and self-made doer and shaker in Houston. Minerva knew him through a friend, some guy she had known back on the reservation in Kansas, said they were once lovers, her and this guy."

Lucas's heart almost leapt from his chest. Greyson must be talking about the man that Minerva had left the reservation for, following him to Houston, the man she'd given her heart to and abandoned her son for. "Tell me everything you know about this other man, the one she knew on the reservation."

"She didn't say much about him. Seemed bitter, angry about the fact he had gone to work for this Noussaint character. She once told me that Noussaint turned people to evil, and that he was the devil's own child, and that she had information about him that could topple him. Of course I was interested, but she had nothing on Noussaint, nothing usable. I'm sorry to say I kinda, you know, teased her about it. Next thing I know, she's murdered, and I knew that Noussaint had enough clout to control City Hall and the police commissioner combined, but I was alone and clearly marked. I dropped it out of . . . out of cowardice, I suppose. I didn't want to die like Minerva did. Moved away for a while. Came back years later and already the incident had been forgotten."

"Do you know the name of her friend who'd become involved with Noussaint?"

"No . . . couldn't tell you the guy's name. She'd been intimate with him, though, and he was making good money in Noussaint's organization. For a while, she accepted his charity of clothes and rent, but she couldn't live the life he wanted, so she left him. She never wanted to talk about him."

Lucas pulled forth the amulet that Roundpoint had left with him, asking Greyson to take a good look at it—unnecessarily, for Greyson's eyes grew big at the sight, and he said, "That's . . . she wore that all the time, even when she was naked. Showered with it."

"The night she was killed, was it found on or near her body?"

"No, least I never heard. I always assumed some bastard at the scene stole it off the body. How'd you come by it?"

"Her son, the one she left on the reservation. Somehow it got back to him. Left on the altar at the reservation church."

"I'll be damned." He reached out and touched the necklace as if it were a religious icon; he seemed to draw a mix of wonderful and painful memories from the turquoise amulet.

Lucas stood, took the old man's hand and said, "I think you're a brave man, Mr. Matt Greyson, and obviously a survivor."

"Only because Alvarez Noussaint thought me insignificant."

Lucas dropped his gaze. "Maybe I'll go have a talk with this Noussaint character."

"You'll never find him, unless you search hell. Disappeared, presumed dead. Before there was Jimmy Hoffa, there was Noussaint. Body missing for a decade. Where've you been?"

"Dallas."

"Oh," he replied, as if the single word explained all.

Lucas didn't want to leave the old man without learning more. He wanted to know more about what sort of information Minerva Roundpoint had had that she died for it. He further wondered if the man who killed her knew that she carried a baby, wondered if the man who killed her had inadvertently let slip some pillow talk that had cost Minerva her life, wondered if the man who killed Minerva—and not Matt Greyson—could have been the father of the unborn child.

Lucas suggested as much to Greyson, who sat in numbed silence. "You intend to pursue this wherever it leads?"

"I do, sir."

"It could get you killed. Me, I don't much matter, seeing as how I'm at death's door anyway, but what about you? You willing to die for the truth, to demonstrate real courage, Mr. Detective Stonecoat?"

"I am. . . ." Lucas waited over the man's bed, his eyes insistent.

"I've lived with the same and similar thoughts as you now carry about the case, but no one wanted to hear it then."

"Now's the time to right it."

"There's a guy," Greyson suggested, "another guy she was seeing at the time."

"And you knew about him?"

"I couldn't say no to her. We argued about the other guy, but she felt, I don't know, connected to him, tied to him; but again, according to police, he had an airtight alibi, sworn to by a host of others. Seems he was hundreds of miles away, visiting his boyhood home, the reservation where she had lived in Kansas."

"The man's name?"

"A part-Indian Mex named Torres. I never met the guy, but I was suspicious of him. Bastard went on to become a major player in the underground here in Houston. Has a record, but nothing that ever stuck. Today, he heads the Native American end of the Mafia here. He took over when Noussaint 'disappeared,' or died of cancer, or whatever, but who knows. You go looking into this guy's background, though, son, and you could find yourself in a grave without a pine box."

Lucas knew of the stories of how the cacti and sagebrush in the desert flourished because the desert was littered with the good minerals provided by the untold number of bodies buried there.

"Will you be going to see Torres?"

"I will."

"He's a dangerous man. Don't turn your back to him."

"Thanks again, Mr. Greyson, for your time and honesty."

"It doesn't come without a price, Detective. Just be careful or that price will become too high. A week before she was killed, I had told Minerva that I couldn't help her expose Noussaint in my newspaper without solid proof that he had committed a crime, despite what the whole city knew—that he was a murdering, thieving son of a bitch. I told her to forget it, to leave it to the authorities, but obviously she did not heed my advice. My theory is that she somehow got hold of incriminating evidence against Noussaint through Torres, but it's all conjecture. . . . Still, I've had a lot of years to think it over and over and over. . . ."

Lucas shook Greyson's hand, bid him farewell and then quickly exited the depressing retirement condo. The open air of the brightly lit world outside refreshed Lucas's every sense, and from the corner of his eye, he saw a dark limousine pull away from the curb across the street, someone inside it marking him. He'd like to follow the sons of bitches, whoever they were, pull them over and confront them. He didn't care to be tracked like an animal. But a glance at his watch made him realize it was already time to meet with Dr. Desinor and Meredyth Sanger at Meredyth's downtown office.

He climbed into his car, gunned the engine and raced off for the rendezvous with the two women in his life.

SEVENTEEN

Ward off evil spirits

Lucas, Meredyth and Kim greeted one another at Dr. Sanger's downtown psychiatric offices to go over the Coleson case evidence once again, and for Meredyth to hypnotize Kim once more.

"If you're feeling up to it, that is," said Meredyth.

Kim took in a deep breath and said, "We must continue to try, but I'm fearful that Lamar has shut down."

While Lucas again taped the session, Meredyth worked quickly to get Kim under, her voice soothing and mellow, Lucas finding himself wanting to succumb to the suggestion of floating off to the netherworld Meredyth's words promised.

Then suddenly Kim was again *inside* the Coleson boy's suffering skin, alone with the devil that tormented Lamar. Dr. Desinor screamed, realizing that she was covered with spiders, all crawling over her burnt flesh and open wounds. "I can't take any more! Let me go!" she shouted.

Meredyth acted quickly, loudly asking Kim to focus on the sound of her voice and her questions. "What does your tormentor look like? What is he doing? Where is he standing?"

"Just outside my cage—rope cage. White hands filled with crawling things."

"Step away from Lamar, Kim, and step into his tormentor's skin. Tell me what you feel inside the killer's skin."

Kim went silent for a long moment. Dr. Sanger asked Kim again to switch her point of view, to focus instead on what was going on in the mind of the man tormenting the boy.

"He handles the animals and insects with more care than he does anything else, almost a reverence for any life other than human life. He has white hands."

"Are the hands gloved?"

"Maybe . . . perhaps . . . can't tell for sure."

Kim Desinor suddenly felt spasms of pain washing over her as she again felt the boy's suffering and pain. She could not reveal any more, not even while under hypnosis, so long as the excruciating pain blurred her sight.

Reluctantly, Meredyth brought Kim back from the abyss, giving her the commands to return to the here and now.

Thoroughly exhausted, Kim drank a tall glass of water Lucas had fetched from Meredyth's desk. The threesome decided they must look further into the idea of the animal menagerie. Obviously, the killer had access to animals and spiders and reptiles.

"Got a phone book?" Lucas asked Meredyth, who instantly produced one.

Lucas began riffling through the pages as if it were a comic book, each turn another slap. "Why not animal shops, pet stores, that sort of thing? If he's got so many pets, from snakes to spiders, then he has to purchase them somewhere."

"There's got to be literally hundreds of pet stores in greater Houston, Lucas," returned Meredyth.

"We concentrate on those in the vicinity of the killer's geographic boundaries, as before, but now we concentrate on pet supply stores. The coroner said he found traces of fish food in the throats of the victims, remember?"

Kim smiled, nodding her approval and saying, "Now you're thinking more clearly."

"Like a detective," agreed Meredyth.

"A little rest can do that for the brain," countered Lucas.

Meredyth's phone rang, and at the other end was Randy Oglesby. "I'm calling from County General."

"What, Randy? What happened?"

"I was attacked, and I think it was your Indian friend of this morning, that Roundpoint character."

"Roundpoint? Attacked you?"

"Knocked me cold, several stitches to the scalp! Cranial hemorrhaging now under control, but if Patsy Walker from Personnel hadn't come up to flirt . . . Well, let's just say I'd be toast by now."

"That bastard hit you over the head? For what?"

"I think he got into the police computer, searching for something. I'm heading back to the office now to check it out."

"I don't know what to say, Randy. Lucas Stonecoat is investigating the case. I'm going to put him on with us. He's here with me now."

Kim Desinor, ignoring Meredyth's phone conversation, was saying to Lucas, "All the same, the animals and insects could be mere symbolic representations of the various wounds inflicted on Lamar's body, so we need to go cautiously, Lucas."

But Lucas had been half listening to and monitoring Meredyth's conversation, his ears having pricked from the moment she used Roundpoint's name. "Just go through the book. See if anything clicks," Lucas suggested, handing the Yellow Pages over to Kim and joining Meredyth in a three-way phone conversation.

"Did you see Roundpoint? Could you make him in a police lineup?"

"No, not really. A guy just stepped into the office, and I kept focused on what I had on-screen, working, you know, and next thing I know they're scraping me up off the floor. Bastard hit me with some sort of metal pipe, they think, or maybe a long hog-leg-styled gun barrel. Put me right under—under my desk. Then he stripped the system of anything to do with Minerva Roundpoint. That's been confirmed per my request. That's how I know it was Roundpoint."

Lucas's eyes shone with realization. "He shadowed me to Greyson. He talked to Greyson, no doubt."

Meredyth screwed up her face, asking, "Greyson, the reporter on the '48 case?"

"One and the same."

"How did you find him?"

"That's what I do, remember?"

"So, you think Roundpoint followed you there and took from Greyson the way he took from Randy?"

"Yes, I'd better call Greyson . . . See if he's okay."

"Why don't you do that. But in the meantime, it appears that Roundpoint may not be whom he claims to be. I've caught him in several significant lies now, so we don't really know who we're actually dealing with here, or if he wishes to destroy all record of Minerva to protect her memory—which I doubt—or to protect someone from her memory."

"Like his employer, maybe?"

"What do you know about his employer or his line of work?"

"He's a paid assassin, a hired gun, a killer for hire."

"Jesus, I didn't know."

"I told the bastard to back off, to let me do my job. Now it appears that maybe he's just been using me in order to locate his target. I may have gotten Greyson killed. Meantime, he's going around destroying evidence. Jesus!"

"What?"

"The Cold Room file on Minerva. It's still down there. I put the file on computer with Randy's help, but I held on to the original and returned it to its shelf in the stacks. If Roundpoint's as smart as I think he is, he won't overlook the original file. He'll be down there looking to destroy it. I've got to get the hell over to the precinct at best possible speed, now!"

"Go!" said Meredyth. "But be careful!" she further admonished him as he was going through the door. "I'll get someone at the precinct down to the Cold Room to seal it off!"

On the wild, siren-blaring ride from Meredyth's to Precinct #31, Lucas had Dispatch put him through to Greyson's retirement condo switchboard. He demanded to speak with the man.

"Sorry, sir," came the controlled but sad voice of a female on the other end, "but Mr. Greyson died a few hours ago."

"That's crazy. I was just talking to him a few hours ago."

"It happens that way sometimes, sir."

"I'm a Houston police detective, and I'm ordering you to hold the body and hold the man's room for crime-scene analysis. He may have been murdered."

Shocked, she replied, "Murdered? Kindly old Mr. Greyson? Murdered?"

"It's a possibility, yes."

"But we can do nothing about it here, not now."

"Whataya mean?"

"The coroner's office picked up the body, gave its blessing that Mr. Greyson had died peacefully in his sleep, in his bed. Funeral arrangements are already being made by his next of kin, and there was no evidence of foul play or abuse perpetrated on the man, so . . ."

"Where's the body now?"

"Flynt's Memorial Home on Eustis."

"Do you have their number?"

"Of course, we do a lot of business with Flynt's."

"Give me the number, now!"

"No need for rudeness, sir."

"The number!"

Lucas then had Dispatch contact the mortician at this place called Flynt's to do nothing whatever with the body until another medical examiner had an opportunity to check for foul play.

Lucas then cursed himself for a fool. If Roundpoint needed a greater patsy, he need only look up Lucas Stonecoat. The bastard had wanted Greyson from the beginning, and the story he concocted about being Minerva Roundpoint's abandoned son worked like a charm. Lucas felt like a fool, but all he could do now was to get over to the Cold Room and preserve that file.

He momentarily wondered how Greyson had died, and if Greyson, in his last moments, had cursed Lucas Stonecoat for bringing the Angel of Death to his doorstep.

When Lucas got to the Cold Room, he lifted his key to the back basement door, but found the lock had been cut off by someone using bolt cutters. He pulled his gun and entered the darkened corridor leading to his Cold Room.

In the shadows, just outside the Cold Room, Lucas saw the outline of a tall, angular man, and he lifted his gun, ordering the man to put up his hands.

"Stonecoat? What the hell're you doing pointing a gun at me?" It was Captain Lincoln. "Holster that weapon now, Detective."

Lucas saw no one but Lincoln, and so he lowered his weapon. But he kept it at the ready, kissing his hip there in the dark. "Put it away, I said," Lincoln repeated. "I got a call from Dr. Sanger that you suspected a break-in down here. Officer Meany and I came down. Meany's on the inside and will remain there until I say otherwise. Meantime, it appears nothing's been touched."

Lucas wondered about the lock, and if Roundpoint had come this way first, and then made his way up to Randy's office. If so, he'd had the original file from the get-go, and short of finding Roundpoint and killing him, they weren't likely to ever see Minerva's file again. Someone had paid big bucks to see to it all, to hide a dirty little secret in a better place than the Cold Room. It seemed probable that someone, learning of the new COMIT program feared that Minerva's file might be reopened.

Lucas saw Lincoln's eye twinkle in the semidark corridor, and for a split second, Lucas wondered if Lincoln could be dirty, if he could be on someone's payroll, if he had something to do with seeing to it that both the file and an ancient, decrepit reporter remembered by no one should both disappear from existence.

"Lucas, you've given over all your time to this Snatcher case, and now someone's supposedly interested in locating and destroying a Cold Room file. I think it's time I got a full report on my desk regarding just what's going on around here."

"Just a report of a break-in, sir, a possible break-in. I'll have to inventory everything before I know one way or another if anything's been taken."

"Be that as it may, where does all this leave the COMIT

program if we can't commit ourselves to cooperation with the FBI? You've placed the entire project in jeopardy, Stonecoat. Do you realize that?"

"I'll give Vorel a call."

"You'll do more than that. Get over there and do some major ass-kissing, Detective, now!"

"But sir—"

"No buts. Just do it." And with that, Lincoln stormed off, leaving Lucas to watch his wake.

Lucas then opened the Cold Room door and stepped inside, expecting to be greeted by Meany, a large, robust Irishman with a red-splotched face, a man who liked his drink. But the silence in the room wasn't total, and Lucas realized that someone was here, hiding in the shadows of the stacks—and Francis Meany it was not. "Who's there?"

Lucas took tentative steps toward the shadows ahead of him, his 9mm. Glock now back at the ready, when suddenly he felt the barrel of a gun pressed against the back of his head and heard the roll of the gun's chamber. "Hold still, amigo," came a sinister voice.

A second masked assassin stepped from the black far wall and stared with luminous black eyes, the eyes of a local tribe. "You're a dead man, Stonecoat, if you continue to pursue the Roundpoint case," this one said. Then he spoke to his partner, saying, "You'd better relieve Detective Stonecoat of his gun, Jorge."

The first assailant slammed the butt end of his gun into Lucas's head, and Lucas went to his knees, his gun skittering along the stone floor.

Lucas heard laughter. Dazed, he heard the second thug say, "That's much better. An Indian dog should be on all fours, right, Jorge?" More laughter followed.

"Who? What the—" As Lucas attempted to get to his feet, he was again struck, this time a terrible second blow with the pistol, knocking him back down.

"Stay down, Cherokee dog, fool," advised the man in charge. Turned around now, in the periphery of his vision, Lucas saw a third hit man in the doorway, a jeweled necklace around the man's throat. But his face remained in shadow. Lucas wondered if he'd been set up by Lincoln, but he had to concentrate now on his assailants, every detail. He studied the man in the doorway, his height, build, possible weight. Lucas's eye fell on a huge diamond ring on the man's left ring finger and another on his pinkie finger.

"Stay out of the past, Indian. Live for the present only. It is not a good day to die for no cause," said the boss man, mimicking an ancient Indian saying.

The other man, as if on cue, uncocked his gun, but the muzzle still rested on Lucas's temple.

"All right, all right, whatever you want," muttered Lucas, blood streaming over his black hair. It was a promise made in order to remain alive.

"If you don't, that pretty little police shrink friend of yours may get hurt next," threatened the man in charge, his accent clearly a mix of Spanish and Native American, Lucas decided. "As they say, let sleepy dogs sleep."

Immediately, Lucas realized that this was the same man who'd threatened Greyson with death in 1948, and possibly the man who today had quietly and efficiently murdered Greyson, that perhaps Roundpoint had had nothing to do with Greyson's death after all. But who was this self-righteous bastard killer?

The boss man added, "Remember this day, amigo." The man then revealed an arthritic limp as he moved away from the shadows and out the door, while his thugs left with lithe, quick movements, the last one sending a booted foot into Lucas's cheek with a ferociousness that drew blood and brought on nausea and dizziness.

Lucas couldn't help but feel a distasteful but grudging admiration for the very men who'd assaulted him, for the hooded assassins had a great deal of coup to count—quite gutsy to storm into a police precinct this way and rough up a detective, threaten him and people he cared about, only to nonchalantly back away from the room.

Lucas's eyes focused on Francis Meany, Lincoln's idea of a

guard for the Cold Room files, lying in a corner. He wondered if Meany were dead or not. Then he saw Meany's chest heave in and out, and he knew the burly cop would be all right.

Now, recalling anew what Greyson had said about his Spanish-accented assailants, and the line about sleepy dogs, Lucas instantly propelled himself from the tiled concrete floor and grabbed his loaded weapon from the corner where it had skidded. He instantly regretted the sudden movement. His head splitting with pain, he fought back the agony to clear his vision. Still, he staggered crookedly to the door, snatched it wide and peered down the corridor leading to a service elevator, a stairwell, some storage rooms and an alley exit, which until recently had been nailed shut. Lucas had earlier pried the damn thing open and had placed a padlock on it. He'd taken to using the exit as an easy out at those times when he might go out of his mind if he stayed a moment longer in the Cold Room. Lately, it had also become an easy access door *to* the Cold Room as well. He had arranged for the door to be usable as a convenience, and that convenience had nearly gotten him killed.

He went darting for the exit, tore open the heavy door, his head still throbbing like an inflating balloon, threatening to burst with the pain inflicted there. As he fell forward onto his knees, his gun clenched tightly in his fist, he watched the long-haired Indian man get into the passenger's side of a well-polished Cadillac that sped away as Lucas blacked out.

Randy Oglesby had been working in the mainframe computer room when someone had gotten into his terminal and stole the Minerva Roundpoint news clippings, and whoever he or she was, Randy could not imagine. He, assuming it was a guy, did sterling hacker work; no doubt he was hired specifically for the job. Only hours before, that creepy guy Roundpoint had been in the office and had attacked Randy, sending him up to County General for stitches. Now back at the office, Randy wondered if Roundpoint or someone he had hired had done the thievery.

It had been from the mainframe room that someone noticed

the activity on Randy's machine, and once it had been pointed out to him, he ordered an immediate stop on any information going out from his terminal, because Big Brother indicated something was being tapped in to and deleted, using Randy's code name, which every freaking person in the precinct could get hold of now that it was printed out on scads of reports allowing traces to be done on every employee and cop using the computers.

Randy had sworn up a blue streak, racing for his terminal, but when he got there, the machine hummed peacefully with no one in sight. Now Randy had returned to the mainframe room, in search of anyone who might know something or help him to establish just what had been lost and how irreparable the damage might be. He'd originally come here to "fix" the Big Brother program so that his time and activities *couldn't* be monitored. Randy detested knowing that everything he did was monitored whenever he logged on to the Net or did any internal or external E-mailings. The bastards might just as well bug the fucking walls, he'd told his friends in the mainframe room, all of whom agreed, but none of whom wanted to help him do anything about it.

He'd worked it all out on paper, and he was certain that it must be possible to debug his terminal, but he also had to set up the proper bypasses necessary to fool Big Brother—or Big Mother, as the case seemed to be.

From where Randy stood, working and discussing the matter with a fellow computer expert, he could look out on a building just opposite the alleyway, and in the reflection of the windows, he now saw three black-clad men rush to a Cadillac, all wearing masks, and then he saw Stonecoat burst through the door and fall flat on his face.

Randy raced to Lucas's aid, calling a couple of uniformed cops for help as he ran through the precinct corridors for the back alley behind the Cold Room.

Lucas, dazed and confused, his head wrapped in a turban bandage, his jaw aching where the boot had struck him, came to, only to become further confused to find himself stretched out on Meredyth Sanger's couch with a cold compress on his forehead. He raised his hands and grabbed Meredyth's in his own, telling her, "Quit fussing over me. I'm all right, damn it."

Meredyth, who had been hovering over him with words of motherly encouragement, frowned now and pulled back.

"How did I get here?" he asked.

Randy replied, "You had a nasty go-round with some bad dudes who disappeared in a limo."

"Did you get the license number?"

"I was too far away . . . sorry."

"You were talking gibberish when Randy got to you. Something about Roundpoint's not being the killer although he was hired to kill?" said Meredyth. "And you tried to stand, but you passed out again, according to Randy. We only arrived after he and some uniformed officers helped you back inside. Kim and I had just come to find you."

Lucas saw that Kim Desinor stood nearby, concerned as well. *Now she, too, knows my secrets*, he thought. "I took a pretty severe blow to the head, but I'll be fine."

The lie didn't convince Kim Desinor, who stared at Lucas. Again, almost in a whisper, an inner voice said, *She knows about the blackouts. One word to the right people and she controls your future.*

"Randy," began Lucas, his eyes still pinned on Kim as Meredyth, worried sick, still hovered over him. "Randy, tell me what you saw, precisely. How many were there? What were they wearing? How were they built? Color of skin, hair, all of it."

"I think there were three, four maybe, if you count the driver, but it happened so fast. They wore black and they all had long, dark hair, black or brown. As for their sizes, it varied, but two of them were goons for sure. I was too far away to see their eyes or smell anything on their collective breath. Again, sorry, but I didn't get my ass kicked, either."

"What's going on, Lucas? And what's this got to do with Roundpoint?" Meredyth asked point-blank.

Lucas looked past her and into the psychic eyes of Kim Desinor, and something there told him that he was among friends. He relaxed and relented, telling them all that he knew, qualifying his remarks at every turn with apologies for knowing so damned little, and asking Randy to check the wire services for any news on the death of Matt Greyson. He told them of his visit just that day to speak with the elderly man and what he'd learned from speaking to him. The information given him by Greyson had only created new twists in an already twisted trail, and he was no longer sure of Roundpoint's position in all this, unsure even if the man calling himself Minerva's son was really who he said he was.

Lucas explained further, saying, "Roundpoint—or the man calling himself Roundpoint—well, it could all be a ruse to murder whomever might be at the end of this twisted trail."

"What're you saying? Zachary Roundpoint, the man who came to see me for help, appeared gentle, kind, like a lost child."

"That's precisely what he wanted you to believe, Meredyth. The man is in fact a self-styled hit man, an assassin. Whatever reasons he's given you for wanting to know more about his mother—if she indeed is his mother—are suspect," Lucas warned her. "He just used you."

Meredyth shook her head, unable to accept this.

"Knowing of your connection with the police, he used you to get to the file and me."

"And whoever these three thugs were today, they were decidedly local men, Native American, possibly Spanish or of mixed blood, and they have lots of money, or they work for someone who does. Someone high up on the food chain." Lucas pulled himself up to a sitting position, turned to Randy and asked, "Tell me, of all the cops in the city, who best knows the local rackets and vice lords?"

Randy didn't hesitate a moment, barking out the name, "Carruth. Detective Jack Carruth. I see more vice busts with his name on them than anyone in Houston. He works out of the thirty-first, too."

"Get him up here. I want to talk to him, now."

Lucas, feeling woozy again, lay back down for the moment.

"Randy, get Detective Carruth up here to my office like Lucas says, now."

Randy hurriedly left for his desk to locate Carruth and to get him to Sanger's office as quickly as possible.

Detective Jack Carruth ate well, slept well, lived well and it all showed in his robust, round and dimpled face; he was a grown-up cherub, seemingly all wrong for the part of a vice squad detective, and yet he had the highest clearance rate of any vice detective in the city. People who took the time to ask him how he did it learned his standard, stock answer: "Attention to detail, son. The secret of anything is attention to detail. Same was true when I was doing decoy work for the twenty-fourth," he told Randy as they entered Dr. Sanger's office to find Lucas Stonecoat now sitting up, sipping black coffee.

"What can I do you for?" asked Carruth, taking a seat across from Lucas.

"I need names."

"Well, I'll do what I can."

Lucas retold the story of his mugging downstairs, describing his assailants as Mexican-American with perhaps some Native American blood interspersed as well.

"Right in this building? In our precinct? That's a hell of a nerve. Captain Lincoln know about this?"

"He does. When Randy called for help in all the excitement, he came down to the alleyway, even helped Lucas to his feet. Lucas mumbled something about Meany needing help, so the captain turned Lucas over to Randy and the others, and he rushed into the Cold Room and found Meany there and called for an ambulance. Lucas stubbornly refused to go for an ambulance ride, so we brought him up here after the medic bandaged his head. It was either that or a fistfight between Lucas and the ambulance attendant."

"You took a pretty good beating, Stonecoat. Maybe you

should've listened to the medics and gone with them," commented Carruth as he studied Lucas's bruised face.

"Never mind that," Lucas shot back.

Meredyth laughed nervously and said, "Even the captain couldn't persuade him to get into that ambulance. It came down to a staring match, and the captain blinked first. You don't remember any of this, do you?" she asked Lucas, studying his squinting eyes and questioning face, seeing the confusion there like a pall that'd suddenly descended.

"No, I don't," he admitted, while at the same time thinking how Lincoln had just left the Cold Room moments before. "What about Meany? Is he going to be all right?"

"He's resting at Memorial Hospital. They say he'll be just fine by morning. Took a severe blow to the head, like you, but apparently yours is the thicker of the two," Meredyth teased.

"Sounds like it could be the work of Louis Fernandez or maybe this guy named Torres."

"Torres, huh," replied Lucas, his eyes lighting up as he recalled the name from his conversation with Greyson. "Tell me more about this guy, Torres."

Carruth first provided Lucas with several more names, but Lucas asked him again to tell him all he knew about Torres. "Well, he is a Mexican-Indian guy, not a bit of Irish in 'im. He's the head of a . . . well, only way to describe his organization is as a Native American and Mexican self-styled Mafia here in Houston, with just enough white to make it an evil mix, you might say."

Lucas nodded knowingly, and he said, "I believe it is more often the partial whites in the Indian tribes all across America who buy in to the white man's black market ways, and it's these 'breeds' who make money hand over fist in illegal goods, border dodging, gambling, prostitution and other corruption."

"You think this Torres character maybe put Minerva Round-point out on the street to turn tricks for him in 1948? How old would that make him now?"

"Doesn't matter how old the bastard is. Statute of limitations never runs out on murder."

"Nineteen forty-eight?" asked Carruth. "Whataya chasing a murder from 1948 for? You're really taking that Cold Room job to heart, aren't you, Lucas?"

"I am. Now, tell me more about Torres. What's he called on the street?"

"*Autoridad*, Spanish for—"

"The authority; I know enough of the language to get by."

Carruth smiled in response. "Bastard is known for his cunning and for taking no prisoners. You're actually lucky to be alive, lucky that he didn't kill you."

"Then he's a murderer in your estimation?"

"Oh, no doubt about it, but nothing sticks to him. He's got his own personal revolving door down at the courthouse."

Lucas took a deep breath and said, "I hate it when someone in my race makes me embarrassed to be a member of my race. I'd like to think of it as the white and maybe the Mexican genes, and not the Indian genes that turn a person into a murderer."

"Race hardly qualifies one as a killer," replied Meredyth, who had heard enough on this issue.

"Hey, after all, it is a statistical fact that the mixed-blood Indians, on the whole, run successful casinos and other, often nefarious businesses and use questionable means of achieving their ends far more so than do full-blooded Native Americans."

"Is that right?" she returned facetiously. "I'd like to see those statistics."

"The full-bloods think so, and there've been rifts in Indian tribal society since white men began intermingling and inter-marrying, from Puritan New England to the present, because those with low-octane blood, as it's called on the res, are the ones who sold Manhattan to the enemy, and they're people who have a flair for making money, a gift for wheeling and dealing, but who are also cut off from the mainstream of Indian life in this country, usually by their own choosing. Many are embar-rassed to be recognized as Native Americans."

"That fits Mendoza Torres," said Carruth. "He dresses white, acts white, likes an opulent lifestyle, but Torres has the added ingredient of the Mexican cleverness behind him. Every cop in Houston knows he is dirty, but for more than forty years now, this old bastard has owned the 'Indian Rights' to Houston's underground trades. It's believed Torres has had any number of people snuffed out. And he employs thousands with his casinos and other businesses—all legit, of course."

It occurred to Lucas that the young assassin named Roundpoint might well work for this man, Torres, the very man who quite possibly murdered his mother in 1948. Lucas wondered if perhaps it wasn't the old man, now in his seventies, who wanted an end to Roundpoint's pursuit of his mother's killer, and for good reason. But where was the why. . . . Why did a man like Torres give a damn? He would have been a young man in 1948, just young enough to be interested in a pretty young thing like Minerva Roundpoint, but why kill her and mutilate her body?

"The tar pit just got larger," Lucas said to no one in particular. "And if it is Torres, I know that he can take the threat to my life and yours, Meredyth—"

"Mine?"

"Yes, they threatened to kill you if I didn't end my investigation into Minerva Roundpoint's murder. I can't take that as idle prattle, not with this kind of man."

Carruth, his large jowls trembling, agreed, saying, "I second that, Dr. Sanger."

"You think you can get me an audience with Torres, Detective Carruth?" Lucas asked, his hand on his bandaged head.

"I think so, yes."

"Set it up, will you?"

"Right on it, Detective."

With that Carruth left, followed by Randy Oglesby, who said he'd get everyone coffee. Lucas looked up into the eyes of Kim Desinor and they gazed at one another until her eyes pulled away, and she went to a window and stared out at the busy streets below. Clearly disturbed, Lucas went to her and placed a hand on her shoulder. She turned and again their eyes met.

"Something wrong, Dr. Desinor?"

Meredyth looked on, wondering what was happening.

Kim cleared her throat and, shaken, said, "I saw death just now, sitting on your shoulder, Detective Stonecoat."

"Oh, is that all. Where else is he going to sit?" Lucas tried to make light of what Kim had imparted, but the joke fell flat.

EIGHTEEN

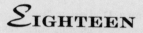

Eagle feathers: chief

Lucas listened intently as Meredyth and Kim brought him up to date with regard to the Coleson case and reiterated what Kim's recent hypnosis session had divulged. Lucas, impressed only up to a point, remembered the useless scavenger hunt of the day before, and the news from the ladies felt repetitious at best, sounding like another scavenger hunt, all symbols and nothing concrete to go on.

Unable to hide his displeasure, he said, "All these signs and symbols can be taken so many ways that they're virtually useless, and I still feel that the killer must be a black man and not a white man."

Kim dropped her head, taking in a deep breath of air at the same time, disappointed herself. "I'm afraid Lamar simply can't send any more clues. He's exhausted, and I'm afraid he's giving in . . . giving in to death. It's a welcomed alternative."

"So, what do you two want to do now?"

Meredyth and Kim exchanged a look. Meredyth explained, "Kim still wants to concentrate all efforts on a white suspect, any whites working or living in the areas of interest who might otherwise fit the profile."

"Put it out there. See what happens. Get Randy on the computer to do a check with our records, run the same requests we've been running but with the added ingredient our suspect is white," replied Lucas, "but I doubt you'll have much luck."

"Lucas always was the eternal optimist," Meredyth said, and it sounded like an apology for him. "Isn't that true, Lucas? Even as a child growing up on the Coushatta Reservation?"

"We're not here to discuss my childhood, Mere."

"You should get further medical attention for your bruises and maybe have a CAT scan done on your head, Lucas," suggested Kim. "Don't let foolish pride keep you any longer from medical help."

Lucas nodded and placed a hand across his turban bandage, which he felt was holding his head and brains together. He wasn't sure he'd ever want to remove the bandage for fear his head would crumble apart. It was, while a silly notion, looming large in his psyche.

Randy, also sporting a head bandage, returned with a large coffeepot filled with the black liquid, and Lucas downed his while it steamed. "You're right, of course, about getting closer medical attention for my head. I think I'll go across the street to Mt. Sinai Hospital where my insurance card is worth something."

Meredyth quickly asked, "Do you need . . . want company?"

"No, no . . . I'm a big, stout boy. I can take myself across the street." His reply came out a bit curt. "Thank you all the same, Mere."

From the doorway, Lucas looked back at Randy and the women, who continued sipping from their coffee cups and discussing the new direction for the investigation into Lamar Coleson's disappearance.

"All right," Lucas reluctantly agreed to meet with Meredyth and Kim to canvass the Bellaire District this night just as they had canvassed the Jacinto District the night before. "See you later at Kim's hotel room."

Detective Carruth called Lucas at the Cold Room where he'd gone to be alone with his thoughts, having decided against going to the hospital. Carruth told him, "Torres says he hasn't got time for you, Stonecoat."

"Fuck that."

"He's a busy businessman, Lucas, what can I tell you? You have to make an appointment to arrest this guy. He seems to dislike you. Have you two met before?"

"Yes and no. I've seen his kind all my life. He gives my race a bad name. He's capable of anything—any means to an end."

"You really can't compel him to speak to you, not without a court order, and even then, he has a right to remain silent if he should fear incriminating himself. Even rapists, murderers, psychos and sociopaths, even pedophiles have a whole array of civil rights in America. This is a damned wonder-filled place and the judicial system is beginning to make about as much sense as the popularity of *The Brady Bunch* or *The Wizard of Oz*."

"Where does he live?"

"What?"

"Mendoza Torres . . . Where does he live?"

"You can't just drop in on this guy, Lucas. His place is like a fortress."

"Damn it, where is he?"

Carruth sounded startled. "You go after this guy like some cowboy, Lucas, and you lose all that you've built here, you know? You know that, so why jeopardize all your progress, your COMIT program, all of it for this kind of scuzz that crawls on all fours?"

"Carruth, I didn't ask for advice. I asked for the man's address."

"The San Mateo Casino and Hotel, along gamblers' row on the river. You know where it's at?"

"I'll find it, and thanks."

"Maybe I ought to go with you."

"No, no, this is something I have to do alone, on my own."

"Jesus, Lucas, you're not going over there to kill the guy outright, are you?"

"No, never entered my mind. I just want to get to know the

enemy, so to speak. Anything wrong with that?" Lucas didn't know what he might do on meeting Torres face-to-face, or what he might do if he discovered that Torres was the man who had had him roughed up. He really didn't know what he'd do if he found the man guilty of Minerva's murder, but he wanted to test the waters, perhaps find out.

"Wait, let me tell you all I know about the place. Maybe give you a chance at survival over there."

"All right, save me from myself. Tell me about this place."

After fifteen minutes of instruction, Carruth wished Lucas good luck, sounding as if he didn't expect to see Lucas in this life ever again.

Lucas nearly sprinted to the motor pool to get a car, realizing that his own car must surely be familiar to Torres and his henchmen if they'd had him under surveillance all this time.

Gathering the keys to a nondescript Ford sedan, Lucas wondered anew if Torres knew of or had dealings with the man calling himself Zachary Roundpoint, and if so what the nature of their relationship was.

The trip out to the gulf coast area, called gamblers' row by the locals, gave Lucas time to think about how he intended to infiltrate Torres's world. Lucas wanted to throw a scare into the bastard, as Torres had wanted to throw a scare into Lucas.

Lucas wanted to count some coup.

The bastard had added to Lucas's collection of aches and pains, and he had embarrassed Lucas in front of his handful of friends, making him look vulnerable. There were few things he hated worse than feeling vulnerable; one of them was *appearing* vulnerable.

Lucas's aches and pains, the hip in particular, along with the back, had returned with a vengeance, and he'd become angry with himself for having been taken down so damned easily and angry with himself for ever having gotten involved in the Minerva Roundpoint affair, and ever agreeing to look into the 1948 slaying for Zachary Roundpoint. Still, here he was— pursuing it further, chasing the ancient case to see Mendoza Torres on the man's own turf, throwing all caution to the wind, pissed off and ready to take scalps on all sides, not caring about what Torres wanted, ignoring Carruth's warning to steer clear of the man, completely out of control, giving in as he had to his emotions. On the edge, the final edge, he told himself, anxious to take out some of his pent-up aggressions for the Snatcher on Mendoza Torres, if he should get his hands on the bastard anytime soon.

Dusk settled over Houston and the gleaming river along the strip when Lucas arrived at Torres's casino and digs.

Lucas had listened intently to Carruth, doing his homework on Torres, now aware of Mendoza's built-in, protective barriers at the San Mateo Casino, which thrived as a floating palace on Buffalo Bayou, not forty minutes from Precinct #31, a marvel of construction with no expense spared. Torres lived the good life, all of it located at the top of an enormous pyramid of depravity and riches, none of which his Indian brothers enjoyed, unless they happened to work for him. Carruth had informed Lucas of all this during their earlier contact, but much of it Lucas could have surmised for himself. He believed he knew Torres's kind.

Lucas walked in as if he owned the place, straight through the front door, his shoulder holster and gun bulging. He knew he was forcing the issue, that if any of Torres's men had stomped on his head earlier today, these same men would quickly approach him now. He knew the knee-jerk reaction of low-life criminals, and that crime translated meant the ultimate in stupidity and soullessness, that in large measure such gofers for mob types were eunuchs whose thought processes had gone the way of their testicles.

Lucas immediately stepped up to the information desk and asked for help.

"And how may we help you, sir?" asked the genteel young woman behind the counter, her sparkling teeth and Texas accent meant to please.

"I'm here to meet with a Mr. Roundpoint, Zachary Round-point, but I'm afraid I've lost the room number where he stays when he's in town. It's urgent we see one another, business matter, you know. I'm his new partner, so to speak. Could you ring him for me or point me in the direction of his room?"

"We . . . I mean *I* can telephone him, give him a message, tell him you're here in the lobby, but I can't give you his room number or his phone number. Rights, privacy, all that, you see."

"Yes, of course, I see. Would you then ring him and tell him that Mr. Lucas Stonecoat is here to see him, please?"

"I'll do that." And she proceeded to do so, but apparently there was no answer. "He must be out, sir. Sorry. Perhaps later?"

"Perhaps."

As if on cue, a heavyset, dark-haired Spanish fellow pushed his way through the crowd in the casino to confront Lucas, his eyes narrow and his right hand indicating a gun below his coat. "Whataya nuts, man, coming here like this? Torres's going to find a place in the desert for you, fool."

"He sent for me."

"What?"

"Torres. He sent word for me to meet with him, face-to-face. He's expecting me."

The lie confused the man—the idea that his boss would do such a complete about-face so suddenly. The utter confusion that masked the man's face almost made Lucas feel sorry for him. "He said now, tonight, so take me to him."

"I don't know, man. I'll have to check first."

"Call him on the house phone. He'll confirm it."

"Walk ahead of me, and no funny business," replied the thug, going for the house phones.

"What's your name?" Lucas asked the man.

"Armand."

"Maybe we'll get to know each other better, Armand, before the night's over. You got some nice boots on there."

"Hey, man, I just take orders, do what I'm told. The boot, you had it coming."

"Call your boss," said Lucas, now standing before the house phones.

"This better be legit."

Armand dialed 1172 and never saw the fist coming. He slumped to the floor in one large pile like a sack of potatoes. Lucas told onlookers that the man had had too much to drink.

Lucas redialed 1172 and Torres came on the line, a bit angry at the second nuisance call, asking, "Who the fuck's fuckin' around with the fuckin' phones?"

"This is Lucas Stonecoat, Mendoza," Lucas said, straight out.

"Stonecoat? I don't know anybody by the name of—"

"I'm here to see you, Mendoza. I've already taken out one of your bodyguards, Armand. Now, get this straight . . . You can see me here and now, and we can get our differences ironed out, or you can refuse to see me, and you'll be looking over your shoulder every minute, every hour, wondering when I'm going to get you alone, like I did Armand, only you I'll get outside this place. What's it going to be?"

"Stonecoat . . . Okay, so how did you figure it was us who roughed you up?"

"Not too hard to figure, Torres. You people leave a crumb trail wherever you go."

"All right. So, you're in the lobby? I'll send Roscoe down to you. He'll guide you up, but you'll have to surrender any weapons."

"I'm waiting." Lucas hung up, and when Armand moaned, coming to, Lucas viciously kicked him in the jaw with his booted foot, sending him into a deeper, calmer peace. A passing elderly couple, their hands full of coins from winnings at the slot machines, gasped in unison on seeing the kick.

"He needs it from time to time," Lucas assured the elderly couple, who kept going, hurrying for the nearest elevator.

Lucas patiently waited by the phones for Roscoe's arrival.

After giving up his weapon, and after being led through a labyrinth of corridors, elevators and more corridors by the huge, muscled-up Roscoe—a man without a neck, so far as Lucas could discern—Lucas was finally brought before Torres. Immediate distaste for Torres filled Lucas's being, largely due to the man's pretense at flattery directed at Lucas, whom he referred to as a "brother of the same campfire."

However, Lucas swallowed the bile that galled him about this pompous little Napoleon, with whom he must play along.

"We have mutual interests in seeing the Minerva Roundpoint case solved, laying out the circumstances of the case," began Lucas.

"Oh, and what interest do I have in a whore's death?"

"The whore's son, perhaps?"

"What the hell're you driving at?" Torres, in a smoking jacket, grabbed nervously for a cigar, bit off the end, lit it, puffing like a winded ostrich, the flame going large, dying, revitalizing itself until the tobacco became a glowing ember, smoke curling from the end as if from a smoking gun. Lucas realized that Torres liked the effects he created even in the simplest of gestures such as this.

"Roundpoint, your assassin and employee, wants peace with it." Lucas's bluff worked. He could see that it worked.

The result reflected in Torres's eyes and in a nervous facial twitch, almost imperceptible along with the clenching of his free fist. He gestured with his cigar as he spoke, saying, "Zachary is like a son to me. If . . . if only I could give him what he wants . . . believe me, I, of course, would."

Lucas believed him, up to a point. "So, that's why you so strongly objected to my continuing the investigation into the murder of his mother? Don't you know that Zachary won't rest until he finds the truth?"

"I see we made very little impression on you, Detective. I hope you don't think my threats are idle ones. They still stand, and as for Zach, I know everything about my employees. I am a caring employer."

"No doubt."

"Roundpoint has enough money to buy *peace* several times over. Dredging up old ghosts like this, Lucas—may I call you Lucas, amigo?—you and I know how very painful this can be. You, for instance, would you care to have the world know how your father died penniless and drunk in a hovel on the res? And your mother not much better? That your grandfather, uncle, aunt still survive but they, too, eke out a poor living on land not fit for pigs, land not rich enough to grow anything but sagebrush and weeds? Would it do the world any good to know that you, the great hero of the Helsinger's Pit case here in Houston, known the world around, allows his relatives to live like swine in a sty?"

"My family freely chooses reservation life over the white world."

"Most fools do." Mendoza Torres relit his cigar, back in form as it were, and he now blew smoke toward Lucas. "Look around you. Do you see any skin-and-bones people here, any hungry Indian children in *my* tribe?"

Carruth had told Lucas that Torres lived with a large family that he lavished riches upon, sparing no expense, and that he acted as a don for any and all Indians and young Spaniards who came to him in need, that he sometimes offered loans, jobs, a place in his organization, always making his judgment calls with an eye to profit and where an individual, male or female, might best earn the organization more money. He made his judgments like a presiding judge in a court of his own making.

"You ever think of making money, Mr. Stonecoat? Of living well, Mr. Stonecoat?"

"Who doesn't?"

"You are a smart man, a clever man. I could make you an officer in my organization, you know. Wealth beyond your dreams, women every night, drugs—which I understand you enjoy?"

"I'll give it some thought. Is that how you interested Roundpoint in working for you? Drugs and money?"

Mendoza seethed with an anger just below the surface, but palpable, like a creature hiding in the nearby closet. "Already you know so little that you believe you know everything. What is the saying among the Anglos? A little knowledge is a dangerous thing, no?"

"In the hands of the wrong man, yes."

"You believe yourself the right man?"

"I am."

"Roundpoint was a boy when I took him into my family, and now, years later, he is like a son to me. It breaks my heart to see him this way, so sad always . . . always with Min . . . her on his mind."

"How well did you know Min . . ."

"I did not know her well. No one did. She allowed no one close."

"Apparently, she allowed someone close enough to kill her and her unborn child, and to take a certain item of jewelry, something precious, from her."

"She withheld her heart from all men after leaving her husband, a thing a woman did not do in those days—a brave and perhaps foolish thing." Torres turned away to hide an emotion, pretending interest in a wall painting of Native American Indians on the plains during a forced winter march, the Indians closely and warily guarded by blue-coated soldiers. Torres began adjusting the painting. A haze of smoke clung cloudlike around him, forming something of a halo now.

"She came to Houston to make a new life, send for her son when she could," Lucas continued, drawing on Greyson's words, feeling his way and guessing aloud.

"It was a mistake; ultimately it cost her her life."

"You were in Houston when she arrived, waiting for her. She came because she could not say no to you."

"That's not entirely true."

"Then what part of it is?"

"I could not say no to her. I loved her dearly, passionately."

"Then you were intimate with her?" Lucas didn't give him time to deny it. "And you must have taken her death hard. Especially in view of the way her spirit left this world."

"It almost killed me. For a time, I thought of suicide, to follow her."

"How . . . romantic. Are you saying, sir, that you came after her from Kansas? When she left the reservation, did you give chase?"

"No, the other way 'round. I came here in the fall, she followed in the spring. She . . . she loved me as I loved her. I wrote to her, pleaded for her to join me here. She could not remain on the reservation with her husband—in that life—any longer."

"She had a wildness about her, didn't she? A reckless, childish nature, didn't she?" asked Lucas.

"How can you know these things from so many years past?" Torres, once again, answered with his eyes as much as with words.

Lucas recalled the hand signal left behind by Minerva, the one cry of truth in all this morass of lies. "She resented your coming here without her? Leaving her on the res to raise a son, Zachary, and another, by you, on the way. Saddled with a drunken and abusive husband, she fled, believing a better life waited for her here, true?"

"If he dared abuse her ever again, I would have killed her husband, so I had to get away. My anger with Zach's father was that great, so overwhelming that I knew I'd kill him with my bare hands if I ever saw the kind of bruises he caused on Min again, you see, so I left the situation. I dared not believe she would follow me, although we spoke of it. I really never expected to see her in Houston."

"What're you saying? That Zach's father killed his mother? That he followed her down here to Houston, found her and cut her up?" Lucas gave thought to Minerva's hand signal. Might it apply to her estranged husband? He hadn't as yet died in that shallow pool on the res where he, bathed in alcohol, drowned like so many other despondent Natives. Lucas had accepted the man's death as suicide all along, as everyone else apparently had, but here stood a man who was capable of murdering the senior Roundpoint just to make it look good. And when Torres referred to Roundpoint, his eyes flamed red.

Lucas pursued Torres. "Answer the question, Mr. Torres."

"No, we were close, as close as two people can be. We continued to be lovers. I began to build my empire, slowly at first, working much as the boy, Zachary, now works for me."

"And you worked for whom at the time?"

"A man of no consequence now, a man long dead."

"His name?"

"Noussaint, a dangerous man, now a dangerous spirit."

Lucas wondered just how much of the old ways Mendoza Torres could not escape, just how superstitious and traditional he was at the core. "Then you believe in our ancestral past, the spirit world?"

"Of course. My parents raised me in the tribal laws."

"So you believe, too, in the law of blood?" Lucas referred now to the utterly unbreakable chain of vengeance and revenge that became a cycle of killing between families and among tribes that said when a man's brother was killed he must avenge that death at all costs.

"Noussaint arranged for John Roundpoint's accidental death, just as he arranged for Minerva's awful murder."

"And you killed this Noussaint fellow to avenge their deaths?"

"Her death. I did it for her. I killed Noussaint myself, for Min. I did love her, you see."

"Then you have no doubt whatsoever that it was this Noussaint who killed her?"

"Yes, he had his butchers tear her to pieces for information she stole."

"His butchers? There were more than one hired to kill her?"

"Yes, and I killed them all, one by one."

Lucas knew this to be a lie. Forensic evidence, as bad as it had been on the case, had made one sure promise: that the killer, whoever he was, acted alone. There had been only one set of footprints in that muddy bottom where she died, and none found around the perimeter that said otherwise. "Forensics showed only one assassin," Lucas coldly replied.

"Forensics has been wrong before." Torres carried on with his charade, saying, "But believe me, Lucas, Noussaint did not go peacefully in his sleep. But, yes, you are right. Noussaint ordered her assassination, but now Minerva's murderer is also among the shrouded."

Case closed, Lucas now thought, nice and tidy. "You killed Noussaint, then?"

"I did. As I said, yes."

"For the woman and *your* unborn child?"

"For Min . . . yes, and my unborn child. Zachary took the child's place in my heart. He is, in every sense, my son now."

"Did she confide in you about the unborn child?"

"I did not know that Min was carrying a child until after her death, no."

It was a fatal error, Torres's reply in the negative. Another lie, Lucas guessed. Was the unborn child another reason for being so fervent with the knife-wielding?

"Someone went to great lengths to cover the fact an unborn child died with the murdered woman," Lucas matter-of-factly added. "Lot of money exchanged hands."

"Aha, Noussaint again," replied Torres, calmer now that he had his story straight. "In those days, even among thieves and murderers, there was an unwritten law—you didn't kill family, especially women and children. It's doubly so in the Mafia."

"Why did this Noussaint have her murdered? What was she killed for?"

"Noussaint had every politician in Houston on his pad, as I do today. I took over Noussaint's empire. I killed the bastard for vengeance . . . for power and for Minerva."

"What did she have on Noussaint?"

"Books, transactions. She was too smart for her own good. She read the papers. She knew who ran Houston in those days, and she thought for a brief time that she might stand to win some power for herself. That's all you need to know."

"How did she come into possession of these ledgers you speak of?"

"We lived together, we slept together. She left her man for me, left her only son for me. Some people might say that's extreme behavior, but she hungered for more and more from me, from life, certainly more than what that fucking reservation and her husband could ever possibly offer."

"I see, she wanted much from life, more than perhaps any

one man could give her. So she started seeing the reporter, Greyson, then, and she was talking to him about you and Noussaint, the organization?"

"She was no saint herself. She enjoyed life, you might say, and she wanted more of a good thing, but she wanted too much too soon. I tried to tell her to be patient, but she was without patience, you see."

"Did you ever put her out on the street to bring in money, Mendoza?" Lucas intentionally used the man's first name to bore at him.

"That's a lie! She was never a prostitute. It was planted that way by Noussaint, who had powerful connections throughout the city, including the city desk editors of the largest newspapers at the time."

"You were running numbers for Noussaint, keeping book on his drug and prostitution rings, and she stole your ledgers, information that could put a lot of people away, and this Noussaint fellow just took care of it himself, personally?"

"The bastard did, yes. Eventually, he *paid*. It took time, but he paid."

"He had his slaughter men tear her into so many pieces, you say?"

Mendoza began shaking at the memory, his resolve shattered as the images fluttered back, like so many dry and brittle leaves. Lucas recalled his own initial reaction to the photos, alongside the sickening bile in his throat that followed a conviction that whoever killed this woman knew her, perhaps intimately, that the killing strokes were laid on by *passionate* hands.

"Tell me, did she ever sleep with this Noussaint character?"

"No, never. She despised him, and he had no feeling whatsoever for her. She would not willingly sleep with him, no."

"But why murder her? Why not simply retrieve the books?" pressed Lucas. "Why kill her? Why not simply send a message as he did with the newspaperman and the detectives investigating the case?"

"All right, all right, you uncover my shame!" he erupted. "Noussaint murdered her to keep *me* in line. She had no information on him. I did. I told her of it, but she had nothing in her possession. He killed her to teach *me* a lesson!"

Lucas gently pressed now, "Go on, Mr. Torres."

Torres suddenly looked old and shrunken in his smoking jacket, a figure for derision. He collapsed now into a blue velvet cushioned chair and continued. "I had certain information on Noussaint's activities, a tape recording, a photo of him meeting with the mayor of the city. It was enough to bring both men down. I made Min keep the evidence, you know, as an insurance policy, so to speak, against the day when I might need it. Somehow Noussaint learned of this. How he learned of it remains a mystery. The man read minds—not unlike yourself, Detective."

Lucas pulled forth Minerva's necklace, dangling it before Torres, asking, "Do you recognize this, Mendoza?" He continued the familiar use of Torres's first name to keep the man off balance.

Torres gasped, buckled and began to dry heave, then snatched out a large, colorful handkerchief and composed himself. "Yes, it was her most prized possession, given her by her . . . her mother. It really should go to Zachary."

"I suppose Noussaint ordered his men to take it from her?"

"Yes, to shove it in my face. Like you are doing now."

"I'm sorry if I've upset you, Mendoza, but we both know that Zachary will not rest until the story is told."

"As I have power now, Noussaint had power then. He had the power to find out everything that goes on in Houston. He summoned me to a private room, sat across a table from me and tossed the recording and the photos on the table with Min's hair and her necklace, the one she wore always. He told me that he wanted to trust me again, wanted me to continue as his right hand, but that he hated above all things a betrayal. He said he understood how conniving women were, and that he slept only with men as a result. He made me plead for another chance, for life itself. He said that since he thought of me like a son, he would give me a second chance, and that we would talk of it no more. But I must show him allegiance in every way."

"And you agreed to this?" Lucas's voice overflowed with disgust, realizing that Torres had just confessed to sleeping with Noussaint in order to rekindle the trust between them, and that there'd been a love triangle among the three. "Jesus, talk about your dysfunctional families," Lucas blurted out.

"What choice did I have? Agree or die like Min." Mendoza began to sob with the memory.

"When the police questioned you about Minerva's death, what did you tell them? They had to know you were her boyfriend. They must've suspected you. Yet there's not a single mention of a boyfriend in the case book."

"Noussaint was a thorough man. I was conveniently out of town at the time of the killing. Noussaint arranged everything. He had long arms, and he saw to it that the investigation went straight down a blind alley from the start. He gave me an alibi, telling me that he could quite easily have me convicted of murdering Min myself and hung for my transgression. He threatened me with having killed Min and the child, how it would play in the press. Meanwhile, he arranged for the necklace to be left at Father Avi's altar and for John Round-point to commit suicide, and Father Avi put the two events together, going to his death believing that Zach's father had murdered his mother, unable to tell the boy so."

"If all this is true, and you were innocent of her murder, why haven't you shared this with Zachary Roundpoint, to settle the matter for him? And why are you so adamant about shutting my investigation down?"

"But I am not innocent. It was my foolish actions that got her killed, don't you see? The boy will never forgive that. He is looking for vengeance, as I sought vengeance on Noussaint. Besides, this ugly picture does not paint me well, you must agree."

"How did you wreak that revenge on Noussaint?"

Mendoza Torres smiled at the memory. "He disappeared so completely that his body has never been found. I woke him from sleep and slowly crushed all life from the bastard as he stared at me. By then all of his men were *my* men."

"Where might I find Noussaint's body?"

"His body?"

"To verify your story? Have an M.E. look it over?" Lucas half assumed the body lay somewhere in a hole in the desert, where most Mafia victims in the sovereign state of Texas wound up.

"You'd have to implode the old Western Union building downtown. He's somewhere in the mix."

Now a landmark, there was no safer place for the mobster to hide his deed.

"You must believe my story. It is true. Now, you must let it end, brother."

Lucas knew that the last thing this old man wanted on his hands now was a cop killing, and that explained why he hadn't killed Lucas when he'd had the chance. It would be far easier if Lucas could be bought off or appeased in some other way, like an employee in Mendoza Torres's huge organization. . . .

"I'll back away if you'll inform Roundpoint of the how and why of his mother's death. Somehow, he must be told," Lucas said, his hands opened wide in the symbol of reconciliation.

"I am an old man. It is written in my hand for him to see, on my death."

Let it go, Lucas now told himself in a moment of exasperation. Then he asked, "Where were you exactly that your alibi held up so well?"

"I had an illness back home to attend to, my ailing . . . dying mother. That was the story."

"On the reservation? With hundreds of eyewitnesses to place you there? Did you actually make the trip?"

"Yes, of course, but my mother had passed on to the next life before I could get to her. Already dead, funeral arrangements in progress, my whereabouts were fixed with the detectives working the case by Noussaint!"

There was always an old mother conveniently dying on the reservation; Lucas knew that Torres hadn't a literal mother dying on the reservation but one of the community of mothers who had raised him, something of an aunt. "How did Minerva's amulet—this one"—he held it up before the old man's eyes once again—"how did it get on the altar back at the Fox and Sauk reservation the day after Minerva's body was found hacked to pieces if this Noussaint handed it over to you?"

"I . . . I placed it there, of course, but like I said, it was thrown in my face when Noussaint had my woman killed to test my allegiance to him."

Lucas pictured Torres doing the actual killing, thinking, *Now that would be a test of loyalty, the sort Mafia dons appreciated.* Lucas could believe it. For all the accumulated wealth and power, this man before him had likely committed hundreds of murders.

Unsure what to say next, Lucas mumbled, "So, you did return to the reservation with the amulet."

"To find the boy, yes. I made an arrangement with Father Avi that the boy receive money, a decent education, all that he needed, and in time, I sent for him, when I took over here, after killing Noussaint. Father Avi told the boy of his past, but I am not sure how much Zachary knows."

"So you secretly placed the amulet on the altar as an offering to her church?"

"I did."

"And did you pray for Min's soul?"

"I . . . I did, yes."

"And you left her necklace with the prayer, as an offering to the church," Lucas repeated, pretending an appreciation for his devout love for Minerva.

"I thought she would have appreciated that. It was her one valuable asset. Avi, the fool, obviously held on to it for the boy instead of using it for the church, but I never knew of this. I hadn't seen that amulet since, until now. But the priest knew I didn't intend her any harm. I swore on his Bible that I had nothing to do with it—which, you see, was and is a lie. She died because of me, because of my ambitions." Mendoza's eyes marked Lucas to determine his reaction to this news.

"So, let me get this straight and even. You secretly placed the amulet on the altar? Her most prized possession as an offering to her church."

"Yes."

"And you prayed for Min's soul?"

"I . . . I did, yes."

"And you left her necklace with the prayer, as an offering to the church," Lucas repeated in his best Columbo imitation.

"Again, yes."

"And Avi never suspected you in Minerva's death?"

"Any suspicions he may've harbored were set to rest by my contrition. I was torn up about her . . . the way she . . . her life ended."

"Father Avi held on to the necklace all these years, and he gave it to Zachary on his deathbed," Lucas said. "So, she was no whore then, Mr. Torres? All part of the fabrication by Noussaint and willing authorities?"

"Noussaint was extremely powerful. No, she was not a prostitute. She was my woman, but I had *nothing* then. I worked my way into the organization."

"And now you're at the top of the dung heap, and it pains you that you let them label her a whore, doesn't it?"

"You know the times . . . a loose Indian squaw on her own in a big city, serving drinks at a bar . . . all that. There was no one to believe otherwise."

"Except that nagging, thorn-in-the-side reporter, Greyson? The one I spoke to today, where your thugs followed me, saw to it he was silenced for good and then lay in wait in the Cold Room for me."

"I know nothing of Greyson's death."

Lucas instinctively read this as the lie it was, and he felt a pang of guilt at having led Greyson's killer to his bedside. "I saw you in the darkness there at my office, Mendoza. Your rings, your limp—they give you away even in the dark."

His face grew enraged. "If you're through questioning me, I have a full night ahead."

"Min could not persuade you to get out of crime, Mendoza, could she? So she thought she'd do it for you, right?"

"No, nothing of the sort!" His flinty, hard-edged eyes filled with a sudden startling hatred of Stonecoat. "She had her bitchy side, I tell you. She wanted more from Noussaint, and she wanted it then and there. She was the ambitious one."

"She took the ledgers, was on her way to Greyson with them when you stopped her. Noussaint knew about it. Like you say, he knew everything that went on in Houston in those days. It became a test of your loyalty and fidelity to the chief. You had to choose her life or your own and your chosen path led you to kill her."

"You lying bastard!" He pulled forth a huge gun from a coffee table drawer, and Lucas lunged at him, grabbing the weapon and wrenching it free from his grasp. He now held the weapon pointed between Mendoza Torres's thick black eyebrows, the trigger cocked and quivering. Torres's cigar began a slow singe of the carpet.

"Go ahead, shoot! Blow my fucking brains out! What do you know of our love? You know no more than Greyson did, than anyone did! *Get out!*"

Lucas had struck a chord, and now Lucas knew that Mendoza Torres was indeed capable of sudden rage and passion, the sort that left multiple stab wounds in a victim, the sort of rage that left a "signature" of the killer behind, a signature that time did not erase.

Lucas, wielding the big western-styled Colt .45 in Mendoza's face, knew now that he and Torres were finally on the path toward truth about how Minerva Roundpoint came to die. He knew this by simply reading the other man's body language, his fidgeting, his clenching and unclenching fists, his grinding teeth, his tired eyes. But how to prove Torres did the actual killing? he wondered.

"I'm not going to kill you, Mendoza, not like this. You'd get blood all over your expensive things."

Lucas brought the gun up and swung it into Torres's cheekbone, at about the place Armand's boot had caught

Lucas's own cheek. Torres slumped back into the cushions of the chair he was in, moaning and dazed.

Lucas looked around the room, his eyes fixing on the expensive Swiss clock on the wall that informed him it was already past five in the afternoon. "If you don't tell Roundpoint what he has a right to know, then I will. His mind will not be settled until he knows the truth, Mr. Torres."

"He will know on my death. That is enough. You are to stay away from him. If you're seen with him again, you will be *eliminated*, Mr. Stonecoat. Do you understand me? Am I being clear enough?"

"You must either fear or love Zachary a great deal to shield him from your guilt."

"He is . . . he is my son by natural birth, although he does not know this. He will one day rule in my place. I will see to that."

More lies, Lucas believed, because this hardly jibed with what the old man had said earlier, *or has he simply begun to believe his own lies?* Lucas wondered. Roundpoint had classic American Indian features, not in the least like Mendoza's Mexican appearance. So why all the pretense, all the lies? A frightened man lied. Torres had long before become Noussaint, ruler over a kingdom, and like some ancient warrior chief of old, he lived now in fear, fear of his son's coming to the throne like some long-awaited Oedipal creature, frightened of Roundpoint's wrath, of Roundpoint's own cunning, the very cunning taught him by his so-called father, and the man feared most of all the truth coming out, because the truth painted him in those so-called true colors as the weak and morally venal thing he'd become.

Lucas finally asked the sad wretch, "Which version of the truth are you most frightened of, Mendoza?"

Staring at Torres as if he were a creature that crawled lower than a desert iguana, Lucas added, "So, you bequeath all this"—Lucas's free hand flourished through the air as he spoke—"as a fitting tribute to Zachary's mother's memory. I see. I really do see, Mendoza Torres." Lucas then hurled the gun across the room.

"Motherfucking Cherokee bastard Stonecoat! Will you do as I say, Stonecoat? Or will they find you *missing*?"

"I'll give it priority one in my thoughts as I ponder the consequences."

"What?"

"I'll give it some thought, goddamn you."

"I want assurances, Mr. Stonecoat, and I want them *now*."

Both men remained frozen, Lucas having tossed the gun onto the sofa, far from his reach. "Or else?" Lucas challenged.

"Or else, I press a button on my desk over there and your ass is surrounded by a hundred guns, and then you are taken to a dark place where you will meet your Gitchie Manitou."

Lucas showed no fear of his threats, instead revealing his huge bowie knife which he carried at all times at his spine. He allowed the weapon to shine in the light before Torres's eyes. The knife loomed large like the tooth of some ancient god. "Any move, you son of a bitch, and you're a dead man before your goons can reach the door. Besides, fool, I'm working in consort with the FBI on the Coleson boy's case, the highest profile case in the city, and I've got a file on you and your connection with a murder that has haunted your worthless ass since 1948 that I've left in the hands of the FBI should anything happen to me or mine, including Dr. Meredyth Sanger, you got that, Torres?" He pressed the knife against Torres's throat, drawing blood. "I asked if you got that?"

"I got it, I got it!" choked Torres.

Lucas relented, the blood rivulet trickling down Torres's neck and creating a trail down below the lapel of his smoking jacket. Lucas then firmly set his jaw and said, "I know that the Houston FBI has long been interested in you and your operation here, and so you're going to make me disappear? And no, I don't think we're going to let your *sleepy dogs* lie still anymore, Mendoza."

"I will have your head and spleen on a platter, Cherokee dog!"

"My superiors in the HPD also know that I'm here to see you regarding a Cold Room case file. In fact, thanks to the modern miracle of the computer and police science today, case file number 671894—as our computers have it—is top-drawer, a test case for a new program that combines FBI files with HPD files, a program called COMIT, a program I rather doubt the all-knowing Mendoza Torres knows a bloody thing about."

"Keep talking. You're still a dead Indian if you go near my son again."

"Sorry, but I don't believe I can make you any promises, Mendoza. Besides, I think you killed Minerva to impress upon Noussaint the depth of your fucking devotion to the bastard, so you could take on the role of *his* devoted son and lover in order to one day inherit this bloody empire of yours. Only you didn't know that Minerva was carrying your child, did you? Not until the medical examiner had a look, did you?"

"Bastard! Lies! Get out!"

"You couldn't rid yourself of the spirit of that unborn child, could you, Mendoza?"

"Shut up!"

"So you've tried your damnedest to make it up with Zachary."

"I didn't know she was pregnant! Why didn't the bitch tell me that she was pregnant?"

"Would it have made a difference?"

Lucas cautiously backed from the room, one eye cocked for Roscoe, yet confident that he would walk from the casino untouched. Torres might send his assassins after Lucas again, but not at this moment. He'd need time to weigh all sides of the move. At the end of the long, regally carpeted corridor, Roscoe awaited with Lucas's 9mm., and the big man's eyes enlarged to saucers when he saw Lucas wielding the bowie knife. Roscoe thought he'd been thorough in his search of Lucas, and he now feared his boss dead, lying on the other side of the wall in a pool of his own blood.

Lucas instantly set the big man's mind at ease. "Your boss wanted to see my blade. He admires good cutlery."

Roscoe half grinned and said he loved knives, too, ending with, "I've always wanted one of these pig-stickers. You any good with it?"

"I can carve up a man or a turkey with it," replied Lucas, putting it into the scabbard that hung in the crook of his spine.

"Think I'll go out tonight and get me some decent cutlery, you know, for those occasions when a blade is advantageous, as they say," continued Roscoe, sounding as if he'd been working all day to improve his vocabulary and couldn't wait to try out the new word.

Behind them, in Torres's room, the sound of breaking glass and things being hurled against the walls could be heard. Roscoe looked from the noise to Lucas, saying, "Sounds to me like you pissed the old man off. Never a good thing to do in this town, Stonecoat."

Roscoe was part Indian, part white, with some mongrel additives, Lucas thought as he stared into the huge man's eyes. "If he sends you after me, Roscoe, be prepared to die."

Roscoe's response was a huge, snakelike grin, like an anaconda before eating breakfast.

Once outside, Lucas breathed the fresh air in a deep sigh of relief, and he began to ferret out the truth and the lies fed him by Mendoza Torres, and he wondered how much Carruth might know of a forgotten Houston thug named Noussaint. Lucas was pleased with one outcome. Father Avi and Zachary Round-point's natural father were no longer suspect in Minerva's murder-mutilation. There remained only one man alive responsible for the ardent, burning, earnest, enthusiastic, fervent, passionate butchering and hacking and rending apart of that beautiful young Indian mother's body, the man who both loved her and could not allow her to live, the man whose seething rage had sent him into a black corridor of no return, the man most threatened by her revelations both then and now, Mendoza Torres.

Lucas's conclusions made perfect sense in light of the meaningful hand signal Minerva had sent Lucas through the years. Her talking hands told Lucas that she loved her killer. The hands told him that Mendoza had a hold on her, had imprisoned her heart. She had taken the dangerous actions she took in the name of love, to free him from his obsession with Noussaint and a lifestyle she feared. She had loved Mendoza, chasing after him to Houston, pleading for him to come away from Noussaint's influence, seeing Noussaint as the purely evil man that he was. She watched Mendoza slide further and further into the cesspool until feelings of helplessness overwhelmed her. Distraught, at wit's end with fear and the feeling of aloneness she must have had, she fell into Greyson's arms, and calculatedly so, for she wanted to use Greyson to good end, so she whispered tales in his ear, stories about corruption and crime, and then she dared take those ledgers to get her story to the Anglo newspaperman on a quiet, calm, rain-soaked night destined to be her last on earth.

Yes, Noussaint was on to her from the beginning. Yes, Noussaint had the eyes and ears of a thousand demons. Yes, Noussaint had her killed, but such a man would not have had her killed by just anyone. Such a man, demanding complete loyalty as a test of his own absolute power over others, would order the murder done by Mendoza Torres himself, and Torres, these multiple chains around him, chains of his own forging, once he lifted the blade to her, allowed all his pent-up rage at the circumstances, at Greyson, at Noussaint, at Minerva to take complete hold of him. He savagely destroyed her, and the multiple strokes with the blade and the soaking in her blood became an age-old ritual in which he cleansed his rage. An all-too-human tale . . .

Now, what to do with this information, and how to prove it, to bring Torres to account for murder some fifty years after the fact, Lucas wondered. Sure, there was no statute of limitations on murder, but there were limits to proving that Torres murdered Minerva Roundpoint in order to sit at Noussaint's right hand. There existed grave limitations in proving any conspiracy-to-commit-murder case, but especially in a case as old and cold as this. What DA's assistant in the city would touch it? Who'd take the lone word of a dead reporter as evidence? The amulet, the shoddy autopsy work, the poor photos of the crime scene, none of it figured as Exhibit A. The DA's office would laugh him out of their plush offices.

He also wondered how much he dared confide in Round-point.

Lucas watched his back as he found the car he'd come in, parked several blocks from the San Mateo Casino. Getting in and starting the ignition, it dawned on him the thing could be wired and he could be blown into a hundred pieces, but he doubted anyone had seen him drive up. The car hummed into life and he pulled from the curb, heading back toward down-town Houston and Dr. Desinor's hotel. As he drove, Lucas considered question after question. He wondered how much sleep he'd be getting in upcoming days, imagining it to be very little indeed. He imagined he'd be sleeping with fewer women and more firepower. He feared for Meredyth's safety. Obvi-ously, Mendoza believed she knew more about the case than she ought to know. Lucas also wondered if Mendoza would order his so-called son to sleep with him for the throne of his kingdom, to carry on Noussaint's disgusting and perverted tradition.

Turning onto the ramp for the highway to take him into the heart of the city, Lucas, half hearing the police band chatter of calls for vandalism, domestic disturbances and an assault in Jackson Park, wondered if Torres would be ordering Zachary Roundpoint to murder Detective Lucas Stonecoat. Lucas re-called that Dr. Desinor had seen death sitting atop his shoulder. He had failed to ask her which shoulder, left or right, and to ask if it mattered. The notion that she'd seen the Angel of Death in contact with him had been enough of a shock to send Lucas into a dumbfounded fugue in which he could neither mentally nor verbally formulate much of a response. He'd only hummed like a stupid college professor confronted with a truth that contradicted all that his lesson meant to convey.

Now, driving across the city in the dark, the irritating headlights of oncoming traffic in his eyes, Lucas somehow found humor in the notion of death sitting on his shoulder, and he laughed aloud and said to the empty car, "What a fitting and ironic twist to the case if Roundpoint, on orders from Torres to prove his loyalty, comes for me. . . ."

NINETEEN

Rain clouds: prospective

Lucas found Meredyth at home, just stepping from the shower, wearing a heavy white terry cloth robe that set off her silky skin and radiant eyes and silvery hair. Meredyth's high-rise apartment exuded order and cleanliness with its Scandinavian furnishings, glass tabletops and the modern art on the wall.

"Help yourself to coffee in the kitchen," she told him. "I'll just get dressed."

"Oh, not on my account, please."

She frowned. "Get any notions of seeing me naked out of your head, redneck!"

Lucas unconsciously touched the long scar that ran the length of his neck, a mark of his near-death experience, and said, "Is it my being an Indian that keeps us apart, Mere? Or is it the social ladder thing? You being on such a high rung, and me on the bottom rungs?"

"Neither, Lucas. We're simply not compatible. It wouldn't work out, regardless of . . . of—"

"The great sex?"

She gritted her teeth. "I was going to say, whatever chemistry we might have, because in time the mixture would turn poisonous, and I don't want to lose your friendship at any cost. Is that clear enough?"

"Yeah, that and the fact you have McThuen, safe and reliable Conrad McThuen, prosperous PR man for—what college is it he's working for now?"

"Texas Christian," she said, disappearing into the bedroom to dress, but leaving the door ajar. Lucas, tempted to peek, thought better of it and went for the coffee she'd offered instead.

Pacing now, coffee in hand, he couldn't help but catch glimpses of Meredyth in bra and panties in a mirror somewhere within her bedroom. He found her nearly irresistible in that half-naked state. An urge to throw all caution to the wind, rush into her room and take her into his arms washed over him, but as he contemplated the possible outcomes of such a rash move, she emerged, fully dressed, brushing out her hair.

"I'm sorry," he began, almost stuttering.

"Sorry? Sorry for what, Lucas?"

"That I got you involved in this whole Roundpoint affair, that your life's being threatened by this arrogant bastard hoodlum Mendoza Torres. Maybe you ought to go on a cruise, get out of the city for a while, Mere."

"Nothing doing. I'm not being chased out of my own town by thugs."

"Don't be pigheaded. Do you always have to be so pig—"

"I'm not running from a fight, if that's what you mean. You ought to know me better than that by now, Lucas."

He put up his hands to her flaring temper, one of her surprisingly endearing qualities, and offered, "Let's smoke the peace pipe, if you're interested in doing some drugs with me."

"That kind of talk . . . that kind of thing, Lucas, it's going to cause you to lose that detective's shield of yours if you're not more careful!"

"Come on, I was only kidding." He suddenly grimaced, a sharp pain cutting through his right hip and down his leg.

"Are you all right, Lucas?"

Frowning, he replied, "Need to take some meds." He took a couple of pills from a small container and downed them with his coffee. "Tylenol," he lied.

She only shook her head, disbelieving.

"How can such a beautiful woman be so uptight? Never mind. Don't answer that. Bring me up to date on what Dr. Desinor's been seeing with that Superwoman X-ray vision of hers, will you?"

Meredyth took a deep breath, collecting herself and her thoughts. "Dr. Desinor's hypnotic trance, now that we two doctors have had time to translate the various images, was, I'm afraid, not so productive. The boy's shut down. There's a disconnection. It's become one-sided."

"So, she still thinks the killer is a white man perhaps posing as a black man?"

"She does."

"Confused maybe by her own paranormal powers?"

"She doesn't appear confused in the least. She knows . . . that is, she believes in her own convictions where the Coleson boy is concerned. She sees the killer as having white hands."

"Hands covered in talc or some other sort of powder, construction dust, starch, or maybe flour?"

"I suppose anything is possible at this point," she conceded.

"Inherent contradictions between the psychic profiler's visions and her profile of the killer lead me to question even her."

"In the meantime, the clock is ticking away too swiftly for the Coleson child for us not to take some action, even if it is wrong."

"All right, let's go with Dr. Desinor's visions and sweep an area known locally as the Holdout, an area of small businesses within the black ghetto of Bellaire, owned and operated by men of other races, men who might be racially motivated to 'clean up the streets of vermin and waste' maybe. . . . Maybe that's the way this nut is rationalizing away any guilt in the murder of young black boys."

Meredyth dialed Dr. Desinor at her hotel room, but she failed to answer her phone. "This is odd," Meredyth said, as if to herself.

"Why so odd?" he inquired, sipping a second cup of black coffee.

"Kim asked that I call her at precisely this time."

"Call the desk clerk back. Ask if she's left any messages for either of us."

Meredyth did so, learning there were no messages, but the clerk also thought it odd since he'd seen her get on the elevator for her room only an hour before and hadn't seen her leave the hotel. A check with the concierge confirmed that she hadn't called for a cab.

"Let's get over there, now!" Lucas shouted, putting aside his coffee cup and rushing for the door.

"Let me get my purse and things!" protested Meredyth.

The drive over to the hotel didn't take long, yet it felt like hours in Lucas's head. Suppose Mendoza had spotted Kim with him earlier, had targeted her instead of Meredyth all along as a way to hurt Stonecoat?

"Do you think she's in some sort of danger, Lucas?"

"I don't know."

Dr. Kim Desinor feels no pressure against her buttocks or thighs where she sits, feels nothing of her own solidness, body or weight, for she is inside the mind of a killer, feeling his body weight, his solidness. She has only a dim sense of her living *self* back at the hotel room where she is in a deep trance, in lotus position. She is in so deep a trance that even the insistent ringing of a bell is far, far away.

She fails in making out any characteristic features of the killer, but she feels his anguish, his tormenting and unrelenting bitterness and pain, and a sense of gripping shame. All traits of the human monster he has become, but she holds judgment, unsure if his shame and his own pain have anything to do with remorse or guilt over the destruction of life he has caused. Rather, his suffering has been a sudden onslaught; something brought on by a blindingly white revelation.

She feels his suffering, weighs it, considers it in her mind, trying desperately to understand it. Unable to reach Lamar any longer, she has turned to his abductor, desperately seeking the monster, the Snatcher.

Dr. Kim Desinor now knows more about the killer than she has previously known due to a number of sudden insights brought together by a series of symbols. For the first time, she believes she knows what her prey is, the confusion of conflicting symbols dissipating into a single, powerful truth that comes from something Meredyth Sanger has told her about psychoanalysis and the difference between *neurotic behavior* and *character disorders.* She realizes that their killer has a character disorder and an identity crisis, both of which he has turned outward against young black children, because he himself was abused and despite his skin tone, he is in fact a black man in a white man's skin. He has passed for white for years. In this lies his bitterness and anger, for he himself has only recently learned this truth about his blood lineage.

Precisely how long he has known about his blackness is unclear, but he has, for the better part of his life, passed for white and has become a racist with a murderous rage against his own kind—the archetypal young black male of the ghetto. Kim hazards a guess that he has known of his blackness for about as long as it's been since the first victim was tortured to death by the Snatcher.

Kim has all along maintained that the crimes are racially motivated in some bizarre way, while Lucas has maintained the crimes are same-race crime. In effect, they have both been right all along.

Sitting here in the darkened hotel room at the top of the skyscraper, an occasional pained moan escapes Kim, the spillover from the giant wounds of the monster himself. This new insight comes straight out of the mind of the killer. Time is running out for the Coleson boy.

Amazingly, as if on cue, Lucas Stonecoat and Meredyth Sanger are outside Kim's door, knocking and asking if she is inside and if she is all right, and she hears them but from afar, as if she is lost in a deep cavern, a maze of conflicting corridors keeping her from returning, the powerful emotions of the killer having forged the labyrinth that might easily become her prison if she loses all control and strength.

She opens the door to them, having no feeling of having gotten up, having crossed the room, yet her glazed eyes look out on them and find them at a great distance. Their hands touch her, console her, pull her back. She sees her own reflection in their concerned eyes and she sees the recognition and light and blood on her face from a strange stigmata: tears of blood; she is weeping blood.

Lucas and Meredyth are instantly shocked, but the psychic says, "I know now that our killer is extremely conflicted, and I've narrowed things down considerably. He's a leopard without spots."

The three of them, detective, psychic and shrink, pinpointed the area called the Holdout, the business district of the Jacinto area, a place plagued by break-ins, robberies, drive-by shootings and drug dealers. Once again they focused on the images in the list of psychometrically envisioned clues. Lucas held his breath as they searched for a giant cowboy or horseman, a railroad crossing, a burned-out war zone, a magician with a lamp riding a magic carpet, a lost cat in a corridor or castle, a dungeon-filled castle built of enormous cement blocks.

Kim Desinor, fearing the boy could be killed now at any time, possibly tonight, could get no reading from Lamar. She feared he might already be dead.

Meredyth Sanger gave silent prayer that they would be more successful tonight than in the past. On their search of this area by car, Meredyth focused on side streets as well, and suddenly she shouted, "Stop! There was a railway crossing sign at the last right. Go around the block."

"This is Houston, Mere. This city's got more railway crossings than a carcass has flies."

"Just do it, Lucas."

"I say we stay on the main drag."

Meredyth persisted, saying, "But if they—the killer and the boy—came from across town from the Raleigh projects and didn't take the Interstate, they'd be entering from that direction, wouldn't they?"

Lucas grumbled under his breath but took a right at the next intersection, doubling back to the point that Meredyth spoke of to find an ancient used car lot with a huge silhouetted cowboy waving at the public, a comical smile and ridiculously huge ten-gallon hat atop his giant head. The sign proclaimed the lot as belonging to Carboy Pete, with his Car-rall of Cars. It was at the same intersection as the train signal and crossing.

Lucas cursed appreciatively, saying, "I'll be damned."

They turned now onto the main drag, Windermere Street, which was lined with storefront windows and the occasional tavern, although most storefront operations here had long since been driven out of business. It represented a most depressed area indeed. Even some of the convenience stores had closed up shop, their windows boarded up.

"Maybe this is the war zone I saw," suggested Kim as they toured down Windermere.

Lucas suddenly stopped the car, halting before a construction site, the sign proclaiming it the future site of low-income housing brought to the neighborhood courtesy of the Housing Authority of Houston in connection with HRS, tax dollars at work. Huge stacks of cement blocks had been dumped here, creating corridors and castlelike portals and avenues, each recess looking like another dungeon.

"You think maybe Lamar saw this?"

They continued onward, more slowly now, all eyes watching for another sign, anything that might lead them closer to Lamar and the Snatcher. "Is your psi sense telling you if any of this is legitimate, Dr. Desinor?" asked Meredyth.

"Yeah," added Lucas, "are we getting any hotter?"

"Nothing yet, but the signs look good, the clues appear to be true psychic hits."

"Home run!" pronounced Lucas, stopping the car a half a block from a pet store, its sign looming above it, faded and old as the cowboy car salesman's sign, reading: SANDCASTLE PET STORE & SUPPLY.

For Kim, the sign instantly brought back all the animal menagerie images, while for Lucas, it recalled the fish meal force-fed to the earlier victims. And in the pet store window, even Meredyth saw elements of Kim's visions.

"This has got to be our target. It's got to be it," said Meredyth.

"Whataya say, Dr. Desinor?" asked Lucas.

"I'm trying to get some reading on it, but nothing so far from either Lamar or the Snatcher."

"Then let's get closer." Lucas inched the car along now, and in a few moments, he heard Kim Desinor gasp as if her air supply had been cut off. She stammered, "I be-lieve . . . pet store is . . . highly charged area."

"Damn it, and us without a search warrant," Lucas bitched.

"How're we going to get one this time of night based on psychic energy flow?" added Meredyth.

"I'm sure no sober judge in Houston will give us one," agreed Kim. "Even getting a federal warrant on the probable cause we have isn't going to be easy."

"We don't have time for judges and papers to be signed and bullshit," determined Lucas. "The place is locked up for the night. Wonder what time he closed his doors."

"Probably posted on the door."

"If he's still awake in there, and it appears someone lives over the store, then maybe he'll open up for, you know, an emergency?"

"It's not a veterinary," protested Meredyth.

"You have any better ideas?"

"But if he opens his door and lets us in under some pretense, couldn't that be construed as some sort of entrapment, and couldn't we get into trouble with the technicalities of lawful arrest later?"

"You've been watching too many episodes of *Law and Order*. If the guy allows us across his threshold, anything inside that provokes us to look further is probable cause."

"Some judges wouldn't see it like that, right, Kim?" pressed Meredyth. "Tell him. Would a federal judge see it like that?"

"These are children being killed, Meredyth. Any judge that

gets in the way of prosecuting child killers won't be a judge for very long."

Lucas worked to contact Randy Oglesby. Dispatch located him and patched Lucas through to his home. "Randy, I need you to run a check on the store owner of a place called—"

"What's this about, Lucas?"

"Shut up and get your computer kissing the police computer. This is urgent. We think we may have a fix on the Snatcher."

"Jesus! Why didn't you say so? Shoot."

Lucas fed Randy the information, which he in turn fed to the computers. Randy gained access to the store owner's name and the fact he'd had no prior arrests; but he had been the victim of several robberies. In one aborted robbery attempt, the store owner, Louis Meachum, shot to death a young black man.

"So far, so good. Go on, Randy."

"At one time, he was a construction worker, making enough to purchase the building and open his pet shop in 1996 when a family inheritance came to him. He's a white male, six foot one, 179 pounds, bald pate and thick, Afro-like hair, from what I can gather from the poor quality of the picture forwarded. The man's thirty years of age. He lives with a wife who helps around the store, and get this, she was injured in the robbery, taking a pistol blow to the head from the same assailant who Louis killed."

"Told you he was white," gloated Kim Desinor, "and black."

"Yeah, except for his skin tone, Meachum matches the profile of the killer," agreed Meredyth. Then she began psychoanalyzing the suspect, saying, "He could simply be working out of a twisted revenge plus racial hatred mode. It might not exactly fit with Dr. Desinor's twisted identity crisis talk."

"It still doesn't *prove* this guy Meachum is working out some racial hatred, and it still isn't enough for a warrant to search the store. Damn it, if we had any evidence at all that the Coleson boy might be inside there, we'd just storm the place, right?" asked Lucas.

"Right," agreed Kim.

"But there simply isn't enough evidence. Remember Toombs? Remember—" Meredyth began cautioning.

"Shhhh! Look!" said Lucas, hearing and now seeing someone banging on the pet store door and calling up to a window overhead, where they got their first look at Meachum, a beefy man with muscled arms, a mustache and a smoker's cough and thick voice. He looked more butcher than pet store owner, Lucas thought.

Meachum, seeing that his late-night visitor—a regular customer whom he recognized—posed no threat, responded to the emergency, coming down and opening his shop.

Meredyth suddenly said, "I have an idea," as she climbed from the car and rushed across the street toward the shop. Kim and Lucas chased after her. Meredyth told them, "Just follow my lead."

"Door's open," commented Kim.

"Let's have a look," agreed Lucas.

"Follow my lead," Meredyth repeated. "We're married. I have a dog named Whoo-Whoo at home, and he's got the colic, and *you* are extremely annoyed with Whoo-Whoo and me. Got it?"

Lucas agreed, saying, "Okay, but Whoo-Whoo?"

Kim joined in with, "And I'm the sister-in-law. I have to get inside there, and then perhaps I'll be sure we're on the right scent."

TWENTY

Lightning & lightning arrow: fast, swift

Louis Whitehall Meachum, in undershirt and coveralls, tried locking them out as his familiar customer, profusely thanking him, stepped out, his hands full of fish pellets and medicine.

Meredyth used her wit and charm to prevail upon Meachum as an animal lover to help her with Whoo-Whoo's serious gastric problems, while Lucas bitched about having to come out so late because of the "mangy" dog. "Let the man go back to his bed, honey! It's not his problem."

"Please, sir . . . The dog's in terrible distress. He needs an enema or something stronger. I need your expertise."

"All right, all right," Meachum relented, adding, "come in, but it will be extra."

Lucas smiled to himself. They'd been invited in; the door was opened for them. Probable cause presented no problem now.

While Meredyth and Lucas pretended to fight over Whoo-Whoo's problems, Lucas saying he hoped the dog would die this night so that he and Meredyth could be intimate without the dog in bed with them, Kim tapped in to the sounds, smells and feel of this place, realizing now that these animal sounds all around her could be the cover for the Coleson boy's screams, and she is suddenly overcome by what she feels/

smells/senses—the terror of this place, like the stench of an ancient ceremonial place for burnt offerings and blood sacrifices.

Kim knows the truth. . . .

She knows in her bones that the child is buried below the cacophony of noise here. *He's in the basement.* She wonders if she's shouted it aloud when a tidal wave of overwhelming sensations of pain and suffering engulfs her.

Kim faints with the crushing, oppressive and devastating stench of impending death and the emotional suffering that rushes in on her like a flood.

Lucas stared down at Kim Desinor, whose fainting spell is no ruse, he knows. She'd become stiff and her hands were clasped in the same Indian signal that she, or some portion of her subconscious, had seen in the crime scene photos of Minerva Roundpoint. Lucas knew it represented a cry for help to free her from her captors, and that she was speaking for Lamar now.

Lucas held no lingering doubts now about Meachum, for Kim's signal clearly indicated that beyond any doubt in her mind, the captive child was imprisoned somewhere on these premises. Meredyth used her "sister's" fainting spell to full advantage, asking Meachum to get water, fast.

As soon as Meachum went for the water in a back room, the animals going crazy with the amount of psychic energy that had been expended here, Lucas darted through a door where stairs led to a basement area. The area was pitch-black and he stumbled and fell halfway down the stairwell and into the pit.

He snatched out a small but powerful flashlight, and its beam sliced through the underground cavern where all the windows had been boarded up. He could see amid the trash piled up here that there'd been some recent construction done on a boxlike room ahead, with a padlock dangling from the door—a soundproof room, perhaps with the Coleson boy inside.

Lucas searched around for a key, but no key dangled nearby. Meachum must keep the key on him at all times, Lucas thought, searching for some way to rip off the lock. He finally found a crowbar amid a plethora of tools, some of which, his light revealed, were caked with dried blood. He also saw electrical devices; one he recognized as a grill briquette starter. He grimaced at the array of cutting and rending tools.

Beyond this, he spied a table covered with cans and jars of makeup, wigs and a clownish old suit of clothes complete with a cane. Lucas's flash picked up a reflecting pair of eyes off the cane, dull yellow wolf's eyes, just as in Kim's vision. He walked over, lifted the cane and examined the wolf's head closely, realizing that the shape of the snout and possibly the sharp ears might well be the mark of the killer left on each victim, a mark that had so eluded identification by the medical examiners.

He took possession of the cane, certain of its being the murder weapon, feeling a sixth sense about it, something akin to Dr. Desinor's psychic sense, and he took a pair of bolt cutters to the lock.

He must do the work as quietly as possible. He could hear the squawking of birds and the barking of dogs upstairs, and he worried about the two women he'd left alone with the devil's own, Meachum.

By this time, Kim, who had come to, and Meredyth Sanger had seen how Louis Whitehall Meachum's murderous rage stood out in sharp contrast to his gentleness with his animals, who'd started a wild cacophony of noise. Meachum tried desperately to soothe the ruffled feathers and the frayed nerves of his various animals. A keen-eyed monkey stared at Meredyth and screeched as if to warn Meachum of her true identity. Meachum had returned with the water for Kim Desinor, and he'd instantly gone about the shop to talk to his birds, cats, dogs and snakes. Now he returned to the two women, his eyes meeting Kim Desinor's. Somehow he recognized that she was someone to fear. He felt naked under her gaze, as if she knew all of his dirty little hidden secrets. Next he caught a fleeting glimpse of the gun in her shoulder holster. This instantly transformed the huge man with the tightly curled hair and a paunch into a maniacal creature before their eyes.

Kim went for her gun, snatching it out, but Meachum had already grabbed Meredyth in such a manner as to insure that her neck would be snapped if Kim made so much as a whimper.

"Toss the gun away, now!" he ordered. But Kim held the gun firmly in both hands, the open muzzle large and looming, aimed at Meachum's forehead.

"I can put you down like a bull elephant with a single shot to the brain, Mr. Meachum," countered Kim.

Meredyth gasped as he tightened his grip, displaying the fact he could snap her neck like a twig in an instant. "Where's the big guy you came in here with? Where'd he go?" Again he made Meredyth squeal in pain.

"Back to our unit. We're police officers, Mr. Meachum, and we came in to ask you a few questions, that's all," insisted Kim, carefully placing her weapon down.

"Cops . . . questions, questions about what, damn you! I should've known you people weren't legit. You don't fit the neighborhood. I never seen you before. What kind of questions!" He dragged Meredyth toward a window and peeked outside into the gloom, unable to see Stonecoat.

"Questions regarding this rash of disappearances of young black boys in and around the area, Mr. Meachum. We thought you might have seen some strange types hanging about, you know, people that don't belong to the neighborhood? That type," Kim tried stalling, knowing that he'd seen the truth in her eyes already.

Meachum's attention remained on the window, while Kim's remained on the gun she had relinquished in order to keep the man calm. "Where's that damned Indian? Where's the car?"

"Out of sight, around the corner," Kim assured him.

Meachum felt trapped, confused, unable to figure out what action to take, and Kim realized at the moment he was extremely dangerous.

Meachum announced, "We'll have to welcome your partner back, then, won't we?" He tugged harder at Meredyth, making her whimper louder, while all around his birds and animals screeched their displeasure at the human opera being played out around them. "Now, damn you both, where do I put you two?"

A shout from upstairs drew Meachum's attention. It was his wife, asking, "Louis? Louis? What's going on down there? What's taking you so long?"

"Go on back to bed! I'll be up when I can. Got an emergency," he shouted up the flight of stairs. He then eyed the basement door, which Stonecoat had closed behind him. "That way, and hurry, you lying bitches," he cursed as he choked more life from Meredyth.

Kim took tentative steps toward the top of the stairs, then seeing Lucas's flash below, she cried out, "But Mr. Meachum, this isn't necessary, and besides, it's black as night down here!"

Lucas instantly extinguished his flash, picking up on Kim's cue. Meachum pushed Meredyth bodily into Kim and together they tumbled the rest of the way into the blackness, Meachum locking the door above them, still awaiting Lucas's return through the outer door, still in a state of confusion and fear of discovery.

Lucas helped the two women to their feet, providing some light from the flash. "I've found the Coleson boy," he said in a tone that brought fear to the women, and he lifted the flash to where the boy remained dangling from the ceiling in a cocoon of thick white hemp and construction tape, much like a mummy, only his nose, mouth, ears and extremities, yet to be exploited and brutalized, exposed.

The sight sickened the people staring at it. Kim's eyes filled with tears as she again literally felt the boy's pain. In a state of silent trauma, the boy was close to death when Kim laid her healing hands on him, sending both a verbal and a psychic message that she had, after all their communication, found him at last and that he was going to be okay, that he was going to survive his terror and suffering. Somehow Lamar, responding to her touch, found strength to open one eye, to look upon Kim Desinor, who saw herself reflected in a single large tear.

Overhead the shrieking animals, from chimps to barking dogs and magpies, began a new wave of horrendous noise. The sudden flurry of animal noises made Lucas and the others look up, and the boards above them began creaking with the monster's thunderous pacing, the leopard nervously pondering the few options left open to him.

"He thinks you went back to the car radio to call for backup. He's freaking up there, Lucas," Meredyth informed him. "Which makes him extremely dangerous."

"Get Lamar down. There're some blankets over by the washer and dryer. Like hell the wife doesn't know there's something weird going on here. I'm going up. I've got my weapon."

"It'll be dark up there, and you won't know where he is until it's too late," Meredyth worried aloud.

"It's time someone put a little suffering on this bastard."

Lucas made his way up the stairs to find the door locked from the other side. He rammed it once, heard Meachum shout, "There's no way out from down there, so you two whores sit still and be quiet!"

Lucas rammed the door again, breaking the paltry lock. Meachum fired, hitting Lucas in the left arm, sending him cascading into a rookery of squawking birds, but Lucas fired as he went down, his bullet biting into Meachum's kneecap and sending him, in great pain, to the floor in the darkened shop.

Lucas saw the flash of metal and heard the other man's weapon skitter away from him, and he quickly got to his feet and rushed to Meachum. He stood over the murderer of young boys, kicking Meachum square in the face, not once but twice. Lucas then stomped on the screaming man's kneecap with all the weight and might he could muster, sending an electrical storm of hellacious pain coursing through the bastard's body, making him pass out completely.

"Stop right there, you murdering son of a whore and devil, or I'll kill you where you stand!" came a scream from a huge, menacing woman behind Lucas.

With his boot poised over Meachum's brain, Lucas held up his shining Houston gold shield for the woman to see.

She responded by shaking the barrel of a huge shotgun, a twelve gauge from the look of it, at Lucas. "I've called 911, and we'll just wait now for the police to take care of you, you gutter scum!"

Meredyth and Kim came stumbling and carrying Lamar up the stairs now, Kim holding the Coleson boy in her arms, his face and head bandages removed, his body now wrapped in a blanket. Mrs. Meachum stared in amazement. "How damned many of you are there?" she asked.

"Mrs. Meachum, we're with the Houston Police," Meredyth replied.

Kim quickly added, "And we have evidence, here in my arms, that your husband is the Snatcher, the man who has brutalized and murdered some—"

"Don't listen to the lying bastards, Ellie," shouted Meachum from the floor, awake now, still groaning in pain, holding on to his broken jaw.

The woman's mouth fell open, and her hold on the big weapon faltered as if it had become too heavy of a cannon for her arms to wield. "That's . . . that's just crazy . . . impossible. He's hardly out of my sight . . . I . . . I'd know . . . I'd've known . . . I'd've called the police long ago if . . . if there was the slightest . . . reason . . . I thought, I mean . . . he said he had to kill some of the animals who got too old, said that's what the room he built downstairs was for."

"Turn on a light, Mrs. Meachum. Look at the child in my arms. Look at his burns, his bruises. . . . He was being tortured in the basement of this establishment."

She found a light, still holding firm to the stock of the double-barreled gun. When the lights came up, she saw the blood pooling about her husband, who himself looked small and broken now, and this shocked her, and then her eyes focused on the murderous rage in Lucas's eyes, and the blood blotting his coat, and then her eyes fell on the traumatized, terrorized and bruised young boy, recognizing him from the pictures she had seen on TV and in the newspapers. "My God . . . it's true. . . ."

Ellie Meachum let the shotgun slide from her grasp and crumpled into a fleshy mound before them, the animals all around her head still squawking. "All because of that damned inheritance," she cried. "All because he found out that he was a black man with a black man's blood."

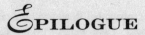

ƎPILOGUE

Four ages: infant, youth, mid and old age

Lucas awoke to the sound of Houston's morning heartbeat, the traffic of the city pounding out its unending anthem. He looked out his front door for his morning paper and found the headlines glaringly bold and screaming, SNATCHER TRIAL TODAY.

Lincoln couldn't fault him for taking the day. It would be a rough one, this first day of the Snatcher case in a public forum. Lucas feared that the three-piece, smart-ass lawyer who took on Meachum's case in order to build a reputation for himself meant to call into question the way in which police and FBI apprehended the accused, and meant to uphold the civil rights of the child killer, citing probable cause and illegal entry, and an expectation of privacy, and a host of other bullshit to get his client the most lenient sentence possible. The mumbo jumbo of the American legal system had swung so far to the side of protecting the so-called "innocent until proven guilty" that murderers, rapists and other violent offenders were daily walking out of jails all across the country on legal technicalities and flamboyantly presented loopholes in the law.

Now, almost six months later, Lucas meant to defend his actions of that night. All the various loose ends of the Snatcher case must be explained in simple and easy-to-follow steps for the jury, and it must be done without rancor but in a professional manner. They weren't asking for much, he told himself now as he dressed for court.

Louis Whitehall Meachum was looking at a death sentence or a lifetime in a lunatic asylum with Meredyth and other shrinks clamoring for an opportunity to study the bastard in order to learn to prevent the creation of such additional monsters in society. Meachum's wife had cut a deal with the DA, that in exchange for telling what she knew and testifying against Meachum—as little as she claimed to know—she would keep her freedom, and the DA would not bring charges against her.

Meredyth had by now learned a great deal about Meachum from interviews she'd conducted with him in his cell, and she believed she better understood his motivation than did all others combined. This pissed Lucas off—her superior shrink's attitude. "Lucas, look at it this way," she had told him. "When he was born, his parents, both mentally insane, used him for sport, torturing him. They kept him chained to a wall in a basement until his grandparents found out and called the police. He was born with white skin into a black family, and as if that were not enough trauma, add to it the abuse he suffered. That's how a monster is created, Lucas."

"So, we're all supposed to feel sorry for him? Plenty of abused children in the world do not turn around and murder others."

"He'd escaped it for years. His mind had shut it out completely. But when his grandmother died, the last of his family, she had named him as beneficiary in her will and on all her life insurance policies and stocks and bonds. It amounted to enough to follow his dream, open the pet store, but it also opened up a trickling of memories that became sharper and more unpleasant with each day until it all came back in a flood of anger and hatred. He'd been living as a white man all those years, with no contact with the broken family, and when he got the news, something snapped. He snapped."

"Learning he was actually black made him snap?"

"He was a known bigot in the neighborhood. He hated black people. That atop the memories of child abuse and torture that he suffered at the hands of a black mother and a black father. It was simply too much. His life, his birth, all an anomaly, an abberation."

So the monster took form, Lucas thought.

Lucas's drive took him by the federal building, where Vorel had been replaced but a number of his underlings remained, licking their respective wounded egos. Dr. Faith was due to testify in court today also, and Lucas found himself pleased at the notion of seeing her again, anxious to ask her if their trip to the desert, taken before she'd left six months earlier, had given her the greater peace of mind she'd sought.

The COMIT program was well underway now with more interest and backing by FBI funds than ever. Cooperation between the FBI and HPD had shown dramatic improvement after a visit from Eriq Santiva to the Houston field office, and behind his visit loomed Dr. Kim Desinor, largely instrumental in the new federal attitude being taken toward the COMIT idea.

Lucas pulled into a parking spot outside the city courthouse, a tall, imposing building, modern in every way. He'd brought the newspaper along with him, his eye having caught the story on the sudden disappearance of casino boss Mendoza Torres. Lucas felt anxious to read about the matter, to see what authorities had on it.

Meanwhile, the Coleson boy was well on the road to recovery, again thanks in large measure to Kim Desinor, but Lucas knew that it would take many positive years to rehabilitate the young man. Once again, Meredyth acted to become extremely involved in this aspect of the aftermath of the Snatcher case, doing pro bono work to help Lamar rebuild his faith in the world around him and to restore his shattered self. He had managed a smile at one of Lucas's half-assed jokes the day before, and was making inroads toward a full recovery.

After sitting all day and seeing that nothing useful had been accomplished in Judge Oliver P. "Unworthy" Worthington's

courtroom, Lucas found himself mentally exhausted and physically ill. He limped the last steps to his door, dusk coming on
the city.

Lucas entered his semidarkened apartment with a bag of
groceries and a six-pack and was about to switch on the lights
when someone in the dark interior startled him, saying, "Don't
touch the light, amigo . . . Stonecoat. And don't drop the bag
or the beer. No need for anything to get messy here. I just want
to talk."

"Roundpoint?"

"Yeah, it's me."

"Sorry . . . I've been meaning to get back to you with
some answers about—"

"I know all about my mother now."

"Oh, really? Then Torres leveled with you?"

A taped voice was switched on in the darkness, the voices of
two men coming clear, that of Lucas Stonecoat and Mendoza
Torres, arguing heatedly. Lucas's accusatory tone seemed on
the tape, here in the darkness, somehow heightened, and the
fact that he came off sounding as if he might be interested in a
bribe or perhaps blackmailing Mendoza gave Lucas a moment's start, as he knew even the appearance of impropriety
could cost him his badge. He wondered what Roundpoint
meant to prove here tonight. "What's your game, Zachary?"

"Shut up and listen."

Lucas did so, helplessly at the other man's mercy, half
certain that Roundpoint was here to put a bullet through
Lucas's heart on Torres's order, but now he again listened in
earnest to the words on tape. He had not known at the time that
he was being recorded by Mendoza Torres; it hadn't occurred
to him. Still, it made sense.

Mendoza's gravelly voice shouted on the tape, "Keep
talking. You're still a dead Indian if you go near my son again."

"Sorry, but I don't believe I can make you any promises,
Mendoza. Besides, I think you killed Minerva to impress upon
Noussaint the depth of your fucking devotion to the bastard, so
you could take on the role of *his* devoted son and lover in order

to one day inherit this bloody empire of yours. Only you didn't know that Minerva was carrying your child, did you? Not until the medical examiner had a look, did you?"

"Bastard! Lies! Get out!"

"You couldn't rid yourself of the spirit of that unborn child, could you, Mendoza?"

"Shut up!"

"So you've tried your damnedest to make it up with Zachary."

"I didn't know she was pregnant! Why didn't the bitch tell me that she was pregnant?"

"Would it have made a difference?"

Roundpoint switched the tape off and said, "Methinks he doth protest too much. . . ."

At the time of their conversation, Lucas hadn't realized just how cocksure and abrasive he sounded when facing Torres, with what he only half knew and had half surmised on the spot.

"I didn't know I was being taped."

"Torres tapes—or rather, taped—every word uttered in that room."

"And you, knowing this . . ."

"When I saw you leaving, I had to know what you two had to say to one another. I didn't know that he'd sent Gonzales and some of the others to rough you up. And I certainly did not know that he had murdered my mother."

"But you'd suspected it for some time, no?"

"I didn't want to believe it, but yes, I suspected. Perhaps he was just a little too good to me."

"I warned you that you might not like where things led."

"It's ended now. I wanted to thank you, and I wanted you to know that in the future, if there is anything you require . . . Well, just ask for my assistance."

"That's very generous of you."

"I can afford a little generosity toward those I admire, especially now that Torres is no longer in charge."

Lucas instantly realized that Torres's body must now be in some remote area of the desert. "You killed him."

"He took a long time dying for an old man, but he also took a long time in reparation, wouldn't you agree?"

"You used Dr. Sanger, and you used me, Zachary."

"I most certainly did."

"So now do you feel whole again?"

"It is unlikely that I shall ever be whole. But like you, I have drugs, and when things become too much to handle, I can always return to the res." Roundpoint's laugh rang hollow. "I leave the tape and the amulet for you, to remember me by."

Lucas's eyes by now had become accustomed to the dark interior of his apartment. He saw the tape, the amulet and a large envelope placed beside them, all through a haze created by the drugs he'd been popping all day to combat the pain that continued to ravage his body. Today the pain was pulsating with a new angry force, directed at Lucas, at breaking him. "I said no cash," he complained bitterly through the drug-induced fog.

"It does not bind you, either in spirit or body."

"It compromises me, my position."

Roundpoint remained firm. "Accept it as a gift from a friend. I have no friends, Stonecoat. I would like to hold on to one illusion, that you are my friend, and that one day you may need to use me as I have used you. I have power now, an army of followers."

"So, you've graduated from the ranks. I'm sure Minerva, your mother, is proud of you."

"Be glad for me. I no longer have to get my hands bloody." He passed closely by Lucas, gliding out the door. He was gone like the fox that was his being, his guide.

Lucas flicks on his light and stares across at the tape, the cross and the envelope. He wonders what in bloody hell he might do with the money, and he worries about the amount. He puts down the items in his hands and investigates, finding that his private-eye work for the assassin has netted him a hundred thousand dollars, the price for Mendoza Torres's head.

It's far too much, he thinks through the fog inside his brain. *If*

I bank it, I'll be suspect should anyone care to even superficially look my way.

He knows he must dispose of the money in some fashion that will cast no shadow on himself. Then, as if in a vision, he sees reservation children playing amid discarded tires in a dump site, many of them, like Zachary Roundpoint and Lucas himself, having had few choices in life. Perhaps a hundred thousand dollars in a special fund, administered by the tribal leaders, will help some of the children at the Coushatta Reservation just outside Huntsville, Texas, where the remnants of Lucas's family live. The money would come from an anonymous donor.

Lucas doesn't remember pressing the On button to his CD player, yet the room fills with Indian tribal chanting and music. His body sways to the music, the envelope of money still in his hand.

For now Lucas must lie down, his mind in a swirl, his body contorting in pain, the drugs finding their mark, easing the pain by increments. As he first kneels and then spread-eagles on his hardwood floor, the money cascades about his loose flowing hair, and the dream time takes hold, yoking him to a starlike comet being ridden by the Angel of Death.

Dr. Kim Desinor is right, he thinks before passing out. *Death does ride on my shoulder.*